HAWK

James Aitcheson was born in Wiltshire and read History at Emmanuel College, Cambridge, where began his fascination with the medieval period and the Norman Conquest in particular. *Knights of the Hawk* is his third novel.

D1138785

520 193 83 7

Also by James Aitcheson

Sworn Sword
The Splintered Kingdom

JAMES AITCHESON
KNIGHTS
OF THE
HAWK

arrow books

Published by Arrow 2014

2 4 6 8 10 9 7 5 3

Copyright © James Aitcheson 2013

James Aitcheson has asserted his right under the Copyright, Designs and
Patents Act 1988 to be identified as the author of this work

This is a work of fiction. Apart from references to actual historical figures and places,
all other names and characters are the product of the author's imagination and
any resemblance to actual persons, living or dead, is entirely coincidental

This book is sold subject to the condition that it shall not, by way of
trade or otherwise, be lent, resold, hired out, or otherwise circulated
without the publisher's prior consent in any form of binding or
cover other than that in which it is published and without a
similar condition, including this condition, being imposed
on the subsequent purchaser

First published in Great Britain in 2013 by Preface Publishing

Arrow Books
Random House, 20 Vauxhall Bridge Road,
London SW1V 2SA

www.randomhouse.co.uk

Addresses for companies within The Random House Group Limited can
be found at: www.randomhouse.co.uk

The Random House Group Limited Reg. No. 954009

A CIP catalogue record for this book
is available from the British Library

ISBN 9780099558293

The Random House Group Limited supports the Forest Stewardship
Council® (FSC®), the leading international forest-certification organisation.
Our books carrying the FSC label are printed on FSC®-certified paper.
FSC is the only forest-certification scheme supported by the leading
environmental organisations, including Greenpeace.
Our paper procurement policy can be found at:
www.randomhouse.co.uk/environment

Typeset by SX Composing DTP Ltd, Rayleigh, Essex
Printed and bound by CPI Group (UK) Ltd, Croydon, CR0 4YY

For Alistair

Contents

List of Place-Names

Throughout the novel I have chosen to use contemporary names for the locations involved, as recorded in charters, chronicles and in Domesday Book (1086). Spellings of these names were rarely consistent, however, and often many variations were current at the same time, as for example for Cambridge, which in this period was rendered as Grantanbrycge, Grantabricge and Grentebrige in addition to the form that I have preferred, Cantebrigia. For locations within the British Isles my principal sources have been *A Dictionary of British Place-Names*, edited by A. D. Mills (OUP: Oxford, 2003) and *The Cambridge Dictionary of English Place-Names*, edited by Victor Watts (CUP: Cambridge, 2004).

Alba	Scotland
Alrehetha	Aldreth, Cambridgeshire
Archis	Arques-la-Bataille, France
Beferlic	Beverley, East Riding of Yorkshire
Brandune	Brandon, Suffolk
Brycgstowe	Bristol
Burh	Peterborough, Cambridgeshire
Cadum	Caen, France
Cantebrigia	Cambridge
Ceastre	Chester
Clune	Clun, Shropshire
Commines	Comines, France/Belgium
Corbei	Corby, Northamptonshire
Cornualia	Cornwall
Defnascir	Devon

Dinant	Dinan, France
Dunholm	Durham
Dure	Jura, Argyll and Bute
Dyflin	Dublin, Republic of Ireland
Earnford	near Bucknell, Shropshire (fictional)
Elyg	Ely, Cambridgeshire
Eoferwic	York
Gipeswic	Ipswich, Suffolk
Glowecestre	Gloucester
Hæstinges	Hastings, East Sussex
Haltland	Shetland
Heia	Eye, Suffolk
Hlymrekr	Limerick, Republic of Ireland
Ile	Islay, Argyll and Bute
Kathenessia	Caithness
Leomynstre	Leominster, Herefordshire
Litelport	Littleport, Cambridgeshire
Lundene	London
Lyteluse	River Little Ouse
Mann	Isle of Man
Montgommeri	Sainte-Foy-de-Montgommery, France
Orkaneya	Orkney
Oxeneford	Oxford
Rencesvals	Roncesvalles, Spain
Sarraguce	Zaragoza, Spain
Saverna	River Severn
Scrobbesburh	Shrewsbury, Shropshire
Sudwerca	Southwark, Greater London
Suthreyjar	Hebrides
Temes	River Thames
Use	River Great Ouse
Utwell	Outwell, Norfolk
Wiceford	Witchford, Cambridgeshire
Wiltune	Wilton, Wiltshire
Wirecestre	Worcester
Yrland	Ireland
Ysland	Iceland

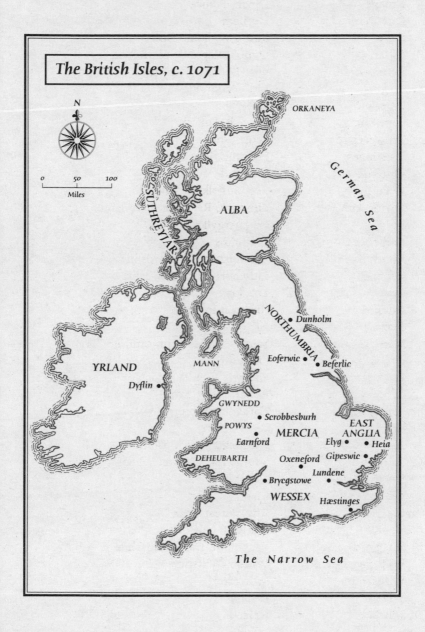

The British Isles, c. 1071

N

0   50   100
Miles

ORKANEYA

German Sea

SUTHREYIAR

ALBA

YRLAND

Dyflin

MANN

NORTHUMBRIA

Dunholm

Eoferwic

Beferlic

GWYNEDD

Scrobbesburh

POWYS

Earnford

MERCIA

EAST
ANGLIA

Elyg

Heia

DEHEUBARTH

Oxeneford

Gipeswic

Lundene

Brycgstowe

WESSEX

Hæstinges

The Narrow Sea

Prologue

A man always remembers his first kill. In the same way that he can recall the time he first felt a woman's touch, so he can conjure up the face of his first victim and every detail of that moment. Even many years later he will be able to say where it took place and what was the time of day, whether it was raining or whether the sun shone, how he held his blade and how he struck and where he buried the steel. He will remember his foe's screams ringing in his ears, the feel of warm blood running across his fingers and the stench of voided bowels and freshly opened guts rising up. He will remember the horror brought on by the realisation of what he has done, of what he has become, and those memories will remain with him as long as he lives.

And so it was with me. Rarely have I ever spoken of this, and even among my closest companions there are few who know the whole story. There was a time years ago when my fellow knights and I would spend the evenings sitting around the campfire and spinning boastful yarns of our achievements, but even then it was never something I cared to speak of, and I would often change the details to suit what I thought those listening would prefer to hear. Why that was, I'm unsure. Perhaps it is because it didn't happen in the heat and thunder of the charge, or in the grim spearwork of the shield-wall, as many might wish to think, and for that reason I am ashamed, although many of my fellow warriors would undoubtedly have a similar story to tell. Perhaps it is because all these events that I now set down in writing took place many decades ago, and when I look back on my time upon this earth there are far nobler deeds that I would rather remember.

Perhaps it is simply because it is no one's business but my own.

What happened is this. I was in my sixteenth summer at the time: more than a boy but not quite a man; a promising rider but not yet proficient in swordcraft, and still lacking in the virtues of patience and temper that were required of the oath-sworn knight I aspired to be. Like all youths I was hot-tempered and arrogant; my head was filled with dreams of glory and plunder and a foolish belief that nothing in the world could harm me, and it was that same foolishness that caused me to cross those men that summer's day.

We had that afternoon arrived in some small Flemish river-town, the name of which I've long since forgotten, on our way home from paying homage to the Norman duke. I had been sent with a purse full of silver by the man who was then my lord, Robert de Commines, to secure overnight lodgings for our party. It should have been an easy task, except that it happened to be a market day, and not only that but it was also nearing the feast of a minor saint whose name I was unfamiliar with but whom the folk of the surrounding country revered, which meant that the streets were crowded and each one of the dozen inns I visited was already full with merchants and pilgrims who had come to sell their wares, to worship and to attend the festivities.

Weary from my wanderings, eventually I found a corner of the main thoroughfare where I could sit upon the dusty ground and rest my legs. Leaning back against a wall, I wondered whether it was better to return to Lord Robert, tell him of my failure and risk his displeasure, or to keep looking, though it seemed a fruitless task. My throat was parched and I drank down the last few drops from my ale-flask to soothe it. The pungent fragrance of the spice-monger's garlic filled my nose, mixed with the less palatable smells of cattle dung from the streets and the carcasses of poultry hanging from the butchers' stalls. Once in a while my ears would make out a few words in French or Breton, the only two worldly tongues I was familiar with, but otherwise all I heard was a cacophony of men and women calling across the wide marketplace, dogs barking, young children shrieking as they chased each other in between the stalls, prompting annoyed shouts from those whose paths they obstructed. Oxen snorted as they drew wagons laden with sheaves of wheat and casks that might have contained wine, or else some kind of salted meat. A young man juggled coloured balls and some of the townsfolk crowded around to marvel at his skill; from one of the side streets floated the sound of a pipe, accompanied by the steady beating of a tabor.

And then I saw her. She sat on a stool on the other side of the wide street, behind a trestle table laden with wet-glistening salmon and herring. Her fair hair was uncovered, tied in a loose braid that shone gold in the sun and trailed halfway down her back, a sign that she wasn't yet wed. By my reckoning she was about as old as myself, or perhaps a year or so older; I have never been much good at guessing ages. She had a fine-featured face, with attentive, smiling eyes, and a friendly manner with the folk who stopped at the stall to ask how much those fish were worth and to argue the price, before grudgingly and at length handing over their coin.

A more beautiful creature I had never laid eyes upon. None of the girls with whom I'd stolen kisses in the woods of Commines or on our travels could match her. The sight of her was like the sweetest, strongest wine I had tasted, and I drank deeply, letting it go to my head, making sure to take in every smallest detail, from the way her eyes narrowed in concentration as she worked a blade between the two halves of an oyster shell, to the deftness of her knife-work as she prised it open, and the quickness of her fingers in scooping out the silver-shining meat contained within and placing it in a wooden bowl beside her.

How long I sat there watching her shell oysters, entranced by her beauty and her skill, I cannot say. It must have been some while, for eventually I realised that she was looking back at me, an odd expression upon her face. Heat rose up my cheeks. Others might have chosen that moment to avert their gaze, and I almost did, but instead, almost without willing it, I found myself getting to my feet and making my way through the crowds towards her, making my apologies to a stout-armed woman carrying a pail of water in each hand, who berated me after I almost collided with her. At least this seemed to amuse the girl, who greeted me with a broad smile when I reached the fishmonger's stall.

'I haven't seen you before,' she said. 'You're not from here, are you?'

She spoke in French, although with a slight accent, as if it were not her first tongue, which meant we had something in common. Her voice was light and full of warmth, exactly as I had imagined it would be.

'We arrived a few hours ago,' I said by way of explanation, and wished I had something more interesting to offer by way of conversation, but I was enthralled by this precious jewel. An idea came to me, and I drew from my knapsack a small, bruised pear I'd purchased earlier from one of the fruit-sellers who plied their trade by the wharves on the river.

'For you,' I said, and held it out as I met her eyes, grey-blue like the open sea. How I ever thought to win a girl's affections with such a paltry gift, I wasn't sure, but I was young and stupid, and that was all I had to give as a token of my admiration.

At first she hesitated, regarding both myself and the pear with a quizzical look as if it were some sort of trick, but after a moment she reached out to accept my offering.

'Thank you,' she said, and gave that smile again as she raised it to her lips, but at the same moment a firm hand grabbed her wrist and she gave a yelp of surprise. A shadow fell across us and I glanced up to see a man as wide as he was tall, with thinning hair, a blood-stained apron across his round belly, and a curved blade gripped tightly in his hand.

'You,' he barked at me. 'Who are you?'

So startled was I by the question and by his sudden manner that no words arrived upon my tongue.

'Do you wish to buy some herring?'

'N-no,' I replied, confused, as I looked up at him. No one would ever have described me as short, but even when I drew myself up to my full height this man still had the advantage of at least a head over me.

'A basket of oysters, perhaps?'

Even at sixteen summers I recognised the smell of ale on a man's breath, and I caught a great whiff of it then. I shook my head.

'So it's my niece you want to buy, then? You want to have your way with her, like all the others who've had their eye on her. That's right, isn't it?'

It had been a glance and a smile and a few words exchanged, nothing more. How could he take insult from that?

'I didn't mean anything by it,' I replied, with as much defiance as I could muster as I remembered who I was: a knight-in-training in the service of the famed Robert de Commines, and more than a match for this brute.

One hand still held his curved knife, but with the other he snatched the pear from the girl's hand. She gave a squeak of protest, but he ignored her.

'I know your kind,' he told me. 'You take a fancy to my Joscelina and think you can tempt her with presents as soon as my back is turned. I didn't take her in and feed and clothe her all these years just to see some filthy lice-ridden beggar take her from me.'

'Uncle—'

Whatever Joscelina had been about to say, she was silenced by a slap across the face. The fishmonger let go of her wrist and she gave a cry as she fell awkwardly on to the muddy street.

He turned the pear over in his hand, examining it with disdain. 'Is this how much you think she's worth?' he asked. 'This worm-ridden thing?' He tossed it into the gutter where the fish-heads lay.

By then a handful of the other stallholders had come to see what the commotion was about. They were men of all shapes: some tall and wiry; others built like the girl's uncle, with strong shoulders and swollen guts and weather-worn faces that bore stern expressions.

'Are you making trouble for Gerbod, lad?' said one of them as they began to form a ring around me.

What I should have done then was see sense and make my apologies, or else try to run before anything further happened; there was no doubt that I was quicker on my feet than these men. That was what instinct told me was the right course, but something else held me there. My blood had been stirred; it ran hot in my veins as anger swelled inside me. It wasn't that the fishmonger's words offended me, for in my life I had been called many worse things than a beggar, and bore such insults lightly. Rather what angered me was the way he'd struck his niece when she had done nothing to deserve it, and even though how he chose to treat her was none of my business, in that moment my head was filled with visions of myself as her stalwart defender, in the manner of the knights of legend, the ones praised by the poets in their songs.

'What are you waiting for?' asked the fishmonger, the man they'd called Gerbod. He waved his bloodied fish knife in my direction. 'Get gone from here before I bury this blade in your gut.'

But I wasn't listening. Instead I slid my own knife from its sheath and brandished it before me, clutching the hilt so tightly that it hurt my palm as I turned to face each one of them in turn. The weapon had been given to me by Lord Robert when first I'd entered his service, and I treasured it above all my other possessions, often spending long hours by light of sun and moon honing its edge with whetstone and polishing the flat of the steel until my own reflection gazed back at me. Of course I'd been in fights before, both in the training yard and outside of it, but rarely with anyone but the other servant-boys in Lord Robert's household, and certainly not with full-grown men such as these, who looked as though they had seen more than their share of tussles over the years. Including Gerbod, there were six of them. Even many years later, when my sword-skills were at their sharpest, when for a while my name was among those sung by the poets and my deeds were known far and wide, I would have thought twice about trying to fight so many by myself. To think I could do so then, when I had not even sixteen summers behind me, was the height of folly, but arrogance had blinded me. That, and a desire to prove myself, to show the girl, her uncle and his friends that I was no craven.

A couple of them drew their own weapons; the others simply laughed.

'Don't be stupid, boy,' the fishmonger snarled from the other side of his stall. 'You can't fight us.'

Behind him the girl was getting to her feet, rubbing her wrist and elbow, and there were tears in her eyes.

'Put your blade away and you won't get hurt,' said Gerbod. He came around the table where the fish lay in their neat rows, and strode towards me, gutting-knife still in hand.

I glanced about, facing each one of those who were surrounding me and starting to wonder whether this had been such a good idea. With every beat of my heart my confidence and resolve began to ebb away, until, almost without willing it, I found my weapon-hand returning to the sheath at my belt and sliding the steel back into the leather.

Gerbod grinned, displaying a row of broken, yellow teeth. He took another step closer to me so that his ale-reeking breath filled my nose, then, after eyeing me carefully, he laid both his hands upon my shoulders and shoved me. I wasn't expecting it and stumbled backwards, into the path of one of the fishmonger's friends, who tried to send me back the way I had come. My feet couldn't keep up with the rest of me, however, and suddenly I found myself sprawling forward, limbs flailing, landing on my side in a puddle to the laughs and jeers of the men. Before I could even think of getting up, something connected sharply with my ribs, and I yelped.

'That's for threatening me,' I heard the fishmonger say. He kicked me again, closer to my groin this time. 'No one crosses me and walks away freely.'

Wincing in double agony, I clutched at my chest as he bent down beside me and in one swift move cut through the leather thong that tied the coin-purse with which Lord Robert had entrusted me to my belt.

'What's this?' he asked. He hefted the pouch in his hand, feeling its weight and listening to the clink of silver inside, before opening the drawstring. His eyes gleamed as he upended the contents into his palm, letting a stream of coins pour forth.

'He must have stolen it,' said one of his companions, a thickset man with lank hair and a large wart on the tip of his nose. 'I reckon he was looking to rob you too, until you caught him.'

'Rob me of my Joscelina, indeed,' Gerbod murmured. He tipped the silver back into the purse and glanced down at me. 'That's right, isn't it? Do you know how they punish your sort here?'

'I'm no thief,' I said. 'That silver belongs to my lord, Robert de Commines.'

But the fishmonger did not want to listen to my protests. He landed another kick to my gut before, at his signal, the lank-haired man stepped forward and dragged me to my feet. I might, I suppose, have shouted out for help, but it seemed the cowardly thing to do, and in any case how many of the market-goers would want to involve themselves in something that was none of their business? Far better, in their eyes, to let things take their course than to risk injury and perhaps worse. And so it was then. Dazed and blinking to keep the tears of pain from my eyes, I glanced around, trying desperately to meet the eye of anyone, man or woman, who might come to my aid, but they all kept their heads bowed low as they hustled past. The pipe and tabor still played; elsewhere merchants continued to call out the prices of their wares. To them it was just another day, another street brawl.

Eventually my gaze settled once more on Gerbod, who stood in front of me. In his left hand he clutched the purse that contained his spoils, while in the other he held the curved knife, and it was with that one that he grabbed my collar.

'This silver is mine now,' he said, and spat in my face.

My arms were pinned behind me, and I could not lift them to wipe away his spit, let alone reach for my knife-hilt, for all the good that would do me. The breath caught in my chest as I glimpsed the glinting edge of his blade, mere inches from my neck. One slip of his hand was all it would take.

'It belongs to Lord Robert,' I said in a small voice. It was useless to argue, even if it was the truth. But the truth was all I had to offer, and no other ideas came to mind.

'Suppose that it did,' the fishmonger said as he clutched tighter at my collar, 'tell me this: where is he now to claim it?'

'Closer than you think,' came a voice from somewhere behind me, and a wave of relief broke over me, for it was a voice I knew well. A look of surprise came over Gerbod's face, which quickly changed to a frown as he let go of me and faced the newcomer. A shiver came over me and I breathed deeply as the knife left my throat. I tried to turn but the lank-haired one still held me. Even when I twisted my neck to look over my shoulder, all I could see was a shadowy, indistinct figure, for the sun was in my eyes.

'This isn't your concern, friend,' said the fishmonger.

The figure shouldered his way through the ring of men around me, his mail chinking. With every step the shadow resolved, until I could make out familiar features: his well-trimmed beard, of which he had always been proud; and his thick eyebrows, which lent him a stern appearance. He was then a little less than thirty in years, and while he was neither especially tall nor imposing in stature, he nonetheless had a manner and a way of speaking that always seemed to command respect, not just from those in his employ but from others too. Silver rings adorned both his hands; he was clad in a newly polished hauberk that glistened in the light, while hanging from his belt was a scabbard decorated with enamelled copper and gemstones of many hues.

'I rather think it is my concern,' he answered. 'My name is Robert de Commines. The boy is one of my retainers.'

He did not meet my eyes as he said this. Instead he fixed his gaze upon Gerbod, who could only give a snort in reply, for the first time seemingly unable to think of anything to say.

'Let him go,' Lord Robert said. 'The rest of you, sheathe your weapons. If any of you should so much as lay a scratch upon him, you will have my blade-edge to answer to.'

He rested a hand upon his silver-worked hilt as if in warning. The other men exchanged nervous glances with each other. They remained six against our two, and probably had a good chance of overwhelming us if it came to blows, the fact that one of us was armed with mail and sword notwithstanding. Yet running through their minds at the same time would have been the knowledge that to begin a fight in this place would not go unpunished. If they drew blood they would be hunted down and forced to pay the fine, and if they could not pay the price required by law, they would be outlawed at best and hanged at worst. None of them wished such a fate.

None of them, it seemed, except for Gerbod.

'Why should I listen to you?' he asked as he advanced upon Robert until there was barely an arm's length between them. It was an impertinent question to ask one of such obvious wealth and status, but ale dulls a man's wits even as it quickens his temper, and a great deal of it must have passed the fishmonger's lips that day. He jabbed the finger of his left hand – the one holding the coin-pouch – towards the other man's mailed chest, but Robert was too quick for him, and snatched hold of his wrist.

'Touch me and it will be the last move you make,' he warned, lowering his voice as he tightened his grip and met the large-bellied one's stare. 'Now, return the money and tell your friend to unhand the boy.'

What possessed the fishmonger that day, I will never know. Perhaps the sight of so much silver had blinded him, or else he was simply used to getting his way and did not much care for being challenged. I have come across many of his kind over the years, and always it has ended badly.

Without warning he stepped forward and in the same sharp movement brought his head down upon Robert's brow, sending him staggering backwards. While my lord tried to regain his footing Gerbod came at him with his knife, but his slashes found only air.

'Lord!' I yelled as I struggled to free myself from the grip of the one who held me, though it seemed he lacked the same appetite for a fight as his friend the fishmonger, since he made little effort to stop me. Nor did the rest of those who had gathered, who were turning tail. They sensed that no good would come of this and wanted no part of any bloodshed.

'Stay back,' Robert shouted when he saw me running to his aid with naked steel in hand. He ducked beneath a wild swing aimed at his head, but couldn't avoid Gerbod's shoulder-charge, and was knocked to the ground. He lay on his back, blinking as he pressed at the spot on his forehead where he had been struck, whilst the fishmonger stood over him, eyes gleaming.

Roaring without words, I hurled myself at Gerbod. My blood was up and I was blinded by hatred and a wild feeling I'd never before known: a feeling that in the months and years to come would grow ever more familiar; a feeling to which men at different times have given different names and which I would come to know as the battle-rage.

Gerbod heard me coming. With surprising deftness for a man of his girth he stepped out of my path and that of my knife-edge. Smirking, he raised his curved steel to bring to bear upon me. I froze, not knowing what to do. My feet seemed to take root where I'd planted them, and in that moment my rage turned to fear; in the gleam of his weapon I glimpsed my death. I could not tear my eyes from it, could not move or think, and I was still watching it when from behind him came the sound of a sword being drawn, followed an instant later by a flash of steel as the flat of Robert's blade connected with the back of the fishmonger's head.

He gave a grunt and staggered towards me, and I had just enough wit remaining to thrust out my blade to defend myself. He tumbled forwards, collapsing on top of me like a block of marble fallen from the back of a stonemason's cart, bringing us both down. The street was muddy and there was cattle and horse dung everywhere, but even so I met it hard, and my head must have hit a stone, since for a few moments everything went hazy and I did not know where I was. Someone was calling my name, but it seemed far away. A great weight pressed down on my lower half, pinning me to the ground so that I could not move, and the only thing running through my mind was the question of where my knife was, the one that Lord Robert had gifted to me, for it was no longer in my hand.

My hand, which was covered in something warm and sticky and glistening. That was when I came to properly and saw the fish-monger lying there, his arms splayed out, his head laid upon my chest, his mouth wide, his eyes open but unseeing. The stench of shit mixed with fresh-spilt blood filled my nose and I wanted to retch, but nothing would come. All around us people were shouting and pointing and running and screaming, but I could not speak or move or do anything at all. Then Robert was beside me, rolling the fishmonger's corpse off me, and holding out his hand to help me up. His face was red from exertion and there was a panicked look in his eyes as he looked about.

Only when I was on my feet did I see the steel buried in Gerbod's chest close to where his heart was. It took but a moment for me to recognise the blade's hilt and see that it belonged to me, and to understand what had happened. The breath left my chest and a chill ran through me.

'Run,' Robert shouted, and then when I did not move, he laid a firm hand upon my shoulder. 'Now!'

But I would not leave without my weapon. I scrambled to retrieve it, closing my eyes and trying to keep the sickness from rising in my throat as I jerked it from the wound, feeling the flesh tear and the edge scrape against bone. Without pausing to clean the blood from it, I returned it to its sheath, and then I was on my feet again, only to meet Joscelina's gaze. I'd all but forgotten her. Desperately she screamed for help, though of course there was nothing that could be done. Her voice and her eyes were filled with anguish the likes of which I'd never before seen or heard, though I have known it many times since.

I had taken her uncle from her: the man who was her keeper and her sole protector in the world. With my own hand I had done this. His blood was upon me.

Once more Robert called my name. That was when I noticed the coin-pouch lying just beyond the reach of Gerbod's outstretched fingers, as if even in death he clutched at it.

'What about the silver?' I asked Robert.

'Leave it!' he said. 'It belongs to her now. Now, run!'

But Joscelina had no interest in the money. Even as I stood there, she rushed to her uncle's side, kneeling down beside him and hugging his bloodstained chest tightly to her own, her cheeks streaming with tears. Swallowing to hold down the bile rising in my throat, I tore my gaze away and broke into a run as I followed Robert through the gathered crowds, fleeing that place of ill fortune. No one dared try to stop us.

We left the town that same hour, riding hard along the tracks towards the woods to the south to escape any of Gerbod's friends who might pursue us and try to bring us to justice or take their revenge. That it had been an accident, that it had been he who attacked us and that we were only defending ourselves would count for nothing in the eyes of those who passed judgment. Although in years to come Robert's star would rise and mine with it, at that time he was still far from rich, and possessed little influence that he could use to sway them. Thus we had no choice but to flee the town. I remember glancing back and watching the houses and the walls disappearing behind us and coming to the realisation even then that, for me, nothing thereafter would be the same.

And that was how it happened. It is strange how the names and faces return so easily to me, when many of the companions and sword-brothers with whom I once shared bread and fought shoulder to shoulder in battle have long since slipped my mind. Strange, too, how vivid it all remains in my memory, although it was but a minor street scuffle rather than a glorious battle, and over in moments besides. Still, it marked a turning point in my life, for that was the day I became a killer and my journey began. Men who previously had looked down on me as stable-hand and cup-bearer and serving-lad started to see me differently and to hold me in greater regard, as if I were a new person altogether. What Robert told them and what they believed took place that day, I never learnt. Certainly I never said anything to them, nor did they ever question me regarding the truth of the matter, and that was probably for the best.

The boy had proven himself a warrior, and in so doing had taken his first steps upon the sword-path; that was all that counted. Of course his lord was hoping that he would grow into a good enough warrior that that kill would become merely the first of many, and so it proved in the years that followed. But the truth is and always has been that no matter how great a man's prowess with spear and sword and shield, or how much silver and gold he may acquire, or how many fine horses he owns, or whether by his deeds he forges himself a reputation to last until the day of judgement, still that first time he took a life will be the one he remembers most clearly.

I should know, for I have walked that path. My name is Tancred, and this is my tale.

One

The smoke on the horizon was the first sign that the enemy were nearby. It billowed in great plumes above the fields, spreading like an ink-stain upon the fresh parchment of the sky. Save for the occasional bleating of sheep in the pastures and the warbling of skylarks hovering high above, there was no sound. A thin drizzle fell, the wind had died to almost nothing and everything else was still, which made the sight of those plumes in the distance all the more unnerving.

Straightaway I reined in my destrier, Fyrheard, and raised my hand to those following as a signal to halt. My men, riding to either side of me, responded at once, as did the mounted archers at the rear of our column, but the oxen-drivers were too busy talking between themselves to notice, and only my shout of warning stopped them and their animals from colliding with us. I cast a glare in their direction and berated them in the English tongue, but they didn't seem to notice. Suddenly their minds were on the distant smoke, at which they were pointing and shouting in alarm.

'A hall-burning, do you think, lord?' Serlo asked. One of my two household knights, he was a bear of a man with a fearsome sword-arm and a temper to match: not the kind of man that I would have liked to face in a fight, and I was glad to count him as a friend.

'If it is, it wouldn't be the first,' I replied. Nor, I suspected, was it likely to be the last. In the last fortnight the rebels had made half a dozen such raids, always in different places but always following the same pattern: striking as if from nowhere to lay the torch to a village or manor, before just as quickly withdrawing to their boats and melting away into the marshes. By the time word of what had taken place had reached us and the king had sent out men to meet them in battle, they were already long gone. Still, it was rare that they should strike so far from their island stronghold. The castle at Cantebrigia was barely two hours behind us; the rebels were either growing bolder or else more foolhardy, and I couldn't make up my mind which.

'What now?' Pons asked, his voice low. The second of my knights, he possessed a sharp wit and an equally sharp tongue, which he often struggled to restrain, but there was nothing light-hearted about his manner now.

'We could try to find another way around,' Serlo suggested.

'Not if we want to reach the king's camp by dusk,' I said. Aside from the main tracks, I wasn't at all familiar with this land: a flat and featureless expanse of pasture and barley fields, crossed by streams and rivers narrow and wide. What I did know was that there were few well-made ways along which fully laden carts could travel, with bridges and fords that they could cross. We could easily waste several hours if we decided to leave the road and strike out across the country.

Pons frowned. 'Do we go on, then?'

'They could be lying in wait for us,' Serlo pointed out.

I considered. On the one hand I had no wish to lead us all into a trap, but on the other it seemed unlikely the enemy would announce their presence so clearly if an ambush was what they had in mind. Besides, it had been several weeks since the rebels had made any serious attempts to waylay our supply trains – not since the king had begun sending out parties of knights and other warriors to accompany them and ward off any would-be attackers.

And that was how I came to be here. I, Tancred the Breton, Tancred of Earnford. The man who had helped win the gates in the battle at Eoferwic, who had led the charge against the pretender, Eadgar Ætheling, faced him upon the bridge and almost killed him. The same man who by night had entered the enemy's camp in Beferlic, rescued his lord from imprisonment at the hands of the Danes, and captured the feared Wild Eadric, the scourge of the Marches. I had stared death in the face more often than I cared to remember and each time lived to tell the tale. I had done what others thought impossible. By rights I should have been rewarded with vast lands and halls of stone, chests brimming with silver, gilded swords and helmets with which to arm myself, stables of fleet-footed Andalusian horses that I could offer as gifts to my followers. I should have been leading forays against the enemy, hunting down their foraging parties, training at arms with my companions, or else helping to hone the shield- and spear-skills of those less proficient in the ways of war.

But I was not, and with every day my anger grew. For instead of being allowed to make use of my experience, instead I found myself reduced to this escort duty, riding back and forth across this featureless country day after day, all to protect a dozen scrawny oxen, their stinking, dung-covered owners and these rickety carts, which were constantly becoming stuck or else collapsing under the weight of the goods they carried. It would have been bearable had the rebels ever dared approach us, since at least then I'd have had the chance to test my sword-arm. Probably sensibly, however, they preferred to go where the pickings were easy and where they could wreak the greatest devastation, rather than risk their lives for the sake of whatever supplies we guarded, which usually comprised no more than some loaves of bread, barrels of ale and rounds of cheese, timber planks, nails and bundles of firewood – all things that our army needed to keep it warm and fed, but which, if the reports we received were reliable, the rebels already had in plenty upon their island fastness at Elyg.

'What are you thinking, lord?' Serlo asked.

'I'm thinking that those smoke-plumes are rising thickly,' I said, meaning that those fires hadn't been burning for long, which in turn meant that those who had caused them couldn't be far off. And I was thinking, too, that this was the closest I had come to crossing swords with any of the rebels on this campaign. The battle-hunger rose inside me; my sword-hand tingled with the familiar itch. I longed to hear the clash of steel ringing out, to feel my blade-edge biting into flesh, to let the battle-joy fill me. And as those thoughts ran through my mind, an idea began to form.

'The three of us will ride on ahead,' I said. 'If the enemy are lurking, I want to find them.'

Serlo and Pons nodded. While they were unafraid to speak their minds and while I often relied upon their counsel, they both respected me enough to follow whatever course of action I chose. The same could not be said of the company of archers that had been placed under my command, who guarded the rear of our column. Lordless men, they made their living by selling their services to anyone who would pay, owing allegiance to their purses and their purses alone. Even now I could make out the mutterings of their captain, a ruddy-faced man by the name of Hamo, who possessed a large gut and a sullen manner, and whom I had little liking for.

I turned to face him. At first he didn't notice me, being too busy exchanging snide remarks with his friends about how I was frightened of a little smoke, and how he'd heard it said that Bretons were all cowards, and that was why I'd been tasked with this escort duty, because I was too weak-willed for anything else. Clearly he knew nothing of who I was, or the deeds I had accomplished. He was lucky that I was too poor to afford the blood-price for his killing, or I would have long since struck him down for his insolence.

As it was, I had to wait a few moments before one of his comrades saw that I was watching and nudged him sharply in the side. He looked up; straightaway his tongue retreated inside his head, while his cheeks turned an even deeper shade of red.

'Lord,' he said, bowing extravagantly, which prompted a smirk from a few of the others. 'What are your instructions?'

I eyed him for a few heartbeats, silently daring him to break into a smile, but luckily for his sake he wasn't that stupid. Although he was not averse to muttering behind my back, he knew better than to defy me openly. I reckoned he was probably ten years older than me, which was a good age for someone whose life was lived on the field of battle. The summer just gone was my twenty-eighth, and although no one could yet call me old, I had ceased thinking of myself as a young man.

'Wait for us here,' I told him, trying to hold my temper and my tongue. 'I want to find out what's happened.'

Hamo frowned. 'We were ordered not to leave the carts undefended.'

'I'm not leaving them undefended. You're staying with them.'

Strictly speaking my duties didn't extend to hunting down enemy bands, a fact of which we were both well aware. But if Hamo thought I was going to let this opportunity pass, he was mistaken.

'Lord—' he began to protest, but I cut him off.

'Enough,' I said, and then pointed to the four of the archers nearest me: a full third of his company. 'You'll come with me.'

The four glanced at their leader, waiting for his assent. He said nothing but for a few moments held my gaze, resentment in his eyes, before nodding and gesturing for them to follow me. No doubt he would add this to his list of grievances, and find some way of using it against me, but I would worry about that another time. For now I had greater concerns.

'Keep a watch out on all sides and have your bows ready,' I said as we began to ride off. 'We'll be back before long.'

'And if the enemy happen upon us while you're gone?' asked Hamo. 'What are we supposed to do then?'

'Kill them,' I answered with a shrug. 'Isn't that what you have arrows for?'

It wasn't much of a reassurance, nor did I expect it to be, but it was all the advice I had to offer. But then I doubted that Hamo and his men would choose to put up much of a fight. Rather, if it looked as though they were outnumbered they would probably turn tail at the first opportunity, abandoning the carts and their contents in order to save their own skins. If they did, they needn't worry about ever showing their faces in our camp again, and at least King Guillaume wouldn't need to keep wasting good silver on them. Although I respected their skills with bow and blade, I didn't trust them, and I was far from the only one to share that sentiment. Sellswords were considered by many to be among the lowest class of men. Exiles and oath-breakers for the most part, they were entirely lacking in honour and scruple. Many would probably kill their own mothers if they thought they could profit from doing so.

With that we left Hamo and the rest of his company, and struck out across the flat country. Seven men did not make much of an army, especcially when I was used to commanding scores and at times even hundreds, but it would have to do. Unlike their captain, the four archers were all young lads. A couple of them were taller even than myself, and I was not exactly short. Each was broad in the chest, with the sturdy shoulders and thick arms needed to draw a string of any great weight. I myself had never mastered the bow, instead preferring as most knights did to hone my skills with sword and lance. But I knew from experience the slaughter that well-trained bowmen could wreak. They had proven their worth in the great battle at Hæstinges, firstly by inflicting great casualties amongst the English ranks and softening them to our charge, and later, it was said, by wounding the usurper Harold Godwineson, who according to rumour had received an arrow in his eye shortly before he fell to Duke Guillaume's sword. Whether that was true or not, no one knew for certain, although I'd met several men who claimed theirs was the arrow that had struck him.

That was five years ago. Since that day much had changed; I had seen friends and comrades die and gained others from unexpected quarters, had striven hard to win myself lands of my own only for them to be laid waste by my enemies, had found fame and honour and love and come close to losing it all.

One thing, though, remained the same, for even five years after we had triumphed at Hæstinges and King Guillaume had received the crown that belonged to him by right – the crown that had been promised him by his predecessor, King Eadward, and had been won with the Pope's blessing – still many among the English refused to submit to him. And so we found ourselves here in this bleak corner of East Anglia, trying to snuff out the final embers of rebellion, so far without success. Already we had been in the field for more than two months, and what did we have to show for it? A mud-ridden camp in which half the king's army was succumbing to fever and flux, while hundreds more lay dead after earlier attempts to assault the enemy upon the Isle of Elyg had ended in failure. Meanwhile the rebels continued to taunt us with their constant raids on the surrounding land. With every week they held out against us, scores more flocked to their banners, so that they had grown from a paltry couple of hundred to a host reckoned at nearly three thousand strong, and perhaps even larger than that. In truth no one knew for certain, and in the absence of any reliable information, the numbers grew ever wilder. Which meant that if we saw even the slightest chance to inflict some damage upon the enemy, we had to take it.

Keeping a careful watch out on all sides, we rode towards the source of the smoke. Soon I began to make out what only a short time ago would have been barns, hovels and cattle-sheds, though there was little left of them now. Amidst the fallen-in posts and roof-beams I spied glimmers of flame. Carrion birds cawed as they circled above the ruins in pairs and threes and fours; from somewhere came the forlorn bleating of a goat, although I could not see it. There was no other sound, nor any sign of movement, nor any glint of mail or spearpoints, which suggested the rebels had already left this place. Even so, we approached slowly. In my younger days my recklessness had often been my undoing, but experience had taught me the value of caution. The last thing I wanted was to rush in only to find ourselves in a snare, surrounded and outnumbered and with no hope of retreat. And so the four archers kept arrows nocked to their bowstrings, ready to let fly if they saw anything that looked like a foeman, while the rest of us gripped our lance-hafts firmly.

The blackened remains of the manor stood upon a low rise. As we climbed, it became clear that we were the only ones around. Anywhere that might have provided a hiding place for the enemy had been razed to the ground. Livestock had been slaughtered in the fields and the pens, while the corpses of men, women and children alike lay in the yards and the vegetable gardens, their clothes and hair congealed with blood. Feathered shafts protruded from the chests and backs of some, while others had gaping wounds to their necks and thighs, and bright gashes across their faces. No one had been spared. The stench of burnt flesh mixed with freshly spilt guts hung in the air: smells at which I might once have retched, but which by now had grown only too familiar. In the past few years I'd witnessed so many burnings of this kind that it was hard to be much moved by them. Still, it was rare that the enemy left so little in their wake.

'They killed even their own kind,' I murmured, scarcely able to believe it, though it wasn't the first time I'd seen it happen. Usually the rebels would kill the lord and his retainers, if they happened to be French, but leave the English folk unharmed. Sometimes, though, their desire for blood consumed them, and they wouldn't stop until all around was ruin and death. Perhaps the villagers had tried to fight back, or else the rebels had judged them guilty of falling subject to a foreign lord. I could only guess the reason.

Usually, though, there would be at least one person left alive. One to tell the tale. One to spread the news of what had happened here. One to foster fear of those who had done this. I knew because it was what I would have done.

We halted not far from what I guessed had once been a church, although there was little to distinguish it from the remains of the other hovels save for a waist-high stone cross that stood at its western end. One wall alone remained standing, but, as we dismounted, that too collapsed inwards, sending a great cloud of dust and still-glowing ash billowing up.

Beside me, Pons shook his head and muttered something that I could not entirely make out but which was most likely a curse.

Serlo turned to me. 'Why do you think they did this, lord?'

To that question there was no simple answer. Even if the lord of this manor had been a Frenchman, as seemed likely, the people living here would have been kinsfolk of the enemy. And apart from a few sheep and goats and chickens, most of which they seemed to have killed rather than take with them, what could there have been in a place like this to make it worth attacking?

Only one explanation came to mind. 'They wanted to send us a message,' I said.

'A message?' Serlo echoed, frowning.

Slowly it was beginning to make sense. The reason why they had come to this place, so far from their encampment upon the Isle.

'The enemy weren't looking for plunder or captives,' I said. 'If they were, they could have chosen to attack any number of manors closer to Elyg.'

'A show of force,' Pons put in, understanding at last. 'That's what they wanted. The more damage they wreak and the more ruthless they appear, the more panic they spread.'

I nodded. 'They want to prove that they don't fear us. That they can strike anywhere, at any time.'

And that was a bad sign, for it suggested that they were not only growing in confidence but also that they had men to spare for such expeditions. Before, they had preferred to keep to their corner of the marshlands and wait for us to come to them, only raiding occasionally and even then in places where they judged the risks to be fewest. But no longer. Now they laid waste the land with impunity, taunting us, and all the while we were powerless to stop them.

I swore aloud. I'd hoped that we might find some of the enemy still here, but in fact they were probably several miles away by now, which left us nothing more that we could usefully do except return to Hamo and the carts. All we had accomplished was to waste an hour or more on our journey. Back at the king's camp in Brandune the clerks would be waiting: pale, weasel-eyed men who recorded with quill and parchment every last crumb of bread and drop of ale that entered the storehouses and was distributed to the army. They wouldn't thank us if we arrived late and they had to complete their work by candlelight. While I always took a certain enjoyment from annoying them – one of the few pleasures afforded by this escort work – it would mean that I'd have to put up with even more of their carping, and I wasn't convinced it was worth it.

Fyrheard pawed restlessly at the ground. I shared his sentiment. I was about to give the order to turn back when amidst the calls of the crows, which had descended to pick at the bodies, came what sounded like a voice, not far off but weak and indistinct.

'Did anyone else hear that?' I asked.

'All I heard was my stomach rumbling,' muttered one of the archers, whose name I had forgotten but whose gaunt face and large ears I recognised. 'The sooner we return, the sooner we can eat.'

'You'll be going hungry unless you keep quiet,' I snapped. That prompted a snigger from the archer's comrades, but they fell quiet the instant I glared at them, and it was as well that I did, or else I might have missed the voice when it came again: a low moaning, like someone in pain.

'Over there,' said Serlo.

I looked in the direction of his pointed finger. Through clouds of smoke and ash I glimpsed a broken haywain and, lying beside it, what at first I took for a dead body; yet the corpse was moving its head, just slightly but enough that I could be sure that my eyes weren't deceiving me.

I strode across the muddy churchyard towards the figure. He lay on his back, coughing up crimson gobs. His tunic and trews were torn, while his face was streaked with mud. An arrow had buried itself in his torso, just above his groin. Around the place where the shaft was lodged his tunic was congealed with so much blood that it was a wonder he still lived. He looked about fifty or so in years; his grey hair was flecked with strands of white and cut short at the back in the French style, which suggested he was a Norman. On a leather thong around his neck hung a wooden cross that suggested he had either been Mass-priest here, or possibly chaplain to the local lord.

I knelt down by his side. The others gathered around me and I called for one of them to fetch something for the priest to drink. No sooner had I done so than his eyes opened, only by a fraction but enough that he could see me looking down on him.

'Who . . .' he began, but faltered over the words. His voice was weak, no more than a croak. 'Who are you?'

'Friends,' I assured him. 'My name is Tancred. We came as soon as we saw the smoke.'

'You came too late.' His face contorted in pain as once more he groaned and clutched at the shaft protruding from his gut. 'Too late.'

I tried to lift his hands away so as to get a better look at the wound. If we could only remove the arrow, I thought, it might be possible to staunch the flow and close up the hole. But no sooner had I prised his trembling fingers from the sticky cloth than I knew it would be no use. In my time I'd seen men recover from all manner of injuries, some worse than this, but not many. I'd learnt a little about wounds and how to treat them from the infirmarian in the monastery where I grew up, and over the years since had often watched leech-doctors at work. That small amount of knowledge was enough to tell me that he was too far gone, even for someone skilled in the healing arts, which none of us were.

Serlo crouched beside me, holding a leather flask. 'Ale,' he said. 'There's not much left.'

'It'll be enough,' I replied as I took it and removed the stopper. From the weight and the sound it made as I swirled the liquid about I reckoned it was probably about a quarter full. I turned back to the priest. 'Can you sit up?'

He shook his head, teeth clenched in pain. His breath came in stutters, making it hard for him to speak. 'I am beyond the help of ale. Besides, soon there will be no more pain. I shall be with God, and all will be well. There is only one thing you can do for me.'

'What is it, father?'

He gave a great hacking cough, and as he did so his whole body shuddered. Thankfully the fit did not last long and, sighing wearily, he lay back once more, at the same time motioning with his fingers for me to come closer. I leant towards him. There were tears in the old man's eyes, running down his cheeks.

'Bring to justice the ones who did this,' he said. 'Their leader too, that spawn of the Devil. The one they call Hereward. Promise me that.'

'Hereward?' I repeated, wanting to make sure I had heard him rightly. 'He did this?'

'So they called him, yes.'

That name was well known to me, as it was to everyone in our army, but I hadn't expected to hear it today, in this place. Hereward was one of the leaders of the rebels; it was he who had instigated this particular rising here in the fens. Some said he was a prominent thegn who had held land in these parts under the old king, Eadward. Others claimed he was a creature of the forest, abandoned at birth by his mother and raised by wolves, which explained his ruthless nature and his lack of Christian mercy. In truth no one knew where he had come from; his name had been first spoken only last autumn. While we had been campaigning with the king in the north, Hereward had raided the abbey at Burh, slain several of the monks and carried away all their treasures, including shrines and gilded crucifixes, richly bound and decorated gospel books and even, it was said, the golden crown that had rested upon Christ's head on the rood beneath the chancel arch. With the help of some Danish swords-for-hire he'd torched the town and monastery, and afterwards had fled by ship across the marshlands to the Isle of Elyg, where he now chose to make his stand against us, bolstered by the hundreds of other English outlaws who had flocked to his banner.

It was because of him that we were here in this godforsaken corner of the kingdom. It was because of him that, barely half a year after we had defeated the Northumbrians and their Danish allies at Beferlic and sent the pretender Eadgar scurrying back to the protection of the King of Alba, we'd found ourselves once more summoned by the king to join him on another of his campaigns.

Yet if the old priest was right, and it was indeed Hereward who had done this, and if we could kill or capture him—

A new sense of purpose stirred within me. 'How many of them were there?' I asked.

The priest's eyes were closed again, and his skin was as pale as snow. His time was near. But if I was to do what he had asked of me, he had to give me answers. I clasped his wrinkled, bloodstained hand, squeezing it firmly to try to keep him with us a little longer. At once he blinked and came to, a look of confusion upon his face, as if he did not quite know where he was.

'How many, father?' I said again.

He groaned as if with the effort of remembering, and after a moment managed to answer, 'A dozen, perhaps fifteen. No more.'

Roughly two men to every one of us, then. Fewer than I had been expecting, but still more than I would have liked to face, especially when one of them was Hereward himself, whose sword-edge had already claimed countless victims, if the stories told about him were true. No warrior ever won himself great fame without some measure of risk along the way, however. The difficulty came in learning which risks to embrace and which to avoid, and this seemed to me one worth taking.

'When did they leave?' I asked the priest.

'Not an hour ago,' he said, his eyelids drooping. 'They went . . .'

'Where?'

At first I thought he was slipping away and that we wouldn't get an answer, but then I spotted the faintest movement of his lips. I leant closer, having to put my ear almost to his mouth in order to hear him.

'Promise me,' he said, barely managing a whisper. 'Promise me.'

'I will bring them to justice, father,' I said. 'I swear it upon the cross. But you have to tell me where they went.'

'North.' The words came slowly now. 'They went north. That much I know. Now, let me rest.'

I nodded and squeezed the priest's hand one last time, then rested it carefully back upon his chest, which still rose and fell, though so slightly as to be almost imperceptible. Between breaths he whispered something that I could not entirely make out, but which from a couple of Latin words I guessed was probably a prayer for the safekeeping of his soul. Not that he had the chance to finish it, for he was still in the middle of whatever he was uttering when a pained expression came across his face and a long groan left his lips. His eyes closed once more; moments later his chest ceased moving, and that was when I knew he had left this world and that he was, at last, with God.

I made the sign of the cross across my breast as I got to my feet, and out of the corner of my eye I saw Serlo and Pons do the same. Around us the houses still burnt. The wind was rising, tugging at my tunic, blowing the smoke towards us and causing tongues of vibrant flame to flare up amongst what remained of the smoking timbers, wattle and thatch.

'What now?' asked the archer with the gaunt face, his expression now devoid of humour.

'We ride,' I answered.

Hereward and his band couldn't have got far in an hour. No doubt they would be making for wherever they had moored their boats. Since few vessels large and sturdy enough to carry a horse could navigate the marshes, I guessed they would most likely be on foot, which meant that we still had a chance of catching up with them.

Without delay we mounted up. I would have liked to bury the priest if only to save his body from the crows, but there was no time. Instead we left him by the haywain where he lay, his expression serene as if he were simply sleeping.

Only later, when the wreckage of the village was far behind us, did I realise that I hadn't even learnt his name.

Two

T he rebels had left few clear tracks, but there was only one path leading out of the village to the north, and so that was the one we followed. We rode swiftly, past stunted trees and the fallen-in roofs of cottages that were now abandoned, across rain-sodden earth and through shallow streams, our mounts' hooves kicking up mud and stones and water. We were close, I knew, to the southern edge of the marshes, where the land ended and gave way to a broad expanse of sedges and reed-banks, of myriad channels and meres, which stretched all the way from here to the German Sea. It seemed a different world entirely from the March at the other end of the kingdom where my manor lay, with its high hills and moors, and its valleys rich and green. No one but fisherfolk and eel-catchers lived here in this desolate place, and even then they did not live well. Only the higher ground upon the Isle of Elyg had anything much worth defending, which was one of the reasons why the rebels had made it their stronghold, the other being the fens on all sides that rendered any approach impassable to horses and treacherous for anyone on foot who was unfamiliar with the safe passages.

The land fell away as we neared that marsh. The wind pressed at our backs and every gust pushed us ever onwards, ever faster, through fallow fields where the grass had grown tall and pasture-lands that sheep and cattle had stripped almost bare of grass. With every furlong we covered I could feel the ground beneath Fyrheard's hooves growing softer, until in the distance it was possible to see the fields giving way to bogs and river inlets that marked the beginning of the marsh. But that was not all I saw. Close by the water's edge, amidst the reeds that rose up around those creeks, were the dark figures of several men unhitching packs from the panniers of two sumpter ponies, no doubt stolen from the village. The clouds were beginning to part, and as the first glimmer of evening light broke through, I spied the telltale glint of spearpoints and helmets that signified a war-band, and I knew we had found them.

There was no cover to be had anywhere, and across that flat land they saw us as easily and as surely as we saw them. They glimpsed our lances and our hauberks shining in the late sun, and all at once they began raising cries of alarm. Leaving the ponies behind, they made for one of the inlets, dragging what looked like small rowing boats out from their hiding places amidst the sedges and bushes and taking them down to the water. They knew that mailed horsemen meant trouble, and they had no wish to fight us and risk their lives if they could help it.

'Faster,' I urged the others. 'Ride harder!'

My blood was up, the familiar battle-joy coursing through my veins as the seven of us raced across the water-meadows towards the enemy. I spurred Fyrheard on, drawing every last fraction of speed from his legs, trusting him not to stumble over the thick tussocks or falter in his stride across the damp earth. I controlled him now with my legs alone as I unslung my shield from where it rested across my back and worked my arm through the leather braces, clutching the crossed straps that ran behind the boss, while in the other hand I gripped the haft of my lance. On my flanks Pons and Serlo roared battle-cries of their own, but their exact words were lost amidst the rush of air, the thunder of hooves and the sound of my heartbeat ringing through my skull.

Already one boatload was getting away, using paddles and longer-handled oars to push their vessel away from the bank and out on to the open water. A few were still struggling to free their vessels from the undergrowth, while three, ignoring their kinsmen's shouts of warning, had run back to the ponies as they tried to rescue more of their plunder. They fumbled at the buckles and straps of the harnesses, spilling the contents of the packs across the ground, where they fell amidst the tufts of grass and clumps of thistles. Desperately they scooped up armfuls of gilded plate and bronze candlesticks and shoved silver coin into their pouches before, at last, they turned in flight.

Too late. From above my head came a sharp whistle of air, quickly followed by another and another and another still. I looked up to see four goose-feathered shafts soaring towards the enemy, then glanced behind to see Hamo's archers drawn up in a line. Without even dismounting they drew arrow after arrow from the bags at their sides, letting them fly no sooner than they had put them to their bowstrings. Most of those attempts overshot, either falling amidst the banks of reeds or else dropping into the mere beyond, but one found its target, burying itself square in the back of one of the greedier Englishmen as he scurried across the field towards the waiting boats. The force of the impact pitched him forward; the gathered plunder slipped from his grasp in a shower of gold.

To my right, Pons gave a whoop of delight, lifting his shield-hand to the sky as he drew ahead of myself and Serlo. The strength of the charge lay in weight of numbers, in massed knights riding knee to knee, and normally I would have shouted for him to keep forma-tion, but the only thing that mattered now was speed. We couldn't afford to let them get away, not this time. Not when fame was ours for the taking.

'On!' I yelled. The wind whipped against my cheeks and the black hawk pennon nailed below my lance-head fluttered. 'On, on, on, for God and for Normandy!'

That single arrow-strike was all it took to spread confusion amongst the Englishmen. Those already afloat were paddling furi-ously to get out of bowshot, leaving behind the two boat crews still on land, who seemed to be confused as to whether they should carry on dragging their vessels down to the water, or else try to make a stand against us. All the while we were bearing down upon them, no more than half a furlong away now: a mere seven men sowing fear in the hearts of a force twice that number.

And then I saw him. He leapt down from one of the craft into the water, a bow slung over one shoulder and an arrow-bag over the other, and waded through the waist-deep waters towards the shore, berating the stragglers and gesturing towards their boats. A gangly, long-limbed giant of a man, he stood half a head above the tallest of his comrades. His mail shirt gleamed as if newly polished, but he wore no helmet to protect his head, and so I could clearly see the lank black hair hanging to his shoulders. There was purpose in his every movement, and even in that brief moment I had the impression of one well used to leading.

Hereward.

It could be no other. The last of his men had finally managed to cast off from the shore, leaving him alone to face us. Around him steel rained down as Hamo's archers continued to let fly volley after volley, but he showed no sign of fear. He lifted his own bow from his shoulder, and in what seemed like a single movement he drew and loosed a single arrow.

It flew swiftly and it flew true, sailing just above the reed-heads. He watched it all the way, without even troubling to put a second to his bowstring, as if somehow he knew that one was all he would need. At first I thought he had misjudged the angle of the flight, for it seemed it would glide well over our heads, but then the wind must have caught it, for its silver-shining head suddenly turned earthwards towards us, the point glinting wickedly with its promise of death.

'Shields,' I cried as I raised my own to cover my face and upper chest, praying that the others heard my warning as for a moment I charged on blindly.

A violent shriek filled the air, and I looked up in time to see Pons's destrier go down in a writhing mess of hooves, turf, mud and horseflesh. Pons himself was on the ground, yelling for help as he struggled to free his foot, which was trapped beneath the animal as it kicked and screamed, its eyes wide and white. Serlo brought his horse to a halt and leapt down to help him, but that was all I saw, for I had other concerns.

Barely fifty paces in front of me, Hereward stood alone, yelling vehemently as he waved back some of his comrades who were jumping from the boats to come to his aid – whether out of stupidity or arrogance, I couldn't tell, and hardly cared. I stared at him, couching my lance under my arm, levelling the point at chest-height

31

and imagining how I would drive it deep into his heart, twisting it so as to kill him all the quicker. Victory would be ours, and we would return to the king's camp with his head as our prize. He returned my gaze, and as he did so I saw the determination in his dark eyes. Calmly, as if he were merely enjoying an afternoon's practice at the butts, he drew another shaft from his arrow-bag, raised the bow into position, aimed it in my direction—

When something happened that I was not expecting. Something that, even all this time later, I find myself ashamed to recount. Something that in all the time I'd travelled the sword-path had only happened once, when I stood with knife in hand facing the fish-monger in that Flemish town all those years ago. For as Hereward slowly brought the string back to his shoulder, as the feathered end brushed the skin upon his cheek and as he prepared to loose, a vision flashed through my mind. A vision that told me how that arrow would fly and where it would strike, how at this distance it would run through mail and flesh as easily as a needle through cloth.

I stared at that arrow-point and fear gripped me: a fear so powerful that I had never known its kind before. My stomach lurched; my breath caught in my chest. My blood was no longer pounding, filling my limbs with vigour, and I wondered if my heart had stopped. Like water being thrown on a fire, the battle-joy was extinguished. For the first time I could remember since that day when I was a youth, my nerve failed me in the heat of battle. I did not see victory before me now, but something else entirely.

I saw my death.

Why it happened and how it happened so quickly, I cannot say. All I know is that suddenly I was jerking sharply to one side, wheeling around, abandoning the charge, abandoning the fight, all the while expecting to feel a sudden strike between my shoulder-blades, or for Fyrheard to collapse beneath me and for me to be pitched from the saddle.

I never knew where that feathered shaft landed, or whether Hereward even loosed it at all. But I heard the jeers and laughter of the Englishmen in their boats. They taunted me in their own tongue, calling me a craven and many worse things besides, and an angry heat burnt inside me at the knowledge that they were right. I had fled from a fight, not because I was outnumbered or because sensible action had won out over blind rage, but because of fear.

Fear at the challenge. Fear for my life.

Floods of sweat rolled off my brow, stinging my eyes. By the time I had blinked the moisture away, wiped a sleeve across my face and turned to face the enemy again, it was too late to do anything. Hereward was wading back once more through the silt-brown marsh-waters to the cheers of his companions. Several of them helped to haul his mailed form aboard one of the boats, where he proceeded to stand up and grin at us, lifting his arms aloft and spreading them wide.

'Hereward!' his men cried as one. 'Hereward!'

A few of them broke into song, raised their fists in the air or bared their pale arses at us, waggling them from side to side. Most, however, had picked up oars and were anxiously rowing as fast as possible. Hamo's men continued to rain steel upon them, riding down right to the edge of the marsh so that they could get closer. One arrow struck a green-painted shield, but that was the closest any of their attempts came, the rest all dropping with splashes into the murky depths. Still they kept sending volley after volley up into the evening sky, although more in hope than in expectation, I sensed. All too soon the boats were beyond the range of even the most skilled archer in Christendom, and not long after that they had disappeared entirely into the marsh-mist.

Our chance was gone. We had let Hereward escape, and a single paltry kill was all we had to show for our efforts.

One kill, and one fallen horse. Whilst I had been watching the enemy vanish across the water, Pons, with Serlo's help, had managed to free his trapped leg from beneath his mount, which lay quiet and almost still now as its bright lifeblood slipped away on to the grass. Apart from bruises and some scratches to his face, Pons himself was unharmed, but Hereward's arrow had driven deep into the animal's belly, puncturing its lung, I didn't wonder, and so taking it beyond the ability of any of us to do anything. As Pons's lord it would fall to me to find him a replacement, but the cost was not what was foremost in my mind then. A knight's destrier was one of his closest and most trusted friends, and every bit as valiant a warrior. The beasts lived and fought and travelled with us, and while good horseflesh was valuable and prized above even swords and mail, their companionship and loyalty could not be measured in terms of weight of silver or gold. Pons had owned him for as long as he'd been sworn to me, which was to say a little over two years, and there was a tear in his eye as he crouched by the animal's side. He stayed with it, rubbing its muzzle until it moved no longer and we knew it had passed.

'I don't blame you, lord,' Pons said some time later while we were returning to Hamo and the carts. 'We did what we had to.'

But the truth was that I should have known better. I had been foolish. Thinking only of the rewards and not of the dangers, I had rushed into battle, and though some might say that I had paid for that folly, the truth was it could have been far worse. We were lucky that the price hadn't been higher, that more Norman blood hadn't been spilt and more lives wasted.

At that thought a shiver ran through me, for I knew full well that some of that blood could easily have been my own.

We arrived at Brandune later that evening, just as darkness was falling and the stars were beginning to emerge. As expected, the clerks were waiting for us when we reached the king's hall. No sooner had I announced our names and our business to the sentries on duty at the gate and we had led the oxen and carts into the courtyard than they began pressing me with their questions. Where had these goods come from, and how had they been paid for? How many barrels of such a thing had we brought; what weight of this and what length of that? Answers to all these questions and others besides were recorded by a squinting monk whom I recognised, Atselin by name. I had crossed paths with him before and understood him to be chief amongst the clerks. He worked by light of a lantern at a writing-desk set up in one corner of the yard, close to the grain-sheds and the storehouses.

'You're late,' Atselin said when I approached. He didn't deign to look at me but continued to scrawl even as he spoke, his head down so that his tonsured pate reflected the orange lantern-glow. From the set of his wiry eyebrows I could tell there was a scowl upon his face.

'We saw another hall-burning,' I replied. 'I took it upon myself to go and see what had happened.'

He gave a snort of derision. 'The rebels are always raiding. Every day we hear of yet more manors that have been razed to the ground. You wasted your time and ours for that?'

'This one was Hereward's doing.'

My words had the desired effect. His hand stopped mid-scribble; the furrows upon his brow deepened. He looked up sharply.

'Hereward?' he echoed.

Finally I had his attention, although I resisted the urge to smile at that small victory. 'We saw him. He'd come by boat, at the head of a war-band numbering around fifteen men.'

'How do you know it was him?'

'It was him,' I said firmly, meeting Atselin's hard eyes. I had nothing to prove to this man.

He seemed to consider my answer for a few moments. Though much had been spoken of him of late, no Frenchman had so much as laid eyes upon Hereward in several weeks. Until now.

'I suppose, then,' said Atselin, raising an eyebrow, 'that you were able to put an end to their pillaging?'

I sensed a barb hidden in his words, but I was determined not to let him provoke me. 'We arrived too late for that. But we pursued them to the edge of the fens where they had their boats, and there we fought them.'

'And killed a great many, I hope.'

To that I made no reply. Atselin gazed expectantly at me for a few moments longer, but when it became clear that I had no answer to offer him he turned his attention back to his quill and the sheet of parchment before him, at the same time dismissing me with an absent flick of his hand. But I was not about to be summoned and sent away so readily, like some trained dog performing tricks upon command.

'You don't believe me,' I said.

He dipped the end of the goose feather into a pot of ink, and then resumed scratching his spindly letters upon the vellum, as if he hadn't heard.

I brought my fist down upon the top of the monk's desk. It shuddered under the impact. 'It was Hereward. We saw him.'

Atselin did not so much as blink. 'Did you cross swords with him?' he asked. 'Did you fight him in single combat? Perhaps you even managed to wound him, as they say you wounded Eadgar Ætheling.'

At that I recoiled slightly. I hadn't thought a mere monk would be so well informed about who I was or about my reputation, such as it was in those days. Eadgar was the man I had sworn to kill, the leader of the Northumbrians who had twice risen against us and twice been routed. The man responsible for the murder of my former lord and of many of my closest comrades on that bitter winter's night. In return I'd laid a scar upon his cheek that he still bore to this day, though it was scant vengeance.

'What do you mean?' I asked, frowning.

Atselin shrugged. From my dealings with him I knew he was a man of little humour, who rarely showed even the hint of a smile, but even so I sensed he was enjoying this sparring, and enjoying my discomfort too.

'If you had captured Hereward and brought him here in chains, then as I see it you would have accomplished something of value. But since I don't see him here, I assume he managed to escape. Just as the ætheling managed to escape at Eoferwic, and again at Beferlic last autumn.'

Few people were aware that I had been in the battle at Beferlic. Again his knowledge surprised me, although when I came to reflect upon it, perhaps it shouldn't have. Working within the royal household, he would have many opportunities to overhear scraps of knowledge and glean important details to keep for later use, just as all the records he made at this writing-desk were stored away in the chancery.

'It isn't my fault that Eadgar still lives,' I said. 'Neither of those battles would have been won were it not for me.'

'Is that so?' He raised an eyebrow. 'Perhaps a better warrior would have seen that he finished his task.'

Anger swelled inside me and I had to clench my teeth to hold my tongue.

'Besides,' Atselin went on, 'what proof do I have that you did these things that you claim, and which others say of you? Why should I believe that it was you who fought Eadgar upon the bridge at Eoferwic, that you were the one who turned the tide of battle against the enemy? For that matter, how can I believe that you faced Hereward this day?'

'You can believe it because it is the truth,' I said, unable to hold my temper any longer. 'I was there.'

'So says every man with such a yarn to spin.'

I leant over his desk and lowered my voice. 'Don't try my patience, monk. I could run my sword through your belly and gut you in an instant if I so wished.'

'You would kill a man of God and choose eternal damnation?'

'He would thank me for ridding the world of such a worthless rodent.'

Atselin sighed, and it was a deep, weary sigh, as though he had heard many such threats in his time and was no longer troubled by them. He pointed at me with the feathered end of his quill. 'I have met men like you before, Tancred of Earnford. I know your kind. Hot-tempered and wedded to your swords, you brag of your feats and wish others to praise you, to shower you in gold and write down songs of your brutish deeds so that they may pass into legend. It may surprise you to learn, then, that I have no interest in your boasts. I do not write songs. I am interested only in keeping the records for our lord king. So unless you have something truly important to tell me, trouble me no more with your wild tales.'

My blood boiled in my veins, but I sensed that this was not a battle I was likely to win. Without a further word I stalked off, leaving him to his parchments and returning to Pons and Serlo, who were waiting while other officials from the king's household, helped by a pair of stout knights, searched the carts. For each item on their list they counted out the number we had brought to make sure that it tallied with the number expected, that we had not been cheated in our purchases or that we ourselves had not taken the liberty of helping ourselves to any of the supplies. Goods were forever going missing in the camp, and while most men could be trusted, there were always some who wouldn't hesitate to steal if they thought they could get away with it. And so we were forced to stand patiently and submit to their questions, in case they discovered something that required further explanation.

Whenever my back was turned I felt Atselin's eyes upon me. What right did he, a mere scribe and a keeper of rolls, have to question my sincerity? What right did he have to pour scorn upon my deeds, when without me the kingdom might have fallen to the enemy? After all, without a king to serve and chancery records to write, he was nothing. He owed me more than he could possibly realise.

And yet the truth was that by that September, in the year one thousand and seventy-one, my standing was not as great as once it had been. After our victory in the great battle at Eoferwic I had been rewarded with a manor of my own, with enough wealth to attract men to my banner, and a reputation that had travelled before me. Now, however, I found myself all but destitute. My hard-earned silver was mostly spent, while my once-rich manor at Earnford had been burnt by the Welsh and half the folk who had lived there slain by their hands. We had done our best to rebuild it in the months since, but the winter had been hard and many more had perished through starvation or sickness, and the spring had brought unrelenting rains that led the river to overspill its banks and flood the pastures, and caused many of the newly built houses and barns to collapse. Now it was a place of sadness, where those who had survived toiled hard to produce enough food to keep themselves and their families fed, all the while surrounded by the memories of what had happened and of their fallen kinsfolk.

My reputation, too, was dwindling. No longer did men respect me to the extent that they had even a year ago. Fame is fickle, and already the tales of my exploits had grown old; men had found other heroes worthy of their admiration. Nor was my current lord as highly regarded as once he had been. Like the man to whom I had sworn my first oath, he too was named Robert, although the two men were very different in character. Whereas the first had been like a father to me, this Robert was more like a brother, being similar in age to myself. He and his family had suffered greatly during the rebellions of the past couple of years. They had lost many good retainers, including several whom I had known, shared repast with and led in the charge. His father, Guillaume Malet, once a powerful man responsible for governing much of the north of the kingdom, had fallen from the king's favour, been stripped of his position and made to forfeit many of his estates as a consequence of his failure to defend against the Northumbrian rebels and their Danish allies. The stain upon his character was a stain upon the entire Malet house. All of which meant that they had little now to offer by way of land or silver, even for the man who had risked his life to save theirs. I had rescued them from imprisonment at the hands of Eadgar and the Danes in Beferlic, and for that deed alone I deserved some form of recognition.

So far, though, my only rewards had come in the form of promises, which appeared ever more empty with each day that went by. Meanwhile I remained shackled to their service by the oaths I had given them: bonds woven from words and yet stronger than words. Bonds of my own making, that I could not escape, only endure.

Three

The encampment sprawled around the manor at Brandune: a sea of tents and horse paddocks, fenced-off pens for sheep, swine and chickens, and training yards marked out with stakes. Countless campfires dotted what had been pastureland and hay-meadows, and around them men cooked whatever meagre provisions had been given them that day from the royal storehouses. The king had seized the main hall, a high-gabled, timber-built structure, for the use of himself and his own household, while the various lords who had been called upon to serve on this campaign had been left to squabble between themselves for the other houses in the village.

At one time I imagined this would have been a prosperous place, untouched by the wars that had gripped the kingdom these past five years. But no longer. Where once had been pastures and paddocks, now there were only wide quagmires. Livestock had fouled the pens and barns, while outside the slaughtering sheds and on the banks of the Lyteluse carcasses of pigs and cattle had been abandoned, left to the flies and the carrion birds, which swarmed around them, feeding upon the flesh as if it were the most lavish of feasts. The recent rain had only made matters worse, causing latrine pits to overflow and making rivers of all that mud and filth. The passage of several thousand feet had done the rest, churning everything into a reeking sludge that clung to one's shoes and caused wagons to become stuck, horses to lose their footing, and men to sicken and die from the poisonous vapours it gave off.

Bordered on its western side by the marsh and on its eastern by an expanse of heathland thick with gorse, Brandune stood on a ridge of higher ground above the slow-flowing Lyteluse river, where rowing boats, punts and ferrycraft were moored. The low-gabled building that my lord had claimed for his own use lay on the very edge of the village, a good half a mile from the royal enclosure with its stables and gatehouse and surrounding stockade. Barely twenty paces in length and built of wattle and turf, it wasn't much to look upon, although it was in better repair than some of the other houses. One of Robert's household knights stood on guard outside the door, a spear in his hand to which was nailed a pennon in the Malet colours of black and gold. Around his shoulders was wrapped a thick winter cloak, though it was only late September. I didn't know the man's name but I recognised his face, and he recognised mine, and so he let me pass without challenge.

Heavy drapes hung across the doorway to keep out the draughts. I pushed them aside to find Lord Robert holding council with some two dozen or so of his vassals, who stood or sat on various stools, barrels and chests in a circle around him. They were men much like myself, minor barons who had sworn their swords to the Malets, and in return for loyal service had been rewarded with land. Most of those faces were unfamiliar to me, for they had only recently arrived from Normandy or else had been called from other far-flung parts of England to be here, but I spotted my long-serving comrades Wace and Eudo seated on the other side of the hearth, where a peat fire was gently smoking, the only source of light in that grim, dung-reeking hall. They nodded greetings to me but said nothing, for Robert was speaking. His back was turned as he paced around the room, addressing his barons, so he didn't see me enter.

'The banks have been strengthened and the roadway widened, with platforms for our bowmen and catapults to stand upon,' he was saying. 'If the enemy do send another band to try to destroy it, they'll find themselves cut down under a hail of steel.'

One of the barons, a rotund, red-faced man in his middle years, gave a snort as he swallowed a gulp of ale from a wooden cup. 'That's what we were told before. And we all remember what happened when we tried to cross that first bridge, as I'm sure you must also recall, lord.'

'I lost four men,' put in another, before Robert could answer. A tall man, he had thick brows that in the dim light made shadows of his eyes. 'The king has lost his wits if he thinks we're going to risk our necks pursuing the same strategy again.'

I expected at least a murmur of protest, for no one ever besmirched the king's name openly and in so light a manner, but there was none.

'He is fixated on the idea of this bridge,' Wace said. One of my oldest companions, he had a wise head upon his shoulders and was ever a source of shrewd advice, even if, as was often the case, he ended up being outspoken. 'We would do better to attack by water from the north, where their defences are said to be weakest.'

'The rebels have erected chains across the largest of the creeks surrounding the Isle,' Robert replied. 'And the smaller channels are too narrow and too shallow for anything but small punts and ferry-craft. It would take days to convey our entire army across that way, and in that time they would be able to throw up all manner of earthworks to obstruct us. Besides, think how many boats we'll need for an army of four thousand men.'

'Is that the king's reasoning or your own?' the ruddy-faced man asked, prompting laughter from a few of the other barons. Robert waited for it to subside before answering. More tolerant and mild-tempered than many men of noble birth I had known, it took a lot to stir him to anger.

'It is the king's reasoning, Guibert, but in this case I agree with him,' Robert said.

'You agree with the king?' Guibert cried. He raised his cup aloft, sloshing ale over himself and the man sitting beside him. 'This is indeed a rare occurrence!'

Robert stiffened. 'I think you've had enough to drink for one night,' he said as calmly and as evenly as possible, but there was no mistaking the warning in his tone.

'No,' Guibert said. He got to his feet, not entirely steadily. Even as he recovered his balance he managed to spill yet more contents of his vessel over his comrades, but he seemed deaf to their protests as he jabbed a finger in Robert's direction. 'No longer will I blindly obey our bastard king's every whim. I've had enough of these foul marshes, of bedding down night after night on ground that might at any moment slip away into the bogs. I've had enough of—'

'You forget your place,' Robert said, raising his voice as he spoke over Guibert. 'Now, be seated and keep your tongue inside your head, unless you want me to cut it out.'

The other barons were all calling for Guibert to sit down, but he wasn't listening. 'I will not be silenced,' he shouted over the din. 'Everyone here agrees with me, even if they are too afraid to say so. I speak for them as much as for myself.'

A hush fell. The high-pitched calls of waterbirds down by the river pierced the air; from further off the sound of a lyre floated on the breeze, and voices singing a bawdy tune that seemed familiar, although the words were different to the ones that I remembered.

'Well?' Robert asked, his face reddening now as he looked about. 'Is this true? You haven't yet spoken, Eudo. What do you have to say?'

Eudo shrugged, probably realising it made little difference what he said now. His feelings, like those of us all, had already been made plain. I had known him and Wace for many years, and he had always been the joker among the three of us, but the last few weeks had taken the edge off his humour, and his expression was sombre.

'What the king has in mind is folly,' Eudo said, after a moment's hesitation. 'We all think it. If another causeway is built and we try to attack across it as before, the outcome will be no different. Many of us will lose our lives, but what choice do we have, except to do as the king orders?'

A murmur of accord rose up. Although outwardly Robert maintained the same calm expression as before, inside I imagined he must be seething at such open defiance. Surely, though, he saw the truth in what we were saying?

'There is nothing more to be said.' He shook his head, a grim expression on his face. 'It doesn't matter whether you agree or not. The king wishes it, and so it will be. We have our instructions and we will follow them. Do you understand?'

No one answered, or at least not in words. A few of the men

spat upon the ground, a clear measure of their discontent, for it was rare that men would disgrace themselves by insulting their lord with so vulgar a gesture. Others simply cast their gaze towards their feet, not daring to meet his eyes.

'Very well,' Robert said. 'Go. We gather here tomorrow at midday. I expect to see you then.'

I alone remained while the other barons filed past me, grumbling amongst themselves. A few, recognising me, spoke a curt word or two of greeting, although most simply ignored me. With the exception of Wace and Eudo, they had all served the Malets far longer than had I, some of them for twenty years and more. They had heard of my exploits and resented my closeness to Robert, and shunned my company. Nonetheless, I shared their sentiments. Of all the campaigns we had fought since arriving on English shores, this had been without a doubt the most gruelling. And still it went on.

'You try to speak with him,' Eudo said, shaking his head as he passed. His expression was hard, his mouth set firm, his eyes dark in the gloom of the hall. 'See if you can make him see sense, and hopefully he can sway the king's mind in turn.'

'Robert will listen to you if he listens to anyone,' Wace added, scratching at the battle-mark below his right eye, as he often did when he was frustrated or angry. An English spearman had given him that injury at Hæstinges, and ever since he had only been able to half open that eye, so that he forever seemed to be squinting, although it had done nothing to dull his sword-skills.

As the hall emptied I approached the hearth, beside which Robert crouched. A chill had entered the chamber and I wished that, like the man standing guard outside, I had thought to fetch my cloak before coming here. The floor of rammed earth had turned to mud, there were holes in the roof through which water had dripped to form wide puddles, while up in the cobwebbed rafters a mouse scuttled. Its droppings were scattered around the bedrolls where Robert's hearth-knights would sleep tonight. For once I was glad that I had my wind-battered tent to go back to.

Robert looked up as I approached. 'Tancred,' he said, with some surprise. 'I didn't see you come in. When did you get here? You were expected back from Cantebrigia some hours ago.'

I shot him a look, not only because Atselin had said much the same thing, but also because he was the one who had foisted this escort duty upon me in the first place. The king had made Robert responsible for assembling the parties of knights who were to accompany the supply wagons, and he in turn had passed that responsibility on to me. Whether that was because he trusted me more than his other vassals, or because he thought I would value the time spent away from camp and thus meant it as a favour, I wasn't sure.

'We came back by a different route,' I said, and went on to explain what had happened earlier that day, telling him how we had seen the smoke, how we had come across the burnt vill and found the priest close to death, how we had chased Hereward and his men to their boats and slain one of their number. I left out the last part of the story, about how the fear had gripped me, for even all these hours later I could not make sense of it. My instinct was to bury the memory deep inside my mind where it would not trouble me, but I could not, and still the Englishmen's taunts rang in my ears. I wished I might have that moment over again so that I could ram my lance-head into Hereward's throat, silence him and his companions and help bring an end to the rebels' stand and to this godforsaken campaign.

'Even if you had killed or captured him, it would have made little difference,' Robert said, after I'd told of how he had escaped. 'He is the least of the rebels' leaders. If anyone holds command over that rabble, it is surely Morcar. He is the one who holds Hereward's leash.'

At that I couldn't help but laugh. The notion that anyone could hold the leash of a man such as him seemed to me absurd. But Robert was right in one sense, for Morcar was indeed a formidable figure, and one who had caused us much trouble these last five years. Before the invasion he had held the earldom of Northumbria, and he and his elder brother Earl Eadwine of Mercia had been among the first of the English to see sense and lay down their arms following our victory at Hæstinges. As a reward they were received as esteemed guests at King Guillaume's court, albeit deprived of their ranks, but a mere two summers later, hungry for greater influence, they had risen against him. Indeed, for a short while they had been successful, winning more than a thousand spears to their cause as they raided far and wide. More than half of those spears, however, were wielded by peasant farmers, who all dispersed to bring in their crops as soon as the harvest season arrived. After that their revolt quickly crumbled and once more they were forced to bend their knees before the king, seeking his pardon. Fortunately for them he was gracious enough to grant it, giving permission for both to return to their positions at court, and allowing them to keep their heads if not their landholdings.

Such was their pride, though, that the brothers were not content with that for long, and so earlier this year they'd fled his court for a second time. Eadwine had ridden north, to seek help, it was thought, from the King of Scots, only to be betrayed by some of his men and overtaken on the road by a conroi of knights, who slew him and all those accompanying him. Morcar, on the other hand, had made for Elyg to join those rebels already gathered there. With him went many of those who had lent their weapons in support of his earlier rebellion, who saw him now as their only hope for a leader who would drive us out of England.

Robert would argue that it was because of Morcar that we were here, and few would disagree with him. Without the former earl's leadership the rebels' loose alliance of squabbling thegns would surely have collapsed months ago. Not only that, but his arrival had bolstered the enemy's numbers by somewhere between, we reckoned, one thousand and twelve hundred men of fighting age: men who could carry swords and spears and shields into battle but who, more importantly, could also dig ditches, raise earthen banks and fell trees from which they could build palisades to surround their stronghold, so that by the time we'd arrived in force, the enemy were already well ensconced upon the Isle and easily able to repulse our attacks.

None of that, though, undermined Hereward's importance, or made him any less of a threat.

'Lord,' I said, 'if it weren't for Hereward wreaking his ruin, the rebels would do nothing but sit inside their fastness. Morcar, Siward, Ordgar and the other magnates might possess greater wealth and standing amongst the English, and have larger followings, but Hereward is the one who inspires them and gives them confidence. By his raiding he alone brings them victory and delivers them booty, and so exerts an influence far above his rank. Destroy him and many of the others will quickly lose belief. Only when that happens do we stand a chance of being able to defeat them.'

Robert shook his head sadly. 'I wish it were so simple.'

'Do you believe that the king's strategy is any more elaborate?'

'You heard, then.'

'Not all of it, lord, but enough. I understand that the king has been rebuilding the causeway on to the Isle.'

Robert nodded. 'He's moving most of his forces back to Alrehetha, where he has recently finished building a guardhouse to watch over the marsh. He is determined to break the enemy once and for all, and wishes to make another assault within the week.'

The manor of Alrehetha lay to the south of Elyg, separated from the Isle by a mile-wide bog that neither horse nor man could easily cross. We had tried to bridge it twice already, and both times without success. The first attempt, built of timber and loose stones supported by sheepskins filled with sand, had collapsed even as our forces streamed across it, brought down by the weight of so many knights and spearmen hungry for blood and for glory. God only knew the number that had drowned; we were lucky not to have been chosen to spearhead that first assault, or we would have been among them. Instead we'd watched from the banks, powerless to do anything as, shouting and screaming for help that would not come, our fellow Frenchmen floundered in the sucking mire, struggling for breath, burdened by their heavy mail, while their panicked mounts thrashed spray everywhere and the enemy hurled javelins and shot arrows into their midst. Even now, two months later, the marsh was still littered with many hundreds of swollen corpses. Together they raised a sickening stench that gripped men's stomachs and caused them to heave, and when the wind was up could be smelt for miles around.

The second attempt had been barely any better conceived. By then more than a month had passed since the first causeway had collapsed, and the king was beginning to grow desperate, so much so that he had been persuaded by one of his nobles, a certain Ivo surnamed Taillebois, to put his trust in the power of a wizened Englishwoman with a harelip and only one leg, who claimed to be able to work the magic of the old gods. Wooden towers had been constructed by the edge of the bog while some of the marsh folk were put to work repairing and strengthening what remained of the bridge, and upon one of those towers the Devil-witch was set in order to protect them with her charms from the enemy's depredations, and also to weaken the rebels' resolve and sow ill feeling among their ranks.

Needless to say, the plan had failed. Before the causeway was even half repaired, a band of rebels, some said led by Hereward himself, had sallied from the Isle one night. Making their way by secret routes, they had set fire to the reeds and the briar patches that surrounded its main platforms and the bases of the towers, so that they and the crone were all consumed by writhing flame that some claimed had been seen from as far away as Cantebrigia. What became of Ivo Taillebois after that no one knew. Probably he had fled the moment word reached him, although it was also rumoured that the king had killed him and disposed of his body in the marsh.

Angered by this second setback and losing the faith of his barons, the king had gathered most of his forces at his main camp here at Brandune while he contemplated what to do next. For a while he had tried to cut Elyg off by land and water and so starve the enemy into submitting, but there was no sign yet of that happening. Indeed if the few reports we received were correct, their storehouses were sufficiently full to keep them fed for several months to come. And now it seemed he had no more ideas left.

'Tell me what's in your mind,' Robert said.

'Lord, if I may say, Eudo and the others are right. The king has taken leave of his senses. We will not take the Isle by sheer force, not by such a crude strategy, at least. The causeway didn't work before. Why should it work this time?'

Robert had no reply to that and so I continued: 'This attack will fail, just as the last attempt failed. Even if the new bridge proves strong enough to take the weight of our horsemen, the best it will do is channel our forces into a killing quarter where the enemy can easily pick us off. Even if we survive that, there is still the small matter of capturing Elyg itself, and that will be no easy task.'

'What do you suggest, then?'

Probably Robert was hoping that would silence me, but our encounter with Hereward had set me thinking. 'The enemy know the secret ways through the marshes. They know which channels are deep enough at high water for boats to sail down, and where to find the paths at low tide. They're supposed to be the ones under siege, and yet they continue to move freely. They raid widely, waste manors and lay ambushes for our patrols—'

'All this is common knowledge,' Robert said. 'Why are you telling me this?'

'If we could discover some of those same passages, lord, or else capture one of the Englishmen who knows them, then we might be able to attack the Isle that way.'

'If there were any such passages large enough to sail a fleet through or march an army across, our scouts would have spotted them long ago.'

'Perhaps,' I conceded. 'But it wouldn't require a whole army. The enemy travel in small bands, rarely more than thirty strong. If even a few of our men could penetrate the fens and get on to the Isle, they might be able to cause enough trouble to confuse or distract the enemy while the rest of our army attacks across the bridge.'

'The king has forbidden any more raiding-parties venturing close to the Isle. We've lost too many good warriors that way already. You know this. And even if we could find some of those passages and succeed in landing a few men close to Elyg, what would be their chances of success? The men chosen for the expedition would be venturing deep into country that the enemy know well, cut off and with little hope of retreat if anything went wrong. Who would put himself forward to lead such a band? You?'

'Why not?' I asked. 'I did at Beferlic.'

Indeed Robert might not be here talking to me if I hadn't. Looking back, it was probably not the best-considered plan I had ever devised, and it had relied on a certain amount of luck, too, but I had always believed that a good warrior made his own luck. In the end it had worked, and that was all that mattered.

If anyone could lead such an expedition, I could. Of that I had no doubt. Anything to avoid having to cross that causeway.

'No,' said Robert. 'It is the most reckless idea I have ever heard, even from your mouth.'

'Is it any more reckless than the king's strategy?'

I meant it as a challenge, but should have known that he wouldn't rise to it.

'I won't allow it,' he said simply.

I shrugged. 'You asked for my suggestion, and I have given it, lord. As I see it, we have only one more chance to capture Elyg, but we will squander it if all we do is repeat the same strategy as before.'

'In what way?'

'You only need to ask around the camp to see how confidence is waning. Few still believe we can win this fight. Another defeat as great as those we've already suffered and many will decide that they wish no more of this. Regardless of whatever oaths they might have sworn, they'll begin to desert and return to their homes. Without men willing to fight, there can be no victory.'

I didn't need to remind Robert that many of those same men had also been called out to fight Eadgar Ætheling and the Danish host last year too, and had little appetite for another long campaign. Nor did I add that many of the mercenaries the king had hired from across the sea, such as Hamo and his band of archers, would in time probably also leave the king's service. Although they were paid a generous stipend from the royal purse, plunder was what they sought above all else, and if they saw little chance of receiving it then they would have no qualms about seeking employment elsewhere.

'We have only one more chance to take the Isle,' I repeated. 'If we fail, then we'll have no choice but to surrender it to the rebels.'

Four

'S urrender Elyg to the rebels?' Robert asked, his voice thick with
scorn. 'No. The king will never do that.'

'It isn't a question of whether he wishes to do so or not,
lord – merely whether he has the men and the supplies to keep
fighting this war. You know as well as I do that no army can stay
in the field for ever.'

'If we yield the Isle, what's to stop more Englishmen allying
themselves to the rebels? Or, for that matter, the Danes? If they
return, we could find ourselves fighting last year's battles all over
again.'

The Danes, led by their king Sweyn, had finally left these shores
at the beginning of this sailing season, their ships laden with chests
brimming with the silver and gold that King Guillaume had paid
them as an inducement to return to their own lands across the
German Sea. But such peace was fragile. The moment they smelt
another opportunity to win wealth and renown here in England,
they would be back. Of that few had any doubt.

'That's why we cannot suffer yet another reverse,' I said. 'Tell
me one thing, lord: do you really agree with the king's judgement
in this?'

Robert said nothing, and I supposed he was right to hesitate. It
was one thing for petty lords such as myself and the others to speak
ill of the king's strategy, but for him to do so was far more dangerous.
It didn't matter that he spoke in private company; walls were thin
and there were few places within the camp where a loose tongue
was not easily overheard. If ever word got back to the royal household then it might be said that Robert was fomenting treasonous

thoughts amongst his followers. King Guillaume was not the kind of man one did well to cross, and the events of the last two years had only served to harden him and make him more stubborn. From the many tales I had heard, he did not take kindly to being contradicted. Among his chief barons there were perhaps a handful whose counsel and criticism he accepted, and the Malets were not among them. Not any longer, at least.

'What about your own oath?' Robert asked.

I frowned. 'I don't understand, lord.'

'If this latest assault fails, will you keep your oath to me, or might you be among the deserters you spoke of?'

Only then did I understand the real reason why he had hesitated. My words had betrayed my own frustrations.

'If this assault happens, then I have to wonder whether any of us will even live by the end of it,' I answered. It was evading his question, but it was the truth.

Robert, however, was not fooled. 'You know that's not what I asked.'

'Lord,' I said, 'I am bound to your service. I pledged my allegiance upon holy relics, in the sight of God.'

He sighed. 'I realise that I have not fulfilled my duties as lord as well I might. Would that things were different, that I had the means to reward you and your friends for all that you have done for me and my family, and I fervently hope that such means will come back into my possession soon. As things are, I barely have the money to repair my own halls and keep my retainers fed and equipped. I only hope you understand, and that you see I need good men now more than ever. I need your sword, Tancred, and your patience.'

I had been patient for nine months already without receiving so much as one silver penny, I wanted to say, but managed to resist the temptation. He was desperate; I could see it in his eyes. Everything around him was unravelling, while all he wished for was respect, both from the king and from his own followers. As long as I had known him he had been a good lord as well as a good friend, always fair in what he asked of me. A man of sound judgement, and honest too, which was more than could be said of many in these troubled times.

'I will not desert, lord,' I said. 'You have my oath, and you may hold me to it, or my life is forfeit.'

He nodded, satisfied, as if there was any other answer I could have given. I couldn't break my oath to him, especially after I had failed in my duty to his namesake, my first lord, Robert de Commines. He had paid for my failure with his life, and I was determined not to let the same thing happen again. I would not suffer such dishonour twice. Nor had I any wish to surrender Earnford, my home, which I held only as Robert's tenant and which was worth more than anything in this world to me. That was what would happen if I broke my vow. I would become one of those lordless, landless, wandering warriors, despised and distrusted by all. That was not a fate I wanted for myself.

Beneath his cloak my lord's shoulders hung low. His angular features looked more gaunt, and even in the gloom I spotted the dark patches beneath his eyes. Suddenly he seemed much older than his years: no longer as commanding a figure, or as confident. As always, he was dressed all in black from his shirt and tunic to his trews and boots, and even his scabbard. It was an affectation he had always considered fashionable, but which now lent him the appearance of a mourner, and perhaps he was indeed mourning: for the loss of his family's former standing, for the loss of all his hearth-knights who had been slain at the hands of foemen in this last year.

Perhaps, too, he was already in mourning for his father, the once-powerful Guillaume Malet, whose health, it was said, was rapidly worsening. He had first fallen ill during his imprisonment by the Danes last autumn, and although he had recovered somewhat in the months since then, that illness had never completely gone away, but kept returning, and every time it did it left him all the weaker. None of the physicians summoned had been able to say exactly what it was that ailed him, or rather each one had his own opinion and clung rigidly to it, shouting down all the others whose assessment differed. Neither had they been able to agree on any one course of treatment, save for the usual bleedings and poultices and herb-infused ointments, none of which seemed to bring any relief.

Knowing how he was suffering, it seemed strange that King Guillaume should have demanded the elder Malet's services on this campaign, especially since he showed no inclination to call upon his counsel. As with everything, the king wished it, and so it happened. For the first few weeks all had been well, and it was hoped that whatever ailment troubled him had passed. Within days of arriving here at Brandune, however, Malet had succumbed once more, and this time he seemed worse than ever.

'How is your father?' I asked.

'He suffers still. This foul marsh air does him no good. Every day he is plagued with bouts of flux. He eats little and what he does manage he often heaves back up. Let me take you to him, and you can see for yourself.'

I wasn't sure that Malet would wish to see me, and doubtless Robert must have known that, but he was already halfway towards the door and so I kept my feelings to myself as I followed him outside. A scrawny grey cat that must have been left behind by whoever had previously owned this farmstead looked up from licking its paws as we crossed the yard towards a smaller building that stood opposite the turf-roofed hall. Smoke rose thickly from the hole in its thatch, obscuring the stars. I had hardly even seen Malet in recent weeks, let alone had a chance to speak to him. Much of the time he was too weak even to leave the house where he was quartered, while I was often out on patrol or escort duty. For a brief time I had served him, just as I now served his son, but after the business with the priest Ælfwold, he had dismissed me from his employ.

'I fear he will not be with us much longer,' Robert said, his voice low as we neared the building.

'I pray that he recovers.' In spite of the bad blood that existed between Malet and myself, the sentiment was heartfelt.

Robert shook his head sadly. 'He will not recover. It is simply a matter of how long he can cling to life.'

I didn't know what to say to that, but thankfully I did not have to, for at that moment Robert opened the door. Inside it was warm, much warmer than the hall. A freshly stoked fire burnt; against one wall was piled enough wood to last all night and all the next day too, I didn't wonder. Malet, my erstwhile lord, sat on a stool facing the hearth with his back to the door, wrapped in furs as he sipped at a bowl of steaming broth. Beside him, stirring an iron pot that hung from a spit over the flames, crouched a man in his middle years, dressed in loose woollen robes. Around his neck hung a wooden cross carved with an intricate pattern of intertwining vines, and I took him for Malet's chaplain. His face held a stony expression as he saw us come in.

'My lord is not strong enough to receive anyone at this present moment, I'm afraid.' His voice, unlike the fire, was entirely lacking in warmth.

'Not even his son?' Robert asked with a frown.

'Come, Dudo,' Malet said to the priest. He gave a cough and slowly set the bowl down on the rushes beside him. 'I am not as frail as all that. Besides, where are your manners?'

'I simply think, lord, that it would be better if you rest. The hour is late and—'

Malet waved him silent as, with not a little effort, he rose to his feet and turned to greet us, a gentle smile upon his face.

A smile that vanished the instant he saw me.

'It's you,' he said, scowling. 'Why do you continue to plague me? Am I not sick enough already?'

Robert began: 'Father—'

Malet raised a hand against his son's protest. 'What have you come seeking this time?' He almost spat the words. 'More gratitude for your good service? Further plaudits for your prowess at arms? Your weight in gold coin, perhaps? I can tell you now that you will find none of those things here.'

'I ask nothing of you, lord,' I said.

But he was not listening. 'I do not wish to see this man,' he said to Robert. 'Why have you brought him here?'

He had never fully forgiven me for the treachery, as he saw it, that he had suffered at my hands. That was why he had dismissed me from his service: because, in his eyes, I had betrayed the trust he'd placed in me, even though I'd done so for good reason and in good conscience. At the same time, however, he couldn't deny that he owed me, and that was why he resented me. Twice I had rescued his hide in the last few years. More galling than the knowledge of that debt was his continuing inability to pay it. Each time he saw me must have seemed a further insult. Nonetheless, a little more gratitude would not have gone amiss. He'd hardly had a single kind word to say to me since the night of that battle in Beferlic all those months ago.

'I come bearing no ill will,' I tried to assure him. 'I merely wished to know how you were faring.'

He snorted scornfully, as if he didn't believe a word that came out of my mouth. 'Leave us,' he snapped at Dudo.

The priest said nothing but bowed. Without meeting either my eyes or Robert's, he made for the door, although I sensed he wouldn't venture too far in case his lord needed him. Why it crossed my mind just then I do not know, but for some reason I found myself thinking again of Ælfwold, the Englishman who had been Malet's previous chaplain and who had met his end some two years earlier. A kind-hearted man, he had tended to me while I was recovering from injury and fever. From our first meeting I'd taken to him in a way that I could not to this Dudo, which was a strange thing to admit given what Ælfwold had later done, and yet it was true, since for a time at least I had counted the Englishman as a friend.

'This enmity must end,' Robert said when the priest had left, his tone sharp and his eyes hard as he glanced first at his father and then at me. 'I will not have the two of you at each other's throats.'

This was the real reason why he had brought me here, then. To try to forge a reconciliation between us.

'Why should I waste my breath dealing with him?' Malet asked, and turned his back.

'Because I wish it,' Robert said.

Shaking his head, Malet limped stiffly across the room to where a pitcher stood on a table beside a stack of parchments, and poured himself a cup. I remembered when our paths had first crossed, in his richly decorated palace at Eoferwic, a very different place to this. How long ago it all seemed, though only two years had passed. How far his fortunes had fallen.

Certainly it was true that I'd never had any especial love for him. While he was more astute and quick-minded than most great barons, many of whom had won their reputations through the sword alone, he was not nearly as cunning as he liked to think. Indeed Malet had always seemed to me arrogant, aloof in manner and calculating: everything that his son was not. But even though I had little respect for him as a lord and a leader of men, I would never wish any harm upon him, and it saddened me to see him brought so low.

'It was Tancred who came for us at Beferlic,' Robert said. 'How can you hold a grudge against a man who risked everything to help save your life?'

'He never came for me,' Malet said, almost spitting the words. 'He came for you, Robert. You are his lord. He would have left me to my fate otherwise.'

The barb stung, but what stung harder was the realisation that there was probably a grain of truth in his words.

'No, lord—' I started to protest, but he cut me off.

'You would have done better to leave me there,' he said. 'I would have rotted away as a prisoner of the Danes, rather than live only to rot away here. What difference has it made? What good am I to anyone now?'

His face was ashen, his hair had grown long and was turning the colour of snow, and his deep-set eyes had a weary look about them. Even huddled in his cloak he looked thinner than I had ever known him. Thinner, and also somehow shrunken. It was hard to believe that this was the same man I had witnessed not so long ago leading conrois into battle: a fearless fighter, ambitious and lacking nothing in conviction. All the fire that once he had possessed seemed to have gone out of him, which perhaps was no surprise given that he was then almost fifty in years. Whilst I had come across men of sixty and seventy and even older, they were rare, and fifty was in truth a good age, especially for one whose living and whose reputation were made by the sword, as his had been. War exacted its toll, not just upon the body, as my many battle-marks would attest, but also upon the soul, and Malet had seen more battles in the last few years than many saw in a lifetime. And so in spite of his hostility towards me, I felt sorry for him.

'Have the physicians been to see you this evening?' asked Robert, his voice quieter now. He had come not looking for a confrontation but hoping to settle matters. Now those hopes were dashed.

'I sent them away,' Malet said. 'They bleed my veins dry and are continually arguing between themselves, but they do nothing to take away the pain. At least I have Dudo. He reads to me, and prays for me, and sometimes we play chess, which I always seem to win. I suspect he lets me, although he insists that is not the case. I do not want pity, from him or anyone. And besides, my mind still works well enough, even if this husk of flesh is failing me.'

No sooner had he finished speaking than he hunched over and began to cough: a dry, rasping sound that shook his entire body and was painful to hear. A dirty rag hung from his belt and he raised it to cover his mouth. When he lifted it away I saw it was flecked with blood, and even I, who was far from well versed in the healing arts, knew that was never a good thing. Robert passed him the cup from the table; Malet took it in his bony fingers and lifted it to his lips, and after he had taken a few sips his son helped him back to the stool by the fire.

'We will be leaving soon,' said Robert as he knelt by his father's side. 'The king is preparing for another assault upon the Isle and so he is ordering most of the army back to Alrehetha.'

'So I am informed,' Malet said. 'And I shall come with you.'

'No, Father. It is better if you stay here and save your strength. Dudo will care for you.'

'My strength will leave me eventually. I would rather be there to witness our victory over the rebels before I die than simply waste away uselessly in this filthy hovel.'

Robert shot him a reproachful look. 'You should not speak so.'

'And why not? There is no sense in denying it. My time is short. We both know it to be true. The physicians think the same, except of course they will not admit it openly, since what then would be the point of us paying them? And so does Dudo, although he is too loyal to say so. No, I have made my decision and will not be swayed from it.'

Robert nodded sadly as he clasped his hands around his father's, and in the light of the fire I glimpsed the glisten of a tear as it rolled down his cheek. 'Very well,' he said. 'I will return in the morning, shortly before noon. Until then, rest.'

Malet gazed back at him, but it seemed to me that there was no hint of sadness or regret in his eyes, no sense of self-pity in his demeanour, but merely an acceptance of his fate, and notwith-standing everything that had happened, I admired that courage.

Robert rose, and after bidding a final farewell we left Malet to his fire and stepped outside, where, as I had suspected, Dudo was waiting, standing so close to the door that he must have been eavesdropping. We'd said nothing of any importance, but even so, I gave him a cold stare as we passed. His face betrayed no feeling, and he spoke not a word to us, but afterwards I could feel his eyes on my back. An odd little man, I thought, at the same time wondering where Malet had found him and how he had come to enter his service.

'I don't like that priest,' I confessed to Robert when we were out of earshot. 'I don't like him, and I don't trust him either.'

'He is harmless. Strange, I will grant you, but entirely harmless. In any case, it doesn't matter what either of us thinks. My father trusts him and that is all that matters.'

I supposed he was right, although that did nothing to stave off my suspicions.

'You must realise, too, that his anger isn't reserved for you,' Robert said as we walked back across the muddy yard. 'He's angry at the circumstances he finds himself in, and the knowledge that he will never accomplish all that he set out to do. He is a proud man, Tancred, and always has been. He hates for others to see him looking so weak. Seeing you reminds him of a time when his fortunes were better, when men did not spit his name but instead held him in esteem.'

'If you say so, lord,' I said, though I didn't entirely believe him.

We trudged on through the mud until we arrived back outside the hall's great doors.

'I've been thinking about what you suggested,' Robert said as we were about to bid each other farewell. 'About how, if we could only find the right passages through the marshes, we might be able to surprise the enemy, or at least inflict some damage in return.'

'Yes, lord?'

'I want you to take a boat out into the marshes towards the Isle. See if you can capture one or more of the rebels and bring them back alive.'

'Tonight?'

'Tonight,' he confirmed. 'Take Eudo and Wace with you, and as many other men as you think you might need, so long as you go unnoticed and you return by first light.'

'And how do you expect us to be able to do this, lord?'

'I hoped you might have some plan in mind. You were the one who suggested it, after all. Unless, of course, you think yourself incapable of such a task.'

He gave a mischievous smile as he spoke. He meant to goad me, for he knew that I rarely refused a challenge when one was laid before me.

'Well?' he asked. 'For you this should be simple.'

He hardly needed to ask, for he had already worked out what my answer would be even before the words formed on my tongue.

'I will do this, lord.'

His smile broadened further. He knew me too well, I thought. Robert had a way of seeing into men's hearts, of understanding their characters and desires and how he might use that knowledge to his advantage: a skill that his father also possessed. In that respect, if in few others, they were very much alike.

With that we parted ways. Robert returned inside while I went to gather my men. Earlier, as the smell of stew bubbling in cooking-pots had wafted on the breeze, my mind had turned to thoughts of food, but it was hunger of a different kind that gripped me now. For this was the chance I'd been waiting for. At last I would be doing something more useful than guarding cartloads of grain. Perhaps this was how Robert sought to repay me for all those days spent riding back and forth on the road from Cantebrigia, or else he was merely indulging my restless spirit. I didn't know, and I didn't care.

What I did know was that we had to make the most of this opportunity, for otherwise it wouldn't be long before the clash of steel upon steel would ring out across the marshes once again. At one time that prospect would have gladdened me, but not now. For as much as I longed to feel the heat of the mêlée, the rush of blood as I charged into the enemy battle-lines, I could not shake the doubt nagging at the back of my mind. A doubt that grew with every moment that I dwelt upon it, as I thought of Hereward and the rest of the rebels, ensconced in their impregnable fastness upon the Isle, and the king's single-minded desire to crush them whatever the cost. By anyone's estimation we faced a fight the likes of which we had not known since Hæstinges itself: a desperate struggle from which glory or death were the only two routes out. Even if, at the end of it, we emerged victorious, that victory would surely come at a tremendous price, of blood and limbs and life.

And though I did my best to drive such thoughts away, I couldn't help but wonder whether this battle would be my last.

Five

Tall reed-banks slid by under starless skies. A thick layer of cloud had come across that the waning moon's milky light could barely penetrate, which made it all the easier for us to slip unnoticed through the shadows. A faint drizzle hung in the air and I felt its cold touch upon my face. All was still save for a gentle splash as I let the punting-pole slip into the black water, felt it strike the riverbed, pushed against the sucking mud and loose stones and heaved it out again, ready for the next stroke. My arms had grown heavy, my shoulders were aching, and I was starting to wonder whether this had been such a wise idea after all. Many miles of pasture and fen lay between us and the rest of the king's army at Brandune, and I reckoned we couldn't be far from Elyg itself.

I glanced at our guide, Baudri, who crouched by the prow of our small boat. A brusque man in his middle years, he was one of the king's scouts: indeed one of the best, if the rumours were right, with sharp eyes and hearing and a keen awareness of strategy. We were relying on his knowledge of the main river-passages to bring us as close as possible to the rebel stronghold. I wasn't planning to set foot on its shores, not this night, at any rate. What I had in mind was rather different. I only hoped that in the dark and with this mist surrounding us Baudri could still find his way, and that we didn't end up wandering into an enemy patrol. Certainly he didn't seem troubled, and I took that for a good sign. Nevertheless, I kept a close eye on each riverbank, expecting at any moment to spy the shadows of foemen following us, watching, or else to hear a sudden whistle of air as clusters of steel-tipped shafts flew from out of the gloom. But the enemy did not show themselves, nor were any arrows loosed upon us, and so I had to assume that we hadn't been seen.

God was with us.

'Remind me, lord,' said Pons. 'What are we doing here?'

I shot him a reproachful look. He was still angry at the loss of his destrier, which I could well understand, although he would do better to save that anger for use against the enemy, rather than turn it upon his friends.

'We're here because Robert ordered it,' I replied sternly.

'Because you suggested it, you mean,' Eudo said. 'Trust you to say something. If it weren't for you, we could all be asleep in our tents right now. I could be tumbling with my Sewenna. Have I told you about her?'

'Yes,' I replied. He'd hardly stopped talking about her in the last two months, although both Wace and I considered her rather plain. Eudo's eye for women tended to be less discriminating than those of most men. 'Now, quiet.'

Eudo returned to keeping a lookout, while I passed the punting-pole to Serlo, whose arms were fresher than mine. Sitting down in the damp bilge where the silt-laden water soaked into my braies, I took up one of the paddles to steer us closer to the bank where we would be less easily seen, and hoped that Wace and Hamo in the two boats behind us did likewise. For my plan to work we would need to draw the enemy's attention, but not yet. Not until our trap was set. And so we carried on, making our way up one of the many creeks and channels that I hoped would take us a little closer to the Isle.

'I'm going to marry her,' Eudo said suddenly, breaking the stillness, and I realised his mind was still on Sewenna.

'You're a fool,' I said. 'You've barely known her half a year.'

Nor was she the first he'd become besotted with of late. Before Sewenna his heart had been pledged to an English slave-woman named Censwith, who had served in a bawdy house in Sudwerca and who had died of a fever before he could buy her freedom. She'd been pretty, though, whereas the latest object of his affections had a face like a sow's arse. She was young, probably no more than sixteen summers old, fierce in temper and lacking in humour. Why he had brought her with him on campaign I could not work out, especially since he could have had his pick from more than a hundred camp-followers, any one of whom would have made a better match for him.

'She makes me happy,' Eudo said. 'What's wrong with that? Besides, you weren't with Oswynn for much longer than six months. Have you given up looking for her yet?'

'No,' I replied, and felt slightly embarrassed to admit it, for I knew what he would probably say. 'I haven't.'

Oswynn was my woman, or had been. Dark, beautiful, wild Oswynn, with her inviting eyes and her hair, the colour of pitch, falling loosely and unbound to her breasts, as I liked her to wear it. I had cared for her more than any other woman before or since: more, indeed, than I ever dared admit to myself at the time. Even though she was English and of low birth, the daughter of a village blacksmith, and even though we could speak only a few phrases in each other's tongue, and even though our time together had been short, nevertheless I had loved her.

She had first been taken from me that fateful winter's night at Dunholm, when the Northumbrians had ambushed us: the same night that my former lord, Robert de Commines, was murdered, burnt to death in the mead-hall. For over a year I'd thought her dead, but then at Beferlic last autumn I had glimpsed her alive and apparently well, as beautiful as I remembered, albeit a captive of one of the enemy's leaders.

'She's gone,' Eudo said. 'Even if you did see her at Beferlic, you said yourself that she's with another man now. She could be a thousand leagues away. What hope do you think you have of ever finding her?'

He didn't mean it unkindly, but even so his words hurt. He still believed I was mistaken. Indeed for a while I had wondered whether what had happened was merely some kind of waking dream, so unreal had it seemed at the time. But it wasn't just that I had seen her; she had seen me too. Our eyes had met and she had just enough time to call my name before she was taken from me a second time as the enemy fled the burning town. How could I have imagined all that?

No, I had to keep believing that she was still out there somewhere. Her captor, like Eadgar and King Sweyn, had managed to escape the slaughter that night. I could picture him as easily as if he were standing before me now: broad in the chest and with his hair, fair but greying, tied in the Danish style in a braid at his nape, mounted on a white stallion, with rings of twisted gold upon both his arms and a fiery-eyed dragon with an axe in its claws emblazoned on his shield. I didn't know where he hailed from, or even his name, but through the winter and the spring I had paid spies to venture into the furthest reaches of Britain and bring me whatever they could learn about a Dane of that description and bearing such a device. Their help had cost me more silver than I could afford, but in my eyes it had been worth it, at the time if not in hindsight. In fact I might as well have tossed all those coins into the sea for all the good it had done me, since not one of those spies had brought me any useful information. The dragon and axe had recently been seen in Northumbria, some of them had told me, which was no help since I knew that already. Another claimed he had taken shelter at the court of the Flemish count, yet another that he had gone back across the sea with King Sweyn, and two more that he had travelled into the far north, to Ysland and the distant, frozen lands that lay beyond. Each one gave me a different name, and since none had been able to offer any more precise detail, I had sent them all away. They had gone to peddle their lies elsewhere, leaving me poorer and no wiser than before. But that did not stop me hoping.

'If you want my advice, you should try to forget her,' Eudo went on. 'There are plenty of other women who'll gladly help warm your bed. Women who won't cost you as much, either.'

He was, in his own way, trying to cheer me, not that it helped. He considered me a fool for wasting my silver on the tales of rogues and swindlers, none of whom he would trust as far the length of his sword-blade. But love makes a man desperate, and in those days my heart ruled over my head. Even though I had cared for and lain with other women since then, the truth was that I had never fully shaken her from my mind. Death had taken so many people who once were dear to me, and now that I knew that she was alive, I was determined to do everything possible to bring her back to me.

'I'm going to find her,' I said, sounding more confident than I felt. 'I swear it.'

'And how do you plan to do that?'

'I don't know,' I admitted. 'Not yet. But somehow I will.'

Eudo sighed and shook his head sadly, and silence fell once more. The rain began to spit down more heavily. I gazed out beyond the stern, making sure that the following boats were still behind us, and was just able to spy their shadows. Like us, Wace and the men under his command had tied scraps of cloth around their spearheads, and put on dark cloaks to cover their mail, so as to hide the telltale glint of steel. There were six of us in each boat, making eighteen in total, and I hoped that would prove enough. By anyone's estimation it was a dangerous plan that I had in mind, but the greatest rewards often came to those who battled the greatest dangers. Anyone who lived by the sword knew that well.

'There,' said Baudri suddenly. I followed the line of his outstretched finger to where a clump of trees stood upon the slightest of rises above the marshes, a few hundred paces ahead of us and slightly to our steerboard side. 'Towards that thicket.'

Setting down the paddle beside me, I scrambled forward. 'Are you sure?' I asked, keeping my voice as low as possible.

'Certain, lord.'

Even in the darkness I could discern the grim look in his eyes. He wasn't comfortable being out on the river by night, and I didn't blame him, especially given how close we were to the enemy encampment. Indeed at first he'd refused to take us, but the sight of a pouch filled with coin, and the promise of more to come, had been enough to persuade him to lend his services. I only hoped that it turned out to be silver well spent, for I had precious little to spare. With each day that went by it seemed that I grew ever poorer.

I nodded to Pons, who cupped his hands around his mouth and made a hoot like an owl's so that Wace and the others in the following boats would know to stay close. It was important we didn't lose one another now. After a moment's pause the answering call came from both crews, and so, taking care to keep the sound of our paddles and punting-poles as quiet as possible, we carried on, making for that wooded rise: the islet of Litelport, which was the name of the small market town that had until recently stood upon it. It lay a little to the north of the larger Isle of Elyg, the two separated by a boggy channel less than an arrow's flight wide at its narrowest point. The king had tried to occupy it in the early days of the siege, in order to establish a base from which to launch raids and to let our siege engines do their work, but the enemy attacked before he had been able to throw up any manner of earthwork or palisade. Repulsing his forces, they had laid waste the town together with its storehouses, jetties, slipways and the nearby steadings, preventing us from using it again as a staging-post.

Until now, or so I wanted the enemy to think. No sooner had we landed on its shores, running our boats' keels aground on the mud beside a row of blackened posts – all that remained of a landing stage – than we set to work. First we hauled our small craft up from the river's edge into the thicket where they wouldn't be seen, then while I set a grumbling Hamo and his men to gather firewood, the rest of us carried the tent-rolls and bundles of kindling and everything else we'd brought with us down to the islet's southern side, where we could look out over the marshy channel in the direction of Elyg. From so far away and in the darkness it was, of course, impossible to make out anything of the monastery or the enemy encampment, but occasionally the mist would clear and in those moments I spied the glimmer of distant guard-fires, beside which sentries would be warming themselves while they watched out over the marshes. We would be lucky if we could draw any of them out, I thought, especially on a damp night like this. More likely the enemy would keep to their halls inside their stout palisades, where they could bed down by the embers of their hearth-fires and wrap themselves in thick cloaks of wool and fur. But I was determined not to give up yet. Not after coming so far.

Working quickly, we laid and lit the fires, set up the tents around them, tossed bedrolls and coin-pouches inside and then across the ground we scattered leather bottles filled with wine, wooden cups, iron cooking-pots, handfuls of chicken bones and a few splintered shields that we had no use for, so that it looked as though there was a camp here. Hamo and his band of men brought armfuls of fallen branches down from the thicket and we cast them on to the fires, feeling the heat upon our faces as the twisting flames took hold and rose higher and higher, causing the green leaves to hiss as they shrivelled away to nothing. Great plumes of white smoke and orange-glowing sparks billowed up into the night, and even through the mist I reckoned they must be visible from the Isle. Once the enemy saw them, they would surely send a scouting-party to find out what was going on. Like moths to a candle they would, I hoped, be drawn in. As soon as I was satisfied that the fires were burning brightly enough, we retreated to the cover of the thicket, within easy arrowshot of our false camp. Our snare was set and we could only wait now for it to be sprung.

In truth I was relying on a certain amount of good fortune that night. The fires had to be great enough in size and in number that they would be considered worthy of attention, but not so great as to invite their entire host upon us. A band of ten to thirty men we could probably fight, but more than that and we would be fortunate to escape with our lives. And therein lay the problem. If the rebels had any sense, they'd realise we wouldn't be so foolish as to place a camp in clear sight of their own stronghold. They would suspect that something was amiss and so either ignore us entirely or else send so many men that we would stand no chance against them. The longer we crouched in silence in the damp undergrowth, watching the pyres flare as the wind gusted, the more such doubts crept into my mind. Much as I tried to remain patient, it was hard, for as soon as it was light, our plan would be revealed. The moment the first grey glimmer appeared in the eastern sky, we would have to leave, or else risk becoming trapped. The nights were growing longer these days as summer faded into autumn, but even so, by my reckoning, we had only a couple of hours until dawn. A couple of hours for the enemy to show themselves.

Tiredness pricked at my eyes like a thousand tiny pins. It seemed as if a week must have passed since we had left Cantebrigia, since we had met Hereward's band by the edge of the fen, and yet it was only earlier that day. How long we must have waited there I do not know, but it felt like an age. Dawn crept ever nearer and I kept glancing towards the east, at the same time praying for night to keep the earth in its grip a little longer and for day to be delayed. Bowing my head, I closed my eyes, listening to the rising wind as it rustled the leaves above my head, feeling its touch upon my cheek as silently I implored the saints to bring us luck tonight. As if in answer there came the call of a moorhen, and I looked up to find the cloud clearing from the sky and the moon and stars emerging, casting their wan light upon the marsh-mist and the channel that separated the two islands.

Where, at last, I saw the unmistakable glint of steel. A spearpoint, most likely. No sooner had it appeared than it was gone again, but it was enough to know that the enemy were on the march.

'Make sure your men are ready with their bows,' I whispered to Hamo, who was beside me. 'Let fly as soon as I give the signal.'

'They'll be ready,' he retorted. 'Have no fear about that. Just make sure that your men do their part.'

I didn't care for his tone, but this was no time for us to argue. As much as we disliked each other, I needed him and he needed me. I was relying on his archers and their bows, since without them this ambush would not work, but equally it was in Hamo's interest to help us, since if we died then there would be nobody left to pay him for his services tonight.

'After you've weakened the enemy, I'll lead the charge,' I said. 'You and your men will follow behind us. Do you understand?'

I spoke slowly so that he did not mistake my words, addressing him as one might a child, and like a child he scowled. 'Yes, lord.'

I narrowed my eyes but said nothing more as I left him and his men to string their bows while I made my way along our line. I found Baudri crouching behind a fallen tree just a few paces from the edge of the copse, within clear sight both of the campfires and of the channel.

'Do you see them?' I asked. I could discern nothing amidst the night's shadows, but his eyes were better than mine.

'I see them.' He squinted into the gloom. 'Two dozen of them, by my reckoning. Possibly more than that; it's hard to tell.'

'Four of them to every three of us, then,' put in Wace, who had been listening.

Two dozen. More than I would have liked to face, although it was about what I'd been expecting.

'We've faced far worse odds before, and still we live,' Wace pointed out, possibly sensing my anxiety.

He was right, of course, although we'd rarely done so out of choice; usually when the only alternative was certain slaughter. Wace knew as well as I did that this was a battle we didn't have to fight. If we threw ourselves into this fray, then good men might lose their lives who did not deserve to. Enough people had died because of me in recent years, and I didn't want to add to that tally if I could help it. We still had time to return to our boats and leave with our sword-edges unbloodied and ourselves unscratched; all I had to do was give the word. But then I'd have shown myself for a craven in front of not just my friends and my own oath-sworn hearth-knights, but also Hamo, who would quietly rejoice in my failure and, no doubt, make sure that all the other mercenary captains heard tell of it the moment we arrived back in camp.

'What do you want to do?' Wace asked, no doubt sensing my hesitation and perhaps some of the thoughts running through my mind.

Wace was more even-tempered and less hasty than either myself or Eudo, and I could always rely on him to give me sound advice. If he had any misgivings about our plan, or considered it a risk not worth taking, he would tell me. I trusted his judgement, and he trusted mine.

He and his knights were looking at me, waiting for my instruction. I felt the weight of expectation upon my shoulders. But we could hardly retreat now. Not after we'd come so far. I would not flee from this fight as I'd fled from Hereward.

'We keep to the plan,' I said. 'But remember that the quicker we do this, the better. We're stronger in numbers than we are if each man fights alone, so stay close to one another. That way we're all

70

more likely to make it through this with our heads still attached to our shoulders. I don't want to be dragging anyone's corpse back with me to Brandune.'

'Nor I,' Wace added. 'So listen carefully, and heed what he says.'

The wind gusted suddenly, rustling the branches above our heads, and from somewhere out in the darkness came the piercing *kew-wick* of an owl. Otherwise all was quiet.

'Not a sound,' I murmured to Wace. 'Stay still, and don't show yourselves until I say. We go together.'

He nodded, and proceeded to pass the same message down the line. I knew well what the battle-rage could do to a man. Too many times in my life had I seen able and well-respected knights, many of them sword-brothers of mine, charge alone from their ranks on to the bosses and blades of an enemy shield-wall, abandoning reason and long years of training in a desperate moment of folly, deaf to the warning cries of their comrades, their heads filled with the bloodlust and with visions of glory. More than once I'd come close to doing the same. I didn't want any of the men with me that night to end their lives that way, and so I gave them this reminder, regardless of whether or not they thought they needed it.

Our fires still burnt, although not as fiercely as before. The wind, slight thought it was, was changing direction, blowing now from the south and sending thick swirls of smoke and ash towards us, making it difficult to see much farther than the circle of tents we'd set up. I raised a hand to cover my mouth, aware that any sudden noise now might give us away. Before long I began to make out what sounded like voices above the crackle of the flames, and shortly afterwards, through a gap in the grey tumbling coils, I spied the dark forms of men moving amongst the shadows of trees and reeds down by the channel, making their way, I guessed, by some of the secret paths that led from the Isle. They were about a hundred paces away now, which meant they were nearly within bowshot.

'Wait,' I said to Hamo, who was reaching for his arrow-bag. 'Not yet.'

'I know,' he replied irritably. 'Do you take me for a dullard?'

'Just make sure your men know it too.'

A few members of his company – the younger and less experienced ones, from what I could see of their faces – were already nocking black-feathered shafts to their bows. The last thing I wanted was for their impatience to get the better of them. At this range the best we could hope for was one or two lucky kills, whereas what I wanted was to sow terror in the enemy's hearts. To do that we needed to draw them in, where they would make easier targets. As soon as they saw those silver-tipped shafts bearing down upon them, they would know they'd walked into a trap, which meant that the longer we could delay our attack, the better.

Cautiously they climbed the rise towards the tents and the campfires. Steel helmets shone in the dancing orange light. Few of them possessed mail that I could see, but instead wore lighter corselets of leather. From their belts hung sheaths for blades both long and short, while a few also hefted stout axes and broad-bladed spears. They looked a disparate lot, but that did not necessarily make them any less dangerous. They held their shields in front of them, moving ever more slowly as they approached, glancing all the time to left and right and behind. One shouted out an order in English, gesturing at his fellow warriors to keep close to one another. I'd hoped Hereward himself might come so that I'd have a chance to atone for my failure to kill him before, but this man was neither as lofty nor as imposing in stature. Nevertheless I guessed from his wargear that he was not only the leader of this scouting-band but also someone of considerable importance. His helm's cheek-plates and nasal-piece were inlaid with gold, while glistering scarlet and azure stones were set into his scabbard. His hauberk shone, and he wore mail chausses in the manner of a Norman knight, all of which suggested he was a person of considerable means, and probably, although not necessarily, a more than competent fighter too.

'I want their lord alive and unhurt,' I murmured to those either side of me, and urged them to pass the message on. 'Kill or maim the rest, but leave him for me.'

They were nearly at the camp we had set up, a little more than fifty paces away: so close that I could almost smell them. The enemy had spotted the empty cooking-pots, the discarded wine-flasks and everything else we had laid out, and now their leader sent three men ahead to search the tents.

'Wait,' I repeated as Hamo rose and raised his bow into position. Concentration soured his expression as he fixed his gaze upon the enemy, no doubt choosing his first victim. 'Wait until I give the word.'

One of the Englishmen emerged and brandished a coin-pouch with a whoop of delight, and the other two shortly followed with their own finds held aloft. Inside those pouches was the last of the silver and gold that I'd brought with me on campaign, together with some more that Serlo and Pons, Eudo and Wace had lent me for the purpose. Altogether it was a considerable treasure, and enough to bring the rest of their band rushing forward. Some tried to snatch those purses away from their finders, whilst others fought over the wine-flasks, or to be the first inside the remaining tents. Exactly why they thought we'd abandoned our camp, I had no idea. Perhaps they reckoned we were away scouting the land, or that we had fled at the first sight of them approaching. Probably most didn't care: they saw a chance to obtain easy spoils, and for most that was all that mattered. Most, that was, except for their lord – he of the chausses and the inlaid helmet – who was left standing alone, bellowing for them to hold back, to stay close to him.

But his warnings were in vain, and now his men would pay for their greed.

'Now,' I said to Hamo. No sooner had the command left my lips than he'd drawn back his bowstring and let his first arrow fly. With a sharp whistle of air it shot up into the darkness, closely followed by those of his comrades. A cluster of glittering steel points soared out from the trees across the open ground, vanishing briefly into the night before plunging earthwards once more, towards the camp-fires and the Englishmen squabbling amongst themselves.

Too late they saw the arrows spearing down towards them. Too late a cry was raised. One man was struck between the shoulder-blades as he scrambled out from one of the tents, and he went down. Another, swigging from one of the leather bottles, took a shaft in the neck and fell backwards into one of the campfires, sending up a shower of sparks. Men were running, shouting, screaming as the silver-tipped shafts rained down in their midst. Volley followed upon volley as Hamo and his men drew the shafts from their arrow-bags. In all probably only three or four out of those twenty-odd foemen were killed, but it was enough to spread panic among their ranks.

And into that throng we charged, filling the night with our fury. We fell upon them before they could recover their wits and work out what was happening, before they could come together and form a shield-wall to fend us off. Usually I find that those final few moments before battle is joined are when my mind is clearest, and that I'm aware of the slightest details, from which way the wind was blowing to the sound of my own heartbeat resounding through my body. But not this time. Exactly when I gave the order to break from our hiding place, or what battle-cry I roared, I cannot recall. The next thing I remember is seeing the first of the foemen standing before me, wide-eyed and open-mouthed, unslinging his red-painted shield from where it hung by its long strap across his back. I lifted my blade high, then struck down so quickly and with such force that it sliced through his leather sleeve into his shoulder. He bent over, yelling out in agony; I brought my knee up into his groin and buried my sword-point in his gut, twisting it so as to finish him all the quicker, then wrenching it free. The steel glistened crimson in the firelight. My first kill of the night.

We tore into the enemy, bringing weeks of pent-up anger to bear. Steel clashed upon steel, ringing and shrieking like the dissonant cries of some hellish beast. The hail of arrows had ceased and Hamo and his company were running to join us, adding their strength to ours, hurling themselves into the fray with knives and hand-axes and all manner of weapons: men both young and old eager to prove their worth alongside trained knights like myself. I raised my shield to deflect a spear, then twisted away and landed a blow across the back of a foeman's head, and he was dead before he hit the ground. These were stout warriors we faced, and not lacking in skill at arms, but for all that they were ill disciplined and no match for knights of Normandy.

'For St Ouen and King Guillaume!' someone roared, and it might even have been me, except that the words seemed somehow far away, and I didn't remember having willed myself to speak.

'God aid us,' another shouted. The traditional war-cry of Normandy, it was quickly taken up, until we were all roaring as if with one voice: 'God aid us!'

The battle-calm was upon me; everything was as simple as practising sword-cuts against the stake in the training yard. Time seemed to slow: each moment stretched into an eternity, and I knew every movement of my foes before it even happened. From their stance and the way they held their weapons I knew whether their next strokes would be low or high, feint or parry or thrust or cut, and armed with that knowledge I lost myself to the will of my blade, striking out to left and right, feeling free in a way that I hadn't in longer than I could remember, all my earlier anxiety having fled. Dimly I was aware of Serlo and Pons on either side of me, protecting my flanks, but I didn't care whether or not they were there, for I was laughing with the ease of it all as we scythed a path through the enemy towards their lord.

He stood beyond the fires, trying desperately to rally his troops, but for the most part his orders fell on deaf ears. All around him was confusion. The enemy were in disarray, in two minds whether to retreat or to hold their ground, whereas we were united in our desire to spill enemy blood. A few of the thegn's more steadfast warriors chose to stand by him, but already a large number were making as fast as they could manage for the safety of the marsh-channel, some limping with gashes to their sides and thighs where they had been struck, others clutching their arms or shoulders, fleeing out of fear for their lives, and I knew we had to take full advantage of this moment.

'Kill them,' I cried. 'No mercy!'

After that it was all over so quickly. One instant I was in the midst of battle, leading the attack against the few who bravely fought on, and the next I was looking into the eyes of the thegn himself. I rushed him with my shield, slamming the boss into his chest and jerking the iron rim upwards into his jaw. The force of the blow sent him stumbling backwards, his mouth and chin running with blood. His sword slipped from his grasp and he lost his footing on the muddy ground. The weight of his mail did the rest, bringing him crashing down on to his back. Breathing hard, I looked up, expecting to find his companions coming to his aid, but they were all on the ground, either finished on the blade-edges of my knights or else writhing in pain and desperately calling out for help that wouldn't come.

Sweat dripped from my brow, stinging my eyes, and the blood of my enemies, warm and sticky, streamed down my sword-hand. A few of the Englishmen still lived, but not many. Having seen their leader fall they knew better than to continue the struggle, and now they too were turning in flight, pursued by Eudo and Wace and their knights. This was the first chance any of us had had to exercise our sword-arms in a long while, to wreak our vengeance upon the rebels, and they seized the opportunity to quench their bloodthirst, whooping with delight at the chase and the glory of the kill.

The thegn tried to get up, scrabbling beside him for his weapon, but I kicked the hilt away before he could reach it. It spun away across the stony ground. I levelled the point of my sword towards the bare skin at his neck and straightaway he stiffened. Beneath his helmet his eyes opened wide, the whites reflecting the moonlight.

'Move and I'll slit your throat from ear to ear,' I said, hoping he would understand me. My blood was still up and it was hard to think of the right English words, and so I spoke in my own tongue instead.

He swallowed. His face carried few scars of the sort that I knew from my own reflection, and that was when I saw him for the youth that he was, no more than seventeen or eighteen summers, by my reckoning, and possibly younger even than that, stoutly built and round of face, with a brace of golden rings on each hand. Clearly he was wealthy, and used to fine living, and yet I doubted if he had won that wealth through battle. Not if his sword-skills were anything to judge by, and while it was fair to say that some men were better leaders than they were fighters, I found it hard to imagine a mere pup such as him inspiring much confidence in anyone.

'*Hwæt eart thu?*' I barked. *Who are you?*

At last he found his voice. 'Spare me, lord.' He stumbled a little over the words as he replied in French, trying to appease me, I supposed. 'Please, take my rings, anything you wish, but have mercy, I beg of you.'

'What's your name?'

'Godric,' he said as tears welled in his eyes. 'Thegn of Corbei and son of Burgheard.'

I'd never heard of a place called Corbei, or of his father Burgheard, but that did not particularly surprise me. I was beginning to build an impression of Godric. A petty landholder with pretensions to grandeur, he equipped himself as handsomely as he could to disguise his lowly status. I recognised his kind.

'I'm not going to kill you,' I assured him. 'But you can give me your rings. I'll have those. Your helmet and scabbard too.'

Godric glanced around him, but he was surrounded by Frenchmen and there was no way he could escape.

'Do it,' I said.

Reluctantly he divested himself of his helm and weapons, laying them down carefully on the ground beside him. I stood over him, my sword still drawn, watching carefully in case he possessed any hidden blades – knives on a belt underneath his tunic, perhaps – and was foolish enough to try to use them. As soon as he'd removed them all, I instructed Hamo and his men to carry them to our boats, together with as much as they could carry of the goods we'd brought with us. We didn't have time to take away everything, or to strip the corpses of their possessions. Already what I thought was a faint smear of grey was beginning to appear on the horizon. It might have been my imagination, but I wasn't willing to take that chance. I wanted to be well away from here by the time day was upon us.

'A few of them managed to get away,' Eudo told me when he and Wace returned from their pursuit. 'They fled into the marsh-channel where we couldn't follow them.'

Another reason to leave this place as quickly as possible. Soon they would rouse their countrymen and return, no doubt in larger numbers. Indeed reinforcements might already be on their way. The clash of steel and screams of the dying would carry easily across the marshes. If there were any sentries on watch on the other side of the channel, they would surely have heard us.

Wace handed me the coin-pouches that had formed part of our bait, which he and his knights had managed to recover from where they'd fallen amongst the enemy dead.

'It's mostly all there,' he said. 'We might be a few pennies short, but not many.'

Probably some had been spilt during the fight. Their loss didn't concern me all that much. Our capture of the Englishman ought to bring us reward enough to pay for everything this expedition had cost us, hopefully with a good amount left over too, although the king's treasurers weren't known for their generosity.

'On your feet,' I told him. At first he did not respond, and it took Pons striking him across his shoulder-blades with a spear-haft to jolt him into doing as instructed. I wished I'd thought to bring some rope with which to bind his wrists, but he didn't look the sort who was likely to put up much of a fight. Not after seeing so many of his countrymen cut down before his eyes.

I shoved him in the back to start him moving as, guided by Baudri, we made our way back across the islet towards where Hamo and his men were waiting with the punts. They had worked quickly, dragging the small vessels down from the thicket and pushing them out into the shallows so that they were already afloat by the time we arrived.

'Whatever price you demand for my release, my uncle will pay it,' Godric said as we reached the shore. 'I swear it.'

'Why should anyone pay a single penny for the sake of a wretch like you?' I asked with a snort as we splashed our way through the murky knee-deep waters out to the boats.

'I'm his only nephew, and the closest to a son that he has.'

'Many men hate their sons,' I replied. 'He might not want you back. Besides, how are we supposed to get word to him?'

Godric had no answer to that, and since he wouldn't get into the punt willingly I had no choice but to shove him over the gunwale. He gave a cry as he tumbled forward, landing awkwardly on his side. I took my place next to him, where I could keep a close watch over him.

'Don't speak another word unless you want to feel my blade between your ribs.' I laid a hand upon the knife-hilt by my waist. 'Do you hear me?'

He said nothing, and I took that to mean that he did. Wace and Hamo in the other boats were already pushing off from the shore and I gave the signal to Serlo, who once more had the punting-pole, to do the same. And so we left the island of Litelport behind us. Not half an hour could have passed since I'd spied what I thought was the first glimmer of dawn, but already the skies were noticeably brighter.

We were barely a dozen boat-lengths out from the shore when Godric, speaking more quietly, began again: 'My uncle—'

'I heard what you said,' I interrupted him, before he could go on. If he had any sense at all he'd have realised it was far better for him to shut his mouth and not to provoke us further.

'But, lord—'

He broke off as I grabbed the collar of his tunic. 'Tell me, then,' I said. 'Who is this uncle of yours, who's so wealthy that he can afford to waste good silver for your sake?'

Obviously he had something he wished to tell me, and I wasn't prepared to have him chirping all the way back to Brandune. Neither did I want to have to make good on my promise, since if I killed him this entire expedition would have been for nothing.

His mouth opened but his tongue must have been frozen, for no sound came out. There was fear in his eyes, and I realised then just how short was the distance he'd travelled along the sword-path. This was no warrior. Certainly I would not trust him to stand in any shield-wall. I wondered if his sword had ever run with the blood of his foes, or if he had ever unsheathed it outside the training yard before tonight.

'Tell me,' I repeated. 'Who is he?'

I saw the lump form in Godric's throat as he swallowed. My patience was fast running out. Eventually he managed to compose himself enough to speak, although the words that emerged from his lips were not at all what I'd been expecting.

'My uncle, lord,' he said, 'is Earl Morcar.'

Six

'H e's Morcar's nephew?' Robert asked later that morning, once we'd brought Godric to his hall and told him everything that had happened that night.

'So he claims,' I replied.

Already it all seemed an age ago. The thrill of the fight had long faded, and tiredness was beginning at last to catch up with me. My limbs felt like lead, fatigue clawed at my eyes, and I wanted nothing more than to find some quiet spot in which to lay myself down and sleep.

Robert fixed his gaze upon the Englishman, who sat on a stool beside the smoking hearth-fire, his hands bound with rope in front of him, his flaxen hair plastered to his skull. Since leaving Litelport behind us he'd uttered barely a word, except occasionally to murmur what sounded like a prayer, but he spoke now.

'It is the truth, lords,' he protested. 'Upon my life, with God and all the saints as my witnesses, I swear it!'

To some men lying came naturally, while others learnt the art through years of practice. Nonetheless, to spew falsehoods when one's very life was at stake was a skill that few possessed, and required no small amount of nerve, too. Perhaps I was wrong about the Englishman, but I doubted he was so daring, and for that reason alone I was inclined to believe him.

'If you want to change your mind, you'd be wise to do so now, before you meet the king,' Wace warned him.

'Yes,' Eudo added. 'If he finds out you've lied to him, he won't be best pleased.'

That silenced Godric, who no doubt had heard of King Guillaume's unpredictable temper, and knew all about the fits of rage to which he was rumoured to be prone. It was often said that no man ever crossed him twice and lived, for while the king was sometimes prepared to overlook a first offence, he was rarely so forgiving the second time. By taking up arms in rebellion, Godric had committed his first transgression. Already, then, his fate rested on a knife's edge.

The drapes across the hall's entrance parted, allowing in a sudden burst of sunlight: something we had seen little of in recent days. Through the parting stepped a pale-faced, dung-reeking lad of perhaps twelve or thirteen, whom Robert had sent to the royal hall with news of our prisoner. He stood, panting heavily as if he had just run all the way to Cantebrigia and back.

'You bring news?' Robert asked him.

The boy nodded. 'Yes, lord,' he said in between breaths. 'I returned as quickly as I could.'

'Well, what is it? Did you give the message as I instructed?'

'I did, lord.'

'And?'

'He is on his way, lord. The king's steward told me himself.'

Robert nodded and dismissed the boy, who looked relieved that his questioning was finished, and that he wasn't about to be sent with any more messages for the royal household. The officials of the palace were powerful men, useful to have as allies but dangerous to have as enemies, not just because they had the king's ear but also because their orders carried his authority. They were respected by lords both petty and distinguished, and the boy had shown determination to have secured the attention of the royal steward.

In honesty, I wasn't much looking forward to facing the king either. For as much as I admired the will that had brought us here to England, and as great as his achievement was in winning this kingdom, nevertheless I feared him, as did many men in those days, both French and English alike. Although few had seen it with their own eyes, we had all heard the stories of how he and his raiding-bands had gone into the north last winter. We had heard how they'd harried the land and its people and despoiled both town and country, burnt storehouses newly filled with the autumn's harvest, slaughtered sheep and cattle in the fields where they grazed, put entire families to the sword, from hobbling greybeards to the youngest babes in arms, and left the meadows to run with blood as they spread fire and ruin, all in the name of retribution for the Northumbrian uprisings. It was, of course, a long-spoken truth that wars were fought with rape and pillage as much as they were with sword and shield, but the ferocity of his vengeance on this occasion sowed great alarm among his followers, and I was glad to have had no part of it. That one act revealed an aspect to King Guillaume that had rarely shown itself before, but which with each passing day became clearer as this campaign dragged on, as his desperation deepened and his mood grew ever more foul.

And so it wasn't just Godric who was nervous as we awaited the king. Fortunately it wasn't long before he arrived. I had barely enough time to slake my thirst from the ale-barrel Robert kept in the hall before I made out the sound of hoofbeats in the yard outside, shortly followed by someone bellowing: 'Make way! Make way for your king!'

He was here.

'Get up,' Wace said to Godric, but the Englishman seemed frozen to the stool, for he did not move, and my friend had to take his arms and bodily haul him up before he would stand. Even then the boy's feet seemed hardly able to support his weight, and at any moment I thought he would spew.

Wace shoved him in the back to start him moving, and we followed Robert out, pushing aside the linen drapes and ducking beneath the low lintel of the doorway before emerging into the heat of the mid-morning sun. For a moment I was blinded by the brightness, although I noticed dark clouds approaching, threatening rain. As if we hadn't had enough of it lately. Raising a hand to shield my eyes, I made out a conroi of some fifteen horsemen, most decked out in hauberks freshly polished, their features masked beneath helmets inlaid with swirling designs in gold and silver, their shoulders draped with the blood-red ceremonial cloaks, embroidered at the hems with golden thread, which marked them out as knights of the royal household.

At the head of them was the king himself. I had met him only once before, but his was not a face that one forgot easily, for it was drawn and entirely lacking in humour, with heavy brows above keen eyes that missed nothing: eyes that seemed to look into one's very soul. He was around forty-four in years if I recalled rightly, only a handful of summers younger than Malet, but had lost none of his youthful vigour or his passion for the pursuit of war. Tall and set like an ox, he possessed stout arms that were the mark of long hours spent in the training yard, where he was said to practise daily at both stake and quintain, and in mock combat with his trusted hearth-troops.

'Kneel,' I hissed at the Englishman. Thankfully he needed no second telling, but did as I bade him without hesitation, and the rest of us did the same as the king jumped down from the saddle, handed his destrier's reins to a retainer and strode towards us. Where earlier the yard had been filled with the sounds of timber being chopped and the clash of oak cudgels as men trained at arms, now a hush had fallen, broken only by the lowing of cattle in the fields and the calls of sheep in their pens, the clang of steel from the smith's workshop some way off and the thumping of my own heart. I breathed deeply, trying to still it.

The king's shadow fell across me. To begin with he said nothing, and I wondered whether he was expecting one of us to speak first.

Robert must have thought the same, for he began: 'My lord king—'

'I gave clear instruction that there were to be no more expeditions against the enemy without my permission,' the king said, cutting him off. 'Is that not so?'

'It is so,' Robert replied, not daring to meet the king's eyes, probably wisely.

'You know full well that we need every man we can muster for this next assault on the Isle, and that we cannot afford to waste good warriors on such reckless adventures. And yet I am told that you saw fit last night to send a raiding-party out into the marshes, almost within arrowshot of the Isle itself. This, too, is true, isn't it?'

'Yes, lord, but—'

'I would have thought that you more than anyone, Robert Malet, would take care to heed my instructions, given your family's current standing. Instead you choose to defy me. By rights I should order you strung up by the nearest tree, or at the very least have you stripped of your landholdings. Perhaps that would be a suitable punishment. What do you think?'

Robert opened his mouth as if to speak and then promptly closed it again.

'Yes,' the king continued. 'You would be wise to think carefully about your next words, lest they be your last.'

Never before had I seen Robert forced to bend his knee for anyone, and I confess the sight was strange, though there was no reason why it should have been. That was the order of the world, after all: every man, from the poorest swineherd to the most powerful baron, was bound by oaths to someone else, and in the same way the king was bound to God's service, obligated to govern his subjects well and to uphold the virtues of our faith. This I knew, and yet in spite of that I couldn't help the anger welling inside me as Robert, the lord whom I respected, was forced to humble himself. Anger, and not a little guilt too, since it was because of me that he found himself in such a position.

'Have you nothing to say?' the king asked. 'Well, perhaps that is for the best. Fortunately you find me in good humour this morning, so I am prepared to overlook your misdeed on this occasion, especially since you have brought me this gift.' He turned his attention upon Godric, whose head was bowed, his whole body trembling. 'So this is your captive,' he said. 'Godric, thegn of Corbei.'

'He claims to be the son of Morcar's brother,' Robert said.

'I know well who he is,' the king snapped, his tone as sharp as a butcher's cleaver. 'We have met before, although the last time our paths crossed, he was, I believe, still a boy under the fosterage of his uncle, not a man full-grown.'

His voice was thick with scorn, but if he was trying to provoke a response from Godric, he was disappointed.

'Look at me,' he said, and when the Englishman did not obey, he repeated more forcefully: 'Look at me!'

Slowly and with not a little reluctance, Godric raised his head, his gaze eventually coming to rest on his king, and I saw the lump in his throat as he swallowed.

'Not so long ago you and your uncle gave oaths to be my loyal servants,' the king said. 'Now, however, you renounce those oaths and ally yourselves with the rebels upon the Isle. You are a worthless creature, a perjurer and a traitor.'

'No, lord,' Godric protested. 'I will p-pledge my allegiance to you anew, if you will only . . .'

He didn't finish, for the king had drawn his sword from its sheath and was turning it over slowly, showing the Englishman the swirling smoke-like pattern embedded in the steel, and the keenness of its point. It was indeed a fine weapon, as one would expect, although clearly meant for display rather than fighting, since there was not a single nick anywhere along the edge, or any other mark to suggest it had ever seen use on the field of battle.

'By rights I should kill you now and be done with you,' said King Guillaume, and raised the tip of the blade so that it gently touched against the skin beneath Godric's chin, not enough to draw blood but enough that a single slip of his hand would spell the Englishman's death. 'Perhaps I will send your head back to your uncle Morcar as an example of how I deal with those who dare rise against me.'

'Please, lord, no,' said Godric, his eyes closed tight as if expecting the killing cut to come at any moment. 'Have m-mercy, I beg of you.'

'If you wish mercy,' the king said, 'then first you must earn it.'

'Whatever you ask, lord, I will do it.'

The king regarded him for long moments. Around us the first few raindrops pattered upon the mud, while the breeze tugged at the scarlet cloaks of the king's guard and caused the pennons nailed to their lances to flutter. Eventually he withdrew the weapon, returning it to its sheath with a whisper of steel, while with his other hand he gave a signal to one of his retainers. The sun was behind him and so at first I could not make out the man's features, save that he was dressed in long, black robes, but then he stepped

85

closer and I made out his shining pate and the small, hard eyes squinting out from beneath owlish brows.

Atselin.

I stared at him, and he at me. A quizzical look came across his face as he recognised me, as if he hadn't been expecting to find me here, but it quickly disappeared as his brows hardened into a frown. In truth I was just as surprised to see him. Although he was chief among the clerks and scribes of the royal household gathered here at Brandune, for some reason I hadn't thought he would be known to the king himself.

'Brother Atselin,' the king said, 'may I rely on you to bear witness and to write down anything of note that our English friend may say?'

The monk broke off his stare, blinking once as a raindrop struck the end of his prominent nose, and then again as another bounced off his tonsured head.

'Of course, my king,' he said stiffly. From somewhere within the folds of his robe he produced a wax writing-tablet, along with a stylus carved from what looked like either bone or ivory. 'Although perhaps it would be best if we venture inside,' he added, pointing towards the sky just as the sun disappeared behind the dark cloud. 'Before we are all drowned.'

Hardly had he finished speaking than the deluge began, so suddenly and with such force that it seemed all the heavens were crashing down upon us. Hard drops bounced upon the yard and lashed my back, plastering my hair against my head and my tunic to my skin. Without delay, the king made for the hall, leaving his retainers to see to their horses, and the rest of us followed him.

Godric alone was reluctant to move, but Eudo and I hauled him to his feet and dragged him inside, where his fate would be decided.

The rain pummelled upon the thatch. From one dark corner of the hall came a steady drip-drip as it seeped through a hole and fell upon the floor, where it formed a pool, in which fragments of rushes floated.

'Speak, then,' the king said when we were once more gathered around the hearth-fire. 'Tell me everything you know about your army.'

Godric sat with hands tied on the stool before the fire, his face lit by its flickering glow. 'Everything?'

'Everything,' the king repeated, his expression hardening. 'I want you to tell me how many men you have, how well they're armed, how they're divided and who commands them. How well is Elyg defended? Are there walls, a stockade and a castle mound? What is the mood within your camp?'

'What do you wish to know first?'

'Give me numbers. How many men of fighting age do you have?'

'A thousand?' Godric hazarded. 'Possibly more than that.'

The king snorted, as well he might. 'A thousand? You expect me to believe that?'

The real number, we suspected, was probably three times that. In the absence of any reliable information, however, it was admittedly something of a guess.

'How should I know, lord?' Godric said, a note of despair in his voice. 'I haven't counted them myself.'

From another man's lips that might have sounded insolent, but it was the fact that he spoke with such sincerity that made me laugh. Straightaway I tried to stifle it. The noise that came out was some-where between a cough and a choke. The king glared at me, and I glimpsed the fire that lay behind his cold demeanour.

'Has your uncle not spoken to you of such things?' Atselin suggested. 'Perhaps you can recall something of what he might have mentioned about their numbers and disposition.'

'He tells me little,' Godric answered. There was a look in his eyes that might have been anger or hurt, and perhaps it was a mixture of the two. 'He says I am still young, that he values my loyalty but I am not a warrior yet, that I should worry about honing my sword-skills first before troubling myself with such details. I had to beg to be allowed to lead the scouting-band last night.' He shook his head and sniffed. 'I failed even at that.'

Atselin narrowed his eyes. 'How old are you?'

'Fifteen summers this year.'

He was barely out of boyhood. Were he not my enemy I might have felt sorry for him. Eager to impress and to win respect, he was nonetheless a long way from fulfilling his ambitions. Doubtless I'd been much the same at his age, although he held one advantage over me, for he was only too aware of his shortcomings, whereas I had never been able to see them. That youthful arrogance had nearly proven my undoing on more occasions than one.

The king, however, was unmoved. 'Tell us something you do know.'

After swallowing to clear his throat, Godric began to speak of the enemy's defences, while Atselin scrawled upon his tablet, although in truth we learnt little that was new. Once in a while the king would interrupt to press the Englishman further, but otherwise he seemed content to let him talk. And so we learnt that nothing resembling a castle had yet been erected – not that we had expected any among the English to have the expertise to do so – but that Morcar and the other leading thegns had thrown up all manner of walls and earthen banks around the monastery, dug ditches and arrayed sharpened stakes in them to deter against attack, and behind those defences they waited for us to come to them. They had food enough to last until winter and even beyond, Godric assured us, although how he could possibly say that when he had no real notion of how many mouths they had to feed, I wasn't sure. Perhaps that fact had come from his uncle, since it didn't sound like the kind of judgement he was likely to have made on his own. Indeed he seemed almost as ignorant as the eel-catchers and other marsh folk, upon whose sparse knowledge and occasional observations of the enemy positions we had thus far come to rely.

Still, everything he told us confirmed our worry, which was that the rebels were secure in their fastness and unlikely to be prised from it in the foreseeable future. Indeed, if their defences were as formidable as young Godric made them sound, we had only one choice: to lay siege to that stronghold, bombard them with our mangonels and try to starve them into submission, but that might take months: months that we didn't have, and I suspected the king was coming to the same realisation. He paced in front of us, every once in a while tapping a finger against his chin as if in thought, no doubt wondering, as I was, what we should do with the Englishman now, and whether he might make a reliable guide through the marsh-passages that led to the Isle. I could not speak for the king, but certainly I wouldn't want to entrust my life to him.

Godric went on to describe the rich halls of the monastery at Elyg, which the abbot and monks had surrendered to Hereward and Morcar to use for their councils of war and as private chambers for themselves and their households. Had he any sense, he would have shut his mouth before going on any further, but desperation was loosening his tongue, and he could not stop himself. Oblivious to the king's darkening expression, he told of the lavish feast his uncle had held there three nights before, of the various dishes of hare and boar that had been laid out, of the wine, ale and mead that had flowed and how men had fallen about insensible with drink, of how a poet had sung of the great victory that would soon be theirs.

'I have heard enough,' the king said eventually, cutting Godric off as he was telling of his uncle's great hoard of gold, and the largesse he had bestowed upon the abbot of Elyg in gratitude for his generosity. 'Unless you have anything worthwhile to offer, I have no more time for you.'

He signalled to two of his scarlet-clad knights, who stepped forward from the shadows where they had been waiting, took hold of the Englishman's shoulders in spite of his protests and hauled him to his feet.

'Take him outside and kill him,' the king said. 'Then hang his corpse somewhere by the marsh's edge where his countrymen might come across him. He will serve as an example.'

Godric tried to struggle, but his arms were pinned. 'No, lord!'

'You are of no use to us, and I have wasted my breath speaking to you. I do not wish to look upon your loathsome face any longer.'

'Wait,' I said, as the king's knights dragged him towards the entrance. They stopped, glancing first at me, and then at the king. Out of the corner of my eye I saw Robert cast a warning glare my way, but I was not to be discouraged.

I could have held my tongue and left the Englishman to his fate without risking incurring King Guillaume's wrath, but an idea was beginning to stir within my mind: an idea that just might help bring a swift end to this war. In all the weeks we'd been fighting, the rebels had never once sent us an envoy, nor us them, since showing one's enemy that you were willing to talk was often taken as a sign of weakness, and neither side wished to admit to that. In Godric, however, I realised we had been gifted an opportunity, and one that we had to take.

The king rounded upon me. 'What is it?'

'My lord king,' I said. 'If I may speak, I have a suggestion to make.'

He stared long and hard at me, then at Eudo and Wace, who were standing beside me. 'I recognise you,' he said. 'Your faces are familiar, though I cannot say from where. Our paths have crossed before, haven't they?'

They had, though I hadn't expected him to remember. It had been the briefest of encounters, and more than two years ago besides.

'They were among the men who opened the city gates to your army on the night of the battle at Eoferwic,' Robert said. 'It was Tancred who led the charge on to the bridge, who faced Eadgar Ætheling in single combat and almost killed him.'

The account as he gave it was more or less true, although others had embellished those feats in their retellings of the battle. Robert, Wace and Eudo all knew well that if anyone had nearly met his death that day, it was I and not Eadgar, but I had rarely admitted this to anyone else, and thought it wise not to say anything now.

'Of course,' the king said, studying me with narrowed eyes. 'Tancred of Earnford. The Breton. I've heard tell of your exploits.'

I did my best not to flinch beneath his gaze, and to quell my anger at the note of scorn in his voice. 'Only good things, I trust, lord king,' I replied as evenly as I could.

He ignored that remark. 'Should I understand that you three are responsible for capturing the Englishman?'

'There were others as well, lord, but yes, it was we who led the expedition,' I said.

The king nodded as if in contemplation. 'Very well, Breton. What is this suggestion of yours?'

I swallowed to moisten my throat. 'I was thinking, lord, that we should send Godric back to Elyg.'

There was silence for a moment, in which only the sound of the rain and the geese in their pen outside could be heard. The king's eyes narrowed but he did not speak.

'Send him back?' Eudo asked. 'After all this, you would let him go?'

'Think for a moment,' I said. 'Why does Morcar persist in stirring up trouble? Why does he ally himself to filth-ridden wretches like Hereward? What is he looking to gain?'

I turned to Godric. The colour had drained entirely from his face but there was renewed brightness in his eyes. If he wanted to leave this place alive, though, he would have to help me.

'I – I don't know,' he mumbled, his voice quiet.

'I think you do,' I said. 'You might be a poor excuse for a warrior but you know him well enough. If Morcar truly wanted to drive us from these shores, his best opportunity was to raise his banner in support of Eadgar Ætheling last year, but he didn't. He doesn't care whether an Englishman or a Frenchman wears the crown, so long as he profits. Am I right?'

Godric did not reply, but his silence told me all that I needed to know.

'I think I understand what Morcar has in mind,' I went on. 'As much as he might act the war leader, the truth is that he is barely more experienced a fighter than his nephew. Remember that in two months not once has he dared meet us in open battle or so much as send a single raiding-band against our camp.'

Wace shrugged. 'He is a coward. What other explanation is there?'

'Maybe he is, but that doesn't mean he is stupid. I'd wager he knows exactly what he's doing. He's content to let others harry us and wreak destruction, while he shuts himself up inside the rebels' fastness at Elyg and, week by week, wears us down. Hereward and his band might have made it their cause to shed Norman blood until the marshes run red, but for Morcar this rebellion is merely a way of furthering his own ambitions. He doesn't want to dirty his hands if he can help it. In the end he's not looking to fight us, but to bargain.'

All eyes turned to the king, who was looking into the hearth, his hands clasped together and his forefingers steepled in front of his pursed lips. The fire-glow reflected in the whites of his eyes.

'If you're right, that means that he can be bought,' he murmured.

I nodded. 'Every man has his price. But the longer this campaign continues and the more desperate we grow, the greater the advantage he and the rebels hold, and so the greater their demands will be if we find ourselves forced to sue for peace.'

I said if, but truthfully I knew that it was a matter of when. As I'd said to Robert yesterday, we could not keep fighting this war for ever.

'You would try to come to an arrangement with Morcar,' said the king. 'You would pay a small price to him now, to avoid having to pay a larger one later. Is that it?'

'That is it, lord king.'

'You have no confidence, then, in our prospects of taking Elyg by force?'

'I don't doubt that it can be done,' I lied, having to choose my words with care. 'But it will be costly, and will mean the deaths of many hundreds if not thousands of our own men. Whether victory is worth that cost is not for me to say.'

The king turned to Godric. 'For the right price, can your uncle be persuaded to renew his oath to me and abandon the rest of the rebels?'

'I don't know,' the Englishman answered. 'It is possible, I suppose. There has never has been any friendship between him and Hereward. They hate one another, and there are often fights between their followers.'

That was news to my ear. We'd long known that the rebels were an unruly and disparate lot, but that their disagreements were spilling over into open violence surprised me. I was about to press him further, but the king spoke before I could open my mouth.

'You know Morcar better than most. What does he want? Does

he wish me to furnish him with chests filled with silver and precious stones? Or does he want ships to take him far across the sea so that he may never trouble these shores again?'

'His earldom,' Robert put in: the first he had spoken in a long while. 'He seeks the restitution of his old province of Northumbria, as it was granted to him by your predecessor, King Eadward.' He glanced at our prisoner. 'That's right, isn't it?'

'It is all he has ever wanted, lords,' Godric said. 'He wishes for his rank, title and landholdings to be returned, and for his honour to be restored.'

The earldom of Northumbria. It had once belonged to my former lord, Robert de Commines, until he was murdered that night at Dunholm. Now it was held by the corpulent and grasping Gospatric, an Englishman who hailed from one of the ancient northern families and who commanded a great deal of influence in those parts. His loyalty to us had always been vacillating at best, and openly treacherous on occasion, and all he seemed to care about was adding to his already considerable treasure hoard and acquiring ever more slave-girls to help warm his bed. I knew the king had long been looking for someone to install in his place, although no Norman wanted to venture into that cold, wet province and risk meeting his end at the hands of the wild men who lived there.

'Northumbria,' the king said mockingly. 'What would he want with such a miserable corner of land? Has he not heard what happened last winter?'

'He has,' Godric said. 'But he believes he would be a better man to govern it than Gospatric.'

Despite the ruin the king had wrought there, he hadn't managed to lay waste the entire province, and I imagined there were parts that had escaped the slaughter and the flames, where a man could easily prosper. Whether Morcar would prove any more dependable than Gospatric, or whether he could subdue the seditious folk who lived there any more successfully, remained doubtful, but none of that mattered at the present moment.

Atselin cleared his throat as if he wished to say something, but promptly fell quiet when the king held up a hand in warning. A stillness hung in the air. I hardly dared move, or even swallow to moisten my throat. Not until the king spoke.

After what seemed like an eternity, he told Godric, 'If that is what your uncle wishes, I will give it to him gladly. You may go back and tell him that.' He turned to Atselin. 'Draw up a writ immediately confirming Morcar as earl as proof of my word. I will put my seal to it.'

The monk blinked in surprise. 'Are you . . .' he began, but then faltered, his brow furrowing. 'My lord, are you certain of this?'

'Do you question my judgement, Atselin?'

'No, lord, but—'

'Then simply see that it is done.'

The monk bowed. 'Of course, my king.'

'Now, in return for this generous gift, Godric of Corbei, your uncle must be willing to renounce whatever oaths he may have sworn to his countrymen, and to swear allegiance to me, and me alone.'

'I will tell him.'

'Good.' The king smiled. 'If your uncle agrees to these terms, he must send word within three days. Do you understand?'

'Yes, lord.'

He turned to me. 'You, Breton, are responsible for escorting our friend back to the place where you captured him, or as close as you can manage if the enemy are afield. There you will let him go, and he will make his own way back to Elyg.'

'When would you have us do this?' I asked.

'Tonight, under the cover of darkness. The sooner he is reunited with his countrymen, the less reason they'll have to be suspicious. He has been gone long enough as it is. I will send further instructions this afternoon, along with the writ for him to deliver.' He pointed a thick finger at Robert. 'I entrust the Englishman to your care until then. He is your responsibility. If anything should happen to him, you will be answerable to me. You will receive your reward for his capture only if he returns, and does so in possession of favourable news from his uncle.'

'Yes, lord king,' Robert replied, more than a little stiffly, but if King Guillaume noticed then he said nothing of it.

'Make sure that you remain true to your word, Englishman,' he said as he gestured for his knights to unhand Godric. 'Consider yourself fortunate and remember that I have been generous on this occasion, but remember, too, that even my generosity is not without limit. Should you cross me and find yourself at my mercy again, I will take great pleasure in seeing that your death is both slow and terrible.'

He did not wait for Godric to reply, but stalked out of the hall, closely followed by his two guardsmen, their scarlet cloaks swirling behind them. Atselin paused long enough to fix me with his customary hard stare, but then he too was gone, leaving us alone with the Englishman. A part of me wanted to breathe a sigh of relief, although I knew that our work was barely begun.

For in a few hours we would send the boy to ply his uncle with promises of rich reward. In his hands rested our fates.

Seven

For the second time in as many nights, then, we found ourselves out on the fens, making our way through the maze of rivers and channels that made up the marsh country. After our ambush the night before, I expected the rebels to be more wary. Indeed had I been commanding them, I'd have made sure to set more sentries on duty, and sent more and larger scouting-parties out to roam the surrounding fens and keep a keen eye out for any signs of trouble. With that in mind, I dared not approach the Isle so closely this time around.

The mist hung a little more thickly over the water that night, with any luck veiling us from sight from the riverbanks, but it meant that once again we were relying on Baudri to steer us through the mist, to find the right channels and show us the way. We were all still bone-tired from the previous night's foray, and even though it had been my idea to send Godric back as errand-boy to Elyg, another expedition into the marshes was the last thing I had wanted. I'd tried to rest for a few hours that afternoon, but the day had been sweltering and I hadn't been able to settle for all the noise outside the thin walls of Robert's hall.

'He should be here,' I muttered, and it was only after I'd said it that I realised I'd spoken aloud.

'Who?' asked Wace, who was sitting next to me.

'Lord Robert,' I said. 'Godric is his responsibility as much as ours, and yet here we are, risking our skins once again for his sake.'

'His father is sick,' Eudo said. 'Who knows how much longer he'll live?'

Earlier that evening the priest, Dudo, had come to inform Robert that the elder Malet's illness had grown suddenly worse. He could not sit up; his fever had returned and he had been coughing up blood again. And so Robert had decided to stay by his bedside rather than join us tonight.

'How often has Malet's health waned in recent weeks?' I asked. 'Each time we were told he was close to death, but each time he recovered. What makes Robert think it will be any different on this occasion?'

'These could well be his father's final hours,' Wace put in. 'Surely you don't begrudge him this time with him?'

'Of course I don't,' I said, although it frustrated me, for I couldn't shake the suspicion that Robert was shirking his duties. Not all men were born to be warriors; I had long known that he lacked the thirst for adventure of one whose life was lived by the sword. I understood that and thought no less of him for it, but I also knew that a good lord would have taken charge of this undertaking himself, showing his vassals that he was deserving of their service. No one ever received respect without earning it first, and in my eyes this was an opportunity squandered.

Doubtless the others thought I was being unkind, and so I kept my thoughts to myself after that. An eternity passed before we spied the wooded crest of the isle of Litelport. At my instruction Baudri took us not back to the place where we had made the fires, facing Elyg, but around to the far shore, where I reckoned there was less chance of us being spotted. We had all come in a single boat this time, without Hamo and his company, and we ran it aground in a narrow inlet overhung by willows, where we would be easily hidden amongst the reeds and the drooping fronds.

'Get up,' I said to Godric. His hands were bound, but he managed to get to his feet without too much trouble. Until the moment that we finally let him loose, he was still our captive, and I was determined to make sure he was reminded of that fact, lest he have any misapprehensions about his importance.

'We won't be long,' I told Wace, who had agreed to wait and keep watch along with Baudri, Serlo and Pons. 'If you see anything in the meantime, give the signal.'

The rest of us climbed from the punt. My feet subsided into the soft, sucking mud, and it took me a moment to find my balance. Chill marsh-water soaked my trews up to my ankles and crept into my shoes, curling its icy tendrils around my toes. There came the startled cries of a pair of moorhens woken from their sleep, followed by two splashes as they entered the water, but those were the only sounds to be heard. I gave the Englishman a shove in the back to start him moving, and Eudo and I followed behind him, keeping our hands close to our sword-hilts. None of us had seen anything to suggest the enemy were here at Litelport, and it would be bad fortune indeed if we happened to stumble upon them, but all the same it was better to be ready, just in case.

We ventured some hundred paces or so inland, to a patch of open grassland, in the middle of which a solitary marker stone rose to the height of a man's waist, and I reckoned that would serve as a good landmark.

'This is as far as we take you,' I said. 'You'll find your own way from here.'

He nodded, understanding. Not wanting to linger here any longer than we had to, I set straightaway to loosening his bonds. I'd tied them tighter that was probably necessary, and I imagined his wrists must be raw from the rope chafing against his skin. Still, he'd made no complaint before and he made none now. Long moments passed while I picked at the knot, but eventually it came loose.

'Here,' I said, unbuckling Godric's sword-belt with the gem-studded scabbard from where it hung around my waist, and passing it to him. We'd already returned his hauberk and chausses, on the king's orders, and now Eudo tossed him his silver-and-gold-inlaid helmet as well. It would do no good to deprive the Englishman of such treasured possessions when we were trying to win his friendship. For the same reason I also gave him back his four gold rings, although with some reluctance, since they were beautiful things, engraved with a fine runic script and polished to such a shine that they gleamed like the sun. They would have fetched a handsome price. As would Godric himself, had we simply ransomed him to his uncle as he'd begged.

'Take this, too,' I said, drawing from inside my cloak the parchment scroll that bore King Guillaume's writ and seal. 'Allow no one to see it save for your uncle.'

The Englishman nodded, trembling slightly as he took it. 'What should I say? When I return to Elyg, I mean. How do I explain where I've been?'

I'd been thinking about that. I hadn't forgotten that some of his scouting-party had fled when they saw their leader captured, and presumably had given their accounts of the ambush when they arrived back at Elyg. His story would need to accord with theirs.

'To anyone but Morcar,' I said, and I spoke slowly so that he could hear me clearly, 'say that we almost succeeded in capturing you, but you managed to slip away into the trees. We gave chase, of course, but eventually you managed to lose us. Then you hid during the day, waiting until darkness fell so as to make certain that you wouldn't fall into our hands again. Do you think you can remember all that?'

'I'll try,' he replied.

From anyone else's lips such an admission of cowardice might have sounded strange, but from his I felt sure it would seem convincing enough.

'This, then, is where we part,' I said. 'Remember this place. For the next three nights, there will be someone waiting here for you to bring an answer from your uncle. You will come unarmed and you will come alone. Do you understand?'

'I understand.'

'Very well,' I said. 'Now, go, before I decide that the king was wrong after all and that you're of more use to us dead.'

He didn't need telling twice. I barely had time to blink before he had turned his back and scurried off, half running and half stumbling, through the long grass. He was slowed a little by the weight of his mail, but the mist obscured the moon's light and so it wasn't long before he disappeared into the darkness. Thus Godric, thegn of Corbei, went to deliver his message and persuade Morcar to change his allegiance.

A part of me wondered whether we would ever see him again. I wasn't alone, either.

'You realise he won't come back, don't you?' Wace said when we'd returned to the inlet where the willows grew and pushed out on to the water. 'He knows he was fortunate to escape with his life. He won't dare put himself at our mercy a second time.'

'Even if he does deliver the message to his uncle as he promised, what if Morcar refuses King Guillaume's offer?' Eudo asked. 'Where will we be then?'

'We'll be in exactly the same situation as we were before,' I replied. 'We lose nothing by trying, and if it works it might well give us the key to victory.'

I sounded more confident than I felt. Wace and Eudo were right. If I were Godric I would think twice about returning to the lion's den. At the same time we were relying on appealing to Morcar's ambition, the depth of which we could not possibly know. What if our offer wasn't enough to overcome his suspicion? What if he judged the risks to be too great for the reward?

There was little point in wondering. The seeds had been cast, and there was nothing more we could do now, save to wait.

And hope.

Godric failed to show himself the next night, or the night after that. Twice we ventured out to the island, and twice we returned with heavy lids and empty hands.

'I told you he wouldn't come,' Wace muttered as we made our way back that second morning under the grey light of dawn. 'We're wasting our time.'

'He'll come,' I said, although I was steadily growing less sure of that. 'If Morcar has any sense at all, he won't let this chance slip from his grasp.'

Once more, then, we set out for the island of Litelport. Since we didn't know whether Godric would heed the instruction to come alone, we travelled in force. With me were Serlo and Pons, Eudo and Wace and all their knights, together with Hamo and a few of his bowmen. That way, if Godric's friends tried to take revenge for our ambush, we would be ready. We were joined this night by Lord Robert, who brought a handful of his household knights, his father's fever having abated a little, for now at least.

'He grows weaker by the day,' he told me. His face was drawn and his eyes hollow. 'The bouts of sickness come more frequently, and though tonight he enjoys some respite, tomorrow he will grow worse again.'

I didn't know what to say to that. I confess I wasn't much used to families, and had never really understood them. Whereas Robert was close to his father, I'd hardly known mine. A Breton lord of no great standing named Baderon, he had been killed in a feud with a rival when I was only five or six summers old. Of my mother, Emma, my memories were even more vague. She had passed from this world a year earlier while giving birth to the girl who would have been my sister. The only kinship I knew, and had ever really known, was that which existed between myself and my sword-brothers: the bond of the conroi.

'I see such pain in his eyes,' Robert went on. 'He is determined to live to see our victory over the rebels, but God only knows when that may be, if indeed it happens at all.'

'I pray for him,' I said. 'We all do.'

He smiled in thanks, but it was a smile that quickly faded. 'I sent word a few weeks ago both to my mother at Graville, and to Beatrice. I hope they will have a chance to see him before he passes away, although with each day that goes by, it seems ever more unlikely.'

'We can but hope, lord,' I said, although to speak truthfully I wasn't looking forward to meeting Malet's wife, Elise, again. A stern-faced woman lacking in humour, she hadn't much taken to me the last time we'd met, and I had little reason to suppose she would be any better inclined now. With Beatrice, Robert's sister, I was on better terms, and indeed counted her as a friend, one of the few I seemed to have in those days. She was married now, or so Robert had told me, to the vicomte of Archis in Normandy, a baron of moderate wealth and noble parentage, who was both a close friend and a tenant of the Malets. It could easily be a week before word reached them across the Narrow Sea, however, and another before they were able to make the crossing, depending on the wind and the tides, and perhaps another still to reach us here in the fen country. Whether Malet had strength enough to last out until they arrived, none but God could know. Doubtless Robert was making the same reckoning, for he had fallen quiet now, lost in his own thoughts.

In silence, then, we rounded the northern shore of the island until we found the familiar inlet where the water ran shallow and the willows grew. We guided our punts close to the bank, where banks of tall reeds kept us out of sight from the river and the low-hanging branches provided a good mooring place. Leaving a few men behind to guard the boats, we ventured away from the inlet, up a gentle rise through long grasses and thick bramble hedges until we were just within sight of the marker stone that I'd chosen as our meeting place. And there, for the third night, we crouched in the shadows and we waited.

And waited.

Hours passed. The glittering stars became obscured as cloud spread across the sky. The wind rose, rustling the grass so that it seemed there were voices all around us, whispering, and the rain soon followed, hesitantly at first but quickly growing heavier. We huddled down inside our cloaks, our hoods raised, letting the water roll off the wool. The smell of moist earth rose up, reminding me of the green pastures of Earnford, and for a moment I was back there again, as it was during the spring with the new shoots breaking the soil and the first leaf-buds appearing on the trees in the woods.

Thunder pealed out, like the roar of some fearsome beast unleashed from the caverns of hell to wreak its fury upon the world. I made the sign of the cross to ward off any evil spirits that might be lurking, hoping that it wasn't a sign of ill fortune to come. No sooner had I done so than the rain began to ease. Another roar resounded through the night sky, but it seemed further away. It was followed some moments later by another, and another, each one quieter than the last, until all was still again.

And through that stillness came a sound. A sound like a voice, except that this time I was sure it wasn't just the wind. It came from the direction of the marker stone, though from so far away I couldn't make out what they were saying.

'Did you hear that?' I asked, taking care to keep my voice low.

Robert nodded and put a finger to his lips, while out of the corner of my eye I saw Pons rest his hand upon his sword-hilt. Through the heads of the grass and the all-enshrouding mist I glimpsed twin points of orange light, the sort that could only come from torches or lanterns.

Godric had not come alone.

Shadowy figures moved around the light; in the darkness and from such a distance it was hard to tell exactly how many, but at a guess I would have said they numbered about ten, most of them warriors, if the glint of their spearpoints and their helmets were anything to judge by.

'Show yourselves,' a man shouted out in French, but I didn't recognise his voice, which was deep and harsh and carried the proud tones of one who was used to being obeyed. 'I know you're there.'

Serlo looked at me. 'What do we do, lord?'

I glanced at Robert, whose face bore a grim expression. 'Don't move,' he said. 'Wait until I say.'

'I have no time for this,' the man called. 'I've come to talk, not to fight.'

That sounded like the kind of thing Morcar was likely to say, although I hadn't been expecting him to come in person. I'd thought he would prefer to stay where there was no danger, in his hall in the monastery at Elyg, rather than speak with us himself.

'You've come to talk, have you?' Robert shouted out. 'You have a strange way of showing it.'

He rose and strode forward, towards the flickering torch-glow, at the same time signalling to the rest of us to get to our feet, which we did, albeit a little stiffly after so long spent crouched in the cold and the damp. Hamo and his men nocked arrows to their bowstrings in warning, and I laid my sword-hand upon my hilt as I followed Robert, my boots sinking into the soft earth. A thin drizzle still fell; droplets rolled off the leaves, pattering on to the sodden earth.

'I didn't come with a whole army to protect me,' the man pointed out. He stepped closer to the light and I saw him properly for the first time. What I was expecting, I wasn't sure. There was little resemblance between nephew and uncle, for while the boy had been short of stature, fair in complexion and round in the cheek, the elder one was tall and dark-featured, with a face composed of hard lines that drew together to form a stern expression. How many he was in years, I could not say exactly, although I might have guessed around thirty-five.

'Are you Morcar?' Robert asked, coming to a halt about ten paces from the Englishmen.

'Were you expecting someone else?'

Robert shrugged. 'At least you had the nerve to come yourself this night, rather than send a boy to do a man's work.'

'If you're hoping to win my allegiance, you're not doing very well,' Morcar said. 'I might decide I don't want to parley after all, and go back to the Isle. Then you would have to face your king's displeasure for having let your one chance at winning this war slip away.'

'Or else I could kill you now and be done with it.'

'You could, but you would as likely die trying,' Morcar said with a sneer. 'And several of your men with you, besides. Your little raiding-band might have managed to surprise my nephew the other night, but we both know that an open fight is another matter entirely.'

Had the numbers lain more in our favour, I might have thought like Robert, but as it was I found myself agreeing with Morcar. Giving battle was always a risky business, and never a course of action to be undertaken lightly, unless victory could be all but assured, which in this case it could not.

'Where is your nephew?' Robert asked. 'Is he here, or have you left him back at Elyg where he can do no harm?'

'He is here,' Morcar said, and gave a snap of his fingers. 'Godric!'

One of the men I'd taken for Morcar's hearth-troops stepped forward, untied his chin-strap and removed his helmet, revealing a plump-faced youth whom I recognised at once. He looked even more nervous, if that were possible, than he had three days ago while kneeling before the king. I could not recall ever seeing anyone so finely dressed for war and yet looking so uncomfortable, and so terrified.

'Don't forget that if I hadn't let Godric lead the scouting-party that night, we might not be standing here now,' Morcar said mildly. 'Your king ought to be thanking me for making this meeting possible.'

'I will make sure to tell him when we return to camp,' Robert said, and there was no mistaking his sardonic tone. 'Should I suppose that you have an answer for him?'

'I do. I have listened to his offer and received his writ, and considered it carefully.'

'And what do you say?'

'That I accept his terms, and that I promise to lend my spears in your support when you make your next attack across the bridge in a few days' time.'

'How are you so sure that we're planning another attack?' I asked.

Morcar snorted as he turned to me. 'Do you think we are blind? We have all seen your men labouring to repair the causeway and the siege platforms, and to clear the ground all about of reeds and sedge. It is hardly any secret that King Guillaume is preparing for another attempt to capture the Isle, and soon, if the number of tents and banners that gather daily around the guardhouse at Alrehetha are any clue.' He turned to Robert. 'I'll tell you what will happen. As soon as I hear that the first of your conrois has crossed the bridge, I'll turn my spears against my countrymen, and send word to those of my loyal followers to do the same. The Isle will belong to us within hours. I will surrender Elyg to your king and at the same time make my formal submission to him.'

'What makes you think you have the right to direct the course of the battle?' I asked.

A frown descended upon Morcar's face, as if in his eyes I were a mere gnat, for whose buzzing he cared little. 'Are you leader here, or is he?' he asked, gesturing at Lord Robert. 'Which one of you should I be speaking to?'

'To me,' Robert said before I could open my mouth. 'I speak for the king.'

'Then tell him what I have just told you.'

'What if he has a different strategy in mind?'

'Then of course he is free to pursue it if he wishes, but he will not succeed,' Morcar said, swelling out his chest and drawing himself up to his full height. 'Without my help he faces an impossible task. I have more than a thousand spears at my command. Without those spears he cannot succeed.' He glanced at me. 'That', he said, speaking slowly, 'is what gives me the right.'

'You ask a lot of our trust,' said Robert. 'You say you will do nothing until we reach the other side of the bridge. By then our army will be committed. If you decide not to make good on your promise—'

'That is a chance you must take. From what I hear, the king is determined to press ahead with this latest assault regardless of whether he has my support or not.'

I frowned. 'How do you know this?'

He grinned. In the torchlight his teeth gleamed as white as a Welshman's, and I wondered whether he obsessed about cleaning them in the same way. Certainly he seemed to think highly of himself; there was a look of self-satisfaction about him, as if he had us all acting according to his desires.

'It doesn't matter how I know it, only that it is true, and you have as good as confirmed it for me.'

Robert glared at me, but I knew that Morcar was only trying to taunt us. He wouldn't risk appearing foolish in front of us by saying such a thing unless he could be reasonably confident he was right. Possibly he had gleaned that knowledge from Godric after his return to Elyg, or it was merely an assured guess. Whichever, I was fast taking a dislike to his arrogant manner.

'Come, though,' said Morcar. 'Let us not sow any seeds of suspicion between us. You have my word that I will fulfil my part as we have discussed, and as surety of my good faith, I give you my nephew as hostage. Should I break my word, you may kill him. Is there any greater guarantee I can give you than that?'

That was why Godric looked so frightened, then. He already knew what his role would be. Although, I thought, should Morcar fail to keep his side of the agreement, his nephew's death would be scant vengeance for the loss of hundreds of Norman knights.

'Uncle—' Godric started to protest.

'Go with them, nephew,' Morcar said, interrupting him before he could continue. 'You will be safe. Upon my own life I swear it.'

The flatness of his tone gave the lie to his reassuring words. Somewhat hesitantly the boy stepped forward, and not for the first time I felt something close to sympathy for him. He was but a playing-piece in a game he was too young yet to understand, although he knew well enough the penalty if he happened to find himself on the losing side.

'I also present to your king a gift that I hope he might take pleasure in,' Morcar said, smiling, and he gestured to his hearth-troops, who brought forward two women.

I say they were women, but really they were no more than girls, both in the early flush of womanhood and probably around as many in years as Godric. So alike were they that they had to be twins. They were slim, delicately featured and obviously unmarried too, for their hair, wavy and chestnut-brown, was not braided and covered but instead hung long and loose to their waists. Were it not for the tears in their eyes, they might have been great beauties. Both were shaking, and not just, I suspected, because it was cold and their dresses were thin.

'Their names are Acha and Tuce,' Morcar said. 'I forget which is which, but I'm sure they will tell you, if you care to ask.'

Robert gestured for Hamo's men to down their bows and seize both Godric and the twins, which was probably wise, before one or more of them decided to make a bid for freedom and lose us in the mist.

'Bind them,' he said, and then to Morcar: 'Why should King Guillaume take any interest in these girls?'

'Why do you think? For the same reason as any other man would.'

'In all the years of his marriage he has never taken another woman to his bed. I thought you might have known that.'

'So he says. You know as well as I that, kings or not, we all have needs, and these are the prettiest of all my slave-girls. But if he doesn't want them, perhaps he will let you have them, Robert Malet.'

If my lord was surprised that Morcar knew his name, he did well not to show it. 'Have you any other gifts for us, or is our business here finished?'

'I have nothing more to say.'

'Very well. With any luck our paths will cross again soon.'

'I look forward to it, and to meeting King Guillaume in person.' Morcar grinned again, and I caught another gleaming flash of his teeth. He had a look in his eyes, at the same time both rapacious and sly, that put me in mind of a wolf. If I didn't trust him before, I trusted him less then. 'I fervently pray, too, that your father recovers soon from whatever ailment it is that troubles him.'

Robert opened his mouth but no sound came out. Before he could find the words with which to reply, Morcar had turned on his heels and marched away, beyond the marker stone into the darkness. As he did so his hearth-troops closed ranks about him, protecting his rear and flanks and keeping a close watch upon us, until the mist closed around them and I lost sight of their torches in the gloom.

'He seems to know a lot,' Eudo remarked after they'd gone. 'Do you think he has spies in our camp?'

'I doubt it,' Robert said. 'Even if there are, it's unlikely that they would be able to get near enough to the king to find out anything of much worth. He keeps close counsel, as you know.'

'What about Brother Atselin?' I asked. 'He's a weasel, if I ever saw one.'

'The clerk, you mean?'

'He's part of the royal household, and has the king's ear,' I pointed out. 'I don't like him, and I don't trust him, lord.'

Robert looked sternly at me. 'There are many men you don't trust. That doesn't make them all traitors. No, I don't believe there's any spy in our midst. All Morcar's looking to do is sow doubt in our minds and that of the king. To turn us against one another, to make us hunt for enemies where there are none, to foment further dissent in our ranks and so strengthen his own position.'

There was sense in that, I supposed. I only hoped he was right.

'Come on,' Robert said as he turned in the direction of the inlet where the willows grew, where Baudri and the others were waiting with the boats to take us back to Brandune. 'Let's leave this place.'

Eight

Fortunately the king seemed to be satisfied by Morcar's terms and the gift of the two slave-girls, for the next morning, under cloudless skies and a fierce sun, we made ready to quit Brandune, and I prayed it was the last we would see of that fetid cesspit.

Awaiting us was Alrehetha, where the bridge was being rebuilt. Most of our host had already assembled there, and we were among the last few hundred men to make the journey, along with the king and his retinue. A token force would be left to guard the boats moored there, together with enough provisions to keep them fed. Everything else we took with us: bundles of firewood, timber planks, sacks of grain to feed our horses, barrels of salted fish and pickled eels, spare spearheads and mail hauberks, all of which were loaded on to carts or sumpter ponies. With us, too, travelled all the leech-doctors and fletchers, wheelwrights and armourers and priests who attended upon an army, as well as the ever-present rolls-keepers who recorded every last bundle of wool and roll of cloth taken from the royal storehouses, every chicken and goose placed in a cage for the journey, and made a tally of every cart and haywain as it was harnessed to a team of oxen and sent on its way to join the main column.

And among those rolls-keepers, as always, was Atselin. He sat at his usual desk in the yard outside the king's hall, except that a canopy had now been erected above his head to shield his bald head and his precious parchments from the sun and the rain. He was overseeing the other clerks, who scurried about from building to building with bundles of scrolls under their arms on which presumably were written lists of goods, which they brought to him for his approval and his seal. A crowd was forming about his writing-desk and I hoped to escape his attention as I made my way past, towards the paddock where my destrier, Fyrheard, was grazing.

I wasn't so lucky. My gaze must have lingered a little too long. Even as I looked away, he called my name. For an instant I hesitated, deciding whether to heed him or pretend I hadn't heard, but then he called a second time, louder this time, and I realised I couldn't ignore him. Sighing, I turned and made my way over as, with a wave of his hand, he dismissed the queue of grumbling underclerks.

'What do you want, Atselin?' I asked, without so much as a word of greeting. He would not have offered me that courtesy, and I saw no reason why I should do any differently.

He did not look up but continued to scrawl, squinting intently at the page. The grey of the goose-feather quill in his hand matched the crown of hair around his tonsure.

'I merely wished to congratulate you,' he said, although there was no warmth in his voice. 'I understand that Morcar agreed to the king's most generous offer.'

I frowned, suspecting some manner of snide remark to follow. 'That's right. What of it?'

'Nothing, save to remind you that you are fortunate that your idea was successful, that young Godric remained true to his word and that his uncle was willing to listen to what he had to say. But don't expect that King Guillaume will grant you or your lord any special favours because of it.'

'What do you mean by that?'

'The king still remembers how you defied him by venturing out on your little raiding expedition without his approval. Your good fortune changes none of that. Don't forget, either, that had your plan failed, it would have been on your head. He would have given up a valuable hostage for no good reason.'

'You're wrong,' I said. 'He had no intention of keeping Godric prisoner. Had I not spoken when I did, the boy's corpse would be swinging from the highest branch overlooking the fens as a warning to his countrymen. We wouldn't have Morcar on our side but instead would surely be marching towards almost certain defeat.'

Atselin's quill stopped, his hand suspended above the page, but still he did not look at me. 'You think very highly of yourself, Tancred of Earnford.'

'You were there,' I said, almost spitting the words. My blood ran hot, as it always did whenever I found myself trying to reason with this weasel. 'You were there, in Robert's hall, when the boy's fate was decided. So tell me, monk, which part of what I've said isn't true?'

I waited for long moments, but no words were forthcoming. Instead he dipped his quill in the inkwell and carried on writing as if I weren't there.

'Speak to me, you miserable, shit-stinking rat,' I said, and snatched the parchment he was working on out from beneath his hand. 'Am I or am I not telling the truth?'

At once he leant across the desk, trying with his free hand to claim the sheet back, but I held it just out of reach.

'Give that to me,' he said, wearing a tired expression on his face.

'First apologise, and answer me.'

He stared at me as if I were speaking in some foreign tongue. 'Why should I apologise to you?'

'Why?' I echoed. 'You call me over only to sneer at my deeds, and then you all but accuse me of telling lies. That's why.'

He rose from his stool and made another attempt to grab at the parchment, but I was too quick for him, and he succeeded only in getting a fingertip to it.

'No more of these games,' he said. 'Give that back to me now.'

'Or what?' I challenged him.

In the brief time I'd known Atselin, I had never seen him roused to anger. Always he had maintained a serene expression, as if he had seen all there was to see in the world and there was no longer anything that surprised or vexed him, but there was fire in his eyes then, and in his cheeks, too, which were burning red.

'I will offer you some advice, Tancred. You do not wish to get on the wrong side of me.' He spoke though gritted teeth. 'You do not want me as your enemy.'

I'd heard words to that effect before, although not from his lips. I gave a snort of disdain. 'Am I supposed to take that as a threat?'

'It is a warning. Heed it or ignore it, as you wish.'

'Do you think I'm frightened of you?' I asked. 'You, with your quill and your rolls? What are you going to do? Drown me in ink, perhaps, or else bore me to death by reciting your records?'

Atselin's eyes were like knives. 'I'm not concerned whether or not you fear me. But I will tell you now that I've suffered enough of your insults. For too long I have tolerated your boorish manner and withstood your contempt. No longer.' He made another attempt to seize back his precious sheet of vellum, and this time I was too surprised by his outburst to stop him. 'Now, leave me in peace,' he said. 'The morning is wearing on and I have work I must attend to.'

I gave him a final glare, but he was unmoved, and so I left him to his parchments, striding away towards the paddock as the clerks in their black robes once more descended, crowding about his desk with scrolls and writs for his attention.

As I walked away, I tried to make sense of what Atselin had said. From what I recalled, we'd been assured of reward as long as our ploy worked and Morcar agreed to join our cause, but the monk had suggested otherwise. Had the king since changed his mind on the matter? If so, it seemed strange that the first any of us would learn of it was from Atselin. Unless he were lying to me, but what reason would he have for doing so?

And what did he mean by his threat, or warning, or whatever one cared to call it? I didn't know, but resolved to keep my distance from the monk over the coming days: not because I feared him, but because I had no patience left for such distractions. Soon we would be riding into battle, and if I was to make it through alive, I wanted to be as ready as possible, to spend every moment I could honing my sword-skills and imagining what I would do when we met the enemy battle-lines. Nothing else mattered. My own fate, not to mention those of my knights and companions, depended on it.

*

The march to Alrehetha took the rest of that day, and all of the next, too. Though the route was probably only thirty miles, we were prevented from travelling as swiftly as we would have liked by the baggage train, which was forever drawing to a halt whenever an ox fell down lame, or a horse lost its shoe, or an axle became detached from one of its wheels and we had to move the offending haywain or wagon off the track so as not to block those that were following. But the king was determined that we would not spend more than one night separated from the rest of our host, and so any who dawdled and fell too far behind the main column for no good reason were visited by his household guard, who spurred them to greater pace with threats of violence upon their persons.

Those were not the only reasons for our slow progress, however. Barely had we been riding an hour that second morning when we spied the smoke rising to the north and west. At first it was no more than a dark smear in the distance but then, as we came closer, it became possible to pick out individual columns of black, roiling cloud, billowing some distance beyond the woods: not just a single spire but many, in a jagged line stretching all the way to the far horizon and beyond.

Straightaway the order went out to halt while the king sent out parties of knights to scout the road ahead, to investigate those burnings and, if possible, root out those responsible for the savagery. They came back some hours later, with dire reports of entire vills that had been put to the torch, barns and storehouses sacked and all the inhabitants slain, but otherwise empty-handed, save for one band which had managed to find two souls alive and unharmed: a thin, white-faced man in his middle years, and his ancient mother, who had no teeth and seemed half-mad for she was constantly muttering to herself. He spoke of a band of wild men who had come upon them from the marshes, led by a black-haired, bow-wielding demon of incredible height, whose eyes were a window upon the depths of hell, and whose arrows were bolts crafted from its flames.

'Hereward,' I said, after Robert had finished relating this information to us. 'This was his doing, wasn't it?'

'Who else could it be?' he said with a shrug, before riding on to seek out his other vassals and pass on the news. He was there when the two marsh-dwellers had been brought in, having been summoned by the king to offer his counsel. I wondered if that was a sign that his reputation was once more on the rise, though it went against what Atselin had told me. At the very least the king no longer seemed to regard him with the same contempt as he had but a few days ago, and I hoped that was a sign of better fortune to follow.

'You mentioned before that there is no love between your uncle and Hereward,' I said to Godric once we were back in the saddle. 'Why is that?'

The king had entrusted him for now to Robert's care and protection, and so he rode with us, having finally been relieved of his bonds. None of us thought him likely to attempt an escape, not with so many pairs of eyes watching him. Besides, even though he seemed to be a more adept horseman than he was a fighter, I doubted he would be able to outpace us.

'Isn't it obvious, lord?' Godric asked.

I shrugged. Perhaps it was obvious to him, but it wasn't to me.

'To begin with, as you know, it was Hereward who led the rebellion. When we arrived, however, he was made to surrender his leadership and give his oath to my uncle.'

'He was made to give his oath? How?'

'That was what my uncle demanded, in return for his support and the men that he'd brought. At that time, Hereward and his allies had gathered a sizeable army, but they saw that if they were to fight King Guillaume then they needed Morcar.'

'And Hereward was content simply to bend his knee and let your uncle assume the leadership?'

Godric shook his head. 'For days he refused even to meet him or speak to his envoys. Had his been the only decision that mattered, I think he might have turned us away.'

Perhaps he was less clever than I had supposed. 'Are you telling me he was willing to deprive himself and the rebellion of twelve hundred men?'

Had he done so, then the course of this war might have been very different. One thing was certain: we would not still be here now.

'He dreams of glory,' Godric explained. 'He hates your people for stealing his lands and those of his countrymen, for despoiling the kingdom. He wants his name to pass into legend as the man who won England back for its people.'

At that I laughed so hard I almost choked, and Pons and Serlo, riding ahead of me, both shot me bemused looks over their shoulders. 'Is this true?'

'So his retainers say. They claim that St Æthelthryth, whose remains are buried beneath the church at Elyg, appeared to him in a dream and charged him with protecting the Isle and with destroying King Guillaume.'

'And he believes this?'

'He seems to. He certainly thinks highly enough of himself. Every time I see him at Elyg he is parading himself like a king. He wraps himself in fine-spun cloaks trimmed with otter fur, and everywhere he goes he is accompanied by a retinue dozens strong.'

I shook my head in disbelief, although as ridiculous as it sounded, men had been known to convince themselves of far stranger things.

'How did Morcar manage to persuade him to swear his allegiance, then?' I asked.

'He didn't, lord.'

'Then who did?'

'It was Hereward's own friends who convinced him. Siward Bearn, Bishop Æthelwine, Thurcytel and all the other thegns. Together they spoke to him and made him see that my uncle would make the better leader.'

That was no small feat, especially considering that it had been Hereward who had led this rebellion from the beginning. To hand it over to someone else's command – and, worse, to have those he'd previously considered among his staunchest supporters conspire to wrest the leadership from him – must have seemed a tremendous insult.

'Pride,' I murmured. 'That's it, isn't it?'

'What, lord?'

'That's why he continues to burn a swathe through the marsh country. He's proud. He wants his name to be known. Now that Morcar has taken his place, he feels he has to prove himself, and this is how he does it.'

I imagined the fire raging inside his heart: a fire sparked both by the enemy besieging him, and by his own countrymen for having undermined and betrayed him. He could just as easily have sent his sworn swords out to wreak the same destruction, but instead he chose to risk his own hide and lead these raids in person: so that he could show himself to be doing something of worth, and give enemies and allies alike cause to respect and fear him.

He and I were more similar than I'd realised. We both strove for recognition for our deeds, and struggled against the weighty oaths that bound us. Both of us had at one time led whole armies into the field, yet now found ourselves in somewhat humbler circum-stances, lacking the respect we craved and which for a while at least we had commanded. But pride could be a dangerous thing. It could make a man blind to reason and at the same time sow the seeds of his own destruction.

'If what you're saying is true, and he sees himself as the man who will drive us all back across the Narrow Sea,' I asked, 'why is it that we haven't heard of him before now? Where has he been these past five years?'

Godric shrugged. 'No one knows.'

'What do you mean?'

'He and his retainers claim he fought both at Hæstinges as well as under Eadgar Ætheling's banner, but no one who was there on those campaigns remembers seeing him. Some say he took ship with a band of Danes shortly after the invasion and has been raiding across the German Sea, and others that he stayed in England, where he roamed the forests, waylaying travellers on the roads and growing rich on the spoils.'

The feared Hereward was little better than a bandit, then, albeit one with pretensions to greatness. Not that that made him any less dangerous; the fires burning in the distance were testament to that. I continued to watch the silent smoke rising, its tendrils coiling around one another and turning the blue skies raven-black: his warning to us. I knew then that there would be no mercy, and that whether or not Morcar held true to his word, this was a struggle that we would be fortunate to survive.

It was near sunset by the time we finally reached Alrehetha and the newly built guardhouse that stood watch over the marshes. The ground was too soft for any castle worth the name to be erected, and so in place of a mound and tower a simple ringwork had been erected, not unlike the hill forts that the ancient folk had left behind them and which we often saw on our travels around the kingdom. A stout palisade ran the length of the circuit, atop low earthen banks, at the foot of which lay broad ditches, in some places as much as fifty feet wide, into which the fen-water had been channelled, so that any would-be attacker would first have to swim beneath a hail of arrows before beginning his assault.

Not that we expected any such attack. The enemy had nothing to gain and everything to lose by sallying from the Isle. Defending the opposite shore of the marsh, running along a ridge of higher ground, stood stout ramparts and palisades, behind which the enemy were no doubt watching and making ready to repel our assault. Between them and us lay two miles of gold-glistening fen, and so I couldn't judge the condition of those defences or of the men who held them, but even without seeing them at close hand I knew it was a hard task that we faced. I wondered how many men the enemy had posted there, and whether they feared the battle to come, as we did, or whether they believed in the power of St Æthelthryth to lend strength to their sword-arms and, in Hereward, to give them someone who would deliver them victory.

In the morning I ventured down to the marsh's edge together with Robert, Eudo and Wace to see for ourselves the bridge about which so much had been said, and upon which rested any hope we had of capturing Elyg. To call it a bridge was, to speak honestly, to give it a grander name than it deserved, for it wasn't a single structure but many, linked together to form a continuous path from our shore, by way of a few patches of dry ground that stood proud of the fen, to the Isle. Where the marsh was shallowest, dykes had been built up from gravel and earth before being overlaid with turf, or else sturdy posts had been driven into the marsh-bed to support timber causeways. Across the deeper parts, meanwhile, rowing boats, barges and makeshift rafts made from barrels had been lashed together, and then wooden planks secured across the top of them, so that they formed pontoons perhaps thirty or forty paces in length. These were then linked with rope and chain so that together they made a kind of floating road.

'Will it hold?' Eudo asked as we led our horses out along those pontoons, towards the largest of the islets, which stood roughly midway between the two shores. 'All it needs is for one of those boats to start leaking, or for a few of those posts to give way, and the whole thing could sink into the marshes, and us with it.'

'It'll hold,' Robert said, although he did not sound entirely convinced. Neither was I, as the timbers creaked beneath Fyrheard's hooves. He was anxious, too, his steps tentative, but I rubbed his muzzle in reassurance and kept a firm grasp upon the reins. The last thing I wanted was for him to panic on first sight of the bridge and the water, and so it was important that he grew accustomed to them before I took to the saddle. Fortunately the causeways were wide enough for three and, in a very few places, four horsemen to ride abreast without difficulty. Even so, for now we went in single file as we approached the islet, where a stout mangonel was mounted on a square platform that also served as a watchtower, one of several that had been built along the length of the bridge. All sedge and undergrowth within twenty paces had been cut and cleared, so that the enemy couldn't try to set fire to the structure as before. Nevertheless, even a small band armed with axes could wreak considerable damage in a short space of time, which was why companies of archers had been posted, both here on this island and on those other watchtowers, to observe the marsh by day and by night and to dissuade the rebels from coming too close.

Only when we grew a little closer did I realise that I recognised some of the faces among those archers, and one ruddy-cheeked face in particular. Hamo. He stood atop the watchtower, laughing with his friends while at the same time gnawing on a bone that looked like it had once belonged to a chicken or some other bird, but when he spotted us approaching he tossed it into the bog.

'You owe us, Robert Malet,' he shouted from behind the parapet. 'Do you hear me? You still owe us for the part we played in your little expedition.'

'You'll have your money in time,' Robert called back as we neared the foot of the tower. 'Don't think I've forgotten.'

'When?'

'As soon as King Guillaume pays me.'

'That's no good to me or my men. Don't forget that we risked our necks for your sake.'

'Didn't you hear what he said?' I asked. 'You'll have your money in time.'

'You have my oath,' Robert said sternly. 'In return, I ask that you have patience.'

Hamo spat across the parapet; his spittle landed a few paces in front of us.

'Words,' he said, sneering firstly at me and then at Robert. 'That is all oaths are. But a man can't live on words. I want what was promised to me. I want my share of the reward for the capture of that English runt. I know who he is, remember, and how much he's worth, too, so don't think for a moment about trying to cheat me. Where is he now, in any case?'

We'd left the English runt, as Hamo called him, back at camp in the care of some of Robert's household knights, who were spending the morning in the training yard that they'd marked out, honing their skills ahead of the battle to come, practising with wicker shields, oak cudgels and spear-hafts from which the heads had been removed. As we'd left they'd been busy teaching Godric some simple stances, cuts and thrusts. From what little I'd seen he was an enthusiastic learner, if not an especially quick one. Clumsy on his feet, he often lost his balance, which resulted in him opening up his guard and ending up on his face in the dirt, much to the laughter and cheers of the others. Not that he seemed to mind; rather he took it all in good humour, each time raising himself with a sheepish grin before resuming his stance. Now that the threat of imminent death no longer hung over him, he seemed less afraid in our presence. And he showed determination too, which was important, for it took years of practice to make a warrior, if indeed that was his ambition. Whether he would ever fulfil it, I wasn't sure. I'd seen boys three years younger more proficient at arms, and it wouldn't have surprised me if he'd barely picked up a blade in all the time he had spent under Morcar's tutelage. But as I'd watched him stumble backwards, arms flailing, before finally landing on his arse in a puddle, I found myself in a strange sort of way warming to him. Ungainly he might be, but there was something in him that reminded me of myself at that young age, though I couldn't quite work out what that was.

'Why should it matter to you where Godric is?' Robert asked.

'He lives, though?' Hamo asked in return.

'Yes, and he is under our protection.'

The big-bellied man gave a curt laugh. 'Your protection? Since when did we start offering shelter to the enemy?'

'Since King Guillaume ordered it,' I cut in, tiring of this exchange. I was trying to decide whom I disliked more: Hamo or Atselin. 'Now, do you like the taste of sharpened steel? If so, keep talking and I'll ram my blade down your throat. Otherwise leave us in peace.'

That shut him up. After a final sneer in our direction, he turned away from the parapet towards his comrades, who were still sniggering, although whether at our exchange or at some private joke, I couldn't tell.

We continued on our way. Even now, men were working on various sections of the bridge: revetting the dykes with timber to hold the earth more firmly in place; and repairing parts that had slipped away into the bogs – tipping gravel and stones into the breaches, and then shovelling soil on top of that foundation and packing it so that it was even and firm.

'This is a foolish idea,' Eudo said, shaking his head as we passed those labourers. 'If these banks are already collapsing under their own weight, think what will happen when a thousand mailed knights are riding over them.'

'It'll hold,' Robert repeated. 'The king has summoned his best engineers from Normandy to oversee the work. They have knowledge of these things. We have to trust in their expertise.'

Eudo returned a grim expression.

'Robert's right,' I said. 'If the bridge were to collapse and we lose this war because of it, then their lives will be forfeit. They won't fail.'

I could only pray that their work was finished before we made our assault, which could now be only a few days away at most. Thus far there had been no word, only rumour, but restraint was not a quality that men often ascribed to King Guillaume. He would be hungry for battle, eager to let his fuller run with the blood of those who dared defy him, and for that reason many, myself among them, suspected it would not be long.

Soon we came to what was, for now at least, the final stretch of the bridge, for it came to an abrupt end a few hundred paces short of the Isle. In front of us stretched a wide, glistening mere.

'And how are we meant to cross the rest of the way?' asked Wace as he scratched at his injured eye. 'Does he mean us to swim?'

'The plan is for our foot-serjeants, spearmen and archers to lead the attack,' Robert explained. 'They'll cross the fen in punts and rowing boats and hold the enemy at bay while the last few boat-bridges are drawn into position. Once they're secured, the way will be clear for the rest of us to begin the assault proper.'

Eudo snorted. 'Is there no simpler way of doing this?'

'If there were, don't you think someone would have suggested it by now?' Robert replied tersely.

We gazed out across the marshes in silence. On a ridge of higher ground perhaps a quarter of a mile to the north rose the enemy's ramparts, twice as high as the ones surrounding our own guard-house, I reckoned. Arrayed atop them were banners in all colours and sizes and shapes, with designs that at this distance I couldn't make out, all flapping resplendently in the breeze. Beneath those banners were hundreds upon hundreds of glinting shield-bosses and helmets, men in mail and men without, their spearpoints gleaming, in a line that stretched the entire length of the wall. Watching us.

'All I know is that I don't want to find myself in the leading conroi,' I said. 'If those boat-bridges aren't properly secured, whoever arrives upon them first is going to find himself a watery grave.'

Even now I recalled only too well the screams of those who had perished when the original causeway collapsed, as the weight of their mail dragged them beneath the murky waters. Fyrheard only needed to lose his footing or to panic for the briefest of moments, and I might find myself sharing the same fate.

I glanced at the others. Their faces bore grim expressions, and I could tell they were all of the same mind. All except for Robert, that was, who alone would not meet my gaze.

I knew him well enough by then to be able to sense when something was amiss. 'What is it, lord?'

'I ought to have told you sooner.'

'Told us what, lord?' asked Wace.

'I spoke with the king earlier this morning,' said Robert, shaking his head. 'I did my utmost to try to change his mind, but he wouldn't listen—'

He broke off and turned away to look out across the glittering marshes.

'Whatever it is, say it,' I said impatiently, even though I wasn't sure that I wanted to know.

'Very well. This is what I have learnt.' He glanced at each of us in turn. 'As reward for your good service, and for your efforts in delivering Godric to him and bargaining with Earl Morcar, the king has decided to grant us the honour of leading the army across the bridge.'

Eudo swore under his breath. Wace shook his head, as if denying what we were all hearing. I just stood there, powerless to speak or move or do anything at all, feeling numb as a chill crept across my skin and worked its way into my bones. I had always hoped that when my end came, it would be a noble one: that I would die with sword in hand and battle-joy coursing through my limbs, fighting to the last for a cause that I believed in. This way, however, we were as likely to perish from being swallowed up by the swamp as upon the spears and swords of the enemy.

I spat upon the ground. 'This is no reward. He might as well string us up and leave us to hang!'

'Haven't we done enough already, lord?' Eudo asked.

'Even assuming that we make it across the bridge without injury,' Wace said, 'we'll have the enemy ramparts to contend with, and then their shield-wall, with no possibility of retreat if things go badly. We'll be dead three times over before we get the chance to lay a scratch upon them.'

'I do not pretend to understand the king's mind,' Robert said. 'Would that things were otherwise, but these are his wishes.'

'This is how he repays us?' I asked, doing my best to restrain my anger. 'Were it not for us, he would now be facing almost certain defeat. Provided that Morcar holds true to his word, we still stand a chance of winning this campaign and finally bringing an end to this rebellion.'

'He realises that,' said Robert. 'And he is grateful—'

'He has a strange way of showing it,' Eudo muttered.

'Let me ask you this, lord,' I said. 'He has more than a thousand knights at his disposal, and yet out of all of them he chooses us. Why?'

'Because he has seen what you can accomplish. Because you have all three of you proven your worth in his eyes. And because he believes there is no one better to spearhead the attack and break the enemy lines than the men who opened the gates and fought the ætheling at Eoferwic; the same men who last year ventured into the heart of the enemy camp at Beferlic, who risked their hides to save mine and those of my kin, who helped to rout the Danes and force them to make terms.'

'What are you saying?' I asked, feeling the blood starting to boil in my veins. 'Did you commend us for this task?'

'Of course not,' Robert said, recoiling at the insult. 'Do you really believe I'd do such a thing? I entreated him as best I could, and almost thought at one point that I'd persuaded him to give the honour to someone else. But then his clerk spoke up.'

I thought at first that I must have misheard him. 'His clerk?'

'The monk. The one with the squint, who accompanied him when he came to question Godric, if you remember.'

Atselin. Heat rose up my cheeks. It felt as if there were firebrands behind my temples, under my very skull, burning me from within. Without willing it my hands had balled into fists.

I remembered how hot his temper had flared the last time we had met, before leaving Brandune, though at the time I'd thought nothing of his threats. Only now, when it was already too late, did I finally understand. He'd been planning this, biding his time, waiting for the reason and opportunity to bring about my downfall.

And I had delivered both to him.

'What did he say?' I heard myself asking. My voice sounded somehow distant, as if it no longer belonged to me.

'He merely reminded the king of your deeds, as I've told you,' Robert answered. 'He seemed to know a great deal about you, and indeed had nothing but the highest praise for all your accomplishments. Is he a friend of yours?'

'No,' I said, knowing that to admit the truth would only invite rebuke, and I was in no mood for that. I saw now so clearly everything to which pride and frustration had blinded me. I should have guessed, somehow, that the monk would be whispering in the king's ear. I should have heeded rather than scoff at his warnings. I should have known better than to bait him and stoke the fires of his enmity. And yet, as so often, once my blood was up I could not restrain myself.

It was not Atselin who had done this. I had brought this fate upon myself. And not just myself, but my sword-brothers too. Because of my pigheadedness we all would suffer, and if this attack went badly then their blood would be on my hands. I would have as good as killed them by my own sword, and the guilt would burden me for ever.

'When do we begin the assault?' asked Wace, oblivious, as they all were, to these thoughts raging within me.

'Tomorrow, at dawn,' Robert replied. 'At first the king wanted to attack by night, but he was persuaded to wait until it was light so that we would be able to see more easily the way across the marsh, and that fewer men would lose their lives needlessly.'

He had some sense, then, which was more than I could claim. If I hadn't been so desperate for adventure and a chance to free my sword-arm – if I hadn't grown so fixated with recovering the respect that once I had commanded, the fame from which I'd fallen – I wouldn't now be standing on the verge of losing everything.

'The enemy will be ready for us,' Eudo pointed out. 'They'll see us coming and have more than enough time to form up in their ranks.'

'That cannot be helped,' said Robert. 'Besides, we only have to hold out until Morcar turns his spears upon his countrymen. When that happens, our task will become much easier.'

'We, lord?' Wace asked. 'Do you mean you'll be riding with us?'

'Why not? You've risked your skins often enough on my behalf in the last few years. It's only right that I return the favour. I will not shirk my duties any longer. If I don't show willingness to place myself in danger, how can I expect my vassals and followers to do the same on my behalf?' He didn't wait for us to answer, but went on: 'Besides, so long as Morcar keeps his promise, we will all make it through this alive.'

'I still don't trust him,' Eudo muttered.

'Neither do I,' Robert replied. 'But what choice do we have?'

To that none of us had any answer. For a while longer we stood in silence, looking out towards the enemy ramparts, and I wondered how we would make it through this battle. Eventually, however, Robert mounted and turned back towards the guardhouse where the smoke of blacksmiths' furnaces billowed and our banners flew.

'Come,' he said. 'We have only the rest of this day to prepare ourselves. We should make the most of the time that we have.'

Straightaway he turned to ride back across the bridge, his destrier's hooves clattering upon the timber roadway, and he was closely followed by the others. The sun wasn't lacking in warmth that morning, but nevertheless I still couldn't rid myself of the chill, which by then had worked its way into every inch of my body. I gave one final glance at the marshes and the Isle, then swung myself up into the saddle and spurred Fyrheard into a canter so as to catch up with them.

After weeks of waiting and wondering and hoping and despairing, it was finally happening.

Nine

I remember that night so clearly. I remember every such night before a battle, for always there is a keenness in the air, a mixture of anticipation and dread, of restlessness and anguish that is never voiced but is shared amongst all present, and that, once experienced, is never forgotten. And yet that night was different, for in all the seasons since first I rode under my lord's banner into the fray, never had I felt such trepidation as I did in those few hours.

Even long after the sun had set and the clash of arms had faded and the soft-spoken Latin of the priests giving absolution had ceased, I found myself unable to settle. I wasn't alone. Despite having spent most of the day in the practice yard, and notwithstanding our drooping eyelids and our heavy limbs, still none of us could sleep. There was nothing more for us to do: our blades were sharpened; our helmets and hauberks polished until they gleamed; our destriers fed and groomed. And so we sat cross-legged, huddled in our cloaks beneath the stars, and watched our cooking-fire dwindle while we recounted stories of battles past, of women we had known, of the marvels we had seen on our travels, of things that had happened when we were young and still in training, of fine weapons and horses, of sword-brothers long since fallen, of the various dreams and desires to which we all clung; and we revelled as much in the listening as in the telling.

We were men of all ages: seasoned fighters like myself, my friends and the Malets' other vassals; a few young warriors of Godric's age or thereabouts. For some this would be their first battle, while others had long lost count. But we were all equals that night, for when morning arrived and we rode out across that bridge, our fates would be bound together. Only Lord Robert wasn't there, having preferred to spend the night by his father's bedside. Still Malet succeeded in clinging to life, albeit barely. He could no longer raise himself from his bed without help, let alone walk or ride even the most docile of horses, and so a covered cart had been found in which he and his chaplain had travelled from Brandune. I had caught a brief glimpse of him, but that had been enough. His pallor was as grey as ash, like a fire that was all but spent; the faintest of sparks remained in his eyes, which were now mere hollows. His face was gaunt, his wiry hair straggling past his chin. Soon there would be nothing left of him, I thought.

'He is in such pain,' Dudo said when I was finally able to accost him that afternoon, in between bouts in the practice yard, and to ask how the elder Malet fared. The chaplain was as slippery as a toad, with a manner so quiet that one sometimes failed to notice him, and a habit of slipping away unseen when one wanted to speak with him, only to reappear later unannounced. 'Every day he grows worse, and he only makes it harder for himself, too.'

'How so?' I asked.

The priest regarded me with a contemptuous look. Probably he had come to share his master's dislike for me. 'He remains as determined as ever not to commend his soul unto God until the rebels have fallen and the whole of England is ours.'

'He might be waiting some time,' I said, not in a flippant way but seriously.

'Indeed. Every day I pray that he will allow himself to be received into our Lord's arms soon, rather than continue to suffer as he does. I do what I can for him, as do the physicians and wise women, when he allows them to see him, but I fear that all our infusions and remedies are powerless to offer him any succour.'

All this he said without blinking, his beady eyes fixed unnervingly upon me. Even though there was compassion in his words, I couldn't hear it in his voice. He seemed to me an unlikely sort of man to take priestly orders, although equally there were many I'd known and fought alongside whom I had considered unlikely knights when first I'd met them.

'I understand that he might not wish to see me,' I said. 'Perhaps, though, you could tell him something for me.'

Dudo said nothing, and I decided to take that for his assent.

'Tell him that I have never wished any ill upon him or his family. Tell him that in all the time I've been sworn to him and his son, I have only ever sought to serve him loyally, and that I ask for his forgiveness before it is too late. Can you do that?'

I didn't really see that I had done anything needing of forgiveness, but the rancour that he reserved for me weighed heavily on my mind. Despite everything that had passed between us, I still had a certain respect for him and in particular for his determination to see out this war. If I were to meet my end in the battle tomorrow, I would rather go to the grave having dispelled that enmity, or at the very least knowing that I, for my part, had tried.

'I will tell him, but I cannot promise anything more,' the priest said.

I supposed that was the most I would get from him, and so I sent the toad on his way. Hours had passed since then and still I'd heard nothing in reply, and that was another reason for my disquiet that night, as I wondered whether the priest had even passed on my message at all. In the meanwhile I partook of the ale and wine that the king had ordered distributed to raise our spirits ahead of the fighting to come, although I made sure not to quaff too heavily. I was experienced enough to know that to fill one's belly with drink the evening before a battle is never wise, for there is nothing worse than having to don mail and helmet, raise shield and sword, to run and turn and twist when one's mind is hazy, one's skull is throbbing and one's belly is churning and threatening to empty its contents at any moment. I have succumbed to that folly, but it is not something I would ever counsel.

Still, I understand why others do it. They do it to escape the fear: the fear that comes from anticipation, which is the part of a warrior's life that I have always liked the least. For it is in those final hours, when the prospect of battle has become real and the time for hard spearwork is suddenly close at hand, that a man feels most alone, and when doubt and dread begin to creep into his thoughts. No matter how many foes he has laid low, or how long he has trodden the sword-path, he begins to question whether he is good enough, whether he can maintain the strength of will necessary to see him through, or whether, in fact, his time has come.

That was why we talked about the things we did: not out of boastfulness, although a few of the younger ones among Robert's knights were only too eager to impress us with tales of their feats of arms and their various conquests, which seemed to grow wilder with every passing hour. Rather, we talked to distract ourselves and each other from the task at hand and, in so doing, to keep those fears from entering our hearts for a few more hours. After a while some of the others went to seek distraction in the arms of their women, and later they returned to join us by the fire, sidling up close to one another and sharing in the meagre warmth. We talked and we laughed and we ate and we drank and we talked some more, and when there was nothing left to say and our sides were hurting and we had each eaten and drunk all that we could stomach and the fire had all but died and silence reigned, Eudo brought out his flute from his pack. He put the beaked end to his lips, closed his eyes and, after a deep intake of breath, began to play.

At first I didn't recognise the song, which started soft and slow, as Eudo's fingers stepped gently and with precision from one hole to the next, lingering on each note, adding from time to time a wistful flourish that spoke somehow, in a way that I couldn't quite explain but simply felt deep within my soul, of faded glories, of yearning and of home. My thoughts turned to my manor at Earnford. I wondered how Ædda and Father Erchembald and Galfrid were faring, and everyone else I'd left there. And I thought of my Oswynn, a captive in some unknown, far-off place, and wondered if she were thinking of me too. What small hope I'd held out of ever finding her seemed even smaller now.

Before I could lose myself in self-pity, the tune erupted like a tree blossoming into colour. Eudo wove sharp flurries and trills in between the longer notes, his hands running up and down the length of the pipe, and suddenly from out of that cautious and brooding song emerged one more familiar, that even in those days was popular in the halls and palaces and castles of France, from farthest Gascony in the south to Normandy and Ponthieu and Flanders. It was a tale of noble deeds and fearless sacrifice, which gave inspiration to all, from the lowliest hearth-knight to the greatest of barons. At once I forgot everything troubling me and instead found myself smiling. Men began to clap their hands upon their knees, keeping time with the rhythm set by Eudo as it rose once more both in speed and in vigour, his brow furrowed in concentration, until abruptly he broke off and began to sing the words that were so familiar:

> The king our emperor Charlemagne
> Has battled for seven full years in Spain.
> From highland to sea has he won the land;
> His sword no city could withstand.

It was a lay that every Frenchman who lived by the sword knew well: the Song of Rollant, the knight who, some three hundred years before our time, had given his life in the service of his king, defending to his dying breath the narrow mountain pass that they called Rencesvals against the vengeful pagan hordes.

> Keep and castle alike went down
> Save Sarraguce, the mountain town.
> The King Marsilius holds that place,
> Who loves not God, nor seeks His grace:
> He prays to Apollo, and serves Mahomet;
> But they saved him not from the fate he met.

But for the difference of a few words, Eudo could have been singing of King Guillaume and his struggle against the rebels holding out on the Isle. But whether the court poets would praise our names and set out lays of our deeds three centuries hence, were we to prove victorious tomorrow, or even were we each to meet a death as noble as Rollant's, I very much doubted. More likely our names would not go recorded in any chronicle or verse, and if we were remembered at all in the years to come, it would be merely for being the first unfortunates to have our blood spilt in this great folly. On such things I tried not to dwell. There was nothing more that could be done or said about the king's strategy and our place within it. God had already chosen my destiny, whatever that might be, and I could not escape it. I would not run from this fight, nor would I abandon Robert, my lord. He needed me, as he needed all of us.

Thus tomorrow we would ride, to glory or to death. For good or for ill, tomorrow we would fight.

Eventually I managed to sleep, though by the time I did finally close my eyelids there could have been only a couple of hours until first light. In my dreams I was Rollant, gazing down from the mountain pass towards the plains where the enemy massed beneath their banners: a horde of snorting horseflesh, painted shield-faces and gleaming steel; thousands upon thousands of men, together raising a clamour loud enough to raise the dead from their graves. In my hand was Durendal, the sharpest sword in all of Christendom, and hanging at my side was the Olifant, the great gilded war-horn that Charlemagne himself had gifted me, carved from the tusk of an elephant. And then came the foe, marching in a single column up the winding and stony road, steadily growing nearer, until their conrois broke free, their riders raising a battle-cry to the heavens as they dug their heels in and couched their lance-hafts under their arms, with every stride gaining in speed, gaining in confidence—

I never found out what happened next, for at that moment I was brought from my dream by a voice at the opening to my tent. It was not yet day, but as the flaps parted I caught a glimpse of the skies outside, which already were turning from black to grey, and in that faint light I made out Robert's face.

'It's time,' he said, his voice low. 'Wake the others. Dawn is nearly upon us.'

As quickly as he had appeared, he was gone. Hurriedly I shook myself free of the coarse woollen blankets in which somehow I had become entangled, pulled on a tunic over my shirt, took a swig of ale from the flask at the foot of my bedroll to moisten my parched throat, and then scrambled out into the half-light. Across the camp men were stirring and dressing for battle, taking whatever food they could stomach and mounting up. Bleary-eyed, I went to Serlo and Pons's tents and roused them, before donning hauberk and chausses and coif, fastening my helmet-strap, buckling my scabbard upon my waist, checking that both my sword and knife slid easily from their sheaths, and going to help the servant-boys saddle Fyrheard and the other horses.

We led the animals to our conroi's arranged meeting place by the twisted stump of a wide-bellied oak. There we waited for the rest to assemble. First came Wace together with his three men, and he was soon followed by Eudo, who was doing his best to prise himself free from the grasp of Sewenna, much to the amusement of his knights. Her face was streaming with tears, her hair was loose, and in her eyes was such anger as I had never seen before. With one hand she clung to his arm, while with the other she kept trying to strike him, though he was able to bat each blow away easily, until another of the women – a fair-haired Danish beauty who had pledged herself to one of Eudo's men – at last spoke some words in her ear and managed to tear her away, upon which the Englishwoman turned and, wailing, fled back towards the tents. Eudo bit his lip as he watched her go, but did not make any attempt to follow her.

'What happened?' Wace asked.

Eudo let out a weary sigh. 'She said that before I rode into battle, we ought first to be wed, as I'd vowed. That way if I happened to die today, at least our souls would find each other in heaven. She even went this morning to find a priest.'

I understood. 'But you couldn't.'

He shook his head sadly. 'You were right. I've been a fool. She claims that I misled her with false promises, but it's not true. I loved her, only not as much as I thought.'

I rested a hand on his shoulder in sympathy, but only for a moment, since Robert's vassals were almost all assembled, which meant that we were ready to ride. Among them I spied the ruddy-faced Guibert, who had spoken so loudly against the king in the hall at Brandune so long ago it seemed like months, though in fact it was only a week. Whatever ill feeling he might have held towards anyone as a result of that clash was now dissolved, or else buried deep. We could not afford to let petty quarrels divide us. Not now.

Robert himself was the last of all to arrive, flanked by ten of his hearth-knights and one of his stable-hands, who bore the banner I had grown to know almost as well as my own: the same banner beneath which for two whole years and more I had rallied, charged and served. It was divided into alternating stripes of black and yellow, and the yellow was shot through with threads of gold so that it would catch the light and be more clearly recognisable in the midst of battle.

Robert passed his lance to one of his retainers, before dismounting and making towards me. His expression was solemn as he extended his arm in greeting. I gripped his wrist, and he mine, and then he embraced me, not as a lord might embrace a vassal of his but rather as if I were of his own kin.

'I want you to know that you have my gratitude for all that you have done in my name and that of my family,' he said. 'I only pray this is not the last time we ride together.'

'And,' I replied. 'A better lord I have never served.'

The falsehood tasted sour upon my tongue as I remembered some of the grievances I'd uttered against him recently, but what else was I supposed to say?

He attempted a smile, but it was a weak attempt and I knew his heart was not really in it. As nervous as I felt, he looked to me a dozen times worse. He was dressed like the rest of us, but somehow the helmet appeared to sit uneasily upon his head, as if it were too large for his brow, and the hauberk seemed to weigh heavily upon his shoulders. He had never looked entirely at ease in a warrior's garb, and he looked even less comfortable then.

'May God be with us, Tancred,' he said, and with that he left me, mounting up and riding to the head of the conroi while I took my place with my knights. Everyone fell quiet as he unlaced his ventail, letting the flap of mail hang loose by his neck.

'I've just had word that our foot-warriors have set out for the Isle,' he said, raising his voice so that all could hear. 'The moment we receive the signal that their attack is under way, we will begin crossing the bridge. From then on there will be no turning back.' He paused to allow the import of that to settle, before continuing: 'In all my years I have never known warriors more valiant than you. Regardless of what fate awaits us, I consider it the greatest honour to ride amongst you today, and to fight by your sides. May God and the saints bring us victory, and lend us the courage and the fortune to see this day through.'

It wasn't the most rousing battle-speech I had ever heard, but it was heartfelt, and powerful for that alone. In any case it would have to do, for the skies were quickly growing lighter, the stars fading, which meant that the time for words had passed. Robert led us from the shadow of the guardhouse, its high ramparts and the crowning palisade, down to the flat stretch of land beside the marsh, where dozens upon scores upon hundreds of horsemen were already gathered, their many-coloured banners and pennons barely fluttering in the still air, their horses tossing their heads and pawing restlessly at the turf. Their exact number I could not say, though it was probably close to a thousand, with more arriving still. These were some of the finest knights ever to ride in the name of Normandy.

And we would be leading them all in the charge. Had someone told me when I was a youth and a warrior in training that such an honour would one day be mine, I wouldn't have been able to stop laughing. Even now I scarcely believed it. Yet here I was.

I half expected to find Atselin and his clerks overseeing the muster, tallying up knights on his wax tablet, but if he was there I could not spot him. It was hard to miss King Guillaume, though, surrounded as he was by his household guards, his helmet adorned with a tail formed from two scarlet strips of cloth that marked him out, lest anyone lose sight of him in the fray. Holding the banner bearing the lion of Normandy in one hand, he galloped up and down the ranks of horsemen, bellowing instructions, drawing the assembled host into ordered ranks and grouping smaller bands of four and five into larger conrois of twenty, thirty, forty. A few glanced up as we passed on our way to the front of the column, and someone must have recognised our banner, for I heard him call out Robert's name, and then a cheer went up, and a hundred men and more were raising fists and weapons to the sky. Hearing the commotion, the king turned and watched us for a long while, though he did not speak. His mouth was set firm, his countenance betraying no feeling, and at that moment I glimpsed with my own eyes the iron resolve for which he was renowned. Never once had he failed in any task he took upon himself, and in the same way I understood that he would not fail now. For five years he had striven to defend his right to this kingdom. This would be the morning when he would finish what had begun with the slaying of the usurper at Hæstinges. This would be the morning of his victory. Whatever misgivings the rest of us had, he truly believed it.

We took our positions at the head of the column. Behind us lay an army to wreak terror in the hearts of all but the most hardened of foes. Ahead lay only the fen, with the so-called bridge winding its way towards the Isle, with small pinpricks of light dotted along its length where watch-fires had been set to ward off any would-be attackers. Of the fleet of boats and punts carrying our foot-serjeants, or the opposite shore, the enemy behind their walls, I could see nothing.

I turned to Robert, who was alongside me. 'What now?'

'Now we wait for the signal.'

As a conroi we had rehearsed the sequence of events over and over the previous afternoon, committing it all to memory so that every man knew exactly what he was to do and when. We had been told what that signal would be, and what pace we would set across the bridge so that our host did not bunch together and at the same time did not become too stretched out. But sitting there in the saddle, waiting for the word to be given and the attack to begin, suddenly I wanted to hear it all again.

Enough, I told myself. I knew what needed to be done. I closed my eyes, breathing slowly and deeply, as I imagined our charge upon the enemy battle-lines and how I would drive my lance-head home, how I would bring my sword-edge to bear, how we would drive them back and cut them down and turn the Isle's earth crimson with their lifeblood.

'There it is,' said Robert suddenly, with something like excitement in his voice, and I opened my eyes in time to see a trail of flame shooting high up into the grey skies to the north, a mile or so away. A single fire-arrow: the sign that our spearmen and foot-serjeants were beginning their attack. It made a great arc above the marsh before plunging out of sight into the all-enshrouding mist, and at the same time the bellow of the rebels' distant war-horns sounded out: two sharp blasts that were the usual signal to rally.

And so it began.

'Stay with me,' Robert yelled for his whole conroi to hear. 'Watch your flanks when we arrive upon the Isle. Remember who's along-side you; don't pull ahead and don't fall behind!' He kicked back, spurring his destrier onwards. 'For St Ouen, for King Guillaume and Normandy! God aid us!'

'God aid us,' we all answered with one voice, and the chant echoed through the ranks: *God aid us! God aid us!*

We followed Robert out on to the bridge. Hooves clattered upon timber, and I whispered a prayer that the men who had built it had done their work well. We kept close rank, riding knee to knee, three abreast, for that was as many as the roadway would allow. To my right was Robert, while on his other flank was the captain of his household guard. Behind us were Pons, mounted upon a bay that Lord Robert had gifted him to replace the one killed by Hereward's arrow, and alongside him Serlo. My sworn swords, the two of them had served me unfailingly these last two years, had followed me in every desperate charge, had given their all for my sake. Behind them were Wace and Eudo and their knights, then the rest of Robert's hearth-troops and vassals, so that there were more than fifty of us in that leading conroi, all united under the Malet banner.

I had fought in some desperate struggles in my time, but this would be one of the most desperate of all. This was the hour of our reckoning.

We were knights of the black and gold, and we were riding to battle.

Ten

As expected, the first part of the crossing was the easiest. The marsh there was at its shallowest, the causeway its widest and sturdiest, and we made it without trouble.

Before long we glimpsed the island where the watchtower with the mangonel stood, roughly halfway across the marsh-channel. The first glimmer of gold crept above the eastern horizon and I could suddenly see movement on the Isle. Hundreds upon hundreds of Englishmen with weapons glinting and pennons flying rushed in disarray from their ramparts towards the marsh's edge, into a storm of missiles being loosed upon them by archers and crossbowmen and even a few small catapults that were positioned on punts and barges out on the fen. Other craft were bringing our spearmen and foot-serjeants in towards the shallows where they could scramble ashore, wade through the murky waters and form a shield-wall amidst the tall reeds to guard against the hordes bearing down upon them. But suitable landing places were few, while the channels leading to them were narrow and easily blocked, which meant that those in the boats to the rear were having to clamber forward from one to the next, all the while encumbered by their shields and heavy spears. War-horns blew; panicked shouts carried across the water as our foot-serjeants marshalled their men and tried to assemble them in some sort of order.

Around a dozen Frenchmen were posted on the watchtower. All of them waved their arms as we approached. 'Wait,' they called. 'Wait!'

Robert slowed his pace and drew to a halt, raising a hand to those behind so that they passed the message on down the line. 'What is it?'

They were pointing out towards the far shore, and I saw at once the reason for their alarm. The final section of the floating boat-bridge hadn't yet been secured; in fact several of the pontoons seemed to have drifted free altogether, and even now men were working to manoeuvre them back into position and to anchor them.

I swore. This wasn't what the king had planned. Unless the boat-bridge was in place, we had no way of reaching the Isle. Our attack would be over before it had even started, and the battle would be lost.

Shouts of protest came from behind. I glanced over my shoulder and saw the rest of the column bunching up as our advance was brought to a halt. Men were berating those in front, trying to push their way forward despite the narrowness of the bridge.

'Wait!' I bellowed. 'Hold position!'

'Wait!' Eudo repeated, and Wace behind him, and the next man, and the next, and I only hoped that our warnings were heeded. Of course those knights were impatient, as I was, to slake their thirst for enemy blood, but many would die if they didn't keep to their ranks.

'What do we do?' Robert asked me, his brow furrowed, his eyes desperate. 'Do we go on?'

'We have to, lord,' I said. 'We can't turn back now.'

'But if the boat-bridge isn't secure—'

'If we delay any longer here, it won't matter. We'll be too late; the rebels will break our spearmen and then cut the pontoons loose, or burn them, and we'll have no way of reaching the shore. We have to go now, and trust that the bridge will be ready in time. If we don't, all our efforts will have been for nothing. It's now or not at all, lord.'

Robert didn't look sure. I glanced over my shoulder, back along the column, and my gaze settled upon the golden lion upon a scarlet field, the age-old symbol of the Norman dukes, flying proudly in the rising wind. King Guillaume himself had given us this responsibility. If we refused it at this late hour our names would be forever tarnished. We would have cost him his best chance of capturing Elyg and wreaking his revenge upon the rebels who defied him. He would strip us of our lands and the few riches we had to our names, cast us into the deepest, darkest dungeon he could find and leave us there to rot. We could not fail him. Not now.

My heartbeat resounded through my entire body, and I could hear the blood pounding in my skull. My fingers tightened around my shield-straps in one hand and my lance-haft in the other.

And I knew what I had to do. If Robert refused to make the decision, then I would make it for him.

'With me,' I cried, raising my weapon aloft so that the steel glimmered in the light of dawn. 'For Normandy!'

I dug my spurs into Fyrheard's flank and he reared up, teetering on his hind hooves for a moment, before falling back to earth.

'Tancred—' I heard Robert shout, and heard, too, the desperation in his voice, but then his words were drowned out by the cheer that rose up as one thousand voices together shouted out. A bolt of confidence surged through me, and as Fyrheard broke into a canter I found my limbs filled with fresh vigour, my mind with fresh purpose. I had no need to look behind to make sure that the rest of our host was behind me, for I could hear it in the thunder of hooves and the whooping as men revelled in the battle-joy.

A flock of wading birds heard our approach and rose all at once with a clatter of wings and a chorus of alarmed shrieks. I kept a firm hand on Fyrheard's reins, trusting in his sure-footedness to keep us both alive. The mud swirled and sucked at the foot of the earthen banks, and the marsh-waters lapped at the posts and revetments. A short distance to our right ran the course of the original causeway, the one that had collapsed all those weeks ago. I recognised it not just from the ruined timbers that littered the mud all about, but also from the scores of corpses of horses and men that had been left there to rot without Christian burial, their mail and helmets brown with rust, their flesh blackened and swollen, with what remained of their innards spilling out. They stared unseeing from empty eye sockets, their jaws fixed open as if even in death they were still crying out. Yellowed bone protruded where carrion beasts had picked away the skin and sinew. The stench of their rotting flesh filled my nose, more powerful than anything I had known, and I fought the urge to retch.

I tore my eyes away, focusing on the way ahead and the rebels tumbling in their hundreds down towards the shore. A ragged mass of spears and scythes and hayforks and the long English knives they called *seax*es, they charged upon the Norman battle-line, until at last there came a crash like thunder as limewood boards and steel bosses met, and then men on both sides were screaming, shouting, falling, dying. Thus the grim work of the shield-wall began. Behind the protection of their countrymen, the bridge-workers were still labouring to manoeuvre the final few pontoons into place, lashing them together with ropes and anchoring them to the marsh-bottom with stone weights attached to chains, but they did not have much time, for I saw even now that the enemy foot-warriors outnumbered our own, and already it seemed they were forcing them back towards the marsh.

'On!' I shouted above the din, trusting that Robert and Pons and Serlo and all the others were with me as I set out across the first of the pontoons, leaving the earthen dykes behind me. Iron clattered upon oak and I felt the planking bob beneath Fyrheard's hooves, not by much, but enough to send a shiver of doubt through me. 'On,' I cried, trying to put those fears from my mind. 'On, on!'

That was when I heard Robert shouting.

'It's too short,' he cried. 'The bridge is too short!'

For a moment I didn't understand what he was trying to tell me, but as I stared at the shore and those Englishmen charging towards us, suddenly sickness gripped my stomach.

He was right.

The line of pontoons did not quite stretch all the way to the Isle's shore, but came to an end around thirty or forty paces short, in the shallows rather than on dry land. Perhaps the recent rains had swelled the marsh-waters more than the king's engineers had expected, or else the current had taken one or more of those floating platforms and carried them downstream. I didn't know, and it hardly mattered. To reach the shore we would now have to fight our way through water that I reckoned would reach up to our mounts' knees, if not even higher.

'Keep going,' I yelled. 'We can make it!'

I sounded more confident than in truth I felt, but only because I knew we had no choice. Everything depended on us. We couldn't give up now.

Barely three hundred paces ahead, the Norman shield-wall was beginning to break as the English ran amongst them, driving a wedge into their ranks, surging forward with shining blade-edges raised.

'Faster!' I yelled, knowing that if the enemy managed to rout our spearmen, they could hold the shore against us and drive us back into the marsh. With that in mind I spurred Fyrheard from a trot into a canter, which was as fast as I dared ride along those narrow platforms. 'For Normandy!'

Indeed one flank of the Norman shield-wall had already collapsed, and a group of rebels perhaps two score strong was now racing through the shallows towards the pontoons with axes in hand, having spotted our approach and recognised the danger.

'Faster!' I repeated. 'Ride harder!'

The bridge shook beneath the weight of the charge, and the timbers creaked. At any moment, I thought, they would give way, splinters would fly, and we would all, knights and banner-bearers, destriers and palfreys, be plunged into the fen. Surely it could not fail now, not when we were so close. Fewer than one hundred paces stood between us and the Isle. No Frenchman had managed to come so close in three months on this campaign.

Let the bridge hold, I prayed. Let it hold.

I clenched my teeth. Reed-banks and gold-glistening meres flew past on both sides. The thunder of iron upon timber filled my ears as Fyrheard's hooves thudded in rapid rhythm upon the oak planking, so loud that I could hear nothing else. Not the shouts of the enemy or my companions. Not the screams of the dying or the clash and scrape of steel on steel up ahead, or the jangle of my mail, or the blood pounding in my skull, or the clatter of the chains anchoring the pontoons, or the creaking of timbers, or the whistle of arrows being loosed by the bowmen in the punts out on the marsh. Only the unrelenting thunder reverberating through my skull.

I was dimly aware of those two score rebels rushing to meet us, crashing thigh-deep through the marsh-waters with steel in hand and the promise of death in their eyes. My attention was fixed upon the bridge's end, which was growing nearer with every stride. Like any good destrier, Fyrheard was trained to water, so I didn't expect him to falter or to panic, but nevertheless I felt my stomach lurch and my breath catch in my chest as we galloped along the last pontoon, the final dozen strides, and I saw the marshes looming. My fingers tightened around the haft of my lance and the straps of my shield—

As Fyrheard leapt.

All fell silent. For the briefest moment I had the sensation that we were flying. Beneath us was only air, but not for long, before Fyrheard's hooves came down, and then suddenly there was water and mud all around. Showers of spray drenched my shoes and my braies and soaked through my mail to plaster my tunic against my arms and chest. Fyrheard was crashing on through the shallows, the marsh reaching as high as his forearm, but he didn't seem to mind. On my flanks now were Serlo and Robert, and I wondered what had happened to the captain of his knights, whether his horse had stumbled or refused when it came to the water, but there was no time to dwell on that now. I couched my lance under my arm, levelling the point at the enemy. Seeing us charging through the marsh towards them, for the first time the rebels hesitated, unsure whether to attack or to flee.

In the end they failed to do either. I fixed my gaze upon the one who would be my first target, his beard sopping, his long hair clinging to the side of his face, and then it was just as if I were tilting at the quintain. He came to his senses and tried to get out of our path, but too late. Slowed by the water, he only managed to get a couple of paces before I was upon him, ramming my lance into his shoulder. It was only a glancing blow, but it was enough to knock him off balance and make him lose his footing. He sprawled backwards into the water, falling under the surface, under Fyrheard's hooves, and straightaway he was forgotten. Knee to knee, kicking up sheets of spray, we rode on, making space for those behind us to follow. In their desperation to reach the bridge, the enemy had abandoned their serried ranks and were now in disarray. We charged amongst them, filling the morning with the blade-song, freeing our weapon-arms, striking out to left and right as we carved a path through the shallows, making towards dry ground.

An Englishman came at my left flank, bringing his axe around in a wild swing that glanced off my shield-boss, denting the steel and sending a shudder through my arm all the way to my shoulder, only for Robert to ram his lance home into the man's neck. Another, screaming in rage at the death of his friend, ran at my undefended right hand, aiming his seax at Fyrheard's belly, but my weapon had the greater reach, and before he could come close enough to strike, I plunged my lance-head down, into his breast, twisting the weapon as it went in, until I felt the crack of ribs and knew I'd found his heart. I left the blade lodged in his breast and he collapsed with a splash, adding his corpse to all the others floating upon the surface. They bobbed on the waves, turning the surrounding waters a dirty crimson.

'Normandy!' I yelled, drawing my sword and raising it skywards, hoping to rally our spearmen, whose battle-line had been broken. With few places to go except back into the marsh, most of them were fighting on, albeit divided and surrounded. I only hoped that their doggedness would now be rewarded. The rest of Robert's conroi was with us now, and others besides as rank upon rank of knights spilt from the bridge on to the Isle's shore. They fanned out in pursuit of the kill, cutting down those who had broken from their shield-wall to come to challenge us, presenting the rebels with a decision: whether to throw themselves into the battle here, and try to drive us back into the marsh, or whether to return to the safety of their fortifications on the higher ground some three hundred paces or so to the north, where they could make a proper stand against us. Already some of their rearmost ranks had turned, preferring the latter, more sensible choice to death at our hands, and it looked as though the message was spreading to the others.

They realised that the bridge was ours, that they'd lost that particular struggle, and so as one they were falling back.

At that sight I gave a roar of delight. The field was all but ours, because any moment now Morcar would show himself and give the word to his followers. They would turn on their countrymen, and then the real killing would begin. Against all expectations, we had done it. The bridge had held and we had led King Guillaume and his army to the Isle, and soon, if our luck held, to victory.

'What's Morcar's device?' I called to Pons and Serlo as we found ourselves briefly with space around us. They both looked back blankly. Glancing around, I found Robert not far off. His face was pale, his eyes wide, as if he couldn't quite believe he was still alive.

'Lord,' I called, and repeated my question.

'The white stag on a green field,' he shouted in reply as his hearth-knights rallied around him.

I turned my attention back to the fleeing Englishmen ahead of us, some of whom were casting aside the shields and weapons encumbering them, others slowed by injury, hobbling on sprained ankles and wounded thighs, or bearing bright scarlet gashes to their chests and sides. The battle-joy surged through me, filling me with laughter as we raced from the shallows on to firmer ground, riding down our quarry. They looked back over their shoulders when they heard our hoofbeats upon the turf, closing in on them, and in the whites of their eyes I glimpsed their fear. But the ground was soft and uneven, with tussocks of tall grass everywhere, and bulges and dips and pools of stagnant water that were hard to spot from the saddle, all of which slowed us and meant that although we succeeded in killing a good few stragglers, most of the English were getting away, falling back towards their ramparts, which were now little more than a hundred paces away—

That was when I saw it. The white stag, that noble animal, flying proudly above those earthworks, along which were arrayed rows upon rows of spearmen in gleaming mail.

'There he is,' I cried, pointing in its direction, and felt a surge of joy for I knew at that moment that the day belonged to us. 'It's him! It's Morcar!'

Except that his troops were not moving to cut off their countrymen's retreat, as we'd been expecting. Instead they seemed to be merely holding position, watching, waiting.

'What's he doing?' Serlo shouted. 'Why isn't he attacking?'

'I don't know,' I said, as an anxious feeling gripped my stomach. Once our first conroi had crossed the bridge, he would turn his spears against his countrymen. That was what he had told us. That was what he had promised. He had given us his own nephew as hostage, as proof of his good faith. We had fulfilled our side of the agreement. We had crossed the bridge and captured the shore. All that remained was for him to make good on his word. What, then, was he waiting for?

That was when I realised. He had never meant to aid us. The rat-turd had pledged his support only so that he could lure us into a trap. Why hadn't I seen this before now? How could any of us have thought that he, who had broken so many oaths before, should keep to this one?

And a trap it was, for our only hope of withdrawal rested with the bridge and the punts, and neither of those offered a swift escape. While some might get away, others would be left to hold off the enemy at our backs, and we would probably lose almost as many men that way as if we fought the enemy in open battle.

'He lied to us,' I said. 'He betrayed us!'

My grip tightened around my sword-hilt. Without Morcar's help, we faced an almost impossible struggle. For he held the higher ground, and to have a hope of defeating him, we would have to assault their defences, or else somehow draw them out, and I did not see how we could do either. The king's plan, so carefully crafted, lay in ruins, and all because of Morcar.

Perhaps it was because my mind was filled with all these thoughts that I didn't see the danger ahead, or perhaps it would have made no difference. My blood was up and I was thinking only of killing as many of the rebels as I could before they escaped to the protection of their ramparts. Between the grass-heads I managed to glimpse a band of them half running and half stumbling away from us, across the tussocks and through shallow, murky pools.

'Kill them,' I yelled to Pons and Serlo, and all those others who were with me, as we charged through the grass after them. 'Kill them! Kill—'

I was still shouting when a shriek filled my ears and I found myself falling. Fyrheard's forelegs gave way and I clung to his neck until I could hold on no longer and was pitched sideways. The ground rushed up towards me and I met it hard. My head rattled inside my helmet as I tumbled into a gully, where I found myself looking at the sky, with blood and dirt in my mouth and all the breath knocked from my chest. I was trying to work out what had happened when there came a second shriek, and a third, and suddenly horses were falling all about. I ducked just in time as hooves lashed out barely an arm's length above my head. Clods of earth and wet turf showered my face.

Panicked shouts filled the air, and then not far off I heard the English battle-cry: *'Godemite!'*

Blinking, I raised myself to my feet. My shield was still on my arm, having somehow survived the fall, but my sword had slipped from my grasp. My head still spinning, I looked around, searching for my blade amidst the mud, and in so doing nearly missed the bearded, leather-clad foeman rushing at me from the side with a seax in hand, a smirk upon his face and victory in his eyes. I raised my shield just in time to meet his strike. He feinted low before thrusting forward over the top edge of my shield towards my face, but I was too quick for him, turning to one side, grabbing his arm in my free hand and twisting hard so that he dropped his weapon. He staggered forwards, howling in pain, and as he did so I landed a kick upon his backside, sending him sprawling.

'Tancred!'

I looked up to see Wace wheeling about my flank with a spear in each hand. He tossed me one and I caught it, and as the bearded one tried to rise I used both hands to sink it into his thigh, before tugging it free and turning it upwards, driving underneath his jerkin and into his groin. He bellowed out in agony, and I plunged the steel deeper and deeper still, twisting so that it went in all the further, until his cries trailed off and I was sure he was dead.

All was confusion. The rebels, who until a few moments ago had been fleeing, were suddenly turning upon their pursuers, reinforced by a line, three ranks deep, of helmeted and mailed spearmen, who must have been hiding in the long grass, for I could see nowhere else they could have come from. Horses screamed as a forest of blades sprang up towards their bellies; those that were not impaled reared up and kicked their hooves and tossed their heads in terror, only to turn and find themselves with nowhere to go, trapped between the English spears and the rest of the oncoming Normans. Into that chaos the enemy piled themselves. They buried their steel in the animals' bellies and dragged knights from the saddle, setting upon them with knives and seaxes.

'Fall back!' Wace was shouting, though no one but me seemed to hear him.

I looked around for Fyrheard and saw him scrambling out of the gully, which was half as deep as a man was high, and thirty paces from end to end. The rebels had dug ditches amongst the tussocks so as to break up our charge, overlaying them with branches and reeds so as to disguise them, and into those same ditches we had ridden blindly, like fools.

From every direction came cries of alarm and of pain. I left the spear in the bearded Englishman's groin, for I had at last spotted my sword, and recognised it for mine because of the turquoise stone that I'd had set into its pommel. I sheathed it, hauled myself from the ditch and ran to Fyrheard. His eyes were wide, and on seeing me approach he tensed, but then he recognised me. The fall had clearly shaken him, but he looked unhurt, and for that I thanked God as I glanced around and saw those that had been less lucky, flailing in the gullies and struggling to stand on broken legs. I rubbed the side of his neck in reassurance, but knew we could not tarry here. The stench of death was everywhere, and it was the stench not just of blood and spilt innards, but of piss and shit and vomit too. The corpses of our fallen countrymen and their steeds lay strewn across the field, along with many more who were not yet dead but whose end was near, desperately crying out for help in French and in English.

'Withdraw,' cried a familiar voice. The gold threads of the Malet banner glinted away to my right, and beneath it Robert was waving, trying to attract the attention not just of his conroi but everyone else who was with us. 'Withdraw towards the shore, back towards the lion banner!'

Turning, he pointed his sword back in the direction of the bridge and spurred his steed into a gallop. Around a third of our horsemen, I reckoned, had made the crossing by then: some three hundred knights marshalling beneath the colours and devices of their lords. King Guillaume himself rode up and down the battle-line, bellowing exhortations to them and to those of our foot-warriors who still remained.

The enemy were swarming forward like carrion birds around a corpse, taking advantage of the confusion they had wrought. On either side of us Normans were fleeing on horseback and on foot, running, riding, limping, a few being helped along by their comrades. Doing their best to cover their retreat, around fifty paces away, were Serlo and Pons, Eudo and his knights, and I recognised them by the emblems on their shields, but even at a glance I could see they were outnumbered and close to being outflanked. For the conroi's strength lies in its swiftness and in the weight of the charge, but once its force has been met and its drive is halted, it becomes vulnerable, and I knew that they couldn't stand toe to toe for long against all those English spears.

Robert was already riding back to join the rest of our host, but Wace still lingered, along with his hearth-knights: the quiet-spoken Gascon whose name I still hadn't learnt, and a dark-haired lad not much older than Godric but almost twice the size, who was known to everyone as Tor, which in the French tongue means Tower.

'Wace,' I yelled, and as soon as I had his attention: 'We have to get to Eudo!'

He nodded breathlessly. His right cheek, I saw, was streaming with crimson where a fresh cut had been laid across it, to add to those he had taken at Hæstinges, although I wasn't sure if he realised it.

Without further hesitation, I leapt up into the saddle and dug my heels in. Sweat rolled off my brow, stinging my eyes, and for a few moments all I could see was a watery blur, but still I pounded on. Already the enemy had surrounded Eudo and the others, and I knew we didn't have much time. The ground had been trampled flat by the passage of so many feet and hooves, which meant that we could see the ditches easily now, and we swerved around them.

'Normandy!' I cried, hoping to catch the attention of some of those Englishmen, to draw them away, but my voice was hoarse from so much shouting, and they didn't seem to hear me.

In fact it was probably a good thing that they didn't, since it meant that they knew nothing of our charge until we were upon them. With weapons drawn and gleaming in the morning light we fell upon them, throwing our sword-edges and our lance-points into the fray, losing ourselves to the wills of our blades as we struck and struck again, laying about with sharpened steel, roaring as one, clearing a path through their lines, swearing death upon them all, smashing our shield-bosses into their brows, burying steel in their backs, piercing mail and cloth and flesh, riding them down so that their skulls and ribs were crushed beneath the charge, doing our best to drive them back.

Eudo risked a glance towards us, and I saw the desperation in his eyes. His shield was splintered and the hide, emblazoned with the tusked boar that was his device, had half fallen away from the limewood boards, rendering it all but useless.

'Retreat!' I yelled to him and Serlo and Pons and the dozen or so others who were with them, and hoped that they heard me above the clash of arms and the shouts and the screams.

'Back to the lion banner!' Wace was shouting.

For suddenly there was open space at our backs, offering a way out of that mêlée, and I knew we had to seize this opportunity while we could. Our charge was beginning to slow; the enemy were regrouping as warning shouts echoed through their ranks and they turned to face the new threat, and with every heartbeat their numbers were swelling. If we were to beat our retreat, now was the time.

'With me,' I said. 'With me!'

I clattered the flat of my blade against an Englishman's helmet and wheeled about, looking to escape the fray—

Too late.

Already the enemy had come around our flanks, and now they were closing upon us from front and rear, presenting their bright-painted shields and overlapping the iron rims with those of their neighbours so as to form a wall.

We were surrounded, and there was no way out.

Then from the ramparts to the north came a sound that was only too familiar, as hundreds upon hundreds of warriors struck their spear-hafts and axe-handles and swords and seaxes against the rims and the faces of their shields, keeping a steady rhythm. With each beat they roared a single word, over and over and over, like a pack of ravening wolves who had scented easy meat.

Ut. Ut. Ut.

The white stag was advancing, leaving behind it the defences the rebels had built. Under that banner bobbed a thousand shining spearpoints. Morcar's confidence had overcome his caution, and he would wait no longer. He saw a chance to press his advantage, to drive us back into the marsh, to win glory and renown among his people and give his followers and Englishmen everywhere the victory they had long desired: one that they would sing of in their feasting-halls and that would be remembered down the ages. They would praise him as the defender of Elyg, the man who dared to stand against King Guillaume and who did what Harold and Eadgar Ætheling could not. Little would they realise that he was nothing but a worthless perjurer, a foul oath-breaker.

'Tancred!'

I tore my gaze away from the stag banner just in time as the enemy surged forward and I found myself staring at more blades than I could count. Fyrheard lashed out with his hooves and my sword struck and struck again, but for each one I dispatched, it seemed that two more took his place.

'Die, you bastards,' Eudo was yelling as he heaved his blade around, backhanding the edge across an English throat. Blood gurgled forth, trickling down the man's neck as he clutched at the wound and gasped vainly for breath. 'Die!'

One thickset warrior clutched at the bottom edge of my kite

shield, trying to tug it down and out of position, while another, gangly and with dark hair trailing from beneath his helmet-rim, grabbed hold of my spear-arm. I smashed my boss into the first's temple, then jabbed my elbow into the second's chin, sending both stumbling backwards and bringing me a moment's respite, although it had to be only a matter of time before they overwhelmed us.

'There are too many of them,' Serlo shouted, as if I didn't already know. 'We can't—'

'Hold firm,' I said, shouting him down. Whatever he had to say, I didn't want to hear it. 'Stay close and don't let them through!'

My heart was hammering in my chest and my lungs were burning as I struggled to breathe. I was determined, though, not to give in. Not while I still had a sword in my hand and my head upon my shoulders. I would keep the battle-anger blazing in my veins as long as I could. If this was my fate, then the least I could do was take as many of the Devil-spawn with me as possible.

That was when the shouting began. Cries of surprise, of panic and of pain filled the air, together with howls of the wounded and the dying.

It took me a few moments to realise that those shouts weren't in French but in English. That they weren't coming from among my countrymen, but from the ranks of the enemy. I risked a glance towards the source of the screaming, and at first was convinced that my eyes were deceiving me. Surely I had to be imagining this. For what I saw seemed like a gift from God. My heart swelled with relief and joy, my limbs coursed with renewed strength, and suddenly I was laughing.

Laughing, because those men of the white stag weren't marching to aid their countrymen. They were coming to kill them.

Morcar had held to his word after all. He had arrived not a moment too soon, and now the slaughter would begin.

Eleven

Like me, the foemen surrounding us were slow to understand what was happening. When they did, however, the collapse was as complete as it was sudden. No matter how many times I have seen it, it never ceases to surprise me how quickly a battle-line will crumble when fear and uncertainty take hold, and so it was then. One instant they were pressing at us, their war-cries filling my ears, drowning out my thoughts, and the next they were abandoning the struggle, running in all directions: towards the ramparts, towards the shore, towards the copses of alder and willow, towards anywhere they might find shelter. They didn't realise that between our forces and those of their erstwhile ally, Morcar, they had nowhere to go.

Chaos reigned. Bands of Englishmen who only a few moments ago had been friends, united by a common cause and by their hatred of us, suddenly found themselves on opposite sides and unable to tell each other apart. In their panic some of the enemy mistook their own comrades for Morcar's troops, and set about one another. All the while the men beneath the stag banner drove on, as relentless as they were disciplined. At the same time the main part of our host was beginning to advance once more, not just the knights but also the spearmen, all led by King Guillaume himself, his helmet-tails flying behind him. Beside him rode his standard-bearer, raising the lion of Normandy for all to see. The golden threads glinted in the morning light, and to the east the sun shone with the promise of victory.

And so the rout began.

'Kill them!' I heard Wace shouting, and the order was echoed throughout the conroi, passed on from man to man down the line. For the second time that morning we charged down the fleeing foemen, slicing our blade-points across their necks, slashing at the backs of their legs to fell them, only on this occasion there were none of their friends waiting to surprise us from their hiding places, to halt our charge.

Crumpled bodies of the wounded and the dead lay all about, their leather and mail pierced by sword and knife and spear, their clothes matted to their flesh, their weapons and shields beside them, their eyes open but unseeing. Blood ran in rivulets, pooling in the hollows and running into the ditches and pits the enemy had dug, while elsewhere the ground, trampled and torn up by so many hundreds of feet and hooves, had turned into a sucking quagmire. Through it all we rode to the sound of the victory horn and with roars of sword-joy all around. After the heat of the fray, the battle-calm had descended upon me. Nothing mattered but finding the next man whose lifeblood would foul my gleaming blade. I gave myself over to instinct; each thrust and cut, each parry and drive, came without thinking. Long years of training in the yard and at the quintain had ingrained those movements in my limbs. All I had to do was lose myself to the will of my sword-arm, to let it guide me.

What I do remember is glimpsing a blue, mud-spattered banner ahead of us. Beneath it a thegn and his hearth-troops, his *huscarlas*, stood amidst the screams and the chants and the roars and the howls, bellowing instructions that went unheard, desperately trying to rally the panicked hordes, but all their efforts were in vain. One of the rebel leaders, I thought. He was the wrong build to be Hereward, for he was possessed of a stocky frame and hunched stance, and was fair-haired besides, but nevertheless I reckoned he must be someone of importance.

'Take him,' I yelled to my knights and everyone else who happened to be with me. 'Kill the rest, but take him alive!'

No sooner had the words left my lips than the thegn spotted us coming. His huscarls, the ten or so that remained, closed ranks around him, presenting their scratched shield-faces and their gleaming axe-blades, sharp enough to take a horse's head from its neck in a single blow. But they were few, while we had the might of an entire army behind us, and he must have sensed that to fight on was useless. He let his sword fall to the ground and raised his hands aloft.

'*Gehyldath eowre wæpnu!*' he bellowed at his retainers, but they did not seem to be paying him any heed. Obviously they preferred to meet death with steel in their hands rather than suffer the shame of giving themselves up to the mercy of their enemies.

I would have granted them their wish, but we were still some thirty paces away when their lord barged his way through their lines and wrested the axe-haft from the grasp of the huscarl to his left, tossing it down.

'*Gehyldath eowre wæpnu,*' he repeated, gesturing towards the others' axes and spears and seaxes.

One by one, not daring to take their eyes off us even for an instant, his men lowered their weapons and dropped them to the ground with a clatter of steel. Their nasal-guards and cheek-plates made it difficult to see their faces, but even so I could clearly see the scowls they wore, and the hardness in their eyes. Even in defeat, there was much pride there.

I reined Fyrheard in, halting before them, and Wace drew up alongside me. The rest of the conroi did not need any instruction from me, but straightaway formed a circle around the band of Englishmen, just in case they tried to make an escape, though I didn't think they would.

I fixed my eyes upon the thegn, their leader. He unlaced his chin-strap, letting his helmet fall by his feet. Unkempt hair fell across his brow and he swept it back from his face before staring, unspeaking back at me, his chin raised in defiance.

'*Ic eom Thurcytel,*' he said flatly. *I am Thurcytel.*

I recognised the name. He was, or had been, among Hereward's oathmen, if I remembered rightly what Godric had said: one of those who had supported him only to later shift their allegiance to Morcar.

'My name is Tancred of Earnford,' I said, just as flatly. 'Perhaps you've heard of me.'

'Should I have?'

I moved closer. My sword was still in my hand, and I pointed it at his breast. 'Don't try my patience.'

'You won't kill us,' said Thurcytel.

Wace gave a snort. 'Why not?'

'Your king is, at heart, an honourable man. Were he to learn that you received our submission only then to kill us, I think he would not be best pleased.'

Wace laughed. 'Do you think that he cares whether you live or die? After he's spent this long trying to capture the Isle? After all the trouble you and your countrymen have caused?'

Thurcytel didn't answer, which was probably for the best.

'I'll see that your life and those of your men are spared,' I said, 'provided that you do two things for me. First, I want your sword and your scabbard.'

He spat, and grudgingly unbuckled his belt, letting it fall next to his sword. His scabbard was decorated with copper bands inlaid with gold, while in the middle lobe of the pommel was a single emerald. I nodded to Serlo, who dismounted and collected them from where they lay at Thurcytel's feet and passed me first the sheath – though the thegn was wider around the waist than me and I had to pull the belt-strap tight to fasten it – and then the blade. The cord wrapped around the hilt was stained red and blood was congealing in the fuller, but otherwise it seemed in good condition, with few nicks along its edge. It was balanced a little more towards the point than I would have preferred, but otherwise it was a weapon befitting a knight.

I slid it back into the scabbard. 'A fine blade,' I said to Thurcytel, who merely sneered. 'Now, the second thing. Tell us where Hereward is.'

His expression changed, from defiance to something like disgust. 'Hereward?'

'Is he here, on this field?'

The reward for capturing someone like Thurcytel would be reasonable enough, but the prize for bringing Hereward before the king would be far greater. From everything I had heard of him, he seemed the kind of man to lead from the front, rather than skulk in the ranks. Except that there had been no sign of him during the battle, and that was beginning to worry me.

Thurcytel made a sound that was neither a laugh nor a snort, but something in between. He spat upon the ground. 'Hereward will not so much as talk to Morcar, let alone fight in the same shield-wall. Always he must do his own thing—'

'Just tell us where I can find him.'

The battle-anger still simmered inside me, and I was fast losing patience with this Thurcytel.

'The last I heard, he was still at Elyg, praying at the shrine of St Æthelthryth for her to grant him her favour and help him to bring us victory.'

'How many men does he have with him?' Wace asked.

'A hundred and fifty, perhaps two hundred. No more than that.'

'Dead, all of them,' someone called, and at once I recognised the voice, which was deep and harsh and rich in arrogance. 'Or, at least, they will be shortly.'

Morcar strode towards us, a wide grin upon his face, which was flushed with triumph. He was dressed in a leather jerkin reinforced with iron studs, but there was not a speck of blood or dirt on him anywhere, and I wondered whether he had dared enter the fray, or so much as unsheathed his blade during the battle.

He clapped a hand upon Thurcytel's shoulder. 'Alas, my friend,' he said. 'Fortune did not favour you this day.'

'You bastard,' said Thurcytel, shrugging off the other man's hand. 'We gave you our allegiance and you betrayed us!'

'Temper,' Morcar said in a soothing voice, as if trying to still a querulous child.

For a moment the thegn tensed, as if ready to hurl himself at Morcar, but that moment quickly passed. The earl was accompanied by some dozen of his own spearmen, and Thurcytel must have realised that any attempt he made would not go well for him. He contented himself with spitting at the other's feet. Morcar only smiled, clearly relishing in his success.

'How do you know they're dead?' I asked him.

Morcar turned and fixed me with a stern look. 'I recognise you. You're Robert's man.'

I was not to be deterred, and so I said again, 'How do you know they're dead?'

'Because I ordered it,' he retorted. 'As soon I glimpsed your boats arriving upon the shore, I sent my swiftest rider to Elyg with instructions to my hearth-troops there to kill Hereward and all his followers.'

Even presuming he was telling the truth, that could have been around an hour ago at most, by my reckoning, which meant that Morcar's messenger had probably only recently arrived.

'And how can you be sure that all your hearth-troops won't themselves end up killed by Hereward and his band?'

Morcar drew himself up to his full height and inspected me closely, as if I were some manure he had trodden in, but I was not about to back down. He might consider himself an earl, but we both knew it was a title acquired through treachery and only then by the king's grace. Whatever noble blood he'd once possessed had soured in his veins long ago. The man who stood before me knew nothing of honour, and he was mistaken if he thought himself worthy of my respect.

He opened his mouth as if to say something, but before he could speak something else caught his attention. His eyes fixed on a point somewhere beyond my shoulder, and then he and Thurcytel and all their retainers were bending their knees and bowing their heads. I glanced behind me and saw the king riding hard towards us, flanked as he always was by his household knights.

Hurriedly I sheathed my sword. The king paid no attention to us, though, nor indeed to our captives. He was interested only in Morcar.

'Where were you?' he barked without so much as a greeting. 'Where were you?'

'My lord,' Morcar began. 'I don't—'

'The moment we arrived upon the Isle. That's when you were supposed to begin your attack.'

'Have I not given you victory, my king?' he protested. 'Have I not given you the Isle, as I promised? Is that not enough?'

Suddenly I understood why Morcar had waited so long before committing his forces. He'd wanted to see which way the battle would turn before deciding whether to hold to his promise. Only when he could be sure of being on the winning side had he finally marched to help us.

No doubt the king realised this too, since he regarded Morcar for what seemed like an eternity. In his eyes burnt a fire more intense than I had ever seen, and I think that, were it not for the fact that several hundred of the Englishman's sworn followers were watching, he might have struck him down there and then.

'You have given me nothing yet,' the king snarled as he turned away.

'What about my nephew, lord?' Morcar shouted to his back. 'It was agreed that he would be returned to me.'

The king curbed his horse, no doubt startled, as were the rest of us, by such effrontery. 'What makes you think I haven't already ordered him killed?'

'If you have, then our agreement is finished,' Morcar replied, but though his words suggested defiance, his tone betrayed his lack of confidence. Having wormed his way into the king's favour and allowed our army on to the Isle, he would be foolish indeed to risk losing everything by fighting us now, especially over such a small point.

The king smiled and raised an eyebrow in amusement. 'It is as well, then, that young Godric lives. You entertain me, Earl Morcar, and for that I will see that your nephew is brought to you.' He turned towards one of his household guards, a dark-featured man with a broken nose and a scar upon his lip. 'Fetch the boy from Alrehetha.'

'Yes, lord king,' Scar-lip replied, and broke off from the conroi, making back towards the bridge.

'In the meantime,' the king said to Morcar, 'you'll come with me.' He turned his gaze upon myself and Wace, although his expression showed no sign of recognition. 'You too. Bring every man you can muster.'

'Where are we going, lord?' I asked.

'To Elyg!' he shouted over his shoulder as he galloped away. His household guards fell into close formation around him, and they made towards the head of the main part of our host, which was once more forming up in its ranks and columns. Frenchmen cheered as he passed, showing their respect for the man whose vision and unfailing resolve had, despite the months of setbacks and frustrations, despite the misgivings of almost every man in his army, despite the fact that the odds had not favoured us, led us to this victory.

Except that it was not won yet. There remained Elyg and Hereward. For all Morcar's conviction that he was as good as dead, I would believe it only when I saw it with my own eyes. Indeed if I'd learnt but one thing of Hereward in recent weeks, it was that he was not a man to be underestimated.

Morcar, red-faced, was calling for someone to fetch him a horse. When a servant-boy finally brought one to him, he was rewarded for his trouble with a clout around the ear that sent him sprawling. The earl noticed me watching him and scowled, as if I were somehow responsible for having brought the king's wrath upon him.

'Come on,' I said to Pons and Serlo, gesturing for them to follow as I mounted up. 'Let's go.'

'What about them?' Pons asked, meaning Thurcytel and his men. 'We're not going to leave them, are we?'

The disappointment on his face was clear. The capture of one of the rebel leaders would bring us not just glory but riches too, and I was as reluctant as he to give those things up. But the king had spoken. Once the Isle belonged fully to us, then we could begin to think about prisoners, but not before. Not while there was still work to be done.

'We have no choice,' I said. 'Now, with me!'

We were in danger of being left behind. The king's banner was already on the move, striking out across the flat country to the north and east, in the direction of Elyg. I searched among the assembled banners for the black and gold, and found it towards the middle of the column. Robert was there, together with his knights, most of whom seemed unhurt save for some small scratches and cuts, although as we grew closer I could see that our numbers were decidedly thinner than they had been.

Only then did I realise that one of us was missing.

Robert saw us then, and came over to greet us, but before he could say anything I asked him, 'Where's Eudo?'

He glanced first at myself and then at Wace, frowning as if not quite understanding. 'I thought he was with you.'

'He was,' Wace said. 'And now he isn't.'

I turned to Serlo and Pons. 'You were close to him in the fray, when the English had us surrounded,' I said. 'Did you see what happened to him?'

'No, lord,' said Serlo, while Pons merely shook his head.

I swore under my breath, at the same time trying to think when and where I had last seen him. I didn't recall having spotted him fall, but that meant nothing, for in the heat of battle one's world becomes narrowed, and there are many things that one cannot hope to notice amidst the din of steel on steel, screaming horseflesh and the glittering blades of the enemy.

'He'll be all right,' Robert said, laying a hand upon my arm in reassurance. 'He can take care of himself.'

'His knights were with him,' Wace pointed out. 'They'll have seen him to safety, I'm sure.'

I hoped Wace was right, and silently prayed that the cost of victory here today did not turn out to be Eudo's life. If it were, I would never forgive myself.

We arrived outside Elyg a little more than an hour later. The skies were ablaze with pinks and oranges and the sun was rising, steadily burning away the remaining tendrils of marsh-mist, and glaring so brightly off the still fens that we had to shield our eyes.

Exactly as Godric had told us, the rebels had fortified the place in preparation for a siege, strengthening the gatehouse and throwing up a stockade around the monastery. Instead of shutting themselves away inside those defences, however, men and women were flocking in their scores and hundreds away from the stronghold, herding their children and carrying the smaller ones in their arms, even as others drove swine and sheep from the pens and the fields towards the woods and the marsh. Others followed, with wagons and pack animals, but they were so laden with goods that they were in danger of being left behind. On first sight of our approaching army they abandoned their goods, instead taking flight as fast as their legs could carry them. No sooner had they done so than the plunder began. Groups of riders split off from the main part of our host, raiding those same wagons and spilling the contents of the packs on to the ground in search of silver and gold and anything else that might be valuable. They would be lucky to discover much of value among the possessions of mere peasants, however. The monastery was where the greater riches were to found.

Or so I thought at first. We soon learnt that when Morcar's order had reached his men in Elyg, they had taken it not just as the sign to attack Hereward and his band, but also as an invitation to begin looting, perhaps thinking that anything they didn't quickly lay claim to would shortly be seized by us Normans. Breaking into the abbey's treasure house, they had filled sacks with coin and gilded candlesticks and anything else they could lay their hands upon, before crossing the cloister to the church where the service of prime was then in progress. There they had drawn weapons and driven the monks out, seized jewel-inlaid crosses, torn down tapestries bearing images of the Passion, stripped altars of their expensive cloths and even stolen the strongbox containing the monies that had been given as alms.

This news was brought to us by one of the king's messengers, who in turn had heard it from Elyg's abbot, an Englishman named Thurstan. Together with the rest of the monks he had met the king at a small village named Wiceford a few miles from the monastery, having had no choice but to leave Elyg to the ravages of Morcar's hearth-troops. On hearing that our army was approaching, he had come seeking his liege-lord's protection, as well as his forgiveness for having harboured his enemies for so long, a circumstance which he claimed had been imposed upon them against their will.

'What of Hereward?' I asked the messenger. He was built like a bear, and was almost as hairy as one, too.

'Gone,' he said.

'Gone?'

He nodded grimly. 'The king is less than pleased. From the sounds of it, Morcar's men were less interested in risking their lives than they were in claiming booty. There was some fighting in and around the cloister, but it seems Hereward and his band had received forewarning that they'd been betrayed and had already started to make preparations to quit Elyg. They were ready when Morcar's hearthtroops came for them, and managed to overpower them and break their way out.'

'They escaped?' I asked.

'Not all of them. Morcar's men killed a good few, and even managed to wound Hereward before his companions could pull him from the fray. So the abbot says, anyway.'

Somehow I'd known this would happen. Not only had Morcar failed to keep to the strategy he'd agreed with us, but he had also allowed Hereward to slip through his fingers.

Wace shook his head in disbelief. 'After everything, who would have thought that the feared Hereward lacked the stomach for a fight? That he would turn out to be such a coward?'

'He's no coward,' I assured him. Wace would have known that if he had crossed paths with him. I turned to the bear-man. 'Where did they go?'

'Out into the marshes to the north of here, by way of the secret paths.'

'And Abbot Thurstan saw all this happen?'

'With his own eyes. He is a broken man. Three of the monks under his protection were killed in the confusion as they tried to flee. He blames himself for their deaths.'

So he should, I thought, for nothing good ever came to those who threw in their lot with King Guillaume's enemies. But that, at this moment, was not what was most important.

'We need to get after them,' I said to the others. 'We can't let Hereward get away.'

'What does it matter?' Wace asked. 'If he's gone, the Isle is ours.'

He was right, I supposed. And yet as long as Hereward remained out there, it seemed to me that our task remained unfinished. I'd been readying ourselves for one last battle, expecting either that he would make a stand within Elyg's walls, defying us to the end, or else that we would arrive to find the struggle between him and Morcar's forces still ongoing. In a strange sort of way, I was disappointed. I'd wanted the chance to free my sword-arm once more, to make Hereward pay for all the injury he and his band of followers had caused, and for the humiliation he had inflicted upon me. Instead, after everything, the rebels had crumbled like a house whose timbers were rotten, shearing into so many splinters.

Of all those splinters, though, the most dangerous was Hereward. He had raised a rebellion against us once already, and would surely do it again if given the chance, if not this year then when the next campaigning season came around in the spring. That was why we couldn't let him get away.

And I hadn't forgotten, either, the promise I'd made: a promise given to a dying man, a man of God, though I hadn't even learnt his name; a promise that so far remained unfulfilled. Anyone who knew me well would attest that I never made such oaths lightly. Whether I liked it or not, I was bound to that promise, and unless I made good on it and brought Hereward to justice, I would have perjured myself before God.

'Which way did he go?' I shouted after the messenger who'd brought us this information. Already he was heading on down the column to spread the news.

'Hereward?' he asked. 'He's at least an hour gone. You'll never catch up with him now.'

He spoke sense, though it pained me to admit it. There was no way of knowing which of the many routes Hereward had taken through the marshes, or where exactly he might be headed.

A cheer rose up from the direction of Elyg's gates. I turned around to find them opening, and a contingent of men whom I presumed must be Morcar's huscarls marching forth to greet the king. Elsewhere fighting was breaking out over some slight I hadn't witnessed. Frenchmen were attacking Frenchmen, wrestling one another to the ground even as their friends tried to prise them apart, striking out with knife and sword, and some were staggering, wounded, clutching at their sides, their arms and their faces. Now that the battle was over, all their rage came pouring out. I had seen it happen before, and once witnessed it is a difficult thing to forget. It is as if a madness, a sickness of the mind, takes hold. Reason and restraint are forgotten, and those who in other circumstances one might count among the most even-tempered of men become wild creatures.

Robert was bellowing instructions to his troops, trying desperately to keep some measure of control. Other barons, not wishing to let slip the chance of plunder, or to let their rivals claim it before they did, were leading their conrois towards the monastery, their banners raised high, kicking up clods of turf and mud as they went.

That was when I saw Godric. He rode a grey palfrey, and was being escorted by three knights, one of whom was King Guillaume's man, the one with the broken nose and the scarred lip. Suddenly an idea came to me.

Waving to attract their attention, I rode to intercept them. 'Where are you taking the boy?' I asked.

'To the king,' answered Scar-lip, drawing himself up self-importantly. I thought he recognised me from earlier, but couldn't be sure. 'What business is it of yours?'

'There's been a change of plan,' I said, aware that to lie to the king's men in such a way was to commit a grave perfidy. I would worry about that later, and if need be suffer the consequences. 'The king wants to keep him hostage until he has received formal submission from all the rebels. Only then will he return him to his uncle. Until then he wants him taken back to Alrehetha.'

'Back to Alrehetha? We've just ridden there and back!'

'I realise that,' I said. 'If you prefer, I'll escort him back there for you.'

He eyed me doubtfully, but evidently he could think of no reason to distrust me. 'If you wish,' he said with a sigh. 'He's yours,' he said, and signalled to the other two.

I watched them go, making sure that they were out of earshot, then turned to Godric.

'What's going on, lord?' he asked. 'I thought I was being taken—'

'You were,' I said, 'but now there's something I would have you do for me first. Hereward has fled into the marshes. I thought you might tell me where he's gone.'

'Me, lord? How would I know?'

'If you were him and looking to escape, where would you go?'

Godric shrugged. 'To the ships, I suppose.'

'The ships?'

'The ones that we've been using to provision the Isle.'

Of course. The king had been trying to find them and destroy them for the better part of three months, without any success.

'And where are they?'

'Some miles to the north of here, deep in the fen country, on the mere near Utwella, where the rivers meet.'

If he had only thought to tell us this a few days ago, I thought with not a little irritation, we might have tried to stage an attack on them. But then I remembered how he had spoken of the lavish feasts that the rebels had been holding. If they were already that well provisioned, what difference would it have made even had we been able to cut off their supplies? It would not have prevented King Guillaume with pressing ahead with the assault, nor would it have made our task any easier.

'Could you show us the way?' I asked. 'And answer honestly. The last thing I want is for us all to end up cut off and drowned when the tide rises.'

'I think so, lord.'

That was good enough for me. It would have to be, for who else was there that I could rely upon? Who else knew the ways? Strange though it seemed, I had come to trust Godric.

'Very well,' I told him. 'We don't have a moment to spare.'

As it was, we would be hard pressed to catch them. Our quarry had a good lead on us already, and even though we were mounted, whereas it sounded as though they were travelling on foot, this was difficult country for horses. Still, I would rather make the attempt and fail than not try at all.

I searched about for the black-and-gold banner and Lord Robert, but couldn't find him anywhere. Bands of men on horseback and on foot rushed past on both sides, most making for the monastery, while a few were tearing thatch from nearby hovels in search of treasures that the folk who lived there might have hidden before they took flight. All was disorder, as our proud and noble army dissolved into packs of wolves.

I saw Wace with the Gascon and Tor, and called to them, waving for them to follow me.

'Where are you going?' Wace shouted back.

'After Hereward!'

He looked at me as if I had lost my wits, and perhaps I had, although the wildness that possessed me was of a different sort to that which had seized the rest of our army. A confidence burnt inside me that I could not account for. Suddenly anything seemed possible.

'You're going after Hereward?' he asked, and wiped another trickle of blood from his cheek.

'Why not?' I replied.

To him this no doubt sounded like a fool's errand, but I knew otherwise. For I wasn't only thinking of the oath I had sworn. I was also thinking that here was our chance to do something worthy of the king's attention, something that the chroniclers would write of when, in years to come, they came to lay quill to parchment about the battle for the Isle. Whether they admitted it or not, fame was what all those who made their living by the sword craved, more than silver or gold or fine-wrought blades or horses with jewel-studded harnesses or land or power. I was no different. I longed to restore my dwindling reputation, and I saw in Wace's eyes that he had the same hunger.

'Why not, indeed?' he said with a smile, and I grinned too, because I'd known he wouldn't refuse.

'Do you really think we can catch them, lord?' asked Pons.

'Maybe not,' I said. 'But we can try.'

No one noticed as, led by young Godric, we slipped away from the rest of King Guillaume's host, leaving behind us the clash of steel, the shouts of triumph and of pain, as we rode in pursuit of Hereward.

And glory.

Twelve

We rode hard, following winding, flint-studded paths so narrow and treacherous that in many parts we were forced to go in single file. Reeds flashed past on both sides as we skirted stagnant pools and leapt fast-trickling rivulets, trusting in our steeds not to falter over the soft ground. In every direction a wide expanse of bog stretched to the horizon, broken occasionally by dense copses of birch and elm, above which jackdaws circled, cawing loudly as if warning those ahead of our approach. I only hoped the enemy weren't lying in wait for us there, since we would make easy targets if they were. I watched the trees carefully as we passed, expecting at any moment to see a flurry of silver-shining arrowheads flying forth from out of those yellow-green leaves, soaring over the reeds, glinting with the promise of death.

But no arrows came. Fyrheard was flagging, his head bowing, but I coaxed him on. In some places the path had fallen away into one of the countless channels that crossed the land, and we had to dismount in order to lead the horses through the muddy waters. Every so often we would spy footprints, and by the number of them and the way the mud had been churned we could tell that a significant number of men had travelled this way. Whether those prints had been set down recently, though, none of us could say for sure. I wished then that we had Ædda with us. My stableman and the ablest tracker in all of the Welsh Marches, he was also my closest friend among the English, but he was back at Earnford. In his absence we had no choice but to follow Godric, and trust that he knew what he was doing. Every so often the path would seem to fork and he would come to a halt, his young brow furrowed while he looked for tracks upon the ground and gazed about the surrounding swamp for landmarks that showed we were on the right course.

'Are you sure you know where you're going?' Wace asked when, for the fourth time that hour, Godric paused. The morning was wearing on and the sun was growing high in a cloudless sky, beating down upon our backs. There was no shade to be found anywhere; beneath my mail my arms and chest were running with sweat, and my tunic and shirt were clinging to my skin. Flies buzzed in front of my face and I tried to swat them away, but they kept returning.

Three ways presented themselves. One continued straight ahead, leading due north, while the others branched out to the east and the north-west.

'Not all of them necessarily lead anywhere,' Godric explained. 'Not anywhere we want to go, at least. Some look safe, but if you aren't careful you can find yourself cut off when the tide rises. Many men have lost their lives that way.'

'But you know which one to take, don't you?' I asked.

He studied the ground closely, and squinted as he gazed out towards what looked like a ruined cottage, a spear's throw away to our right. 'I've only travelled these paths a couple of times, lord.'

'Only a couple of times?' Wace asked, and turned to me. 'Why are we letting ourselves be led by this pup?'

'I can find the way, lords,' protested Godric. 'I need some time to think, that's all.'

'Time is something we don't have,' I muttered peevishly. The lad didn't seem to have heard me, and that was probably as well, because I didn't want to hurry him into making a decision that we might come to regret.

After long moments Godric pointed down the branch heading north. 'This way,' he said firmly.

'You're certain of this?' I asked.

'Certain, lord.'

Wace cast a doubtful glance my way, but I could only shrug, and so we ventured on. Once in a while the path seemed to turn back on itself, or else peter out amongst the undergrowth, but we never lost it entirely, and I supposed that meant we were on the right trail. That suspicion was confirmed when, not long after, we came across what looked to be the same tracks as before, except that this time, trodden into the mud, were smears of horse dung, and freshly laid horse dung at that. We stopped and Serlo crouched down to inspect it.

'Still moist,' he said, rubbing some between his fingers and then sniffing them. 'Still warm, too.'

'If they're mounted rather than on foot, then we've no chance of catching them,' growled Tor.

'They aren't,' Serlo said. He rose and vaulted back into the saddle. 'If they had, we'd have spotted more of their dung before now.'

'Sumpter ponies, then?' Pons suggested, and looked to the rest of us for confirmation.

I nodded and at the same time felt fresh hope rising within me. Hereward and his band would be slowed by their pack animals, and that meant we must surely be catching them.

'Keep going,' I said. 'They can't be much further ahead.'

No sooner had I spoken than there came a distant shout from behind us. I turned sharply to see a band of horsemen, perhaps a dozen strong, approaching from the same direction as we had come, and I tensed at once, my hand tightening around the haft of my spear.

'They've found us,' Godric said. The colour had drained from his face. 'It's them!'

So I thought at first too, but how could they have known we were following them, and how did they end up behind us on the path? My answers came in the form of a greeting, shouted out in the French tongue, and I realised that they were friends, not foes.

Godric looked ready to flee, but I drew alongside him and seized hold of his mount's reins. 'It's all right,' I said. 'They're some of ours.'

Who they were, though, I couldn't tell at such a distance. The sun was behind them and so it was difficult to make out their features, and I had to raise a hand to my eyes to shield them from the glare.

'Lord Tancred!' one of them called brightly. 'You didn't think you were going to claim the whole reward for yourselves, did you?'

'What?' I shouted back.

'The reward,' he said. 'For Hereward's capture.'

The voice was familiar but only when he grew nearer, and I was able to see his ruddy jowls and small, hard eyes, did I finally realise who it was. In that moment my temper soured.

'What are you doing here, Hamo?' I asked.

'The same as you. So I thought, anyway, except you all seem to be more interested in the dirt than in doing anything useful.'

I ignored that, glancing at the eleven companions he'd brought with him, most of whom I remembered from our escort duties. But I saw no one who looked like a guide.

'How did you know the paths through the marsh?' I asked.

'We didn't,' Hamo said with a smirk that spoke of self-satisfaction but which at the same time seemed to mock me. 'But then we hardly needed to. We could see your helmets and your spearpoints a mile off. All we had to do was follow them, and trust that you were going in the right direction. And so here we are.' He flashed me a gap-toothed smile. 'Together once again.'

'Together once again,' I muttered under my breath. Eighteen men were better than seven, for certain, although Hamo was hardly a steadfast ally, or the kind of man that I could rely on to hold his nerve in the thick of a fight. His only loyalty was to his purse, and if things began to turn against us, his first thought would be to protect his own hide.

'Are we riding on, then?' Hamo asked. 'Or are we just going to wait here while Hereward and his band get ever farther away?'

'We ride on,' I replied. 'But first understand this: you'll listen to us, and do everything that either I or Wace here tell you to, without question or hesitation.'

'I am my own man, sworn to no one,' he said with a sneer, drawing close enough that I could see the hairs sticking out of his nostrils. 'I can make my own choices.'

'No,' I said. 'You'll listen and do as you're told, or else we could all end up dead. Do you hear me?'

He returned my stare but said nothing. I only hoped he heeded my words, for I wasn't prepared to waste any more time or breath arguing with him.

'Lead on,' I told Godric, whose colour had returned, although he continued to regard Hamo and his friends with an apprehensive look. He didn't seem to hear me at first, but then I repeated myself and he turned to face me. 'Come on,' I said. 'The longer we tarry, the less chance we have of catching them.'

He nodded and kicked on down the path, and we followed, past tangles of crooked trees and splintered branches brought down by the recent winds, past thick reed-beds and shallow streams in which wicker eel-traps lay. How many miles we'd come from Elyg, I had no idea, although it was probably not quite as many as it felt. My arse was aching; we'd left camp at first light and midday was fast approaching, and most of that time we'd spent in the saddle.

We must have ridden for another half an hour before Godric gave a stifled cry. Perhaps half a mile ahead, a flock of marsh birds took wing, some hundred and more of them rising into the sky, turning as one in a great circle, before descending and disappearing from sight behind a stand of drooping willows. Straightaway I checked Fyrheard, and held up a hand to the others as a signal to stop.

'Something must have scared them,' Wace murmured.

My heart was pounding as I squinted into the distance, trying to make out what that something might be, and whether at last we had found our quarry. If it was Hereward, however, he and his band were well hidden amidst the undergrowth. Yet who else had any reason to be out here?

It had to be them.

'Stay close,' I said. 'From now on, not a sound.' I glared at Hamo's men, who as usual were laughing between themselves at some private joke, probably at my expense. 'We move quickly and we move quietly.'

I didn't wait for any acknowledgement but spurred Fyrheard on. The path led us to the willow thicket, which stood upon one of the many small islets that dotted the fen. Its slopes were slick with mud, but we struggled up them, ducking beneath low branches, pushing our horses as fast as we dared as the track dipped and rose, until we burst forth from the trees into the blinding brightness, and could see the way stretching out in front of us.

And there I saw them. There were, I reckoned, around three dozen of them, although it was difficult to make an exact count, since they were not all together, but rather strung out along the path, the closest of them a mere hundred paces ahead of us. And those were just the ones who looked to me like warriors, for there were also women and even a few children, scurrying along behind their mothers, not to mention those leading the packhorses, who had taken up the rear.

Hamo gave a whoop. Before I could do or say anything, he was galloping past me down the slope, almost knocking me from the saddle. Behind him thundered the rest of his men, their bows in hand.

'Kill them,' he yelled. 'Kill them!'

'Hamo!' I shouted, but it was too late. I'd wanted if possible to surprise the enemy, but there was no chance of that now. I swore aloud.

He nocked an arrow to his bowstring, narrowed his eyes as he pulled back, took aim and then let fly, closely followed by his companions. The air whistled and the midday sun glinted off the steel heads. The first struck one of the sumpter ponies on the rump, tearing through its flesh, and it went down with a shriek, thrashing its hooves and spilling the contents of its packs. The second buried itself in a man's back and the force of the impact sent him tumbling forward, and then came the rest, raining death upon the Englishmen and their families. Children were screaming and crying; somewhere amongst them a dog was barking, and men were shouting to one another as they realised the danger. While some grabbed the hands of their womenfolk and picked up the smallest of the children to carry them to safety, others were shoving their way to the rear, unslinging their round shields from where they rested across their backs and forming a line to obstruct our path and cover their retreat. The way was wide enough for three men at most to stand abreast and they formed the shield-wall across it.

But they could do nothing to stop the hail of steel. The air whistled as Hamo and his men let another volley fly, and another and another, and they did not seem to care whether they loosed all together or not, for they were merely intent on killing as many as possible and staining the marshes with English blood. One of the women stumbled as she ran, and fell upon the ground. A boy who might have been her son turned to try and help her up, only for an arrow to take him in the chest. The remaining ponies were whinnying, rearing up, kicking out at anyone who came too close, the whites of their eyes showing. The wounded lay on the ground, cursing, yelling out to God and the saints.

And then, striding forward through the throng of fleeing women and children, came Hereward himself. It was only the second time our paths had crossed, and on this occasion he wore a helmet that served to mask his face, but I recognised him at once. His dark hair straggled about his shoulders, and there was the same purpose, the same confidence in his bearing that I remembered. He came with a seax upon his belt and his own bow slung across his back, and with a score of mailed warriors behind him. Abbot Thurstan must have been mistaken, for he didn't look injured at all.

He roared an instruction that I couldn't quite make out, but I didn't need to. At once the shield-wall was breaking and the Englishmen were surging forward with steel in hand and death in their eyes.

'Get back!' I yelled at Hamo. The path was too narrow to fight effectively on horseback, but if he and his men could withdraw to join us on the higher ground by the thicket, then we might just have the space in which to give our sword-arms room.

Either Hamo didn't hear me, though, or else he chose not to listen. Barking an order to the rest of the archers, he drew and loosed another two shafts from his arrow-bag. The first fell wide, disappearing somewhere amongst the sedge, but his second found the throat of one of the onrushing enemy. The man's legs buckled and he toppled backwards to cries from the comrades into whose path he had fallen. Two of them stumbled as they tried to negotiate his fallen body and, as they did so, their shields dropped out of position, just for the briefest of instants, but it was an instant too long. One dropped his seax as an arrow pierced his upper arm, while another was struck upon the breast; the head must have found a gap between the links of his mail, for the shaft was buried almost up to the fletching. Suddenly the track was slick with blood and obstructed by the corpses of three men, over which the rest now had to climb.

'*Sceldas!*' Hereward roared at them, and at the same time lifted his own bow.

The same bow with which he had felled Pons's destrier. The same one with which he humiliated me before my own knights.

He drew the string back past his chin and held it there for a few moments before finally releasing it. The arrow sailed over the heads of his countrymen, flashing silver as it flew, spearing towards Hamo and his company. There was a yell and then one of them was tumbling from the saddle to the ground: the gaunt one with the large ears who was forever grumbling about how empty his stomach was.

'Ansfred!' one of his friends shouted, but Ansfred was already dead. He lay on his back with his eyes and mouth open, a surprised look fixed on his face, and a white-feathered shaft flecked with scarlet protruding from his chest.

'Get back!' I yelled for the second time. Whether it was because they heard me, or because they had seen one of their number fall and had no wish to suffer the same fate, I didn't know, but finally Hamo's men seemed to awaken from their bloodlust. As the Englishmen charged towards them, they all began to turn, riding back to join us on the higher ground where the willows stood.

All, that was, except for Hamo himself. Seemingly oblivious to the death of his man, he stood his ground, loosing arrow after arrow as fast as he could draw them from the bag at his side. Most fell wide or else stuck fast in the leather and limewood of the English shields, but a couple found their targets, and I saw that several among the enemy were beginning to waver as they stepped across the bodies of their slain comrades, their feet slipping on the blood-soaked mud, even as those behind pressed forward. Hereward called for them to advance, but while some were paying attention, confusion and indecision had gripped the rest.

Long years of experience had taught me that such moments were fleeting. If we were to take advantage of their confusion, we had to do so quickly. An idea formed in my mind.

'Stay here,' I said to Wace and all the other knights as I pushed Fyrheard into a gallop, racing down from the cover of the trees towards the English ranks.

'What are you doing?' Wace called. 'Tancred!'

'Trust me,' I shouted back, and then to the withdrawing archers: 'Form a line in front of the trees. Wait for my signal!'

Hamo must finally have used all his arrows, for only now did he follow the rest of his company. His cheeks were even redder than usual and his face showed a smirk of satisfaction as he rode past.

I checked Fyrheard about fifty paces from the enemy lines, raising my hands in the air, away from my body, to show that I had not come to fight but to speak.

'Sheathe your swords,' I said in the English tongue. I was aware that I was taking a chance, but I reckoned that they would be intrigued enough to want to hear what I had to say. 'I've come to speak with your lord.'

I'd lost sight of him among the ranks of his men, but I knew he had to be there somewhere.

'Where are you, Hereward?' I shouted. 'Come and show your face!'

My heart was beating fast. This all depended on my sounding confident, but I was not confident at all. One arrow was all it would take, if Hereward decided to use this opportunity to finish what he had begun one week ago.

His men broke ranks and I saw him. He handed his bow to one of his retainers and strode forward, stepping over the corpses as easily and indifferently as if they were fallen branches.

He stopped about ten paces from me, removed his helmet and that was when I saw him properly for the first time. The man who by his sword-edge had probably accounted for more Normans than any other single Englishman had managed in the last five years. The man who had defied us all these months. But if his pride was at all wounded by being betrayed by his allies, by having to flee the place that for so long he had helped defend, it was not apparent in his demeanour. He was probably around the same age as myself, if the number of cuts and scars decorating his face was anything to judge by. Certainly he looked no younger. There was a hardness in his eyes, and a firmness in his stance that gave the impression of someone who didn't know the meaning of defeat. He dressed not in mail but in an archer's leather corselet, reinforced with iron studs that would deflect a glancing blow but little more.

'Have you come to parley or just to gawp?' he asked.

'I've come to talk,' I answered.

'Then talk.'

His voice was strangely measured and even, not at all what I had been expecting after everything I'd heard about him.

'Very well,' I said. 'You know you can't run. We can easily outpace you and pick you off, one by one, until you decide to surrender.'

Hereward shrugged. 'We might not be able to run but we can still fight. You'll run out of arrows eventually and I doubt your men have the same stomach for a fight as mine. We have numbers on our side.'

I forced a laugh, and hoped it sounded convincing. 'You think we're the only men that King Guillaume has sent?'

'You tell me.'

'There's a whole raiding-party four hundred strong following behind us,' I said, hoping that he would fall for the lie. 'King Guillaume is scouring the marshes with fire and sword to try to find you. He has put a price on your head of one hundred silver marks, and he doesn't care whether you're brought to him alive or dead.'

It sounded believable enough that even I was convinced. With any luck he would swallow the morsel whole, and we wouldn't have to risk another battle.

'What, then?' Hereward countered. 'You would have me give myself up to you?'

'That's right. If you do that, and freely offer your submission, then the king might just be willing to show you clemency. There is no other choice, if you want to live.'

He snorted. 'There is always a choice.' He turned his back and made to return to the shield-wall.

'You can't escape your fate,' I called after him. 'Your rebellion is finished. The Isle belongs to us. Your allies have forsaken you, as has your cherished saint, Æthelthryth. She heard your prayers and she laughed at them. She spits on your dreams. Do you hear me?'

He rounded on me. 'What would you know of St Æthelthryth?'

'Only what Godric tells me,' I replied. 'To think that the feared Hereward, the scourge of the fenlands, was reduced to begging for a woman's help to win his wars!'

'Godric?' he asked, frowning. 'You mean Morcar's nephew?'

'Didn't you know?'

I called the boy's name and he came forward, tentatively at first, but I jerked my head and he quickened his pace.

'Were it not for him, we might never have taken Elyg,' I said. 'This is the one who brought about your downfall, who brought an end to your rebellion.'

'You were the one who betrayed us?' Hereward asked Godric. His eyes were colder than steel on a winter's morning. 'I always knew that your uncle had the tongue of a serpent. I ought to have guessed you would be no different.' He sneered as he gestured at the scabbard that hung from the boy's belt. Godric had come from Alrehetha without a weapon, and so I'd given him the sword with the emerald in the pommel that had belonged to Thurcytel. 'That's a big blade for a child to carry. You'd best take care that you don't cut yourself.'

The boy's cheeks reddened, but he said nothing.

'You always were a worthless turd in my eyes,' Hereward went on. 'How can you call yourself a thegn when you don't even know how to wield the weapons with which to defend your lands?'

'Enough of your squawking,' I said to Hereward.

He ignored me. 'Even now you cower behind the protection of these Frenchmen. Why do you let him speak for you? Have you lost your voice, or just your wits?' He spat. 'Your mother was a whore, and the daughter of a whore besides, but even so she would have drowned you at birth had she known the disgrace you'd bring upon your kin and your countrymen. Because of you, our one last chance to regain our birthright is lost. This once-proud kingdom has fallen, we find ourselves ruled by foreign tyrants, and it is your fault. Do you hear me? You did this, Godric of Corbei!'

'No!' the boy cried, and before I could do anything he spurred his palfrey forward, at the same time drawing his sword.

'Godric!' I shouted, but it was too late. The boy had allowed the elder Englishman to goad him to anger, and now he would suffer.

Some of Hereward's men started forward, but he raised his shield-hand to forestall them, while with the other he let his helmet fall and drew his seax. A smile spread across his face as he took his stance, lowering his blade-point towards the ground, leaving the upper half of his body open as an invitation to attack. Godric accepted without hesitation, roaring with rage as he swung at Hereward's head, but his foe had been anticipating such a move. He ducked beneath Godric's blade, at the same time whipping his own up and flashing the edge across the palfrey's hindquarters, tearing through flesh and sinew. The animal buckled and the boy fell, and he was still clinging desperately with one hand to the reins when he hit the ground.

'Stop this,' I shouted above the horse's screams. Hereward stood over the boy with his seax pointed at the skin beneath his chin. Godric's sword lay just a little beyond grasp, but the fall must have knocked the wind out of him, or else hurt him worse than I had thought, since he seemed unable to reach it – for all the good that it would have done him at that moment.

'Stop?' Hereward asked, although he did not take his eyes from the boy. 'Why should I stop? Not only has he betrayed us, he's tried to kill me too.'

'He couldn't kill you if you were weaponless and missing both your legs,' I said. 'You've had your fun, so now let him go. He's worth nothing to you.'

'Please,' Godric said weakly, and let out a cough. 'Spare me, p-please, I beg of you.'

Hereward kicked him in the ribs. It didn't seem to me an especially hard kick, but it was enough to make the boy cry out in agony and bend double as he rolled over, clutched at his side and cursed all at the same time.

'I hardly touched you, weakling,' Hereward growled. Disdainfully he spat at Godric before at last he turned to face me. 'Are you so scared to fight me that you have to send whelps like him to do your work? Don't insult—'

He didn't get the chance to finish. In one movement Godric's hand had found the hilt of his weapon and brought the blade around, aiming at the back of his opponent's legs, and I saw that all that howling and swearing and writhing had been but a ruse.

Hereward gave a yell as the point slashed across his ankle. A glancing blow, it seemed, but the lank-haired Englishman fell to his knees. Straightaway his retainers started forward. Godric scrambled to his feet, took one glance at them and another at Hereward, perhaps thinking to finish him, but instead he froze. For, despite his injured leg, Hereward was struggling to his feet, his teeth clenched and his eyes wild.

'Bastard,' Hereward said, and swung at the boy, but it was a wild stroke that missed by a hand's breadth, and suddenly he was off balance, staggering, hobbling, sliding on the mud. 'Bastard!'

And I saw a chance to end this.

Summoning all the breath in my chest, I gave a wordless roar, and in that roar was all the anger and frustration of the last few weeks. I charged forward, trusting that the others would be behind me. Hereward heard me coming, and despite his injured ankle managed to turn just in time to fend off my strike. Steel shrieked against steel as our blades met, but then I was riding on, leaving him for those behind me to finish. I crashed into the first of Hereward's men before he could so much as level his spear. Iron clattered upon limewood as he fell beneath Fyrheard's hooves. Like a river the battle-joy was flowing, carrying me with it as I struck out on both sides with shield-boss and sword-point. Men must have been shouting, screaming, yelping in pain, howling in anguish as their friends fell before their eyes, but all I remember hearing is the sound of my own breathing and the beating of my heart in my breast and the blood pounding behind my eyes. I rammed the steel home into the throat of the next man and then battered the flat of the blade across the nasal-guard of the one after him, slicing his cheek open, biting into his skull, sending teeth and fragments of bloodied bone flying.

'No mercy!' I shouted.

I heard a rush of air and glanced up to see a volley of goose-feathered shafts arcing high into the blue sky, but thankfully they were headed in the direction of the enemy and not for me. Hamo's archers had not entirely exhausted their arrow-bags, then. It was quick thinking on their part, too, for it happened that at the same moment as Hereward's retainers raised their shields, to protect themselves from the approaching storm, we were upon them, cutting beneath the iron-reinforced rims into their unprotected thighs, driving into their midst, forcing them back. The ploy was one that we had used at Haestinges five long years ago; it had worked then and it was working now, and the enemy did not know what to do. Behind me I heard Serlo and Pons and the others bellowing as they cut down some of the wounded we left in our wake. The enemy were falling before our fury, and in that instant I felt as if nothing in the world could harm me.

Confidence is a strange thing. It can arrive unexpectedly as if from nowhere, for no apparent reason, and inspire men to do things that in their right mind they would never dream of under-taking; and it can desert a man just as quickly, even on the point of victory. And so it was then, for even though they still just about outnumbered us, the enemy broke. A couple threw down their weapons, obviously hoping that we would spare them if they gave themselves up, but those hopes were in vain, and they had barely a chance to open their mouths in protest before we cut them down.

Breathing hard, I found myself with space around me. The rest of the Englishmen were fleeing northwards along the track, following their womenfolk, abandoning the fight.

I checked Fyrheard by the path's edge. 'Go,' I yelled to the others, my voice hoarse and hurting. 'After them!'

'With me,' said Wace. 'Conroi with me!'

He and Pons and Serlo and Tor and the Gascon flashed past, and they were followed by Hamo and half a dozen of his men, who had cast aside their bows and drawn swords and axes and knives. Cries of delight went up as they sensed plunder at hand.

But I had more important things in mind. I glanced about, searching for Hereward. For his corpse was not among those strewn along the path.

And then I saw him, striking out from the path across the mud, crashing through the sedge and the reeds towards a stand of alders an arrow's flight away, hobbling as he went owing to his injured ankle. Godric was pursuing him, swearing as he struggled over the soft ground, while by the willow trees on the island one of the remaining archers – a squat, square-faced lad – had an arrow upon his bow. Already he had drawn the string back and his eyes were narrowed as he took his aim.

'Leave him,' I called, and thankfully the lad heard me and lowered his bow. 'He's mine!'

If ever there was one kill I wanted, it was this one. I would not let Hereward escape my sword, as Eadgar Ætheling and Wild Eadric and Bleddyn ap Cynfyn had done. I wanted to be known as the man who had slain the scourge of the fens, who had gone toe to toe with him in single combat and had bested him. His death would be just reward for all the hardships we had suffered, on this campaign and in the past five years.

Freeing my shield-arm from the leather braces and leaving Fyrheard behind, I headed off in pursuit of the Englishman, charging across the quagmire as best I could manage. The ground sucked at my boots; before long my trews were soaked and clinging to my legs as high as my knee, weighing my tired legs down further, but I clenched my teeth and kept going, hacking at the reeds with my sword as desperately I tried to clear a way through.

I saw Godric ahead of me and called to him. Mud caked his clothes, his tunic was torn, his arms were cut and his cheek was grazed where he had fallen, and all he had with which to defend himself was his sword.

'Go back,' I told him. 'This isn't your fight.'

'Lord—'

'You've done enough,' I said, more forcefully this time. 'Now, go.'

His face fell, but I didn't have time to argue with him as I crashed on, further into the bog.

'Hereward,' I yelled. 'Come and fight me!'

Soon I was wading through water that was knee-deep, and I was wet up to my chest from the splashing, but still I pressed on in the direction he'd been heading, until I found myself gazing out across a sun-sparkling mere, some fifty paces wide and more.

I'd lost him.

'Hereward!'

No reply came. I swore violently, and again, and again. All that could be heard was the swish of the breeze amongst the reeds, and the gentle, rhythmic whistle of a heron's wings as it flew overhead, and the distant cries of alarm as my sword-brothers chased the enemy down.

He was gone.

The bloodlust faded and I was standing alone, panting, feeling the cold waters swirl around my toes and sweat trickle down from my brow. Marsh-grime covered my hauberk and chausses and there were strands of weed tangled around my sword-hand and around my blade. There would be no glory. Not this time.

I was returning my sword to its scabbard when behind me there was a sudden splash, and I half turned, thinking that Godric had decided to follow me after all—

Not a moment too soon. Hereward, his damp hair flailing, heaved his seax around, aiming for my head. Instinctively I ducked, but in doing so I found myself struggling for balance. My foot had become trapped in the mud and I couldn't move it quickly enough. With a crash of spray I toppled backwards, plunging into the marsh, my mail dragging me down, and there was water in my mouth and in my nose and in my throat, and I was choking and swallowing and gasping for breath all at the same time, trying somehow to raise my head above the surface, but there was a weight on my chest, holding me under, and my limbs were flailing and my lungs burning, and I could see nothing except white stars dancing in my eyes.

Then there was a hand on my collar, pulling me free of the marsh's grasp. I inhaled deeply, thankful to find air at last even if only for a moment, and I saw my enemy standing over me, his yellow teeth bared, and in his stone-grey eyes was hatred such as I had never seen.

'You Frenchmen stole my lands,' he said, and he was sobbing as he spoke. Tears streamed down his face. 'You killed my men. Now I'll kill you!'

I tried to struggle, but couldn't find the strength. I had just enough presence of mind to take another breath before Hereward let go of my collar and stamped down upon my chest. I could make out his shadowy form standing over me, and the bright spot of the sun behind him, but all my kicking and waving was to no avail, and that was when the fear took me.

Fear, because I knew that this was it. My time had come, and all I could think was how stupid I had been, and how for that stupidity I would now pay with my life.

My mind began to cloud. With every last beat of my heart I could feel my strength failing, the darkness encircling me, closing in—

When suddenly the weight on my chest was no more. Summoning every last ounce of will that was left to me, I raised myself up, struggling against the weight of my hauberk, gasping desperately for air that at first would not come, but which, when it did, was as sweet as heaven. I blinked as I inhaled, scarcely believing that I was still alive.

Sunlight pained my eyes, making it difficult to see, but as the brightness faded I saw Hereward. He staggered a couple of paces backwards, staring stupidly down at me as if in surprise, his jaw hanging open as if he were about to say something. Whatever that might have been, though, he never had a chance to utter. His legs gave way; he toppled forwards, and I caught a glimpse of the gash decorating the back of his skull as his limp corpse fell with a crash into the water.

And I found myself looking upon the face of the man to whom I owed my life.

Godric.

Thirteen

He stood, breathless, his eyes wide and his face deathly pale as he gazed down at Hereward's body. His hand and the fuller of his weapon were running with his foe's glistening blood, while the swirled waters around his feet were stained a brownish-crimson. He gave a moment's shudder, then his sword slipped from his hand and he began to spew.

Still coughing up water, I hauled myself to my feet. Godric was shivering, though the day was far from cold. He had tasted the battle-rage for the first time, had taken his first steps upon the sword-path, and was not sure if he liked it. I understood the feeling well. It didn't seem so long ago that I had been in his place, claiming my first kill. Twelve years had passed since then, but it could have been yesterday, so clearly was it fixed in my memory.

'I'm sorry, lord,' he said. 'I should have listened—'

'You don't have to apologise,' I assured him. 'You did well.'

At last a smile broke out across his face. A man always remembers his first kill, but few had such a glorious tale to tell as young Godric now did.

Some way along the marsh-passage to the north our war-horn sounded out: two short blasts that I recognised at once as the signal to fall back. Probably that meant Hereward's men were at last beginning to rally. Of course they couldn't know that it was too late to save their lord, but the last thing I wanted was to embroil myself in another mêlée.

'Come on,' I said. 'We have to go while we still can.'

Godric did not move. He stared, transfixed, at Hereward's body lying face-down and motionless as his lifeblood seeped away into the fen, as if still not quite believing what he had done.

'Now!'

At last he did as he was told, following me as I made back in the direction of the path, crashing through the reeds, trying to remember the way. I would have liked to bring Hereward's corpse with us, or at least cut off his head so that we could take it back as our trophy, but we had no time, not if we wanted to be sure of getting away from this place with our lives. And so we left him. Perhaps his followers would find him in time and haul his bloated form from the bog, or perhaps his flesh would provide a feast for the eels and the worms. That would be no better a fate than he deserved.

Before long we found the path again, and Fyrheard, and the others, who were riding back from their pursuit of the rebels.

'There are more of them up ahead,' Wace said when he saw us. 'Fifty, sixty, possibly more. They're coming this way, but we can't fight them all.'

'It doesn't matter,' I said as I let Godric take the saddle, whilst I sat behind him.

'What happened?' asked Pons, glancing first at me and then at the Englishman. I wondered what he must be thinking as he saw me drenched from brow to feet, with my hair clinging to my head and neck and tendrils of weed draped across my shoulders, clinging to my hauberk. 'Where's Hereward? Is he dead? Did you kill him?'

'No,' I replied, and grinned because it was the truth.

'He got away?'

I shook my head, and suddenly, for the first time in what seemed like months, I found myself laughing.

'What, lord?' Serlo frowned.

'First let's leave this place. Maybe then Godric will tell you.'

'Godric?' Hamo asked. 'The English runt? What do you mean?'

But we were already on our way, and I was whooping with delight, for the Isle was ours, England was ours, the sun was shining and all was well with the world. For the first time in longer than I could remember, I was happy, and in all the hours that it took us to journey back to Elyg, not once did I stop smiling.

Thus the Isle of Elyg fell.

I am far from the first to tell the tale, and doubtless many others will follow my example in the years to come, filling sheet after sheet of fresh-cut parchment with their delicate script, much more refined than my own scribbles, which are wiry and poorly formed as a result of my fading eyesight. They may compare the siege of the Isle to that of ancient Troy, and lavish praise upon King Guillaume for his strength of will, or else upon the rebels for having the courage to defy him for so long. And, as is the way of things, with every retelling some details of the story change.

Nowadays I often hear it said that Hereward escaped, that he and his loyal followers managed to flee uninjured from the Isle into the swamps, and from the swamps into the woods, and from there continued to harass his enemies for many summers to come. Wandering poets sing songs of his deeds, claiming that, were it not for the treachery of his own countrymen at Elyg, he would have driven us Frenchmen from England within another year. Across the marsh country of East Anglia, folk still revere him as a hero and a great war leader, even though he was no such thing. Children wield sticks in the manner of swords and make hiding places in the birch copses and the willow groves, and in that way relive some of those battles that we fought, as well as others that happened only in the imagination of certain chroniclers.

It doesn't seem to matter that no one ever saw Hereward after that day, nor that he was but one of many who stood against us at Elyg, for the stories that people choose to remember are rarely those of what really took place, but rather the ones they would prefer to believe. Thus as the seasons turn and the years and the decades pass, the stories grow ever wilder, and the myths grow more powerful than the truth.

The truth, which few men alive these days know, or care to remember.

But I know, for I was there.

'No one will believe me,' Godric said glumly as the belfry of Elyg's church came into sight. It was the middle of the afternoon and cloud had rolled across the sky, obscuring the sun, but that had done nothing to dampen my spirits. The monastery's bell rang out across the fens, not in warning but in celebration of our victory.

'Show them the blood drying on your sword and they'll believe you,' I answered. Out of gratitude to him, and in honour of his triumph, I had allowed Godric to ride Fyrheard, while I walked beside him. 'If anyone still doubts you after that, challenge them to deny it through combat.'

Godric didn't look reassured. 'And what if they accept?'

'They won't.'

'How can you know?'

'Because you're under my protection now, and they'll know that if they so much as lay a finger upon you, they'll have me to answer to. On that you have my oath.'

Godric's eyes brightened. 'Truly, lord?'

'Truly,' I replied. 'Being a warrior is as much about how men see you as about the number of foes your blade-edge has claimed. If you believe in your own accomplishments, then others will believe them too.'

We reached Elyg soon after. That last mile seemed the hardest of all, for our horses were tired and thirsty, and so were we. Thankfully the ale was already flowing when we arrived. I was glad to see, too, that tempers had cooled in the hours we'd been gone, and that the quarrels that had been breaking out were now settled. Great fires had been lit and around them there was dancing and drinking, while elsewhere men were receiving treatment from leech-doctors for wounds taken in the battle.

I asked if anyone knew where we might find Lord Robert, since no doubt he would be wondering where we were. A gap-toothed boy, who was carrying pails of water on a yoke, nodded towards the monastery.

'You'll probably find him in the great hall with the other barons,' he said, and went on to tell us that King Guillaume had returned to Wiceford, where he had received the formal submission of all the English leaders who had surrendered. Behind him he'd left several hundred knights to garrison Elyg, as well several hundred more who were already too insensible with drink to stand, let alone accompany him.

I thanked the boy and we hastened towards the monastery, where we rode through the great stone arch of the gatehouse and gave our weary mounts to the care of the stable-hands, who directed me towards a long stone building with high windows on the south side of the cloister. A throng of men and shit-stinking animals filled the yard, but I forced my way through them.

'If you're looking for Lord Robert, you won't find him there,' someone called as I neared the hall's doors. I turned to see a familiar figure waving in our direction.

'Eudo!' I said, at once forgetting why we were here, so glad was I to see him alive. He was sitting on a stool while a young woman dressed in drab, loose-fitting robes, who might have been a nun, wrapped a length of cloth around his forearm. He rose to greet us, embracing Wace and myself in turn.

'Is it bad?' I asked, gesturing at the bandage.

He sat back down and gave a wince as the woman tied off the loose ends. 'One of the bastards broke my finger and laid a cut here. His axe came down on my shield and smashed straight through. It could have been worse, I suppose. At least it wasn't my sword-hand.'

'We didn't know what had happened to you,' Wace said. 'We feared the worst.'

'Likewise,' Eudo said. 'So where have you been?'

'Ask Godric,' I said. 'He'll explain.' Eudo gave me a questioning look, but before he could say anything, I asked him: 'Where's Robert?'

'He rode back to camp. His father isn't long for this life, or so we heard. A message arrived from his chaplain a couple of hours ago. He left straightaway.'

We'd all known that Malet's days were few, and yet somehow I'd never actually believed that his time would come so soon. Not on this, our day of victory.

'He's returned to Alrehetha?' I asked.

'That's right,' Eudo said. 'Why?'

I started back towards the gates. 'Because that's where I need to go.'

'What? Why?'

It was hard to explain. I was stubborn in those days, and rarely cared what others thought of me, and yet for some reason it felt important that I should have Malet's forgiveness before he left this life behind him. Whether that was simply because he had once been my lord and I had been oath-sworn to him, or because he had given me new purpose and offered me a chance for redemption at a time in my life when all seemed dark, I couldn't say exactly.

I only hoped I was not too late.

The sun was growing low in the sky by the time I arrived at Alrehetha and rode through the gates of the guardhouse, which was where Malet was quartered. A handful of sentries were posted on the gate, but when I told them why I'd come they let me pass and pointed me to a large timber-built hall, a fine place which had existed before the ditches and banks and palisades had been built, and which had been appropriated for the comfort of the king and his household. Certainly it was a more fitting place for a baron of Malet's standing to live out his final hours than the hovel at Brandune in which he'd spent all those weeks. I took that as a sign that the king's feelings towards the family were at last softening. It was about time, too, considering everything we and Robert had done for him of late.

At the hall I gave my weapons to the steward, who directed me along a narrow passage. At its end, guarding the door, stood a man whom I recognised for one of Robert's hearth-knights.

'Is he—?' I asked.

'Still with us, if only barely,' the man replied. 'I can't let you go in, though. Not unless Lord Robert says so.'

'Then why don't you ask him?' I suggested.

I waited while he went inside. After a few moments he returned and with a nod of his head motioned me through.

The chamber was windowless and filled with a powerful, sharp stench of burning tallow, which came from stout candles placed all about. I remembered Father Erchembald, the priest at Earnford and a dear friend, once telling me how the smell helped guard against pestilential vapours, and that was why he recommended keeping one burning whenever someone was laid low with fever or other sickness. But no amount of tallow smoke would save Malet from whatever malady it was that afflicted him. Not now. He looked so thin, and so frail, not at all like a man of fifty, but one twenty years older. He lay upon a bed beneath a bundle of woollen blankets, with his head resting upon a pillow, so still that at first I thought Robert's man had been mistaken, and that I was too late, but then his eyelids trembled, and I saw his chest rise and fall. He was not gone quite yet, then.

A host of familiar faces were crowded into that small space. On one side of the bed were Robert and the chaplain, Dudo, who knelt by Malet's right hand with a bowl of what looked like pottage. On the other were Malet's wife, Elise, her usually stern expression broken by the tears flooding down her cheeks, and Beatrice, her fair hair glimmering in the flickering candlelight. She smiled sadly when she saw me. At her side stood a dark, thin-lipped man I didn't recognise but guessed must be her new husband. They must have all arrived earlier today, even while, on the other side of the bridge, the battle for the Isle and for Elyg was under way.

Robert rose and came to greet me, clasping my hand. 'It's good to see you,' he said, keeping his voice low. 'Where did you go? One moment you were with us, and then you and your men had disappeared. What happened? Is Wace with you?'

This was no time to give a full account, and so I told him simply, 'Hereward is dead.'

'Dead?' he asked. 'You know this for sure? How?'

'I know because we pursued him and his band across the marshes and met them in battle. I saw his corpse with my own eyes.'

He blinked, as if the news were too incredible to take in, then turned back towards the bed where the elder Malet lay. 'Did you hear that, Father? Hereward is dead.'

His father stirred and gave a rasping cough.

'Here,' said Dudo, and offered him an ale-cup. 'Drink.'

Malet shook his head as the cough subsided, and drew the blankets closer around him. No fire was lit, but it was nevertheless far from cold in that room. Beneath my hauberk my arms were running with sweat. I wished I'd thought to return to my tent first and leave it there, and at the same time to exchange my tunic for the spare one I kept in my pack. Although I had dried in the hours since the fight with Hereward, the damp marsh-smell still clung to my clothes.

'Who is it, Robert?' Malet croaked as his eyes flicked open. 'Who comes here?'

'It's Tancred, Father.'

Malet sighed. His eyes closed again. Long moments passed before finally he said, 'Leave us.'

His voice was hardly strong enough to sustain a whisper, but in the silence it was clearly enough heard. At once all eyes were on me. I found myself besieged by Dudo's unfeeling gaze, by the thin-lipped man's indifferent regard, and by Elise's hard, spiteful stare. She had never liked me, from the moment our paths had first crossed. Only Beatrice's eyes held any sympathy, although she made no protest on my behalf. Not that I blamed her. Her father had spoken and his wishes were to be respected. I had done everything I could, and yet even in his dying hours the old man couldn't find it within his heart to finally lay to rest this quarrel of ours.

'I'm sorry, Tancred,' said Robert. 'But perhaps it would be for the best if—'

'It's all right,' I muttered, and looked around the chamber, meeting the eyes of each of the Malets in turn. I was thinking about saying something more, but the only words that came to mind were ones that I dared not utter in my lord's presence, and so I kept my tongue inside my head as I made for the door and grasped the handle—

'No,' said Malet. 'No.'

I halted with my fingers wrapped around the twisted rods of iron, and glanced over my shoulder.

'What is it?' Robert asked.

Malet's chest rose and fell several more times before he was able to muster the strength to speak again. 'I don't mean that Tancred should go,' he said at last.

Robert frowned. 'Then I don't understand.'

'I mean the rest of you must leave.'

'Guillaume,' Elise pleaded. 'You have no need to waste your strength speaking to such a worthless creature. What more do you have to say to him?'

'I will spend the strength I have left how I choose,' Malet said. 'And I would speak to Tancred alone.'

Elise looked despairingly first at Robert and then at Beatrice, evidently hoping for one or both to lend her their support, but none was forthcoming.

'Come, Mother,' said Robert. 'We should go, and let Father say what he must.'

Elise pointed at me, her cheeks red. 'How can you defend him, Robert? You know how he betrayed your father. He is nothing but a perjurer!'

'Peace, Elise,' Malet whispered, while Robert was still struggling for words. 'What has passed, has passed.'

Elise's eyes bored into me. 'Guillaume told me how you broke your oath to him when you were in his service. Even if he has forgotten, I have not! It sickens me how you prosper while our house and our name is brought ever lower. May you be damned!'

'Mother—' Beatrice began, but Elise was not listening. She rose and pushed past us, hastening from the room. I heard her footsteps disappearing down the passage.

'Let me speak to her,' Robert said, and darted out after her.

Beatrice's husband held out a hand to help her to her feet, and then they too made to leave.

'I knew you would come,' Beatrice said when she passed me. She took my hand in hers, just for a moment, and I felt the warmth there. I had loved her once, or thought I had, and she had loved me. Those feelings had faded now, but in their place had arisen an understanding and friendship that I valued far more.

Her husband regarded me with that same indifferent expression as before, as if appraising me in some way, but said nothing. Apart from Malet, only his chaplain remained.

'Perhaps it would be wise if I stay,' Dudo suggested as he fingered the carved wooden cross that hung from his neck.

'If I have need of you, I will have Tancred send for you,' Malet said.

'Lord—'

'Do not argue, please. I am too weak for that.'

The priest pursed his lips and bowed in deference to his lord's wishes. He did not look at me as he went, closing the door behind him.

Now that the chamber was empty of people, I saw how sparsely furnished it was. A threadbare rug covered the floor, while in one corner stood an iron pail filled with water, in which floated a scrap of cloth.

Malet raised pale fingers, beckoning me closer, and I knelt down by his bedside.

'It's good to see you, Tancred.' He managed the faintest hint of a smile, but there was pain in that smile and it was short-lived. 'I'm glad you came.'

'You are, lord?' I asked, surprised and confused in equal measure.

'I am. Dudo told me yesterday evening that you wished to speak with me.'

'He did?' Wonders never cease. The toad had delivered on his promise after all.

'He urged me to summon you, but I, in my stubbornness, refused. I have since been regretting that decision.'

'You changed your mind,' I said. 'Why?'

Malet did not answer straightaway, but gave a deep sigh. 'There are things that privately I have long wished to say, but which I have been reluctant to admit openly.'

He was speaking in riddles. 'What do you mean?'

'Pride,' he said. 'I have always been too proud. You would agree with that, wouldn't you?'

'No, lord,' I said, a little too quickly.

Malet smiled again. 'Just because my end is near, Tancred, don't presume that you must tell me what you think I want to hear. I know what's in your mind. Robert thinks the same. And you are right, both of you.'

I didn't know what to say to that, and so I bowed my head.

'It is a strange thing, pride,' he murmured. 'We are taught that it leads to disgrace, and that anyone who is proud of heart is an abomination to God. These things are true, aren't they?'

Both proverbs were ones that I recognised. They had been favourite sayings of the prior at the monastery where I'd grown up.

'So the Scriptures tell us,' I replied neutrally. Not for the first time, I felt as if he were testing me. 'But they are not meant to bind us, only guide us. There is no shame in taking pride in one's work and deeds, so long as that pride is not excessive. There is always a middle path to be found.'

'And yet it is not always so easy to follow that path, is it?' He breathed deeply, and I heard a rasp in his throat. 'That is why it has taken me so long to say what I will tell you now.'

He held out a pale hand, and I took it. His skin was dry, like the parchment in the gospel books I had sometimes copied from during my studies as an oblate.

'I have been mean-spirited, and undeservingly so, given all that you have done in my name and that of my kin. For that I am truly sorry.'

I felt a tear forming in my eye and tried to blink it back. My throat was dry and I swallowed to moisten it.

'You served me well, Tancred, for the brief time that you were sworn to me, difficult though it was for me to acknowledge that when we parted ways. And you have served Robert well, too.'

'He is a good lord,' I replied.

'He is becoming one, certainly. God knows he can be pig-headed at times, much like myself. Still, at least he understands how to win respect. He will do well for himself, and for those who follow him, in the years to come. Better than I have done, at any rate. But he needs loyal men around him.' He made a feeble attempt to squeeze my hand. 'I ask that you remain faithful to him. That is my one wish.'

'Of course,' I said. 'You know that I will.'

'Do I have your oath?'

I laughed, not with frustration but with amusement. I had lost count of the number of times I'd sworn pledges of one sort or another to various members of the Malet family.

'You have my oath,' I assured him.

He rested his head back upon the pillow, closed his eyes and coughed again, after which he gave a flick of his hand, and I realised he wanted the ale-cup brought to him. Cradling the back of his head with one hand, gently I lifted it to his lips. He sipped at it and his mouth twisted in distaste.

'Whatever this infusion is that Dudo has prepared, it is supposed to be good for me. Or so he insists,' he said when he had finished and I had set the cup back down on the stone floor. 'But the taste of it is foul.'

'I thought it was ale.' I raised the rim to my nose and sniffed at it, but could smell nothing offensive about it, nor much at all, save for the faintest trace of honey.

'Ale?' he asked. 'Alas not, though I have often asked for it. That, and some of the Rhenish wine I used to enjoy. But he will not bring me any. Such things are bad for the balance of my humours. So I am told, anyway. Is that likely, do you think?'

I shrugged. 'I don't know, lord.'

'You could bring me some, perhaps.'

'I could, but Dudo wouldn't thank me for it.'

'Come,' Malet said. 'He does not have to know. He has done all he can for me. I promised myself that I would live to see this day, and with his help I have done so. The battle is over. The Isle has fallen. And now you come with news that Hereward is dead, too?'

'It is true, lord.'

Malet settled down beneath the sheets. 'Then I have nothing more to live for,' he said, his voice hardly more than a whisper now. No doubt the effort of speaking had tired him. 'I am ready to face my Lord.'

He closed his eyes. I laid his hand back upon the blankets and watched for I knew not how long as his chest rose and fell in steady rhythm. Eventually, once I thought he was sleeping, I got to my tired feet and made to leave, moving as lightly as possible across the stone flags so that my footfalls and the chink of my mail did not disturb him.

I'd barely taken three paces when I heard him say: 'Before you go, there is one more thing.'

I turned. 'What is it, lord?'

'I have had Dudo draw up a will.'

Sensing what was to come, I said, 'Your forgiveness is all—'

He raised a finger to forestall me. 'Please, while I still have breath left in my chest. You would have learnt of this in time, in any case, but I wanted you to hear it from me first. I have made provision for you and Wace and Eudo. As you know, I have little enough land or silver at my disposal, but nonetheless I wish to leave you a token of my gratitude. To that end, each of you is to receive two of the finest destriers from my stables, and three palfreys, too. I know that you will make good use of them.'

I didn't know what to say to that. 'You are too generous,' I said once I'd recovered my voice.

'There is more, if you will listen. After all, were it not for you, Tancred, I would have perished at the hands of the Danes and would never have lived to see this day. To see the conquest of England complete. For you I have a particular gift.'

'I want nothing more,' I said, and surprised myself with how honestly I meant it.

'I have already made up my mind, so there is no use in disputing with me. Do you see the chest in the corner?'

An ironbound box stood up against one wall. Wondering what sort of gift he had in mind, I went to it.

'In here, lord?'

He nodded weakly. 'Open it.'

I flicked open the catches and then, finding that it wasn't locked, lifted the lid.

Inside, lying atop stacks of dry, crinkled parchment, was a curved drinking horn, one of the largest I had ever seen, as long as my arm and more than a hand's span in breadth at its open end. Silver binding ran around the rim, on which were engraved a fleet of dragon-prowed ships with sails billowing and decks filled with close-packed warriors. Another band ran around the middle on which was depicted a hunting scene, while the point was ornamented with a bird cast in gold.

'Made from the horn of an urus,' Malet said.

I'd never heard of such a beast. 'An urus?'

'A creature like a bull, only much larger, which I am told is found in lands far to the east of here. This was a gift from my father on the day I came of age. I have not had much use for it of late; there has been precious little to celebrate in recent months. Now I want you to have it.'

'Lord,' I protested as I lifted it up, hefting it in my hands and feeling its weight. It was a heavy thing, far heavier than it looked, and polished smooth so that, even in the soft candlelight, it gleamed. 'This is too much.'

'It is less than you deserve.'

'What about Robert?' I asked. 'Won't he—?'

I was about to say that as a father's gift to his son, surely it was only right that it should be passed in turn to his heir.

Malet must have guessed what I was thinking. 'He will not mind. He has always said it is too gaudy for his liking, and he cares little for drinking, as you know. You will appreciate it more than he will. Please, take it now, with my blessing.'

It was indeed a beautiful thing, more valuable, I didn't doubt, than any other possession of mine save my sword and my mail, my helmet and my horses.

'Thank you,' I said, although the words seemed insufficient to express my gratitude.

'I trust you will take care of it, and I wish you luck in all your undertakings. God be with you always, Tancred.'

'And with you, my lord,' I replied.

'As for that,' he murmured softly, a note of melancholy in his voice, 'we shall soon see. We shall soon see.'

His eyes closed once more. Before long his breathing had grown heavy and I knew for certain this time that he was asleep. A strange feeling overcame me as I left that chamber, the drinking horn in hand, and closed the door behind me, knowing it was to be the last time I saw Guillaume Malet, the man to whom, though I had not always cared to admit it, I owed so much.

*

Again that night I could not rest, and again I was not alone. Even as Pons and Serlo joined in the celebrations of those who had returned to camp, and Godric returned to his uncle Morcar on the Isle, I waited with Eudo and Wace and several of Malet's other vassals, some of whom I knew by name and others I didn't, in the yard outside the hall, where we warmed ourselves beside a charcoal brazier.

Once in a while Robert would come out from the hall with furrowed brow to tell us how his father was faring. His strength was failing fast, he said; with every hour the life was going out of him. His breath was growing shallower, his pulse was weakening and he grew ever colder. The leech-doctors who had seen him did not think he would last until dawn. Already Dudo had heard his final confession and given him the sacrament. It would not be long.

'We'll wait, lord,' I promised.

And so we did. Even though we were all bone-weary from the battle and from the lack of sleep the previous night, we nevertheless stayed awake, hardly speaking a word, even as from outside the guardhouse the joyous cries and music of the revellers floated upon the breeze. A dog barked somewhere and mice rustled the hall's thatch. We watched as cloud veiled the stars and we watched as the skies cleared again. We watched sparks from the brazier rise with the twisting smoke and dance around one another, flaring brightly for the briefest of instants before they vanished and became one with the blackness.

Hours more passed, until eventually, in the grey half-light that comes before dawn, Robert emerged from the hall once more. He didn't speak, nor did he have to, for straightaway we saw in his eyes the news that we had all been expecting.

Guillaume Malet, his father, had passed away.

Fourteen

The following morning, King Guillaume came to make arrangements with Robert for the payment of the relief that would permit him to inherit his father's barony, as well as to give his sympathies to him, Elise and Beatrice, though such gestures seemed to me rather false-hearted after the lengths he had gone to previously to strip Malet of his honour and his dignity. But he did at least give Robert leave to accompany his father's body on its final journey to Heia, which was the family's chief estate in England and was where he was to be buried.

All this took place in the yard of the guardhouse at Alrehetha. Accompanying the king and his retinue were Earl Morcar, grinning like a fool now that his title had been restored to him, his nephew Godric, and the clerk Atselin, who followed his master like a shadow. Whilst the king and Robert conversed, he watched me with hard eyes, as if puzzled how it was that I was still alive. I hadn't forgotten that he was the one who suggested we should lead the attack across the bridge. If I'd disliked him before, I despised him even more now, and was surprised that he so much as dared to show his face in my presence.

So intent was I on out-staring Atselin that at first I didn't hear the king calling myself and Wace forward, and only awoke from my thoughts when Serlo nudged me in the ribs. Fortunately the king didn't seem to notice. For once he was in a good humour, and I supposed he had every right to be.

'Robert tells me that you pursued Hereward and met him in battle,' he said, glancing between the two of us.

'We did, lord,' Wace said.

'And killed him, too, or so I hear.'

'That wasn't our doing, my king,' I said.

He frowned. 'Then whose was it?'

I nodded in Godric's direction. 'That's the man who slew Hereward.'

The boy reddened as all eyes fell upon him, and he cast his gaze down, as if embarrassed. But he had no reason to be. He had done what I and countless of my fellow knights could not manage.

'Godric?' Morcar asked, perplexed. His grin had vanished. 'My nephew killed Hereward?'

'I wouldn't have believed it had I not seen it with my own eyes,' I said. 'Hasn't he told you?'

'Godric barely knows which end of a sword is the killing one, let alone how to use it,' Morcar said, and gave his nephew a cuff around the ear. 'Look at him. He is as timid as a pup and as wet as a fish. He could no more have killed Hereward than he could have built the abbey at Elyg with his bare hands. In any case, what was he doing with you?'

'The Breton lies,' Atselin put in. He turned to face the king, whose smile had vanished. 'He seeks to take advantage of your beneficence, and in doing so to mock you, lord.'

'It is the truth,' I insisted.

'So you are always saying,' he retorted. 'But I have it otherwise. I heard tell that it was a bowman by the name of Hamo who struck the killing blow.'

'Hamo?' I asked.

'He was there also, was he not?'

'Yes, but he wasn't the one—'

'And what proof do you have that this boy was?' Atselin asked. He turned to the king. 'Lord, why do you persist in entertaining such nonsense?'

'Peace, Atselin.' The king held up a hand against the monk's protests. 'I would know what young Godric himself has to say, if anything.'

The boy hesitated, and I saw the lump in his throat as he swallowed. It was as if nothing had changed, as if we were back in

Robert's hall at Brandune, when he had first submitted to the king's questions.

'Well?'

'Yes,' Godric said, lifting his eyes to meet his king's, having at last discovered some courage within himself. 'It is true.' He took a pace forward and raised his voice for all in the yard to hear. 'I killed Hereward. His blood is upon my sword-edge, and if anyone wishes to deny it, I will fight him in order to prove it.'

Silence fell. The king's retainers glanced uncertainly at each other. Morcar, red-faced with embarrassment, glared at his nephew as if he had taken leave of his senses.

A hard expression had fixed itself upon the king's face. For long moments he met Godric's gaze. I feared that he was about to order him to be taken away, when suddenly his expression softened, and then he was laughing and grinning and shaking his head all at once. He strode forward, spread his arms wide, and embraced Godric, much to the Englishman's confusion.

'Your nephew might not be much of a swordsman, but at least he has wit, and for that he has my respect,' he told Morcar, beaming with delight.

His new Earl of Northumbria forced a smile, but his eyes betrayed the fact that inside he was seething.

'Wherever Hereward is hiding,' the king announced for all to hear, 'we will not stop searching until we find him. His acts of violence will not go unpunished.'

I couldn't believe what I was hearing. 'What use is there in searching for someone already dead?' I blurted before I thought better of it. 'We saw Hereward's lifeblood seeping away from his corpse into the marsh. We can take you to the place where he was slain.'

The king's smile faded as he turned towards me. 'I am a patient man, Tancred of Earnford, but even my patience has its limits,' he said sternly. 'You and your friends have had your amusement, but you would be wise not to test me further.'

I couldn't believe what I was hearing. After everything, was this all the acknowledgement we were to receive? There were a hundred things I wanted to say then, and none of them wise. 'Yes, lord king,' I answered stiffly.

'Very well,' he said, and then marched towards the gatehouse, where his mount and those of his hearth-knights were being held. Atselin, smirking, was close behind him, and Morcar followed, looking relieved not to have incurred the king's wrath following his nephew's outburst.

Godric alone remained, blinking as if he were not quite sure what had happened.

'Godric!' Morcar called when he was halfway to the gatehouse. 'Are you going to stand there all day, or are you coming with me?'

The boy regarded his uncle without saying anything, his lips set firm. Long moments passed before finally he turned his back.

'Where are you going?' Morcar asked. 'The king wants me to accompany him back to Elyg.'

'Then go,' Godric said. 'But you go without me. I am not your nephew any more.'

'What?'

'I've suffered your insults long enough,' Godric said, and spat in his uncle's direction. 'You are dead to me. Do you hear me, Morcar?'

'You ingrate!' Morcar shot back as he watched his nephew stalk away from him. His cheeks were flushed red. 'What about all the years I spent raising you? Do they count for nothing? I was the one who took you in when your father died, or don't you remember that? I clothed you and fed you, gave you a stipend from my own treasure chests! I armed you and gave you lands of your own so that you could call yourself a thegn. If you go, those lands are forfeit, and you'll never again get a single penny from me. Are you listening?'

I thought Godric might hesitate, but he didn't. Instead he kept on walking, his jaw set firm, his eyes fixed straight ahead, ignoring the rebukes hurled after him by his uncle.

'That was a brave thing to do,' I told him when he reached us. 'Not easy, either.'

He shrugged. 'It was easy enough. You spoke up for me when my uncle would not. For that I thank you, lord, even if it came to nothing.'

'You saved my life,' I reminded him. 'I should be the one thanking you.'

He smiled weakly. 'I told you no one would believe me, didn't I?'

'You were right about that.' I glanced towards the gatehouse, where Morcar, now mounted, continued to stare in our direction, no doubt shaken as well as a little perplexed by his nephew's disloyalty, until at last he turned and spurred his horse on.

Godric watched him go. His expression was stony, and I saw in the way that he held his chin high a resolve that had not been apparent until then. He had chosen his course, and he would not be swayed from it.

Thus we made ready to leave Alrehetha. I confess a strange mixture of feelings filled my heart. For the first time since we crossed the Narrow Sea that fateful autumn in the year one thousand and sixty-six, our enemies were all quelled. The risings and disturbances that for so long had plagued the kingdom had been put down and the rebels captured, killed or put to flight. England, at long last, was ours. I could scarcely believe it.

Yet Malet's passing soured it all. He had lived long enough to know of our triumph over the rebels, but not to savour the fruits of that triumph. He had striven so hard to govern justly, to serve his king and support him in every endeavour since the invasion, and his reward was death. Not a glorious death in battle, either, with sword in hand at the head of the charge. For someone who had prided himself as a war leader, who had once ranked among the kingdom's leading men, it seemed a wretched way to end one's life.

We were striking camp when I heard someone calling my name. I looked up to see a man on horseback being pointed in the direction of our still smouldering campfires.

'Tancred a Dinant?' he called as he approached. 'Lord of Earnford?'

'So they call me,' I replied, observing the newcomer closely. His face was lined with the scars of battle, and his eyes were hard.

'One of the prisoners from the battle has been asking to speak with you,' he said. 'I've spent all morning trying to find you.'

'Then you can't have been looking very hard,' I snapped, and regretted it straightaway. I had nothing against this man, but I was in a strange mood, and the words had left my tongue before I even had time to think.

Thankfully he paid my retort no attention. 'Come with me,' he said, and turned. That was when I noticed his scarlet cloak, embroidered at the hem with golden thread, and saw the lion of Normandy on his pennon, and understood that he was one of the royal guardsmen.

I followed him across the camp to one of the large tents close to the king's pavilion. He pulled the flap aside and gestured for me to go first.

Inside, sitting upon a stool with her hands bound behind her, sat a girl of around fifteen with dirty, straggling hair and eyes as blue as the sky at midday. She glanced up sullenly as we entered, a scowl upon her face.

'This is the one,' the guardsman said.

'Her?' I asked.

'You don't know her? She seemed to know who you were.'

'I've never seen her before.'

'I was wondering if she might have been a lover of yours, although it would be a brave man who tried to tame her. A vicious one, she is. She sank her teeth into the forearm of the first man who came near her, and didn't stop struggling until we'd managed to tie her wrists. Even then we had to almost drag her from the field.'

'I didn't think the English allowed their women to fight.'

'She isn't English, so far as any of us can tell, though she seems to speak their tongue well enough.'

'Who is she, then?'

Her dress, though smeared with mud, was of fine wool and fastened at the shoulders with a pair of golden brooches inlaid with silver crosses. She was obviously not poor, wherever she came from.

'The wife of one of the rebel leaders killed in the battle, maybe? Who knows? If she weren't so richly dressed, and she hadn't mentioned your name, we might have left her for the men to fight over.'

I stood over her and she dragged her gaze upwards to meet mine.

Even if one ignored the bruises and grazes that decorated her cheeks, one would find it difficult to call hers a pretty face, composed as it was all of sharp angles. Still, she was generously endowed and I imagined that, if she smiled rather than scowled, she would not look unattractive.

'I'm told you wanted to speak with me,' I said in English.

'You are Tancred of Earnford?'

'I am,' I said. 'Who are you?'

'Someone with knowledge that I think you would be interested in.'

'So I've heard. How do you know my name?'

'Who hasn't heard of the great Tancred of Earnford?' she asked with more than a hint of mockery. 'Across the north men fear you, from the mead-halls of the Northumbrian thegns to the household of Eadgar Ætheling and even the court of the Scots' king, Mael Coluim. All know of your deeds and quiver at the mere mention of your name.'

'You flatter me,' I said, without sincerity. I was fairly sure that King Mael Coluim had more pressing things to worry about than me. And while it was true that nothing had been heard recently of the ætheling, I doubted very much whether fear of me had anything to do with his hiding away in the north. 'What is this knowledge you have for me, then?'

'I will tell you, but first I want something in return.'

'If I don't know what it is I'm paying for, I'm hardly going to waste my silver, am I?'

'You didn't seem to mind when you gave your coin to those so-called spies of yours last winter.'

That took me aback. 'You know about them?'

'One of them stayed a night at our hall,' she said. 'He told us all about what you'd charged him with finding out, and asked us what we knew, but mainly he was interested in bragging about how rich you'd made him.'

My blood boiled in my veins. I wondered which of my informants that had been, and resolved to break his legs if our paths ever crossed again.

'Besides,' she said, 'your silver isn't what I'm interested in. All I want is your assurance that if I pass on this knowledge to you, you will let me go free.'

'That isn't my decision to make.'

'You could ask.'

She had the arrogance of youth, this one. Her husband had clearly allowed her too much rein, and that had made her overly haughty. Nevertheless, I turned to the guardsman. 'She wants to know whether or not she'll be allowed to go free, if she tells me what I want to know.'

'She's worth nothing to us,' he answered. 'Since she won't so much as tell us her name, there's no possibility of her kin paying ransom for her. She can go into a nunnery, or take ship back to wherever it is she came from, for all I care.'

I nodded, and faced the girl, who could have understood none of our conversation since we had spoken in French. 'Whether we decide to let you go depends on what you have to tell me.'

She considered for a moment, then said, 'I know that you seek the banner that bears the dragon and axe. I know you're looking for your woman, Oswynn.'

My heart was pounding. I had never told those spies the reason why I'd wanted them to fetch this information for me. I had never told them who it was I was really searching for.

'Oswynn,' I breathed. 'She's still alive, then?'

'That I cannot say, but I know the name of the man who has her, and I know where you can find him.'

'Tell me,' I said, and took a step closer, so that I was looking down upon her.

She did not avert her gaze, or flinch at all. For one so young, she seemed very confident of herself. 'First, give me your promise.'

'You have it,' I said. 'Now tell me.'

'I want to hear you say it.'

'Don't try my patience, girl,' I said, and rested my hand upon the hilt of the knife at my waist. 'I've said that you have my promise, and I do not make oaths lightly, so speak. What's this man's name?'

She did not flinch, but merely regarded me for a moment. Without taking her eyes off me, she said: 'The man you're looking for is Jarl Haakon Thorolfsson. The word I have is that he was last seen in Dyflin.'

Haakon Thorolfsson. A Danish name, and a Danish title, too. Finally I had something more to pursue than simply the face that burnt in my memory and in my nightmares.

'You're sure?' I asked.

'As sure as anyone can be of anything. Although whether he's still there, I don't know. He moves around. I don't know where he has his hall, or even if he has one.'

Dyflin. The favoured haven of outlaws and sellswords everywhere. I'd never been there but I knew it by its ill repute. A port town, it lay across the sea to the west of Britain, a day's sail with a good wind from Ceastre, in a violent land of squabbling princelings.

'How long ago did you hear this?' I asked.

'Back in the spring. Four months ago, perhaps. I don't remember exactly. It was before we came here to Elyg, at any rate.'

Four months ago. My spirits fell. The Danes were well known for their restless spirits, which had seen them settling all across these isles of Britain and far beyond. They were always travelling, rarely staying in one place for very long but moving wherever the winds and the scent of gold took them. This Haakon could be anywhere by now.

'Why didn't you tell the man who came to your hall about him?' I asked.

'You already know why, lord. Knowledge costs and, as I said, he wasn't interested in paying. He was content enough to brag about his success and how he'd managed to cheat you. Next time, lord, you should find spies you can trust.'

That was easier said than done. There was no point in telling her that such a man used to visit my manor from time to time. His name had been Byrhtwald, and as well as a reliable bearer of news had also been a good friend for the time that I knew him. He had met his end because of me, and even after a year the guilt for his death still haunted me.

'How did you come to hear my woman's name?'

'My husband served with King Sweyn last year when he came across from Denmark. He was there at Beferlic, as was I. We crossed paths with Haakon a few times while the two armies were quartered together, although he and my husband were not exactly friends. That's how I came to meet her.'

'You've met her?'

'Only the once, lord. But I can understand why you're so eager to have her back, and why Haakon was so keen to show her off, too. She's a rare beauty. Many men would kill to have a woman like her by their side, or in their bed.'

She smiled, but it wasn't a friendly smile, and again I sensed mockery in her tone, as if, even at her young age, she knew only too well the desires of men.

'Where is this husband of yours now?' I asked, feeling the need to change the subject suddenly. I didn't like the thought of this girl speaking so of my Oswynn, when she hardly even knew her.

'Dead, I suppose,' she replied. 'The last I saw of him was yesterday morning, when he went to fight against your king in the battle. Since he hasn't returned yet, I'm guessing he won't be returning at all.'

Clearly there had been little love in that marriage. What their story was, I could only guess. At that moment, however, I had more pressing concerns.

'Tell me more about this Haakon,' I said. 'Did he also serve Sweyn?'

'No, he was sworn to the ætheling.'

'Was?'

'He isn't any more.'

'What do you mean?'

'They met at the court of King Mael Coluim three winters ago. He supported both Eadgar's rebellions, but there was some disagreement between him and the ætheling after the failure of last year's campaign. He took his leave by ship shortly afterwards. We didn't hear of him after that, until a passing trader happened to mention him, and that's how we learnt he was in Dyflin.'

I was beginning to form an opinion of this Haakon. Like many

Danes, he probably made his living by selling his sword and his loyalty to anyone who would offer him sufficient reward. When Eadgar's efforts to wrest the crown of England from King Guillaume had ended in humiliation, he must have decided he would do better searching for employment or riches elsewhere.

I only hoped I could catch up with him. Eudo might be right, I thought, and Oswynn could be many hundreds of leagues from here, but at least now I had a trail to follow, and a place to begin my search.

'How would you like to go to Dyflin?' I asked the girl.

At once the defiance drained from her face. She paled and cast her gaze down. 'I've been there before,' she said. 'I have no wish to go back.'

'Why not?' I asked, but she didn't answer. 'You've met Jarl Haakon before. Your knowledge could be useful to me. You could help me find him. And if you know the city, then all the better.'

'All I want is to find passage back home, to my kin, if they still live,' she said. 'I've given you what you asked for. Isn't that enough?'

'You can either come with me, or else I can leave you here to the mercy of the king's men. It is your choice.'

'You promised, lord! You said I'd be allowed to go free!'

'And you will,' I said mildly, 'after you've helped me. Then I'll take you wherever you wish, but not before.'

A glimmer of hope appeared in her eyes. 'You'll take me home?'

That had been a rash thing to say, in hindsight. But if it would convince her, then perhaps it was worth it.

'Not straightaway,' I said. 'First we go where I say. But as soon as my business is finished, I'll do what I can. You have my oath.'

She did not look at me for a long while, and I thought she might still refuse. What reason, after all, did she have to trust me?

Eventually she gave a sigh. 'Very well.'

'Good,' I said, and smiled, but she did not return it. 'One last thing. What do I call you?'

'Eithne.'

It sounded like no name I had ever heard. It was neither French nor Breton, nor, from what I could tell, Danish or English.

'Eithne?' I repeated, and she nodded.

I called to the guardsman, who was sitting on an ironbound chest with his back to me, polishing his helmet with an oilcloth.

'I'll take her with me now, with your permission,' I said.

'You're welcome to her,' he said. 'Just watch that she doesn't gouge out your eyes, or slide a knife between your ribs while you're not watching her.'

'Have no fear for my sake,' I said, and jerked my head in Eithne's direction as a signal that she should follow me. The scowl was once again upon her face as she rose from her stool. I gave a nod of thanks to the guardsman as we left the tent and emerged into the sunshine.

A new sense of purpose filled me. At last I knew what it was I had to do, and where I needed to go. To the city across the sea, that ill-famed den of villainy and treachery.

To Dyflin.

Fifteen

Five days later, Malet was laid to rest beneath the chancel arch in the small stone church at Heia, with all the ceremony befitting a lord of his standing. Rushlights lit the nave and candles stood upon the altar, while a thurifer spread incense to mask the smell and also remind those gathered of the ever-presence of the Holy Spirit. Prayers were said and hymns sung as Malet's body, embalmed with cinnamon and salt, clad in a fine crimson tunic and shrouded in plain black cloth, was carried in upon a bier by Robert and five of his household knights, all dressed in white, one of the traditional mourning colours. The coffin was lowered into the hollow space beneath the stone floor, Mass was said, and afterwards alms were distributed to the men and women who worked Heia's lands, while the church's bell rang for nearly an hour, so that long after the procession had left and made its way across the crumbling stone bridge, beneath the browning leaves of the orchard and up the winding path that led to the castle, we could still hear its plangent notes sounding out across the manor.

I was in the training yard with Pons and Serlo, teaching Godric some simple thrusts and parries, and how and where to move in order to outflank an opponent in single combat, when Robert called me to see him. I found him in his solar, on the up-floor of the hall in the castle, kneeling in prayer in front of the slit of scraped horn that served as a window. Ashes smouldered in the stone hearth, candles stood in the corners of the room, and tapestries covered the walls, though they weren't enough to keep out the draughts. He was still dressed in the same white tunic and breeches, which was strange to see, given his fondness for black clothing. He looked up as the wan light of late afternoon flooded in, and rose to greet me. His eyes were red from weeping, or tiredness, or a combination of the two, and he looked suddenly much older than his twenty-eight years.

'It was as my father would have wished it,' he said.

'I'm glad, lord.'

'As am I,' he said. 'Glad, that is, that you had the chance to speak with him before he passed away.'

'I'm not sure that your mother was so pleased. Nor the priest, for that matter.'

'Dudo has been his most devoted servant these past couple of years. All he wanted was to ensure that my father suffered as little as possible in his final hours. As for my mother' – Robert gave a deep sigh – 'she still holds to the belief that you betrayed his faith in you during the business with Ælfwold, as you know. For that she will not forgive you.'

I stiffened. All that was more than two years in the past. How was it that talk of such things continued to plague me, after so long?

'Do you hold to the same belief, lord?' I asked.

'Of course not,' he said. 'And if my father ever truly believed that you'd wronged him, don't you think he might have discouraged me from accepting you as my man?'

'You tell me.'

'Not once. At heart he knew that you did the right thing, hard though that was for him to admit openly. I think in truth he always appreciated what you and your companions did for him.'

I wasn't entirely convinced by that, remembering all too clearly the venom with which he had spoken to me but a couple of weeks ago. The memory of that still stung, despite the kindness he'd shown on his deathbed. He would not be the first to have felt a desire for reconciliation once he realised his time was short.

'In any case,' Robert went on, 'what has passed, has passed. Regardless of what once happened between you and my father, and regardless of whether or not he recognised your good service, you have more than proven your worth to me. That is all that matters in my eyes.'

'Yes, lord.'

He looked troubled for a moment, but I did not press him. A draught blew in and caused the candles on the altar to gutter, and one of them to go out. There was a chill to the air, and a dampness too. Truly summer had departed.

Using a taper, Robert relit the candle that had been extinguished. 'I realise that I am already in your debt, Tancred. Yet there is something more that I would ask of you.'

'What might that be?'

'I have received a message from the king. There is trouble in Flanders.'

'Trouble?'

'As you'll no doubt have heard, the rightful heir to the province was killed in an ambush earlier this year at Cassel. The new count, who has no love for Normandy, is said to be gathering his barons to his banner in readiness for a campaign.'

I knew very well about what had taken place at Cassel. Guillaume fitz Osbern, one of the king's closest and longest-serving companions and advisers, and by most people's reckoning the second most powerful man in England, had been sent across the Narrow Sea at the behest of Queen Mathilda, the king's wife, to aid the young heir, a relation of hers by the name of Arnulf, in his struggles against his enemies. He had been at the boy's side when the attack came, and he met his end there too, which was hardly surprising given that he'd seen fit to take with him a mere ten of his household knights for protection. I couldn't say that I was altogether sad to hear of his demise, as embarrassing a fate as it was for one so formidable. I had met him on more than one occasion and felt him to be among the most arrogant of men, with an exaggerated sense of his own importance that perhaps stemmed from his many years of friendship with the king.

'A campaign against Normandy?' I asked. 'At this time of year? The leaves are already falling. In a couple more months it will be winter. What does the Flemish count think he can possibly achieve in so short a space of time?'

'I don't know. Nevertheless he presents enough of a threat that the king has felt the need to act. He is determined to strike against the Flemings before they have a chance to do the same to us. He wishes to remind them of their place, and to avenge Fitz Osbern's death.'

'Why should that be of any concern to us?' I asked, though I was starting to suspect what the answer would be, and didn't like it. 'That is the king's business, surely, not ours.'

'He plans to sail as soon as possible, and has requested that I join him. I have sent a letter to him this afternoon with affirmation of my intention to do so.'

'We've just spent close to three months in the field,' I said. 'You have fulfilled your duties to him, and more besides.'

'Would that were so. But there is the small matter of the relief that I owe him, if I am to succeed to my father's barony.'

'I thought that had already been agreed, lord, when he came to pay his respects.'

'It has,' he said. 'And, given the emptiness of our house's treasury, and in recognition of the good service I have given him so far this year, the king has generously agreed to waive the requirement for a monetary payment, or renders in kind, if I will join him on this latest campaign.'

'Lord, the outlay required for yet another expedition—'

'Will still be lower than the cost of paying the relief,' he finished for me. 'I have considered this carefully, and weighed up the various expenses involved, and this is the conclusion I have reached. But the cost is not my only reason for doing this.' He took a deep breath. 'If I am to forge my own reputation and build upon the foundations that my father has laid, then I must continue to make every effort to win the king's favour. And I cannot spend all autumn and winter in mourning. My father would not have wanted that.'

I knew then what it was he wished to ask of me. As usual, though, he refused to come out with it and tell me frankly. Instead he always sought to explain everything first, as if he'd already guessed what my response would be and felt the need to try to persuade me.

'You want me to go with you,' I said. 'That's what you've called me here for, isn't it?'

'I have need of your sword, Tancred.'

It was as I'd thought. Hardly had we had the chance to rinse the bloodstains from our mail and our blades than another foe reared his head. Except that the most the Flemish count probably had in mind was stealing a few herd of cattle and burning some storehouses, before retreating to his own lands just as the first snow began to fall: a quick victory to win renown and support from his nobles and to cement his rule. Such raids happened all the time, even when our realm and his were supposedly at peace with one another. They hardly warranted our attention. Moreover, King Guillaume had left his half-brother, Bishop Odo, and his eldest son, another Robert, to govern and defend Normandy in his absence. If there was any fighting to be done to fend off the incursions of the Flemings, they would surely see to it as vigorously as the king himself would. In short, I could think of no reason for us to go.

'No,' I said.

Robert stared at me. 'No?'

'I'm going to Dyflin,' I said.

'Dyflin?' he echoed, with a look on his face as if I'd just told him the sky was green, and the grass pink. 'Of all the places in Christendom, why do you want to go there?'

I'd never told him about Oswynn – there had never been any reason to – and I wasn't about to try to explain now. In all the time I'd known him, he had shown little interest in concerns of the heart, and whilst I didn't doubt he had his share of mistresses, he never spoke of them to me. He wouldn't understand.

'I have my reasons,' I said simply.

'You have your oath to me to consider.'

'Have I not already given you my service, lord?' In return for the lands he had granted me at Earnford, I was obliged to follow him on campaign for forty days each year. I didn't know how long exactly we had spent in the marsh country besieging the Isle, but it was probably closer to twice that. 'Have I not done enough?'

'You have done a great deal for me, and you should know that I am grateful for your loyalty, I truly am. As soon as our foes are defeated, I promise that I will repay you most handsomely. The king will grant me lands in return for aiding him in his victories, and by the time we are back here for the Christmas feast, I will have riches aplenty to bestow. Gold, silver, horses, land. Whatever it is you seek, I will be able to give you. You have my word. I ask only for your patience.'

I could hardly look at him then as I shook my head, disbelieving. He had said that to me before. But Christmas was two and a half months hence. How patient did he expect me to be?

In any case, it would take more than a few chests of coin or precious jewels to convince me that it was worth abandoning my pursuit of Oswynn to spend almost a quarter of the year following the king on yet another of his expeditions. Another two and a half months and I might never find her again. Even now it might be too late.

'Would that we could linger by our hearth-fires and regale others with the tales of our hard-won success,' Robert said in a tone that was no doubt intended to soothe, but which did anything but. 'In time we will have that chance, I promise. But not yet.'

I clenched my teeth to curb my tongue, feeling my ire rising. 'Lord, I cannot.'

'One more campaign before the year is out,' Robert said. 'That is all I ask.'

'And after the Flemings, who will it be next?' I countered, almost spitting the words. 'The Scots, perhaps, or else the French king?'

If Robert wanted to go to such lengths to worm his way into King Guillaume's confidence, then that was his choice. He hardly needed my help in that, and he was mistaken if he thought I would follow him blindly wherever he chose to go, like some dutiful puppy. I was sworn to Robert, trusted him and counted him among my friends, but that did not mean I had to obey his every whim.

'God's teeth, it's hardly as if I'm asking—'

I'd heard enough. 'I have given you my answer,' I said before he could finish. 'And the answer is no.'

I turned and marched towards the door.

'Tancred,' he called after me. 'Tancred!'

I did not stop or so much as look back, but ignored him as I threw the door open and strode away along the passage and down the stairs, out into the yard, my mood as black as the gathering clouds.

Robert did not come after me, nor had I expected him to, but nevertheless I took pains to avoid him the rest of that afternoon. I needed some time alone while I tried to tease out the various skeins of thought that had become tangled in my mind.

As soon as the showers had passed, I went where I thought no one would think to look for me, to a place by the edge of the orchards that I remembered from my previous visit here, at Easter when Robert had welcomed all his vassals to a great outdoor feast beneath the blossoming branches. I sat on the rain-soaked ground, beneath the yellowing leaves of a gnarled pear tree, drew out my whetstone and ran it up the edge of my knife, as I often did when I wanted to clear my mind, pausing occasionally to gaze out across Heia. For all that I had grown to love Earnford's green pastures and golden wheatfields, its woods and its ploughlands nestled in the steep river valley, this was far grander, a place of true beauty, and I could easily see how one might grow comfortable here.

The castle, a fine building of timber and dressed stone, stood on a hill in the triangle of land where two rivers met, commanding the crossing-places. Around it in every direction, bounded by the ancient trackway to the west and the woods to the east, lay broad expanses of hay-meadows and common lands where the villagers grazed their sheep and their goats, with cottages and vegetable gardens, barns and pig-pens and crofts dotted in between. A mill-wheel turned lazily in the distance; there was another further upstream that we had seen as we rode in. In spring, when I had last been here, it had seemed a place of wonder, with the winding river sparkling in the sun's light and green barley-shoots bursting forth from the earth. In autumn, however, it was even more enchanting. The evening mist clung thickly to the land, forming a white ocean out of which the castle alone rose proud, its tower and encircling stockade standing sentinel across that wide land, under skies as clear and pale as they were vast.

All was quiet, save for the tumbling of water over the fish-weirs and the lowing of cattle and the flapping and honking of a skein of geese as they rose from the water-meadows, taking up arrowhead formation as they flew towards the setting sun.

West, I noted. Not south, to Normandy and Flanders, but west, to Dyflin.

The churchmen and scholars who studied the holy texts all shared the opinion that any attempt to divine the future was sacrilege, whether it involved studying the flights of birds, or examining entrails, or scattering runesticks as the Danes were known to do. God's design, as complex as it was mysterious, could not be determined by such crude methods, they said, and I was inclined to agree. I didn't believe in portents, although if I did, those geese were probably the clearest sign I was likely to receive.

'Here you are,' came a voice from behind me. 'I've been looking for you.'

Surprised, I fumbled the whetstone as, instinctively, my other hand clutched tight at the knife-hilt, and somehow in it all I managed to nick my finger, which began streaming with blood. Cursing at the pain, I shoved it in my mouth and began to suck hard, at the same time glancing up to see who this newcomer was.

It was Beatrice.

'I didn't mean to startle you,' she said. 'Is it bad?'

'I'll live, I suppose,' I muttered. 'I've suffered worse injuries in my time.'

She smiled at that. When first we met she had not much liked me, I remembered, and it was a while before I ever saw such warmth from her. She sat down on the damp ground beside me, amidst the leaves and the windfalls. She wasn't wearing a cloak, and I wondered that she wasn't cold.

'Your brother sent you, didn't he?' I asked.

'Why do you think that?'

'He means to convince me to join him on this expedition to Flanders.'

'He tells me you have it in your head to go to Dyflin.'

That was neither a confirmation nor a denial, although, I thought, if he had told her that much, it meant that at least he had been listening.

'Where's your husband?' I asked. 'Isn't he concerned about you seeking out the company of strange men?'

She gave me a wry look. 'He went hawking in the woods with some of my father's other vassals. He's a keen falconer. Robert lent him his swiftest bird, Ligetsleht. He said they wouldn't be back until dusk.'

'All the same,' I said, teasing her, 'if he hears that you've been arranging secret meetings in the orchard while he's away, he won't be pleased.'

Guillaume d'Archis, for I'd learnt that was his name, seemed a humourless sort, although perhaps that was unfair, given that I had only met him properly for the first time that morning, after the funeral. To my mind he was rather cold, not easily approachable, and taciturn, too, with hard eyes that betrayed no feeling. Not the sort of husband I imagined being well suited to Beatrice, who was warm in heart and gentle in spirit.

Was there a touch of jealousy there? Perhaps, but only because it had been so long since I myself had last felt a woman's touch. Whatever feelings Beatrice and I might once have shared, they were long buried.

'My being here isn't any secret,' she said. 'Robert asked if I would come and speak with you.'

There, finally, was my answer. 'You mean he asked you to talk some sense into me.'

'That's not why I came, though.'

'Then why?'

Beatrice picked up one of the dappled pears that lay beside her, looked it over for signs of worms before, satisfied, she took a bite out of it. 'If Robert wants to follow the king on another expedition, that's his business, and his alone. He doesn't need you to always be there to defend him from the evils of the world.'

But what if he did? I remembered only too well what had

happened to Fitz Osbern. Robert was a competent swordsman, but no more than that, and at times he could be, in his own way, every bit as reckless and headstrong as myself. If I and Eudo and Wace and all his other vassals allowed him to venture across the sea alone, with only a contingent of his hearth-troops for accompanying him, what was to say that he wouldn't suffer the same fate?

'Before I ever gave my oath to your brother,' I said, 'you made me pledge myself to his protection. I still remember that promise, even if you've forgotten.'

'I remember,' she said quietly. No doubt she remembered the kiss we'd shared then, too. 'But Robert is a better knight now than he was then; older and wiser, too. He can take care of himself.'

'I hope you're right. For his sake.'

'Why do you want to go to Dyflin, in any case?'

I inhaled deeply. Until now, I had kept everything Eithne had told me to myself.

'Oswynn,' I said simply.

'Oswynn?' Beatrice repeated, frowning. 'Your woman? I don't understand. I thought—'

She didn't say it, but I knew what she meant.

'So did I. But then at Beferlic last year I saw her. She was there, alive and as well as I've ever seen her, in the company of one of the Danish jarls, who goes by the name of Haakon, or so I've recently learnt. Dyflin is where he was last seen.'

'So you mean to go after her?'

'And to bring her back.'

'What if you can't find her? What if she's no longer with this Haakon, or if he's gone so far away that you can never catch up with him?'

Such doubts had been plaguing my mind ever since my meeting with Eithne, but I didn't want to hear them from someone else's lips as well.

'I'll find her,' I said.

A magpie hopped close in front of us and nibbled for a brief moment at a fallen pear, before a crow descended, screeching, its jet-black wings outspread, and chased it off.

'What about you?' I asked. 'Are you happy? With him, I mean.'

She would not meet my eyes. 'I am content,' she said, but the set of her lips betrayed her.

'Are you sure?'

'Does it matter whether I am or not? The fate of women is not to be happy but merely to serve the wishes of our menfolk and to spit out children. My father made the arrangements earlier this year. It was hardly as if I had a voice in the matter.'

There was resentment there, clearly. 'I shouldn't have asked. I'm sorry.'

She was quiet for a moment. 'I am content,' she repeated. 'That is enough for me. Of course I wish that things were different, but if we spend our lives forever craving that which we don't and can never have, then we condemn ourselves to years of misery, and we will never find happiness.'

There was good sense in that, I supposed. Father Erchembald was forever offering me similar pieces of wisdom, and he was usually right.

'Besides,' she said, 'in another few months I will have reason to be joyful again, for I will have a new life to take care of, to hold in my arms.'

'You're with child?' I asked, surprised. It didn't show – not yet, at any rate.

'I think so,' Beatrice said. 'Don't mention it to my husband, should you see him before I do. I want him to hear it from me first.'

'You're carrying his child but you haven't told him?'

'Not yet. He'll be pleased with the news, won't he?'

From the little I'd seen of him, I reckoned it would take more than news of his impending fatherhood to please that man, but it would be unkind of me to say so.

'What husband wouldn't be?' I said instead. 'Especially if the child turns out to be a son to whom he can teach the skills for battle and the pleasures of the hunt.'

We sat in silence for a while as the mist closed in. The sun's rim was almost upon the horizon and the cold of dusk surrounded us.

'It seems to me that an oath is much like a marriage,' Beatrice mused after a while. A smile crossed her face and her golden hair glimmered in the evening light. 'I am sworn to my husband, while you're married to my brother.'

I laughed at the comparison, which had never before crossed my mind.

'It's true, though, isn't it?' she said. 'In their own way they bind us both, and prevent us from pursuing our own ambitions and desires.'

'Only if we allow them to do so,' I replied, although the words seemed hollow. For the purpose of oaths was to maintain order in the world. If men and women were free to do as they would and go wherever they pleased, all would quickly become ungovernable. Oaths help ensure that people follow the laws of the land; they offer protection and security to both parties. For just as a knight swears to defend his lord's life with his own, so the lord in return pledges to furnish him with the arms and equipment to do so, a roof to sleep beneath and a stipend by which he may live, or else with lands and their rents sufficient to support him. Or so, at least, it went in principle.

'When we first met you told me that you were married only to your sword,' Beatrice said. 'You should follow where it takes you.'

Indeed I remembered saying that, and I'd meant it too. In those weeks and months of despair after losing Oswynn and my former lord and so many of my brothers-in-arms in the ambush at Dunholm, I'd had no one to fight for, nothing to lose.

'Things are different now,' I said. 'I have responsibilities. To Robert, to my own knights, to the people of Earnford. They depend on me.'

Beatrice was silent for a while, as if lost in thought.

'Do what you think is right, not what Robert expects of you,' she said eventually. 'That is my advice. He'll respect you all the more for it; if not at first, then in time.'

I nodded, though in truth I wasn't entirely persuaded. 'You came to give me comfort on the day that we buried your father,' I said, and managed a smile. 'I should be offering you words of consolation, not the other way around.'

'We all knew his time was coming.' She spoke softly, looking down at the ground. 'He was so weak, and in such pain by the end. When he finally passed away I was as much relieved as I was saddened, because I knew then that he wouldn't have to suffer any longer, but instead would be with God. Does that sound strange?'

'Not at all.'

Beatrice nodded, and I hoped she was reassured. 'There's to be a feast tonight in his memory,' she said after a while. 'You'll come, won't you?'

'Perhaps,' I replied, although it wasn't as if I had much choice. To refuse the invitation would seem disrespectful. Despite our many differences and all the frustrations I'd felt in recent months, I still admired Robert as a lord and valued him as a friend, one of the few that it seemed I had in those days. The last thing I wanted was for that friendship to sour. Yet he could not forever ask these things of me and expect me to remain content.

Beatrice understood that. Why couldn't he understand it, too?

Sixteen

T here was feasting that night, as Beatrice had promised, and there was drinking, too. Robert ordered the fattest hog from the pens slaughtered and we roasted it on the hearth-fire in the castle's great hall, while barrels of ale and mead and wine were brought up from the cellars. Cups and horns were filled and raised in honour of Guillaume Malet and, afterwards, of his son as well, to whom all present now owed their allegiance. Cheers went up in Robert's praise, but I did not join in, instead preferring to keep to the benches along the sides of the hall, where the shadows lingered, so he was less likely to notice me, and where I could quaff my ale in peace. I watched as he greeted and embraced those who had been his father's vassals, who had come to Heia not just for the funeral and feast, but also to pay homage to their new lord and, most importantly of all, to seek confirmation of their land grants. Occasionally I glanced towards Beatrice, who sat at the high table on the dais together with her husband, her mother, the chaplain Dudo and other guests more esteemed than I. If she saw me, though, she gave no sign of it.

Eudo, ever fond of his drink, was already insensible and lay asleep on the bench beside me, snoring loudly, Wace had ventured outside for a piss, while Serlo and Pons were at the camp across the river, where most of Robert's vassals and their retinues would be sleeping tonight. All of which meant that, not for the first time of late, I found myself on my own, with only my thoughts for company.

Elsewhere men were shouting and hollering out bawdy songs that I recognised by the tunes if not by the words, which were almost indistinct. One of Robert's younger hearth-knights had climbed on to a long trestle table from where he proceeded to declaim his undying love for his sword-brothers. Some were holding contests to see who could drain a pitcher of wine the fastest, who could be spun around the most times in a circle without falling over, who could drink the most before emptying the contents of his stomach. Mice scurried along the roof-beams and in the shadows under the tables and stools, in search of crumbs of bread and cheese and anything else that had fallen amidst the rushes, and men were flinging chicken bones at them, seeing who could come closest to striking one. A few had brought dogs with them, which roamed the hall, eating scraps thrown to them, barking at one another and occasionally yelping when someone trod on a paw or tripped over them.

And then, above the singing and the yelling and the belching and the thumping of fists upon tables and the clatter of wooden wine-jugs and the sounds of someone spewing in the corner, I made out what sounded like Godric's voice.

'It's the truth,' he was saying loudly. 'I'm telling you I killed him!'

I spotted him then, in the shadows on the other side of the hall. The lad was being pressed up against one of the timber posts that supported the roof. Surrounding him were three heavyset men I didn't recognise, and one I did: Guibert, the rotund, ruddy-faced one who had spoken out against Lord Robert and the king that day at Brandune.

Sensing trouble, I rose and barged my way through the ale-stinking throng towards them.

'You expect us to believe that a runt like you managed to kill the feared Hereward?' Guibert asked. He glanced around at his companions and gave a laugh, but there was a hollowness to it that betrayed his lack of humour, and I knew then that this was no jest.

'I swear it,' Godric protested, but that was all he had a chance to utter before the other man grabbed his collar and forced his head back against the post.

'You're a liar,' he said, leaning closer to the Englishman. 'Do you know what I do to men who lie to me?'

'Leave him alone, Guibert,' someone shouted, even as others

were calling for a fight. 'He's had a little too much to drink, that's all. He doesn't know what he's saying.'

'Is that so?' Guibert asked. He eyed Godric closely, but the boy was too afraid to speak, and could only stare back at the Frenchman, blinking with the vacant expression of a drunkard. 'How much have you had?'

'Enough to loosen his tongue.' I pushed my way to the front of the crowd that was forming around them. 'Not enough that he'd be so stupid as to start a fight with you. Now, let's put an end to this before someone gets hurt. The Englishman's worth nothing to you.'

He let go of Godric's collar and turned to face me. 'And he is to you, Breton?'

'He's under my protection.'

'In that case perhaps you need to teach him some discretion. He'll do himself no favours by spouting lies everywhere he goes.'

'I'm not lying,' Godric blurted, and inwardly I cursed him for not keeping his mouth shut. 'Lord Tancred was there. He knows. Ask him!'

The lad hadn't moved. Indeed he had nowhere to go, surrounded as he was by Guibert's friends, whose gazes were all now on me. Everywhere but in our corner of the hall, the revelries went on.

Guibert snorted. 'You'll vouch for him?'

I shrugged. 'What does it matter whether he's telling the truth or not? Either way, he's not worth bothering with.'

He narrowed his eyes. 'How so?'

'Think about it this way,' I said. 'If he's as harmless as you think he is, then you have nothing to fear from him and can leave him be. But if he's telling the truth and Hereward did indeed die at his hands, maybe you should think again before you provoke him.'

I let Guibert puzzle over that for a few moments. If Godric was a little the worse for wear, the Frenchman was several wine-cups further down the road towards drunkenness. I could almost see the thoughts working their way through his head.

He paced unsteadily towards me. 'I say he lies,' he hissed. 'What do you say?'

Probably the sensible thing would have been to agree with Guibert and thus settle the matter there and then. But I wasn't thinking about what was sensible. No, I was thinking that I'd made a promise to the boy, and if I allowed him to come to harm then I would have broken that promise. What was more, the longer I looked upon Guibert's ugly, pox-scarred face and the longer his ale-reeking breath filled my nose, the less I was inclined to back down. If anyone were to yield, it should be him, not me.

'I say Godric speaks the truth.'

He stared at me, as if he couldn't understand why I should lend my support to such a ridiculous tale.

'I was there,' I said. 'With my own eyes I saw him strike Hereward down. So unless you want to fight me to deny it, I suggest you find a stool and sit yourself back down.'

His expression hardened. His already ruddy cheeks turned a deeper shade of scarlet. 'Are you mocking me, Breton?'

I was fast losing patience. 'Mocking you? Why would I mock you?' I drew myself up to my full height and then, speaking slowly to make sure he didn't misunderstand me, said: 'I have no quarrel with you, Guibert, and neither does the Englishman, so why don't you and your friends go and find someone else to bother, and leave us both to enjoy our wine in peace?'

I should have known better than to patronise him. No sooner were the words out of my mouth than Guibert was hurling himself at me, howling in rage, his yellow teeth bared. He might have been drunk but he was also strong, and I wasn't ready for such an attack. He threw me backwards across one of the long tables, sending wooden plates and clay pitchers and candles clattering to the floor. Around us people were shouting, cursing, and Guibert was screaming in my face and showering me with his spittle as he leant over me, his hands gripping my shoulders, pinning me down.

'Nobody mocks me,' he barked. 'You hear me? Nobody!'

Gritting my teeth, I swung my fist at his face and managed to connect with his cheekbone. It was hardly a solid blow, but it was enough to make him let go of me as, reeling, he took a step back. That was all the space I needed. I barrelled into his midriff, hoping to bring him to the floor, but he was more stoutly built than I, and quickly recovered his balance, throwing me off him and towards the open space in front of the hearth. The rushes were sodden with spilt wine and mud; my feet found little purchase, and I found myself sprawling forward, barely managing to keep my balance. Men cleared a space around us, cheering, clapping, jeering, chanting.

I turned in time to see Guibert draw a knife and rush towards me. By tradition it was forbidden to carry swords and other weapons into a feasting-hall, but knives were allowed since without them one would struggle to eat. He attempted a stab, but the move was ill timed and I was able to step to one side, at the same time grabbing hold of his arm and twisting sharply. He yelped in pain, dropping the blade, and I shoved him hard, sending him stumbling sideways.

'Enough of this!' someone yelled, and it sounded like Lord Robert, but the cry came from behind me and so I couldn't be sure. 'Guibert! Tancred!'

Guibert came at me again, this time snatching up a brass candlestick that had fallen on the floor. He swung it like a club at my face, screaming through clenched teeth, and I tried to duck, but the wine had slowed my movements. Searing pain blossomed inside my skull as it struck a glancing blow across the back of my head.

For an instant there was nothing but blackness. Numbly, I felt myself stagger forward. Exactly what happened next I struggle to recall, but my feet must have gone out from under me, since when my sight returned I found myself on my knees, clinging to the edge of one of the long tables as if for support, with white stars dancing in my eyes. I blinked to make them go away, but they would not. The hall was ringing all at once with laughter and shouts of alarm.

'Stop!' the same man shouted, and this time I was sure it was Robert. 'Stop this madness!'

A wordless roar came from behind. My own blade I'd left where I'd been sitting, but a long carving-knife lay on the table. I seized it in clumsy, unfeeling fingers, trying to ignore the throbbing in my skull as I turned—

Shapes and colours swam before my eyes, but through the stars and the haze I saw Guibert's eyes and the drunken hatred that lay behind them. I saw the gleaming brass of the candlestick, raised high, poised to be brought down upon my face. And I saw the opening I needed.

There was no time to consider whether what I was doing was right or wrong. It was my life or his. That was the only thought running through my mind. I lunged forward, gritting my teeth and concentrating all my strength in my weapon-hand, trusting to God that I wouldn't miss, that the steel would strike home.

It did.

The blade found Guibert's belly and I plunged it deep, through cloth and skin and flesh, until I felt it scrape against bone. Blood bubbled forth and a stifled cry escaped his lips, and I drove it deeper and deeper and deeper still, yelling my anger and my triumph. The candlestick slipped from his limp fingers, and he stumbled backwards. I let go of the sticky, crimson-covered handle, leaving it lodged there in his gut.

Breathless, I clutched at the back of my skull, rubbing the place where he had struck me. There was no blood but already it felt as if a lump were forming there. My legs felt weak, as if they didn't quite belong to me, while my head seemed to be on fire.

No longer were men cheering, clapping, jeering, or chanting. I heard the sound of my breathing, and I heard a crash as Guibert met the floor, but that was all. No one moved. No one spoke. Silence reigned for what could only have been a moment, but so vivid is my memory of that moment that it feels as though it lasted an hour.

Blinking to try to clear my sight, I gazed down at Guibert's still form and saw his blood trickling away, staining the rushes and pooling by his side, soaking the front of his tunic. Men rushed to his side, vainly calling his name.

Only then did I realise what I had done.

All at once the warmth seemed to flee my body. My throat felt tight, as if I could hardly breathe. Bile churned in my stomach and I wanted to heave, but somehow I managed to resist the temptation and hold myself back.

And then the silence was broken, and the shrieking began. It was a woman's shriek, shrill and piercing, and it came from the dais at the far end of the hall.

'Murderer!'

I looked up from where Guibert lay and saw that it was Elise.

'Murderer!' she screamed as she pointed at me, her cheeks flushed with fury.

All eyes were upon me. I expected at any moment to be set upon and brought to the floor, but no one moved. Perhaps they all feared shedding more blood in Robert's presence, but I think that they were simply too shocked by what they'd seen to do anything. Most were no great friends of mine, but they all knew well who I was and would have heard the tales of my deeds. They knew, too, that Robert and I were close, and that, I believe, is why they hesitated.

'Seize him!' Elise was screeching. 'Seize the murderer!'

Beside Elise on the dais stood Beatrice, her face pale, one hand raised to her mouth in alarm. She met my eyes for a heartbeat, and quickly turned away, not wishing to look upon me. Her husband was calling for one of the kitchen-boys to fetch him his sword, but like everyone else they merely stood as if frozen, waiting for instructions from their lord.

My eyes met Robert's. He stared at me with an expression that suggested he didn't know whether to be horrified, or angry, or both.

'If no one else will do it, I will,' said Guillaume d'Archis, his scabbard having finally been brought to him. Drawing his blade, he began to advance down the middle of the hall, between the tables towards me.

'No more bloodshed in my hall,' Robert shouted from the other side of the high table. 'Do you hear me? I order you to put your sword away!'

'Guillaume, no!' Beatrice said. She ran after her husband and clutched at his sword-arm, trying to slow him down, but he shook her off easily. The steel gleamed in the firelight, and I saw how keen was its edge. Weaponless as I was, I stood little chance against him. I backed away, towards the open doors.

'A blade,' I yelled at the onlookers, desperately searching for a friendly face among them. 'Someone give me a blade!'

'Lay so much as a scratch upon him and you'll have us to answer to,' Wace said as he appeared on my flank, and with him, brandishing his knife drunkenly in front of him, his eyes bleary as if he were still half-asleep, was Eudo.

'Stand back,' Guillaume said, 'or I will cut you both down as well.'

'No more violence!' Robert repeated, then turned and fixed his gaze upon me. His face was red and his hand made a fist.

'Lord, I didn't mean—'

'No,' he said, cutting me off. 'You will listen to me. You have brought dishonour upon yourself and at the same time insulted both me and my family.'

'He attacked me! What was I supposed to do?' Everyone here had seen it happen, and knew that Guibert's death was an accident. Surely Robert understood that I'd only been defending myself?

'You have spilt blood in my hall, Tancred, and at my father's funeral feast as well!'

'He would have killed me otherwise!' I shot back. 'What would you have had me do? Tell me that, lord.'

Perhaps I would have done better to keep my mouth shut, but my blood was up, and I couldn't stop myself.

'By rights you ought to be on your knees before me, begging my forgiveness,' Robert said. His eyes were hard and unfeeling. 'Instead you merely stand there as if you've done nothing wrong, as if this is all some game to you. Why is it that every time there's some quarrel taking place, I always find you in the middle of it?'

His words struck me hard, like a blow to the gut. 'Lord—' I protested.

'Leave,' he said. 'Leave, and don't return. You are my man no longer. Understand? Consider your oath to me absolved.'

'What? You can't—'

I stopped, not knowing what to say. I could barely believe my ears. What did this have to do with my oath?

'You're letting him go?' Elise screeched. 'This is no time to show mercy, Robert. He killed a man! He cannot go unpunished. He must not!'

'Go,' Robert told me, ignoring his mother's protests. I'd rarely seen him roused to anger, and certainly not like this. 'Now, before I change my mind.'

'Lord—'

'Now!'

I held his gaze for an instant. Guibert must have struck me harder than I'd realised, for I was still struggling to comprehend what was happening. Feeling at the same time numb and cold and sick, I turned on my heels and, without looking back, stalked from the hall.

No one tried to stop me. The doors lay open and I strode out into the yard, into the icy, stinging rain, through the mud and the puddles. No sooner had I gone than I heard chaos erupt in my wake. Shouts were raised, and I heard Elise still shrieking, and dogs barking, but I didn't dare glance back over my shoulder as I broke into a run.

My mind was teeming with a thousand thoughts. Foremost among them was that I needed a horse. I didn't know how long it would be before anyone came after me, if they came at all, but I wasn't prepared to wait and find out. Fyrheard was in the stables close by the main gates, in the outer bailey. I had just passed through the inner gatehouse and was heading down the hill towards the long thatched building when I heard a shout from behind.

'Lord!'

Recognising the sound of Godric's voice, I turned. 'What?'

He came running up. 'I'm coming with you,' he said.

After what had just taken place, I was surprised he dared so much as show his face in my presence. Were it not for him, I wouldn't be in this situation.

'No, you're not. But you can help me. Get word to the others. To Pons and Serlo and Eithne. Find them and tell them we need to leave straightaway. Tell them I'll meet them by the crossroads on the old Roman way.'

'But—'

'Don't argue with me.' My patience was all but spent. 'Just do it.'

He looked uncertainly at me for a moment, but then ran on, down towards the outer gates, and I hurried inside the stables. The doors were unlocked but there was no one about at this hour, and so no rushlights were lit, and I nearly slipped on the wet hay strewn across the floor as I found my way down the corridor to Fyrheard's stall.

I'd thrown the saddle on to his back and was just about to lead him out into the yard when I heard voices and feet splashing through the mud, and saw the glow of a torch flickering on the plastered walls. I tensed, thinking that Robert had given in to his mother's wishes and sent some of his men to apprehend me. They must have seen I'd left the door open.

'Tancred?' a voice called. Two figures entered, one of them holding a torch.

Wace. Eudo.

'You've done it this time, haven't you?' Wace said when he saw me. He shook his head. His eyes were hard and his mouth was drawn tight. He set the torch in a sconce on the wall.

'You know I never meant to kill him,' I said.

'Does it matter?' Eudo asked, and there was no mistaking the anger in his tone. He marched towards me and shoved me hard in the chest. 'What were you thinking?'

'Hey,' I protested, shoving him back. Drink had made him clumsy on his feet, and that small push was enough to send him tumbling to the floor.

He rose and made for me again, but before he could come near, Wace grabbed hold of his shoulder and held him back. 'There's no time for that,' he said.

Eudo swore violently. 'Of all the stupid things you could have done,' he said to me. 'Is there anything inside that head of yours?'

'Enough,' Wace said sharply. 'What's done is done. You have to get away from here, Tancred, and quickly.'

'You think I don't know that?' I asked. 'What did you think I was doing here?'

'Where will you go?'

'I don't know.' I hadn't yet thought that far ahead. 'Aren't you coming with me?'

'Come with you?' Eudo echoed angrily. 'This is your doing, not ours. If we join you, what's to stop Robert expelling us from his service as well?'

They were right, and I knew it. I cursed aloud. How had it come to this?

'We can't come with you, but we'll do what we can to sway Robert and make him reconsider,' Wace said. 'Until then you'd be wise to find someplace quiet where you can weather the storm. I wouldn't put it past Elise to send some of her friends to hunt you down. If she does, it's better that you're as far away from here as possible.'

I nodded, feeling helpless in a way that I hadn't for many years.

'Thank you,' I said.

'You should go,' said Eudo, jerking his head towards the stable door. 'Before I beat you to death myself. I have half a mind to.'

I led a reluctant Fyrheard out into the yard. From further up the hill I heard men shouting, though what was being said was impossible to make out. Dogs were barking, and it sounded as though they were getting closer. Orange lantern-light played across the stonework of the inner gatehouse, where several figures, all in shadow, suddenly appeared, a hundred paces away still but rushing in our direction, some of them with swords drawn. No doubt they'd seen the light of Wace's torch.

Not daring to delay any longer, I vaulted up into the saddle. 'We'll meet again soon,' Wace said. 'Of that you need have no doubt. For now, though—'

'I know.'

I reached down to clasp first his and then Eudo's hand, before spurring Fyrheard into a gallop, across the bailey and towards the outer gatehouse. His hooves pummelled the earth as I galloped beneath its vaulted arch, deaf to the questions of the men on sentry duty that night. I raced on, on, on, down the winding track towards the river's tumbling black waters and the old stone bridge. The rain spat down, stinging my cheeks. My hair was plastered against my skull, my tunic and trews were soaked, and there was a hollowness inside me of a kind I'd never before known.

How could this have happened? I kept asking myself. How?

Only once I was on the other side of the river did I pause to look back towards Heia, at the dark shadow on the hill that was the castle, expecting to find a horde of horsemen riding hard in pursuit. Perhaps I'd lost them in the darkness, for I saw no one, and if there were any hoofbeats to be heard, they were lost amidst the patter of raindrops on the fields and the trees around me.

I tore my eyes away, dug my heels in, and from then on I did not look back as I rode away from Heia. Away from Robert. Away from the Malets.

And a part of me wondered if it would be the last time I ever saw them.

Seventeen

Serlo, Pons and Eithne were waiting at the crossroads for me. No doubt they had heard all about what had happened from Godric, but although I felt my hearth-knights' cold stares upon me, they did not say anything, and that was probably for the best. The Englishman was there too, having decided that he was coming with me after all, and I was too tired to argue any further. We had no time to spare. Every hour that passed was another few miles that we put between us and Heia, and another few miles closer to safety.

We didn't stop until morning, and only then because we needed to give the horses a chance to rest and to eat. There were no stars that night and so in the darkness we kept to drove roads and ancient trackways, which tended to be better kept and where the footing was more assured. We rode on through the rain and the wind, until, a couple of hours after sunrise, with heavy limbs and bleary eyes, we arrived in a miserable river town by the name of Gipeswic, which I remembered had been raided by the Danes when they came last year. There was nothing much left of it now, save for the wharves and the slipways, a few warehouses and cottages that had escaped the fire, and a larger, two-storeyed hall that might have belonged to the port-reeve, but among those ramshackle buildings we managed to find an alehouse close by the river where we could stable the animals, rest our saddlesore arses, sup at the thin broth that the tavern-keeper brought us, and work out what to do next.

We sat in silence around a table close by the common room's hearth. At this hour the fire wasn't lit, but the alehouse's walls were thin, the cob crumbling away from the wattle-work, and that was the only place where the draught didn't seem to reach.

'I never thanked you, lord,' Godric said, in between mouthfuls.

'Thanked me for what?' I asked.

'For vouching for me,' Godric said. 'Again.'

Not that it had done me much good. Because of his reckless boastings and my own foolish sense of honour we now found ourselves here, cast out and wandering the bleak, flat lands of East Anglia.

'I'm sorry,' he said. 'For whatever that might be worth.'

As well he should be. I couldn't help but wonder if perhaps I'd have done better to leave him to whatever fate Guibert might have dealt him. Straightaway I castigated myself for the thought. The boy had saved my life, and for that I owed him. What else could I have done?

My head ached. I rubbed at the lump that had formed, though it did nothing to relieve the pain. Serlo lifted his bowl to his lips and drained what was left of its contents. My own was going cold in front of me. There was cabbage in it, and leek as well, and the smell of both was enough to make me wrinkle my nose, but it was the whiff of salted eel that made me want to spew. For weeks in the marshes we had lived on almost nothing but eel stew, and I was sick of it.

Serlo nodded towards it. 'Are you going to eat that?'

'It's yours if you want it,' I replied.

The big man needed no second invitation. He reached across the table, slid the bowl towards himself and began ladling it into his mouth, so quickly that some failed to reach his mouth, spilling instead down his beard and the neck of his tunic.

He paused when he saw us all looking at him. 'What?' he asked. 'I haven't eaten since last night.'

'You can have mine too,' Eithne muttered in English, scowling as usual. She pushed her own bowl towards Serlo. Like me, she had barely touched hers. 'I'm not hungry.'

'You'll eat what you're given and be glad for it,' I told the girl, and placed it back in front of her. 'I paid good silver for it, and I'm not letting you waste away. You're thin enough as it is.'

'You don't have to speak to me as if I'm a child,' she said, with that same scowl as before. 'I'm fifteen summers old.'

'So is Godric, but he's under my protection just as you are.'

'You're telling me he's the same age as me?' Eithne asked. She gazed doubtfully at Godric, looking him up and down as if appraising a horse. 'He doesn't look it.'

Insulted, Godric frowned. 'What's that supposed to mean?'

'You think yourself a warrior?' she scoffed. 'I could probably best you in a fight, if it came to it.'

'I wouldn't fight you,' said Godric.

'Why not? Because I'd win, you mean?'

'No—'

'Because you're afraid of getting hurt?'

Godric's cheeks flushed red. 'I'm not afraid.'

'Prove it, then.' Eithne rose from her stool and stood over him. 'If you're the fighter you claim to be, prove it to me.'

He glanced uncertainly at me. 'Lord?' he asked, clearly at a loss as to what to do, though what help he thought I might offer, I wasn't sure. In my time I had known many strong-willed women, none more so than Oswynn, but for all that experience, still I hadn't worked out how best to manage them, or if it were possible at all.

'Sit down,' I said, pointing at the girl. 'And eat. No one's doing any fighting today.'

My head was hurting enough as it was, and I didn't need their squabbling adding to my woes.

'What was that about?' asked Pons. He, like his sword-brother Serlo, had yet to learn much of the English tongue.

'Godric's learning his place,' I said. The old saying came to mind. Men might govern the world, but it is women who govern those men. So it had always been, and so it would continue to be.

Having finished my bowl as well as his own, Serlo leant back and gave a loud belch. 'What do we do now, then, lord?'

'I don't know,' I answered. 'If I did, don't you think we'd be doing it, instead of sitting here in this dank place?'

We had, as I saw it, two choices. The first of those was to hole up here for a few more days while tempers in the Malet household cooled, and then return to Heia with heads bowed once Robert's mood had had a chance to soften.

'How long might that take, though?' Pons asked when I suggested this. 'Even with Lords Eudo and Wace interceding on your behalf?'

'If you think about it, Robert's done you a favour,' Serlo added.

'A favour?' I echoed. 'How is this a favour?'

'How many men saw you strike Guibert down, lord?'

I shrugged. 'Fifty? Sixty? More even than that, maybe.'

'And how many of those would have been willing to swear oaths to the same effect, had Robert made you stand trial for his killing?'

I saw what the big man was getting at. While undoubtedly a few of them would argue on my behalf, most were no friends of mine and would probably take great pleasure in bringing about my demise, not least Elise.

'In your absence they'll all be clamouring for your head, lord, and not just Guibert's companions and hearth-knights, but also his kin, once news of what happened reaches them.'

Pons nodded. 'By letting you walk free, Robert has denied them justice. Unless he's willing to recompense them by paying the blood-price from his own treasure chests, he'll come under ever more pressure in the coming days to seek you out and bring you before the shire court.'

I groaned and buried my face in my palms. I'd almost come to terms with the idea of prostrating myself before Robert and begging his forgiveness, much though it grated with me. But Pons and Serlo were right. Were I to return to Heia, I would be delivering myself into the hands of those who sought to destroy me.

'I'm not saying that Lord Robert can't be won round, but it will take some time, if it happens at all,' Pons said. 'Weeks, perhaps.'

Patience had never been one of my virtues, and I wasn't prepared to stay here that long while we waited for news to arrive, even if funds would allow it. For my coin-pouch was growing lighter by the day. Altogether the stabling, lodgings and broth had cost me five of the little silver pennies – far more than it should have done, but this seemed to be the only alehouse in this mud-ridden town, and so it had been a choice between meeting the innkeeper's price or else sleeping in a ditch. I had barely a fistful of silver left, some in ingots and small pieces broken off from arm-rings, and the rest in the form of coins, although many of those had already been clipped to pay for food and horseshoes and other small items over the past few months.

Fortunately Godric had had enough wit about him to gather, as well as his own pack, the saddlebags that contained most of my belongings, including the drinking horn that Malet had gifted me, so I was not quite reduced to the clothes on my back. Not yet, at least. But in the rush to leave Heia we'd been forced to leave behind our tents and our sumpter ponies and anything else we could not gather quickly. That included my sword, which I'd left in the safekeeping of the door-ward at Robert's hall, although Godric had managed to bring my mail and helmet as well as his own, as had the others. Still, once divested of our hauberks and chausses, we didn't much look like a noble lord and his retinue but more like a band of ragged pilgrims. My clothes were torn from the fight, my trews and boots, themselves desperately in need of repair, were caked in mud and filth, while a bright bruise had blossomed high on my cheek, or so the others told me, although I had no idea how that had happened.

'In the meantime I suppose there's only one place we can go,' I said, and both Serlo and Pons nodded. I sighed. 'With any luck all this uproar will have died down by the time we get there.'

'We can but pray, lord,' said Pons.

'Where are we going?' Godric asked.

'Home,' I replied, by which, of course, I meant Earnford. We'd been away so long. The barley was still green in the fields when we'd ridden out to answer the king's summons more than three months ago. Now the harvest would be in. I yearned to be back there, to see its hills and the river winding between the wide pastures, to sleep under my own roof, in my own hall.

I only hoped that Robert's men didn't get there first.

That worry continued to plague me over the following days, as we made the long journey from East Anglia to the Marches. Assuming that Robert didn't go back on his decision to expel me from his service, then sooner or later he would come to take back possession of his lands. For the truth was that, for all that I'd come to think of Earnford as my own, I only held it as his tenant. My hall, my home, belonged by right to him. Without his lordship, I had nothing.

With that in mind we rode hard, or as hard as we could, given both the state of the roads, which were clogged with mud after the recent rains, and the poor directions offered by other travellers and field labourers whom we passed. From Gipeswic we sought out the old Roman way that led to Lundene, where the talk was of the king's victory over the rebels at Elyg and the fleet he was said to be assembling for the expedition to Flanders. We stayed the night in an inn outside the walls, so as to avoid the murage and pavage that all travellers entering the city were now required to pay. Even so, I had to argue at length with the innkeeper before he would finally agree upon a sensible price. Probably he took us for bandits or outlaws, which I supposed was fair considering our unkempt, dirt-stained clothes, our unshaven chins and the weapons we carried, and that was why at first he demanded so much, but eventually I was able to secure us beds for the night. At least the place was in slightly better repair than the inn at Gipeswic, with solid timber walls that kept out the cold and a roof that didn't leak, which meant that when we left the next morning we were a little more rested.

From Lundene we made west along the valley of the Temes as far as Oxeneford, after which we struck out along winding paths in the direction of the market town of Wirecestre, where we crossed the wide Saverna River and obtained directions to Leomynstre from a travelling monk who knew the country well. Day after day we woke at dawn and travelled until dusk, spending the nights in alehouses, in the guest houses of monasteries where they would take us, and, when there was no other shelter to be found, in abandoned cattle barns. And so it was that, on the tenth day after we had first set out from that draughty alehouse in Gipeswic, on the edge of the grey German Sea, we found ourselves, tired and cold and sodden and hungry, riding the familiar tracks that would bring us home, at last, to Earnford.

We rode through a land wrought in bronze and gold. The woodland paths were thick with leaves that rustled beneath our mounts' hooves, while beneath us through the swaying boughs I could make out the river sparkling silver in the afternoon sun, showing us the way. The skies were clear, the day bright, and I hoped that was a happy portent, though of course I didn't believe in such things.

Before long we were able to spy the turning wheel of the mill, which marked the eastern edge of my lands. Sheep grazed contentedly by the riverbanks, and a broad-shouldered man who could only be Nothmund the miller was busily hauling sacks of grain down from the back of a cart and in through the wide doors. So far there was no sign of anything amiss.

We kicked on down the slope and across the ford by the rickety wooden bridge that, with all the rebuilding elsewhere, no one had found the time to repair, towards the mill and towards Nothmund. At the sound of our hoofbeats he stopped in his tracks, letting the sack he was carrying fall to the ground as he regarded us warily, and it was only right that he did so, for it wasn't often that mounted men came to Earnford.

'Lord!' he exclaimed when we grew closer and he saw who we were, and there was both relief and joy in his voice. He shouted into the mill-house, in his own tongue: 'Gode, get out here, woman!'

His plump wife appeared at the doorway, the sleeves of her dress rolled up to her elbows, her round face creased in indignation, but her expression changed the moment that her gaze settled upon me.

'Is it you, lord?' she asked, as if she couldn't quite believe her eyes. 'Is it really you?'

'It's me, Gode,' I said, and managed a smile, though it wasn't nearly as broad as the grin upon Nothmund's face.

'It's been too long, lord,' he said as he reached up to clasp first my hand, then those of Serlo and Pons. He glanced in the direction of Godric and Eithne, who rode behind us, but if he was curious at all about them, he said nothing. Indeed he couldn't stop smiling. 'We thought you would be coming, but we didn't know when exactly it would be.'

At once I tensed. 'What do you mean?'

'Well, we didn't know for certain, but we reckoned you must be on your way here when they said—'

'Who?' I asked. 'Who said?'

'They did, lord,' he replied. 'The ones who came a few days ago, asking for you. When Galfrid told them that you had been gone these past three months, they said to keep a lookout for you, and that they would return soon.'

It was as I'd feared. News had travelled before us. Robert's messengers must have overtaken us on the road, or else taken a different route across the kingdom.

'Did they say what they wanted?' I asked, though I could readily guess.

'If they did, lord, we never heard it,' Gode put in. 'Fierce men, they were, and unpleasant, too, lacking in all manners or Christian grace. Lord knows they put the fear into poor Galfrid.'

I could think of only one reason those men might have come looking for me, and that was to drag me back to Heia.

'They didn't say when they would be back?' I asked.

Nothmund shook his head. 'They asked Galfrid if they might stay here until you returned from campaign, but he refused and eventually they were forced to go away.'

That suggested they weren't any of Robert's men, for if they had been then they wouldn't have needed even to ask. Perhaps he had sent word to the local shire-reeve or else to Roger de Montgommeri, the newly appointed Earl of Scrobbesburh, and he in turn had sent his own oathmen to pay me a visit. That would explain how they had been able to arrive before us. A lone messenger could make the journey across the kingdom far more quickly than a tired and bedraggled band of five, especially if he could change steeds and obtain provisions at friendly castles and manors along the way.

'Who were they, lord?' Gode asked. 'Were they friends of yours, do you suppose?'

'No,' I answered. 'Not friends.'

They might have been at one time, but now I wasn't so sure. I gave my thanks to Nothmund and Gode and then we left them, continuing on our way past the thicket where the pigs foraged, until the village and the church and my hall upon the mound, overlooking the river-crossing, came into sight. The Welsh had completely done for this place, as they had for many estates this side of the great dyke, when they brought their great raiding-army into England around this time last year. In some places one could still make out the fire-blackened outlines where cottages and sheds had once stood. It had taken the full year to recover from that devastation, though the manor was still not as prosperous as once it had been. Even now as we approached I could see men bending withies into wattle for walls, thatching fresh roofs on recently erected cottages, sawing timbers for the new church that was being raised on the foundation stones of the old. But there were also folk working the fields, tilling the earth with oxen and plough, sowing seed, keeping watch over the flocks of sheep, carrying pails of water from the stream to the kitchens across the yard from the hall. For the first time in many months, life in Earnford seemed to be almost restored to what it had been before. Not quite, for I hadn't forgotten how many families had lost their lives to the Welsh attack. Their loss was still keenly felt.

One of the younger lads, Brunic by name, saw us approaching along the rutted track and scurried away to fetch the steward, Galfrid, who was busy overseeing the construction of a new fish-weir a little way upstream. As soon as the lad pointed us out to him, though, he left the men to their work and strode over to meet us. He had never been a cheery sort; he was certainly not happy now.

'I see you're back, then,' he said. 'Not a day too soon, if you ask me. I thought you'd abandoned us altogether.'

'It's good to see you, too, Galfrid,' I said.

'Now that you're here, perhaps you can explain why I've had strangers knocking at our gates, demanding to see you, and threatening our folk with violence if you don't show yourself.'

It was hardly the greeting I'd been hoping for, given how long we'd been gone, although in the circumstances I wasn't wholly surprised. Were I in Galfrid's place, no doubt I'd be asking the same questions. He was responsible not just for managing my household, but also, in my absence, defending the manor against the marauders who from time to time came across the dyke from Wales. I'd first met him the previous year, after his lord had been killed and the manor where he had been steward put to the torch by Welsh raiders, which gave us more than one thing in common. He'd joined me on the campaign in the north that autumn, and afterwards I'd accepted his oath and installed him at Earnford, where I was in need of a man of his qualities, my old steward having absconded some months previously, taking with him a large portion of my silver and one of the finest stallions from my stables.

He was perhaps a little too fond of the sound of his own voice, but that was the worst that could be said about Galfrid. A more than competent swordsman, he was also a lot sharper of mind than at first people often took him for, and loyal besides, which was the most important thing.

'They threatened the village folk?' I asked him. Nothmund and Gode hadn't mentioned that.

'They reckoned you were hiding away in the hall, although why they thought that, I have no idea. I told them you were away with the king's army, but they didn't believe me. They demanded I let them in so that they could search the place, swearing they would run me through and leave my corpse for the crows if I didn't. When I continued to refuse, though, they changed their minds, saying instead that they would be back in a few days' time, with more men. They told me that if you didn't willingly give yourself up then, they would set fire to the hall and all the cottages.'

'When was this?'

'Three days ago, lord.'

'How many of them were there?'

'Half a dozen,' he replied. 'All of them armed and ready for a fight. I had some of the village lads for support, but even so, it was something close to a miracle that they went away as readily as they did.'

Whoever these men were, they had clearly hoped that intimidation would be enough to get them what they wanted. Even if Earl Roger was the one who sent them, as I half suspected, he wouldn't have wanted them to shed blood on lands that didn't belong to him, especially if that blood happened to be French. That, rather than the miracle Galfrid suggested, was probably why they had baulked at the thought of carrying out their threats, and why they had, in the end, gone away. Nevertheless, I wanted to be sure.

'Were any of Robert's knights among them? Did they come bearing the black-and-gold banner?'

'I think I'd have noticed if they had,' he said. 'Why would Robert's men be wanting you, anyway? The last I heard, you were with him fighting the rebels in the Fens.'

'I was,' I said, and gave a weary sigh as I hesitated, trying to work out how I was to explain everything that had happened.

He eyed Eithne and Godric. 'Who are they? You're not bringing in waifs and orphans, are you? The harvest was barely large enough to fill our storehouses. We'll struggle to keep ourselves fed through the winter as it is without another two hungry young mouths eating our bread and guzzling our ale.'

'Peace, Galfrid,' I assured him. 'I'll give you all my news in time, just as soon as we've stabled our horses and had something to eat. We've been on the road for ten days and we're famished.'

'Tancred!'

I turned to find Erchembald, the priest, hustling towards us, raising the hem of his robe so that it didn't trail in the mud. He was stoutly built but not fat, with hair that was greying at the temples and a youthful face that belied his years, of which he reckoned he had nearly forty behind him. I slid down from the saddle and embraced him.

'God be praised that you're here at last, and unharmed too,' he said. 'We feared some ill fate might have befallen you, or was about to. Did Galfrid tell you—?'

'He did,' I said.

'What does it all mean?' he asked, his brow furrowed. 'What business did those knights have with you, and what's happened to you? You look like someone dragged you backwards through a briar patch. Where have you been?'

I felt the weight of their questioning gazes resting upon me, and realised that this could not wait. They deserved answers, and I was the only one who could give them.

I took a deep breath, and then slowly, starting from the very beginning, I told them everything.

Eighteen

I began with the king's siege of the Isle and our assault upon Elyg. At the same time we trudged up the slope towards the new hall, which had been built in the place of the one the Welsh had torched. Somehow it felt safer to talk about everything there than in the open, and besides my throat was parched and I felt as if I hadn't eaten a proper meal in a month. We had spent the last few days on the road eating nothing but hard bread and stale cheese, and my stomach had been paining me since dawn at the thought of the hot food that would greet our arrival. While stable-hands came to see to our mounts and Galfrid sent to the kitchens for ale and sausage and some of that day's bread, I related how we had come to meet first Godric and then, after our victory over the rebels, Eithne as well, followed by the story of Guibert's killing and our flight from Heia. Once in a while Serlo or Pons or Godric would add something that had slipped my mind, but their interruptions aside, everyone was content to listen while I spoke.

After I'd finished, silence lingered. Neither the priest nor the steward seemed to know quite what to say. They sat at the round table that stood in the middle of the chamber, while I paced up and down the length of the hall, from the door to the dais and back again. My legs were aching from our travels, but at the same time my mind was burning with a thousand thoughts, and I could not keep still. So much in Earnford seemed to have changed in the few months I'd been away, or perhaps it was I who had changed. I had become an outlaw, a stranger in my own hall. This place that for so long had been my home was now a place of danger.

'What will happen now?' Erchembald asked after some time. 'What does this mean for you, and for us?'

'Robert wants to bring me to justice. That's why those men came the other day, and that's why they'll be back for me before too long.'

'Because you killed a man?' Galfrid asked, and gave a grunt that I took for a sign of his disbelief. 'You slay a dozen, twenty, a hundred and the poets praise you, but you slay one more and for that Robert wants your head?'

'This is hardly the same thing,' Erchembald pointed out.

He was right, too. 'I killed a fellow Frenchman, and in my lord's own hall. A man who was guilty of nothing, whose only crime was that he was drunk and not in possession of his wits.'

'You said that he attacked you,' Galfrid said. 'Doesn't that count for anything?'

So I had thought, too. Clearly I was wrong.

'I have enemies,' I said bitterly. 'Enemies who, for different reasons, wish to see me brought low, who would poison the bond between myself and Lord Robert, who would take joy in my suffering.'

'What reasons?' Father Erchembald asked.

'Jealousy,' I answered. 'Spite. Because of things I've done in the past.'

'And Robert didn't defend you?'

'He tried.' I saw that now, at least. 'By allowing me to walk away from there, he did what little he could.'

'Anything more, and he might have started a revolt,' Serlo added.

'I can see that,' Galfrid said. 'What I don't understand is why he would let you go, only to change his mind days later?'

I shrugged. 'Maybe Elise and some of the other barons who were there that night prevailed upon him to do so. I don't know.'

I was guessing, admittedly, but what other explanation could there be? Obviously Wace and Eudo's attempts to assuage his anger had been in vain.

That was when another thought crept into my mind. Robert had only just inherited his father's barony, and all the responsibilities that came with it. His new vassals were looking for him to assert himself and to set an example that would prove he was every bit as strong a lord as the elder Malet had been. If he lost their confidence now, he might rue it for years to come. If men became disaffected and wavered in their loyalty, then the elaborate web of oaths and alliances that his father had carefully woven over so many years could quickly collapse. The legacy that he had tried to leave to his son would be ruined before Robert had the opportunity to build upon it.

And suddenly I understood. If he surrendered me to my fate, then he still had a good chance of winning back the respect he needed. So long as his reputation was maintained, he didn't care what happened to me.

I felt sick. After all that we had undergone together, after all the trials we had endured in recent years, after all the occasions on which I'd saved his life and pulled him from the fray, after all the leagues I'd travelled in his service, venturing the length and breadth of the kingdom, after all the times I'd accepted tasks on his behalf that he was too craven to undertake himself, how could he turn his back on me? Did none of that count for anything? Were it not for me, he would be dead several times over by now. How could he contemplate giving me up to my enemies?

'Tancred?' the priest asked, and I realised he'd been speaking without my being aware of what he was saying. 'What do we do now?'

'I can't stay here,' I said. 'That much is certain. They'll come for me again sooner rather than later, and when they do I need to be far away from here. If Robert's men catch up with me, I'll have no choice but to go with them and stand trial, and suffer the penalty, whatever that might be.'

'You don't know that,' Erchembald said. 'Perhaps all Robert desires is to be reconciled.'

I cast him a wry glance. He was a good friend and meant well, I knew, but he was fooling himself if he truly believed that. If I went back to Heia, there could be only one outcome.

'If they find me guilty, which they will,' I said, 'the very least I can expect is that I'll be condemned to exile, in which case I'll find myself in the same situation as I am now. But what if it's decided that banishment isn't sufficient penalty?'

'Your life will not be forfeit,' the priest said. 'You can be sure of that much. The law does not allow it.'

'If I surrender myself to the mercy of my enemies, there's no telling what might happen. Even if they allow me to keep my head, they might still demand my sword-hand, and that's if they're feeling generous. So you see that I have no choice. I have to go.'

'Where?' the priest asked.

That part I'd worked out. Indeed my mind had almost been made up even before I became embroiled in this storm, before what happened with Guibert, before that fateful night had even begun. Now that I had nowhere else to go, no lord to obey, no oath to discharge, no wars to fight, I was free to do as I wished, to go in pursuit of my own desires, my own ambitions. To venture across the sea.

'It's better if you don't know,' I said. 'That way if Robert's men come asking, you can profess ignorance. Pretend I was never here.'

Erchembald was shaking his head. 'There must be a way of settling this. A way that satisfies everyone concerned.'

He had always, as long as I'd known him, provided a voice of reason, and many were the times I'd relied on his counsel in the past. But he was hoping beyond hope for a way to untie this knot that I found myself entangled in.

'If you have some idea in mind, I'll gladly hear it,' I said. 'Otherwise it's better if I don't linger here any longer than I have to. Those men could return tomorrow, or even tonight for all any of us know.'

'You have our protection here for as long as you need it,' Galfrid said. 'No one from beyond the manor need know that you're here.'

'No,' I said firmly. 'I'd rather face exile than be reduced to cowering in my own hall.'

'Stay this night, at least,' Erchembald urged.

I was about to refuse, to tell him that all we needed were fresh horses and provisions for the journey and we would be on our way again before dusk, when I glanced at the road-weary faces of Serlo and Pons, Eithne and Godric. They had followed me this far, across marsh and moor, hills and hollows, and were prepared to follow me even into exile, beyond King Guillaume's realm entirely, across the grey and stormy seas to parts unknown. They needed food and rest, as I did. I owed them that much, and if I could not grant it then I was a poor lord indeed.

'One night,' I agreed. 'But tomorrow, we go.'

'I'll post Odgar, Ceawlin and a couple of the other lads on watch along each of the tracks leading to the manor,' Galfrid said. 'If they spot anyone coming, they'll come running straightaway to give us warning.'

I smiled in thanks, at the same time wishing that there was some way I could repay the loyalty and kindness they had shown me. For all too soon I would be forced to leave this place behind me, and I had no way of knowing when or even if I would return.

Galfrid was as good as his word, and better. I didn't think anyone would try to come by dark, when the paths through the woods could prove treacherous to those who didn't know them well, but he sent those lads nevertheless, and bade a handful of the older ones sleep that night in the hall as added protection for us. He armed them with spears and knives so that if it came to a fight they could defend themselves, though thankfully it never came to that. This business was entirely of my own making, this quarrel with Robert mine and mine alone. While I was grateful to have others on my side, I didn't want to see anyone else killed or hurt because of it.

Sleep did not come easily that night, and when it did come it was broken by swirling, confused dreams, in which I found myself travelling through places both familiar and strange, from Commines in distant Flanders to the fastness on the promontory at Dunholm, where my first lord had met his end, across barren wildernesses, through forests so dense that the sun's light could not penetrate them, on high mountain paths and ancient roads that stretched as far as I could see in either direction. Everywhere I saw the faces of sword-brothers long dead, whose names I couldn't remember, but who at one time had been good friends of mine. By the roadside stood men unknown to me, with scarred cheeks, broken noses and blood-encrusted hollows where their eyes had once been. They shouted at me, accusing me of being the one who had sent them to their graves, and tried to crowd around me, to drag me from my horse. Wildly I struck out with my blade, hoping to dispatch them back to the earth where they belonged, but the moment its edge found flesh they began to flee, running faster than I could pursue them, in every direction, through twisting alleyways and streets thick with mud, between collapsing houses and writhing towers of flame. And then I heard a woman's voice calling my name.

Oswynn.

I glanced about, searching for her face, but could not find her whichever direction I looked in. And then I turned once more and saw his face. The face of the man I had been seeking: the Danish jarl, Haakon Thorolfsson, with his wiry, greying hair trailing down his back, riding a white horse whose eyes burnt bright orange and whose nostrils spouted clouds of smoke, like the dragon that decorated his banner.

He saw me then, but no words came from his lips. Instead he began to laugh: a great thunderous sound that seemed to echo through the very ground and which caused flaming brands to topple from the nearest building, showering me with sparks, blinding me with their light, and my cloak and tunic and hair were suddenly ablaze, and my mount was rearing up and I was thrashing around, trying at one and the same time to tear the clothes from my back and to put out the flames before they consumed me too—

And that was when I awoke, breathless, my brow running with sweat, the linen bedsheets and woollen blanket that covered them wound about me, the chamber spinning. I blinked, trying to clear the image of the blaze from my mind. The hall was dark, although I could see a glimmer of grey light breaking in through the crack under the door, while from outside came the chirruping of thrushes, heralding the dawn.

A few strands of straw from the mattress had become stuck to my tunic, and I brushed them off as I rose and made my way towards the door, stepping lightly between the sleeping forms of the rest of my party, trying not to rouse them.

Out in the yard all was quiet save for a few chickens scratching at the dirt, but I noticed that the door to the stables lay open, which suggested Ædda was already about. I had seen him the previous night, although the last light was fast fading when he returned, having spent the day taking one of the palfreys to be reshod, which meant a journey of ten miles each way to the nearest manor with a farrier. One of my closest friends among the English, he was a quiet man, who kept largely to his own company, and I was pleased to see he hadn't changed since I'd last seen him, except in one respect.

'I have a wife, lord,' he'd said.

'A wife?' I asked, overjoyed though at the same time more than a little surprised. We'd been gone a matter of months, after all. 'Who is she? When did this happen?'

'I first met her at the market in Leomynstre, about a week after you left for the Fens. Sannan, her name is. A tanner's daughter, and a widow at twenty-three.'

'Twenty-three?' I repeated.

He gave a boyish grin, and there was a glint in his one remaining eye, which was a rare thing from someone who was usually so sombre. Ædda had long ago lost count of how many summers he had seen, although to judge by his weathered appearance I reckoned he was probably a good ten years older than myself.

'She met my eye, and I met hers, and for both of us it was love in that moment,' he said. 'I've never known a creature so beautiful. I saw her again the next week and the one after that, and then the one after that I went to her father with the bride-price and we were wed two days later.'

I was glad for him. Men, women and children alike often feared him on account of his disfigured face, partly the result of an enemy spear that had put out one of his eyes as a youth, leaving only an ugly black scar, and partly due to the burns he'd received in an incident he'd never wished to discuss, which had left the skin across one cheek white and raw and painful to look at, though undoubtedly not as painful as it was to bear. Ædda Aneage, he was sometimes called, which meant Ædda the One-eyed, though people were careful not to speak that byname in his presence lest he became roused to anger. He was, at heart, a gentle soul, as any who knew him well would confirm, and it pleased me that he had found someone who could see past his appearance to the person within.

'Do you want to meet her, lord?' he asked. 'Her mother was Welsh, but her father is English, and she speaks both tongues. She'll be glad to meet you at last. I've told her all about you.'

He'd led me to his small cottage next to the sheepfolds, where Sannan was building up the fire with twigs and broken branches gathered from the woods. Truly Ædda had been blessed, for she was a fine girl, red-haired and slender, who blushed as she smiled and who was at every moment attentive to her man. Though it does me ill to admit it, I was a little jealous of him. They invited me to stay and sup with them, there being just enough food to make a meal for three, and I accepted. We filled our bellies with boiled mutton, beans and fresh-baked bread, and though the fare was simple, I was content to be there and to enjoy their company.

All this I would miss.

Now, though it was barely first light, the stableman was already at work, placing feedbags on the doors to each of the stalls.

'Lord,' he said with some surprise when he saw me. 'You're risen early.'

'For the first time in weeks I find myself with a comfortable mattress to lie down on and I can't even sleep the whole night through,' I said ruefully.

Ædda did not join me in a smile. The mischievousness he'd shown yesterday was gone, and his usual sombreness had returned. Last night it had been possible to pretend that all was well, but now the day had come when I would leave Earnford behind, and we both knew it.

'I took a stone from the hind hoof of the girl's palfrey,' he said. 'He'll need to rest that foot for a day or two, but she can take one of the others.' He hesitated. 'I don't mean to pry but I was wondering, lord. That girl, Eithne. Is she your—?'

'No,' I said, laughing, before he could finish that thought. 'Too quarrelsome for my liking. But she's going to help me find the one who is.'

He nodded. 'The rest of the horses are groomed and fed. They'll carry you as far as you need to go to.'

'I'm going to leave Fyrheard,' I said. 'I don't know if I can take him where we're going, and I couldn't bear to sell him to another master. But I don't want whoever happens to be lord here after me to have him either.'

'I'll see that he's well taken care of, lord, and the other destriers too. I have a friend at Clune who owes me a favour. He'll gladly keep them for you, make sure they're well exercised and given the finest grazing, at least until you return. I'll make sure to visit them when I can, too.'

I gave him my thanks. The Englishman went to fetch a bundle of hay from the lean-to that served as a storehouse.

'Has there been any sign of the Welsh while we've been away?' I asked when he came back.

'None. It's been quiet. There was only one raid, if you could call it that. Two lads tried to steal a pig from the pens the night of the feast of St Oda, but the animal squealed and woke half the manor. Galfrid caught them, but they were so young that he took pity on them and sent them away.'

I didn't bother asking when St Oda's feast was. The English had so many saints, some of them barely known outside of the shire they hailed from, that it was a wonder they could remember even half of them.

At least there hadn't been any further attacks, and that was some relief. Probably the Welsh were still licking their wounds after their defeat at King Guillaume's hands last autumn, which had sent them fleeing back to the hovels that passed for halls in their land.

'Has there been any news of Bleddyn?'

The King of Gwynedd and Powys, Bleddyn had held me captive for several weeks last year, and even tried to sell me to some of the

English rebels. His was yet another name on the list of men who had wronged me, and whom I'd sworn to kill, although as yet I hadn't succeeded in delivering on any of those promises.

'Nothing,' said Ædda. 'As I said, it's been quiet.'

'With any luck things will stay that way a while longer.'

'I hope so, lord.'

We embraced. 'I wish you well,' I said. 'Both you and Sannan.'

'And the same to you, lord. God willing, we'll see you again before long.'

'You will,' I said. 'I know it.'

And I wished I believed it.

One final thing remained for me to do before we left. As the first of the sun's rays gleamed through the woods to the east, I ventured down towards the half-built church. In its yard, amidst the fallen leaves, I found what I had come for. There was no stone cross, no grave-marker to show it, but I knew by the way the ground rose and dipped and the way that the grass grew thickly that this was the place.

Kneeling down on the dewy ground, I closed my eyes, bringing back to mind Leofrun's face and all the happy times we had enjoyed together. It was probably true that I had never cared for her quite as deeply as she cared for me, although whether she ever realised that, I wasn't sure. I had known few women as warm in heart or as generous in spirit as she. Now I was leaving Earnford behind to go in search of another. I only hoped that, if we met again in the heavenly kingdom, she would understand. After giving a prayer for the safekeeping of her soul and that of Baderon, our son – the son I'd never known, who had died almost before he had lived, and was buried beside her – I breathed a long sigh, reluctantly raised myself and made back in the direction of the hall. Day was upon us and we couldn't tarry here any longer.

We set off not long after that, as soon as the horses were ready and our saddle-packs had been crammed with provisions for the days ahead. In a chest hidden in the hollow space beneath the timber floor of my new hall were six leather corselets, one reinforced with iron studs, that I'd taken from a Welsh chief and members of his household guard during one of our raids across the dyke a few months earlier. They were made for shoulders broader than my own, but they were in good condition and so we took them with us, thinking that if nothing else we might be able to sell them. There were also several knives and a rusted seax that I wasn't entirely sure why I'd kept. We took the best of the weapons, since one never knew when a blade might shear. It would be useful to have spares, and so we buckled the sheaths upon our waists. I even gave one of the knives to Eithne, hoping that didn't prove to be a mistake and that I didn't end up with the blade buried in my back the next time I let my guard slip. That didn't seem likely; the longer she spent in our company, the more comfortable she seemed to grow. This was my way of repaying her trust.

Lastly, buried at the very bottom of the chest, there was a small pouch of coins that I'd forgotten about. There wasn't much there, but I knew that every slightest shaving of silver would prove useful in the days and weeks and months ahead, or however long it would take me to find this Haakon, and to be reunited with Oswynn, and so I took it too, hanging it by a leather cord around my neck, under my tunic. To that meagre hoard Galfrid offered me a purse containing gold and a few precious stones that had come from selling fleeces and fish to traders at market over the past few months.

'I only wish there was more,' he said as he bade me take it.

'I can't accept this,' I said. 'What if the winter is harsh, like last year? What if the harvest isn't enough, and you need to buy more grain?'

'We have all that we need. That's what's left. Your entitlement as lord.'

'And I want you to take this, too,' said Father Erchembald, who along with Ædda had also risen early to bid us farewell. He unfastened a silver chain from around his neck, from which hung a gold-worked and garnet-studded cross.

'Father—'

He took my hand, pressed the cross into my palm and closed my fingers around it. 'You have been a good lord to us, and a good friend too. A better defender of this manor and these people I could not have asked for. This is the smallest token of my gratitude. God be with you always, Tancred. I only pray that you will be safe on your travels, wherever they take you.'

'I will,' I assured him. 'I promise. As long as we have our swords by our sides, no harm will come to us.'

I tried to sound confident, but the truth was that the thought of venturing beyond the sea to lands unknown filled me with not a little trepidation. Some of that uncertainty must have been betrayed in my manner, for the priest gave me a look that suggested he didn't entirely believe me.

'I hope that you're right,' he said. 'But, please, take care all the same.'

They had been steadfast allies through all the recent tumults, and a part of me wished they could come with me, but I knew very well that they couldn't. Their place was here, at Earnford. Asking them to follow me into exile as outlaws was something I could never ask them to do. Besides, they had already given me so much: more, indeed, than Robert had in the past year, in spite of all his promises. Merely by harbouring me they were making themselves complicit in my crimes and thus putting themselves in danger. Words could not express my gratitude.

Having made our farewells, armed ourselves, gathered what other provisions we might need for the days ahead, saddled the palfreys and the rounceys that would carry our packs, and been offered trinkets and various good luck charms by the alewives and their menfolk, at last we set out along the winding tracks, leaving Earnford behind us for what, for all I knew, could be for ever. In time, perhaps, the rift between Robert and myself would be healed and I would find myself back here once again. But despite my best attempts to convince myself otherwise, I couldn't shake the feeling deep inside that I would never again so much as look out over that valley, or tread its soil.

I'd reasoned that anyone pursuing us would be coming on Earl Roger's orders from Scrobbesburh to the north, and so with that in mind we struck out in the other direction, making first for

Hereford, where we were given directions to Glowecestre, the town on the Saverna in which the king had celebrated Christmas and held his court a couple of years previously. There we sold our horses, and managed to secure a good price for them, too, though not without some negotiation on my part, before buying passage on a wide-bellied Norman trader, which was bound for Cadum, where its captain planned to sell fleeces in exchange for stone for building. He wasn't planning to make port elsewhere, but at the sight of our silver quickly changed his mind, agreeing to take us to Brycgstowe, where I reckoned we were more likely to find a ship that would take us where we wanted to go.

News had only just reached those towns of the king's victory over the rebels, and so I doubted we would find any trouble there, but even so I was wary of attracting too much attention to ourselves. Thus we took care to disguise our appearance as far as possible, carrying rough staves hewn from fallen branches and smearing our faces and covering our cloaks and trews with dust and mud, while those of us who had beards allowed them to grow. That way, if we did by some coincidence cross paths with anyone who might otherwise have recognised the faces of Tancred the Breton and his companions, they would see instead only five dishevelled, road-worn travellers. Or so, at least, I hoped. Thankfully no one challenged us during the five days it took us to reach Brycgstowe, by which time I reckoned we were probably safe. The city was a busy port, and wealthy too, second in all of England probably only to Lundene: a place where merchants from all corners of Christendom and beyond came to sell their wares, where slavers sometimes held their markets, where wealthy pilgrims sought passage to holy places in far-off lands, all of them accompanied by bands of men for protection, so that a group of armed travellers such as us was far from unusual.

We jostled our way along the quayside, past snorting oxen laden with packs and horses pulling carts, around groups of dockhands vying for the attention of captains, who wanted only the strongest lads to help them unload their cargo. I tried asking some of them where I might find a ship bound for Dyflin, but failed to get much of an answer from them, until one of the younger ones pointed a short way downriver to where a broad-beamed ship some twenty benches or so long had been drawn up above the tideline on the mudflats to the west of the city's ramparts.

'That's *Hrithdyr*,' he said. 'Her master is a Dane, from Haltland or Orkaneya or somewhere like that. I don't know his name but I've heard from some of the others who've worked her that this is his last voyage before winter, that he'll be sailing back north before long. If you're wanting passage across the sea to Yrland, he's the one to ask.'

'Are there any others?'

'Not so far as I know, lord. One sailed that way two days ago, and there might be another in a week's time.'

That was useful knowledge to have, for it gave me some idea of the position I'd be bargaining from. I thanked him and signalled to the others to follow me.

'You won't find him there,' he called as we were about to walk away.

I stopped and turned. 'Where, then?'

He gave a shrug, but I saw in his eyes that he knew. The lad wasn't stupid. He'd realised that if we had money for passage across the sea, then we must have coin enough to spare a penny or two for his help.

I drew one from my purse and held it up. His eyes gleamed and he reached for it, but I closed my fist and snatched it away before he got so much as a fingertip to it.

'Where?' I asked.

'Most of the ship captains stay in the town at a tavern called the Two Boars. That where he's most likely to be at this hour.'

'Show me to this tavern and the coin will be yours,' I said. 'Not before.'

He scowled but gave in, leading us through a series of narrow, rutted alleys until we stood beneath a sign on which had been crudely daubed a pair of tusked, four-legged animals that could, I supposed, if one squinted hard and for long enough, be taken for boars. I tossed him the coin I'd promised and he caught it deftly before scurrying away.

Inside, men sat at tables, drinking, playing at dice and at *tæfl*, a game not unlike chess, played on a squared board, of which I had been taught the rudiments but which I'd never been able to master. A woman with a brace of keys dangling from her belt, whom I took for the innkeeper's wife, came to greet us, and I asked her where I might find the captain of *Hrithdyr*. She pointed towards one of the tæfl-players, a bearded, corpulent man in his middle years who was sitting close by the blazing hearth-fire, his brow glistening with sweat, his small eyes peering out from under heavy brows as he contemplated his next move. He and his opponent, a thin-faced greybeard, both glanced up as we approached.

'What do you want?' snarled the fat one in English. 'Can't you see I'm in the middle of a game?'

'I'm looking for a ship to take us across the sea to Dyflin,' I replied, unperturbed. 'I hear that's where you're bound.'

'Who wants to know?'

It was probably unwise to give him my real name, and so instead I gave him one I'd used before on occasion. 'Goscelin,' I said. 'Goscelin of Saint-Omer, in Flanders.'

I extended a hand, but he did not take it. 'I know where Saint-Omer is,' he said curtly. 'A few years ago I happened to meet a travelling monk who came from there. Talkative, he was, always babbling about some saint or another. He was called Goscelin, too, as it happens. He would have been around your size, though I don't remember his face. You're not him, are you?'

'Do I look to you like a man of the cloister?'

He grunted, and I took that for an answer. 'If you're from Flanders, why are you wanting to go to Dyflin?'

'My business is my own. I have silver enough to pay for the passage, and that's all you need to know.'

The greybeard made to rise from his stool, saying, 'If you're going to spend the next hour—'

'Sit down, Wulfric,' said the Dane. 'This won't take long.'

'It doesn't matter,' the one called Wulfric grumbled. 'You've won anyway.' He took an enamelled ring from his finger and laid it down on the table. 'There, as wagered. Perhaps next spring when you come, I'll have the chance to win it back from you.'

'Perhaps.' The Dane grinned in a manner that put me in mind of a wolf while the old man shuffled off, then, when we were alone, he said to me: 'What makes you think I want any passengers? Maybe I do well enough from my trade that I have no need for your money. Have you considered that?'

On my belt was a purse containing a clutch of gold coins that bore a strange curly script I couldn't decipher, which had been part of Galfrid's gift to us. I untied the knot, tossed it on to the table so he could hear the clink of metal within, and gestured for him to open it, which he did, loosening the drawstring and allowing the tiny discs to spill out into his palm. He examined them closely, holding them to the light and testing each one with his teeth.

'Five of you?' he asked, his eyes flicking to each of us in turn before settling on Eithne. A smirk came to his lips. 'The girl as well?'

'That's right.'

He looked her up and down, and I saw hunger of a sort in his expression. 'She'd fetch a fine price, I reckon. Does she belong to you?'

'She's not for sale, if that's what you're thinking.'

'What is she then? Your wife?'

'A fellow traveller.'

If the Dane was at all insulted by my terse manner, he didn't show it. He shook his head. 'I don't have space aboard for that many. Three of you, easily, possibly four. But not five.'

Tæfl wasn't the only game he knew how to play. I supposed I should have expected as much. I removed the smaller and thinner of the two arm-rings that I wore, and placed it in front of him.

'Do you have space now?'

He fingered it, his sweaty brow furrowing while he contemplated whether or not to accept, and I stood watching, waiting, thinking that this was already a steep price to pay, and wondering how much more I could afford. Thankfully that was a decision I didn't have to make.

'We sail in two days, on the morning flood tide,' he said.

'Two days?' I repeated. 'The sooner we could leave these shores, the better. I'd been hoping to find a ship that could take us almost straightaway.

He raised an eyebrow. 'In a hurry to leave, are you?'

I knew that to protest would be pointless, and might only further arouse his suspicions, of which I was sure he already had a few, and so instead I kept my mouth shut.

'It makes no difference to me who you are or what it is you're running from. But I'll tell you this: we won't wait for you. If you're not there by the time we're ready to cast off, you can swim to Yrland for all I care. Do you understand?'

'I understand.'

'You can keep your gold until we're out on the water,' he said. 'So that you don't have to worry about me sailing away with it. I've been called many things in my life, but a thief isn't one of them. I have a reputation to maintain, as I'm sure you'll appreciate.'

I knew only too well the value of reputation, marred though mine was in those days. He passed the gold and the arm-ring back to me, we clasped hands, and it was agreed. We were going to Dyflin.

Nineteen

We spent a restless two nights at the Two Boars while the Dane, whose name we learnt was Snorri, concluded his business. Restless, because I was convinced that those men who had come looking for me at Earnford would not be far behind us, and because I was aware, too, that the longer we lingered in one place, the greater the chance of our being caught.

But they did not come, and so it was with some relief that at last we sailed, *Hrithdyr*'s hold having been filled with bolts of woolcloth, barrels of salted porpoise-meat, Rhenish quernstones and casks of English wine that came from the vineyards further up the Saverna valley. The wind was on the turn, however, a sure sign of worse weather to come, and Snorri kept looking to the grey-darkening skies and muttering in his own tongue, all the while fingering a small chain that hung around his neck from which, I noticed, hung both the heathen hammer and the Christian cross. Perhaps he still held to some of the old ways but was fearful of our Lord's wrath and so wore the cross as well to placate Him, or possibly he thought that by worshipping both our God and those of his pagan ancestors, his soul would be guaranteed a place in one heaven or the other. Whatever he believed, his prayers seemed to work, for the storm that we'd all predicted failed to come, at least on that day.

We entered the Saverna early that afternoon, hugging close to the Wessex shore while the grey waters grew ever choppier and the wind whipped the waves into white stallions. No storm came that evening either, though, and so the following day we crossed to the Welsh side, making port on an island where stood a small stone chapel dedicated to a certain St Barruc, of whom none of us had ever heard. We were just in time, too, for no sooner had we dragged the boat up the shingle on that island's sheltered shore than we were pelted with hail, and a gale rose from the west and the sea foamed and crashed against the cliffs. There we were forced to wait until the wind turned again and the seas calmed and we were able to resume our voyage.

Still England lay in sight to our larboard side, although it was no more than the faintest sliver of green and brown and grey on the horizon. Only then did I realise that in the five years since the invasion, not once had I left its shores. I had ventured on brief forays into Wales and marched into the far corners of the kingdom, close to the borderlands where King Guillaume's realm ended and that of the Scots began, but never in all that time had I made the journey back across the seas, as so many others had done. The Breton had become a Norman, had become bound to England. And now I would leave that land behind me. The land where I'd made my reputation, where I had lived and loved and lost. The kingdom I'd given everything short of my life to defend, and all, it seemed now, for nothing.

I stood by the stern, looking out across the white-tipped waters towards those vanishing cliffs as *Hrithdyr* rose and dipped in the swell and the wind filled its sails, until a sudden squall blew in and cloud veiled that land, and I could see it no longer.

It took more than a week for us to reach Dyflin. Even I, who knew little of the sea, knew that the autumn was ever a difficult time to set sail. The winds were changeable, storms could arrive with little warning, and pirates lurked, looking for easy plunder, knowing that shipmasters were eager to make it home in time for Christmas or Yule or whatever other name they gave to the winter feast, their holds filled and their coin-purses bursting with whatever they had earned from that year's dealing. God must have been with us, for we saw no sign of them, despite all the warnings of the folk who lived on those shores, who said that their low-hulled, dragon-prowed longships had been spotted roving further along the coast. Nevertheless we proceeded with care.

The journey could probably have been made in better time, but Snorri was a cautious man, and one who clung to his superstitions, too. He refused to leave sight of land unless the signs were wholly favourable, and even then only after he had cast the runesticks to assure himself that a watery fate did not await us. Not that I blamed him. Far better to be cautious than dead. Besides, the open sea was already rough enough for my liking. As we left the Welsh coast behind us and, with a following breeze filling our sails, struck a course west towards Yrland, I remembered one of the reasons I'd never made the journey back across the Narrow Sea in the past five years. The horizon rose and fell and rolled and pitched from one side to another, and my belly churned, and I huddled down by the stern, my eyes closed, as I tried to hold back the sickness swelling within. To no avail.

'I thought you Flemings were well used to the sea,' Snorri said after what must have been the third time I'd spewed over the ship's side. He slapped me on the back as I heaved up what I hoped were the last of my stomach's contents, wiped away some that had seeped down my chin, and spat in an effort to rid my mouth of the taste.

'Not this Fleming.' Another swell of bile rose up my throat, and I readied myself to retch once again, but it subsided.

'The last time I was in Saint-Omer, it was still being rebuilt after the great storm, the one that struck that midsummer's night. Were you there then?'

'No,' I said, 'I wasn't.'

He shook his head sadly. 'I was there. I saw the winds bring down the monastery's bell-tower, saw rain such as you have never seen turn the streets into rivers, wash whole houses away. Ships were torn from their moorings, cast downriver and out to sea, though not *Hrithdyr*. She alone weathered the tempest. That's how she got her name. *Stormbeast*, I suppose you would call her in your tongue. A terrible night, that was.'

'I heard the tales,' I lied. This was the first I'd heard of any such storm. If only he would stop harassing me with these questions about a place I'd never so much as visited.

'That tavern is almost the only part of the old town that still stands.' He gave a laugh. 'The Monk's Pisspot, everyone called it, on account of that's what the ale there used to taste like. You know the place I'm talking about, don't you?'

'Of course,' I said, forcing a smile. 'Who could forget it?'

But Snorri was not laughing any more, and that was when I realised my mistake. Saint-Omer was among the richest ports in Flanders. Had there been any such disaster, news of it would surely have reached our ears. There had been no midsummer's storm, and neither, I realised now, was there any tavern by that name. He was testing me.

If he'd had his suspicious before, he knew for certain now that I was not who I claimed to be.

'So what are you?' he asked. 'An outlaw? An oath-breaker, maybe?'

'I've broken no oath.'

'Then what? You're obviously fleeing something. Old Snorri has wits as well as beauty, you know. He can tell these things.'

I returned his stare but did not speak.

'You're entitled to your secrets, I suppose, if that's the way you want to keep it. Your gold's good and that's all that concerns me. I'm not one to pry into another man's business. I knew you were no Fleming, though, from the moment we met.'

'How?'

'The way you speak, for a start. Did you think you could trick someone who's travelled as widely as I have? Anyone who lives his life on the whale-road can easily tell a Fleming from a Norman from a Gascon from a Ponthievin by the sound of their voice.' He sighed the heavy sigh of one who had seen his share of fools over the years, and had grown tired of their games. 'If you want my advice—'

'I don't,' I muttered, but he went on, unperturbed.

'—it's that you should tread carefully, Goscelin of Saint-Omer, or whatever you're really called. Count yourself lucky that I'm not the sort who's easily offended, but there are many that won't take kindly to men who try to deceive them. If there's one place you don't want to start making enemies, it's in Dyflin.'

'I can take care of myself,' I answered, though the conviction in my words was undermined somewhat as I felt another heave coming. Grabbing the gunwale to steady myself, I leant over the side, but by now I had nothing left to give and only the slightest dribble came out.

'Onions,' Snorri said.

'What?' I asked, after I'd wiped a sleeve across my mouth.

'Onions. I always recommend them for anyone who suffers from ship-sickness. Raw is best, but if you can't stomach that then boiled will do. Also rosemary and ginger, if you can acquire them. Grind them into a powder and mix them with water. Better still would be to add the juice of a quince, although you'll be lucky if you find any this side of the Narrow Sea.'

I thanked him for his suggestion, though I'd tried many a remedy for various ailments in my years, few of which I could honestly say had ever seemed to do much good.

'Why Dyflin?' he asked. 'Of all the places to choose exile, why there?'

'I'm looking for someone.'

'Who?'

I hesitated, wondering whether or not I should tell Snorri. But I supposed he had shown faith in me, despite the fact that I had lied to him, and that was worth something. The least I could do was return the favour.

'A man called Haakon Thorolfsson,' I said at last. 'Have you heard of him?'

'Haakon Thorolfsson?' he asked, as if testing the name on his lips to see if it brought forth any memory. 'I can't say the name is familiar, but then there aren't many of us Danes still living in Dyflin these days; it's an Irish town now, mostly. What is he, a merchant?'

'A warlord.'

'A warlord?' He nodded towards my scabbard. 'Looking to sell your sword to him, are you?'

I glared at him in warning and he raised his palms to show that he meant no offence. 'As I said, your business is your own. But I might be able to help you. I know a man who lives in the city, who hears many things and knows many people. Magnus, his name is.

I'll take you to him, if you want. He might have heard of this Haakon, and if he has, there's a good chance he'll know where you can find him, too.'

His generosity surprised me, considering that I was but a stranger to him, but I wasn't about to refuse such an offer. Sometimes fate is harsh and at others it is kind, and all a man can do is take advantage of its kindness while it lasts.

'Very well,' I said. 'I'd like to meet your friend.'

'I didn't say he was my friend. Although that's not to say he's my enemy, either. Truth be told, he's not the friendly sort. He keeps himself to himself. Around your age, he is, probably a few winters younger, fond of his secrets. A brooding kind of man, with a temper hotter than hell's fires.' He gave me a gap-toothed grin. 'In many ways you remind me of him.'

I was about to protest, but at that moment a shout came from the lookout by the prow, who had spied land in the distance, ahead and a little to our steerboard side. At once Snorri left me and began barking orders to his crew in their own tongue. The lookout's eyes were better than mine, and it was a while longer before I was able to see it: at first only a rocky headland rising high above the savage, white-foaming waves, then further along wide beaches of dark sand and shingle, with green meadows and gold-bronze woodlands beyond, and faint wisps of rising hearth-smoke marking out villages and farmsteads, though we were too far away to make out any houses. Cormorants and other seabirds soared in their hundreds, occasionally breaking away from the flock to dive beneath the waves, only to resurface moments later with glistening, writhing fish in their bills.

At last we had come to the land beyond the sea. To Yrland, and, I hoped, one step closer to finding Oswynn, whatever fate had befallen her and wherever she happened to be.

To my eyes Yrland seemed a quiet country, with few villages and halls that I could make out, but such appearances, Snorri told us, belied its true nature. A seething cauldron of violence, he described it, and spoke ill of its people, too, calling them as cunning and rapacious as wolves. This was a land, he said, in which no man's holdings were safe, where chieftains and princelings led marauding bands, despoiling everything in their paths in pursuit of their bloody feuds. Every other man called himself a king, but only one held any real claim to overlordship, and that was Diarmait, who ruled the southern half of the island, including Dyflin and the other ports, and had received the submission of the north. But he was old and frail now, and said to be in poor health besides, and the authority that once he had held over the many squabbling families was waning.

'Already this year there has been open war between them,' Snorri said. 'He nearly lost his kingdom because of it. There will be worse to come when he dies, too. His last surviving son and heir perished last year, so what will happen no one knows, except that there'll be all manner of adventurers and sellswords flocking to these shores, looking to ply their trade. Probably this Haakon you mentioned will be among them.'

Not if I found him first, I thought, though I did not say it.

It took another three days from first spying Yrland's coast before finally we made port in Dyflin. We travelled slowly, hugging as near as Snorri dared to the spray-battered cliffs and stacks where guillemots gathered. He did this, he said, for two reasons: firstly so as to be less easily spotted, and secondly to deter any raiders who might be on the prowl for trading ships like ours. Open water was where we were most vulnerable, for whereas *Hrithdyr* was wide and slow, the ships the pirates favoured tended to be sleek and fast, with slender beams, high prows, and oars as well as sails. Close to land, however, the risks were greater where raiders were concerned. Floating masses of seaweed might become tangled in their oars, while there were sheltered creeks and inlets in which their prey could easily hide. Instead, Snorri explained, they usually preferred to attack when the prey was easy. And so it proved, for although on two occasions we spied sails on the horizon that we suspected might belong to such sea wolves, both kept their distance, obviously deciding that we were not worth the effort of a pursuit, and thus we were spared.

A biting easterly wind was gusting at our backs, piercing our spray-soaked tunics, its chill working its way into my very bones, when we sailed around yet another headland and at long last spotted Dyflin in the distance. Winter was on its way, it seemed. I wrapped my cloak tightly around me. We had to wait a few more hours for the flood tide, and so we anchored in the estuary in the meantime, furled the sail and gazed upon the sprawling city with its crumbling timber palisades, its wharves and slipways and beaches and landing stages where ships both large and small had been dragged high above the tideline and were being caulked in preparation for their last voyages before the snows.

My sickness had at last abated, and it was Eithne who now looked ill. Indeed I'd heard hardly a word from her throughout the entire voyage, the brashness that I recalled in her from our first meeting having ebbed away over the last few days.

'Please, lord,' she said now, and there was fear in her eyes. 'I don't want to go back there.'

'Why not?'

She hesitated, glanced around to check that no one else was watching, and then turned around and pulled at the collar of her dress, revealing a black symbol, roughly as long as my thumb and shaped something like a letter R except more jagged, which had been branded on to her chest, just below her shoulder-bone. At once I understood.

'You're a slave?' I asked.

'Was, lord. I ran away two years ago. There's another, if you want to see it.' She lifted up her skirt to show me her thigh.

'It's all right,' I said. 'I don't need to see.' Some of Snorri's crewmen were beginning to take an interest, nudging each other and pointing in our direction, particularly the younger ones, some of whom were barely more than pups and would probably have counted themselves lucky to glimpse the merest flash of a woman's bared ankle. 'Is that your master's mark?'

She nodded. 'His name is Ravn. He's a merchant. He lives in Dyflin, or used to, anyway.'

'Why did you run away? Did he beat you?'

'No,' she said. 'He was a good master, in that sense. Not cruel.

He gave us warm clothes and fed us well, us Irish ones, anyway. He was fond of us, though some of the others he treated less well. The work he gave us wasn't hard, and he looked after my mother when she was sick—'

'Why, then?'

'I saw the way he looked at me sometimes when I was churning the butter or building the fire. I saw the hunger in his eyes and I was afraid that when I came of age he'd want me to help warm his bed, as my mother did while she still lived.'

'So you fled.'

'Yes, lord.'

As reasons went, that was far from the worst I had heard, and it was hard not to feel sorry for her. We Normans tended not to keep or trade slaves, the bishops having preached that both practices were sinful, though as always there were a few noblemen who disagreed with the Church's judgement and kept them to help with the running of their households. As we had found in the years since coming to Britain, however, slavery was common among the folk who lived in these isles, as it was among the Danes and the Moors, who perhaps once a year would venture north to these shores, bringing boatloads of dark-skinned, black-haired women and children from distant, sun-parched lands, who spoke in tongues no one could decipher and whose strange beauty entranced all who set eyes upon them.

Eithne was no beauty, but she was young, and to many men that was more important.

'How did you end up at Elyg?' I asked.

'Does it matter, lord?'

I supposed it didn't, not really, but I was curious, and when she saw that my interest was genuine, she sighed and told me the whole story. In fleeing Dyflin with the few coins she'd been able to scrape together, she had been able to find passage with a trader, only for their ship to be ambushed when they were less than a day out of port. The captain of the raiders had seen Eithne and taken a fancy to her at first sight, and rather than resist him she had pretended to love him in return.

'I thought it would be easier that way,' Eithne said sadly. 'I didn't realise I'd thrown off one yoke only to place another around my neck.'

He had taken her back to his hall in Kathenessia, and had married soon after. From what she told me it seemed he had been kind enough, treating her well and clothing her in the richest fabrics he could afford and bestowing her with silver bracelets and brooches, and she had kept up the pretence, realising that she was unlikely to find greater happiness anywhere else. Then this year, hearing that there might be glory and fortune to be won in the Fens, he had ventured south, and since he could not bear to be apart from Eithne for long, he had taken her with him.

'And now everything has come full circle and I find myself back here,' she said bitterly. 'The last place I wanted to be. If Ravn sees me—'

'He won't,' I replied confidently. Even if he still lived in these parts, this Ravn might not even remember her after so long.

'But if he does—'

'Even if he does, you're safe with me.'

'You promise you won't take me back to him?'

I was about to say, only half in jest, that that depended on how much he was willing to pay to see her returned, for, though it shames me to say so, I was briefly tempted. I remained desperately poor, and the reward for dragging a fugitive slave back to her master would go some way to replenishing my coin-purse. Yet I had vowed myself to her protection, and I was not one to go back on my pledges, especially given that I'd already tricked her the once, into coming with me. She trusted me, and I would not betray that trust.

'I swear it,' I told her. 'And, after I've done what I've come here for, I promise to see you safely back home. Where is home for you, anyway?'

'A small village that doesn't have a name, where the great river empties into the wide western sea.'

That was no great help, for such a place could be anywhere. 'Do you know where exactly?'

She shrugged. 'A short way downstream from the city the Danes call Hlymerkr.'

I nodded, though I had never heard of such a place. How I'd manage to take her home or even when exactly, I hadn't yet worked out. But I would.

She was still pale and anxious when, later that day, we clambered from *Hrithdyr* on to Dyflin's muddy quayside, hauling our packs up after us. The local reeve, or whatever the word for such an official was in the tongue of that place, came to collect from Snorri the silver penny that was the daily price for keeping a vessel moored here, and after paying it the Dane led us up the city's narrow, dung-reeking alleys to where this Magnus could be found.

Despite everything I'd heard about Dyflin and the folk who frequented it, it was nothing like I had imagined: not nearly as large, nor as impressive to look upon, compared with either Lundene or the great cities of Normandy, with their towering vaulted churches and encircling stone walls that stood the height of six men. Indeed it seemed to me a sorry place. While a few long halls that probably belonged to merchants or noblemen stood proud upon the higher ground to the south, much of the rest of the city looked as if it were being swallowed up by the mud. Crumbling, sunken-floored houses huddled close together on either side of streets ankle-deep in filth. In one place a stream had become clogged with straw and leaves and dung and the putrid remains of an animal that might once have been a hog, and had overspilled its banks, flooding the road and leaving wide pools through which we had no choice but to trudge. One part of the town was burnt to the ground, leaving only blackened timbers and piles of ash, whether as the result of some accident or a recent raid I could only guess. Traders called out in tongues I did not understand, grabbing at our sleeves to catch our attention, pointing to stalls laden with fresh-caught fish or else with bolts of brightly coloured silks from far-off lands. Bone-thin, toothless beggars leant upon sticks as they held out hands in hope of receiving a coin or two, while children played with wooden horses in the alleys between houses, eyeing us suspiciously before they resumed their games.

Snorri led us up the hill in the direction of a wide, flat, grassy mound that looked as though it should have formed part of a castle, except that no tower stood upon it, nor was it surrounded by any palisade.

'That's where they hold the *thing*,' Snorri told me when I asked what it was.

'The thing?' I asked.

'It's our word for an assembly of elders and nobles, like the hundred courts you have in England.' He pointed towards the mound. 'That's where they make the laws, pass judgments on disputes, of which there's no shortage here. Men fighting over money, or women, or both—'

I was only half paying attention to him, for I was suddenly aware of a group of women who had stopped to fix us with stern glares. A few men even went so far as to spit on the ground as we passed, which I thought strange. Obviously they recognised myself, Serlo and Pons for foreigners, either by our manner of dress or, more probably, from the cut of our hair, for unlike the Danes and the English, who tended to let theirs grow long, ours was shaven short at the back and at the sides, in the style favoured in France. Still, I thought such attentions strange, given that they must be well used to seeing people from all parts.

'It's because they're English,' Snorri explained. 'Many thegns came and settled here together with their families in the months and years after Hæstinges, preferring exile over submission to a foreign king. They all know a Norman when they see one. I thought you knew.'

'No,' I replied. 'I didn't.'

Hardly had I set foot in this city than it seemed I was already making enemies. I checked to make sure that my sword was belted upon my waist, which of course it was. Hopefully I wouldn't have any need of it.

Thankfully they were content to stare and spit and nothing more, and we soon left them behind us, arriving shortly at a high-gabled hall with timbers that were half-rotten in places. A boy who might have been a servant or a slave met us at the door and regarded us sullenly.

'*Heill nu, Björn,*' Snorri said by way of greeting, in what I presumed was the Danish tongue, since although it sounded a little like English, the words were not all familiar. '*Er thin meistari her?*'

'*Ma sva vera,*' said Björn with a shrug, eyeing Snorri with suspicion, as if not quite sure whether he was to be trusted. '*Hvi? Hverr vill veita?*'

'*Seg honum at Snorri Broklauss vili hitta hann at mali.*'

Björn glowered and hesitated for a moment, before disappearing into the gloom of the hall, closing the door behind him.

'This Magnus,' I said to Snorri, 'is he a Dane?'

'You might think it to look at him. From what I gather, though, the blood in his veins is English. Truth is, I don't know him well enough to say for sure.'

'And you think this Englishman will be willing to help us?'

'I'm telling you I don't know where he's from. I hear he's from noble stock, but then again I hear many things. He speaks both tongues well, and he has many Danish friends. That's all I know.'

Not to mention a Danish name, I thought, although perhaps that was not so unusual. Men often considered me a Breton, although it was some years since I'd last returned to the place of my birth, but my name was French, given to me by my Norman mother.

'How far do you trust him?' I asked.

'About as far as I trust you,' Snorri replied flatly, which I supposed was only deserved. 'Let me do the talking, at least to begin with. If he's here, that is, and I'm beginning to think he isn't.'

'If he isn't, where will we find him?'

'At this hour?' He nodded in the vague direction of the setting sun. 'Probably down at the stews by the docks. Whores and slaves are what Dyflin is best known for. Fine girls, there are, from all over Christendom and even beyond, as plump or as skinny as you like. You won't find better this side of the sea. Probably there are boys as well, if you're inclined that way; our Lord might judge, but not old Snorri. I'll show you later where—'

He didn't get the chance to finish, since at that moment the door opened again. Standing there was a sour-faced man of around twenty years, by my reckoning, tall and long-limbed, with fair hair that was tied back, a shaggy woollen cloak of a style that I'd seen many Dyflin folk wearing draped around his shoulders, and a flagon in one hand.

'Snorri Broklauss,' he said, without warmth, his words sounding more than a little slurred. He greeted him in English, which, I thought, was just as well. 'I was wondering how soon it would be before you next showed your face here. You knew that wine you sold me had spoilt, didn't you?'

The Dane frowned. 'Spoilt, lord?'

'It made me sick, Snorri. Sick like a pig, all over my hall. I was spewing all that night and the next day too.'

'That'll happen if you try to drink the whole barrel at once, lord,' Snorri said gravely, his expression even.

For an instant I thought Magnus might strike him for such discourtesy, but instead his expression softened and a smile broke out across his face. 'So, what have you come to sell me this time?'

'I'm not looking to sell,' Snorri said. 'I've come looking for your help.'

'My help?' Magnus snorted, and took a swig from his flagon. 'You want my help?'

'I want information, or rather this man does.' The sea captain stepped back and gestured in my direction. 'He calls himself Goscelin, from Saint-Omer. He has some questions which I thought you might be able to answer for him.'

Ale-addled as he was, it took a few moments for Magnus's gaze to settle upon me. He looked me up and down, glanced over my shoulder at Serlo and Pons, Godric and Eithne, and snorted again. 'A Fleming?'

'So he claims,' Snorri said.

The other man sneered. 'And does this Goscelin have a voice of his own?'

He wore no weapons, and yet despite his youth he had the look of a warrior, or at least someone who had witnessed much hardship in his life, and fought many battles, both with the sword and without. There was a certain hollowness in his bleary eyes that matched the ale on his breath, and a world-weariness in his manner that I found strange for one of his age, and for which I couldn't account. He didn't strike me as the kind of person who could help me.

'I'm looking for someone,' I said nevertheless. 'Snorri seems to think you might know where to find him.'

'That depends,' said Magnus.

'On what?'

'How much I know depends on how much you're willing to pay.'

I had travelled that road before. I had wasted half my worldly wealth in paying spies who offered me nothing in return. Nothing, that was, except for lies. I could ill afford to make the same mistake again.

'No,' I said. 'First you tell me what you know, and then I pay you however much I think that information is worth.'

'How about this?' he asked. 'You give me the name of the one you're looking for, and I'll tell you whether or not I know where he can be found, and how much it will cost you. You decide then whether you think I'm telling the truth, and either hand over your silver or leave. Agreed?'

Ale dulled the wits of most men, but clearly not this one. A part of me wondered whether it was better to go and try my luck elsewhere, but how was I to tell who was reliable and who was not? I didn't know this city, and so I was relying on the opinion of one who did. And he had brought me here.

'Agreed,' I said eventually, albeit with some reluctance.

'So tell me.'

'I'm looking for a man called Haakon. Haakon Thorolfsson, of the black-dragon banner. I hear he was last seen here in Dyflin around five months ago.'

Magnus's eyes narrowed. 'Haakon Thorolfsson?' His cheeks flushed an angry scarlet, and he spat. 'What do you know of him?'

'Nothing,' I said, confused. 'That's why I'm—'

'Did he send you to taunt me? Is that it? What more does he want from me?'

'Of course he didn't send me,' I said. 'Why would I be asking you where to find him if he had?'

Magnus swigged again from the flagon, and fixed me with a look of disdain, but said nothing.

'So you've heard of him,' I said.

'Yes, I've heard of him. A friend of his, are you, or else looking to sell your sword to him?'

Snorri had taken me for a freebooter as well. Was it so obvious, I wondered, that I had become a masterless man, one of those landless, wandering warriors that until recently I had so despised?

'He's no friend of mine,' I replied. 'And my services aren't for sale.'

'What, then?'

'He stole something that belongs to me,' I said. 'I want it back.'

Twenty

We sat in near-darkness on one of the benches that ran along the long sides of the hall, while Magnus crouched by the dwindling flames of the peat fire, his tufted woollen cloak drawn close about his shoulders. The air was suffused with the smell of damp thatch and rotting timbers. Instead of rushes as we tended to use in England, I noticed the floor was covered with a loose scattering of woodchips and moss, which clearly hadn't been replaced in some time, if the mouse-droppings everywhere were anything to judge by.

'His fortress is far to the north of here, among what are known as the Suthreyjar,' Magnus said, satisfied now that we hadn't come to taunt him, and having accepted my offer of silver.

'The Suthreyjar?' I asked.

'The islands that lie off the coast of northern Britain,' Snorri offered by way of explanation. 'They used to be under the control of the jarls of Orkaneya and the kings of Mann, but now they are havens for pirates, the dominions of petty warlords. Those are dangerous seas that surround them, and yet that's the way one must travel to reach Ysland and the frozen lands beyond.'

'Haakon is one of those pirates,' Magnus said, and there was spite in his voice. 'And one of the more powerful among them, too. He likes to call himself a jarl, but no king ever bestowed that title upon him. He makes his living in the spring and autumn by preying on the trading ships that sail the waters close to his island fastness, and in summer by raiding along the shores of Britain, sometimes selling his services to noble lords and kings in return for rich reward.'

'How did you come by this knowledge?' I asked.

Magnus was silent for a moment. In his eye, though he tried to hide it by turning away, I spied a glimmer of a tear. 'I know', he said, speaking quietly now, 'because, to our misfortune, my brothers and I tried to purchase his services for a campaign of our own.'

'You did?' Snorri said with some surprise. 'You, a warrior?'

'What happened?' I asked.

'He made off in the night with all the booty we had captured on our raid, leaving myself and my brothers unable to pay our men for their service.' He took a deep breath. 'A fight broke out. My eldest brother was killed, the other gravely wounded. He did not die straightaway, but fell into a fever and left this world three days later. I alone managed to escape with my life, together with a few of my oath-sworn followers, as well as some who had served my brothers.'

'You never told me this,' Snorri said.

'And why should I have done? This was three summers ago, before I even knew you.' Magnus turned back to me. 'So, you see, he took something from me as well. Something more valuable than gold or silver or weapons. He took the lives of my brothers. It's because of him that they're now dead, and I find myself reduced to this.'

A moving story, to be sure, although he was not alone in having such a tale to tell. In a similar way Eadgar had taken from me my lord and all my loyal brothers in arms on that night at Dunholm. What I wanted to know was the one thing Magnus had not yet told me.

'Where is Haakon's fortress?' I asked.

'I don't know the name of the island, although I know how to find the fjord in which it lies.'

'You've been there before?'

'Once,' he said. 'I've seen his stronghold on its crag by the sea. Jarnborg, he calls it.'

'The iron fortress,' Snorri murmured.

Magnus nodded. 'It might as well be made of iron, for all the success that men have had trying to capture it. It's all but unassail-able, protected on three sides by high cliffs rising from the water, and approachable only by a narrow neck of land, but it's so steep and uneven that you could never lead an army up it.'

'Could you take me there?' I asked.

'Take you there? Why?'

'To claim back what's rightfully mine.'

'With this army?' he asked, nodding at the various members of my retinue. 'Four men, yourself included, and one girl?'

'And as many others as I can hire.'

He snorted derisively. 'Hosts numbering in the hundreds have marched against Jarnborg and failed to take it. What makes you think you can do it with five?'

'It needn't come to an assault, if Haakon is willing to deal with me.'

Magnus shot me a look as if to suggest that was unlikely, and in truth I didn't really believe it either. For what could I possibly offer that he would accept in return for Oswynn?

'Haakon doesn't give up anything willingly,' Magnus said. 'I've met him, so believe me when I say this. Whatever he has of yours, you won't get it back without a fight.'

'Then join me,' I said, more confidently than I had any right to, given that I knew little of this fortress Magnus had spoken of, in particular the condition of its defences, or the number of spears that guarded its gates and walls. But I was desperately in need of allies, and it seemed to me that fate had led me to this man. 'You mentioned you still have followers who remain loyal to you. I could use their swords.'

'You're asking me to risk my neck on such an expedition?'

'Why not?'

'Many reasons,' he muttered. 'Not least of which is that I don't know you, Fleming.'

'I'll admit to having little knowledge of war, but even I know that this is not the season to go campaigning,' Snorri put in. 'Assuming that you could gather the men and the ships for such a voyage, all Haakon has to do is withdraw inside this fastness of his, where, if he's sensible, he'll have provisions to last until spring. Do you really plan on besieging him for the next half a year, battered by the winter winds, bedding down night after night on frozen ground?'

I glared at him. The old Dane wasn't helping. 'Think instead what you stand to gain,' I told Magnus.

'And what might that be?'

'Vengeance,' I said, hoping to appeal to his baser instincts. 'Honour. Make him pay the blood-price for your brothers' deaths. If he's as powerful as you say he is, he must have wealth stored away in a hoard somewhere, too. All that can be yours.'

'Don't you think that if I considered this possible, and had the means for it, I would have tried already – without your help?'

'Perhaps. But there are ways of achieving victory without resorting to siege or a direct assault.'

Not many came to mind, admittedly. I was thinking, I supposed, of how we had slipped inside Eoferwic to open the gates to King Guillaume's army two years ago, of how we had distracted the enemy by burning the ships at Beferlic last autumn, of how we had negotiated with Morcar to bring about the downfall of the rebels at Elyg. On each of those occasions it was not sheer weight of numbers that had won us the battle, but cunning and not a little daring. I had done it before. I could do it again.

Magnus sat, chewing upon his lip, slightly and almost imperceptibly shaking his head.

'Assuming that you were to join me,' I said, 'how many men could you marshal, do you think?'

'Twenty, perhaps thirty, given time and depending on who is willing. I have my own ship, too, although she leaks and is in need of some repair.'

That was a not inconsiderable host for one man to command. I had been expecting him to say five, or a dozen, perhaps, not more than that. Excitement stirred within me, as I had a sense suddenly of what was possible.

'How many is Haakon likely to have?'

Magnus shrugged. 'Assuming that he's expecting a quiet winter warming himself by his hearth-fire, not many. A full ship's complement of fighting men, at least.'

Around fifty, then, at a guess. They would be his household retainers, his hearth-troops, his best and strongest warriors: his *huskarlar*, to use the Danish word, which I only knew because it was essentially the same as the English *huscarlas*. Perhaps twice the number that Magnus and I could muster between us, then, although of course as the defenders they would hold a distinct advantage over us. Still, those were far from insurmountable odds.

'There's one thing of which you haven't yet spoken,' Magnus said. 'You've told me what I might gain from this, but what about yourself?'

'As I've told you, all I want is to take back what was stolen from me,' I said. 'I'm not interested in Haakon's hoard, his horses or his ships.'

Magnus sat for a few moments in silence, staring into the hearth while he fingered the pitcher of ale. On his hand, I noticed, lit by the fire-glow, was a gilded signet ring engraved with the emblem of a dragon or some other winged beast, which for some reason seemed strangely familiar. The roof-beams creaked as the wind gusted. Outside in the street, geese were honking, perhaps being driven to the city in time for a market tomorrow.

I turned to Snorri. 'What about you? Would you join us?'

'Me?' he asked. 'I'm no warrior, nor have I ever been. I've no interest in pursuing feuds that aren't my own, and I'm too old for such adventures in any case. I'd only slow you down. All I want is to get back home and spend Yule in my own house.'

'I understand,' I said, disappointed though not surprised. He had already done me a great favour by bringing me here. Another ship would no doubt have proven useful, but then again I supposed that to do this we only really needed one. 'What do you say, Magnus?'

He hesitated, no doubt weighing up in his mind how much he could trust me.

'I cannot promise anything,' he said after a short while, 'but I'll send word to my followers in the morning, and see whether they are willing to come with me. If enough of them are eager, then we sail.'

It wasn't the definite answer I'd been hoping for, nor did I sense much conviction in his tone, but it was something. Of course I would rather have an ally on this expedition, but if the only choice was for myself and my small band to go alone, then that was what we would do. How I thought we could possibly confront Haakon and storm this iron fortress of his, I wasn't sure. One thing of which I was sure, however, was that we would find a way, as we had always done. We had to.

I bade farewell to Snorri and his crew the next morning. I was surprised they were leaving so soon, but understood there was no sense in delaying while the winds were still favourable, especially given how far he had yet to travel to reach his home, which he told me was in distant Ysland. *Hrithdyr*'s hold was full, except that the quernstones and casks of wine had now been exchanged for bundles of the shaggy woollen cloaks that seemed to be considered fashionable in these parts.

'The tufts lend them the appearance of fur, see?' he said, proudly showing off one that he'd kept for himself. 'For those who are too poor to afford deerskin or sealskin or ermine pelisses, it's the next best thing. They're almost as warm, too. In Ysland, these fetch many a penny. Enough for Snorri to feed himself and his kin through the winter, at least.'

I had to admit it didn't look much like fur to me, but if that was what folk wanted to wear, who was I to argue?

'Take care,' I said. 'Especially with men like Haakon Thorolfsson roaming the seas.'

'I'll take care, don't you worry about that. Besides, once we're beyond the Suthreyjar, the only thing we have to fear is the ocean.'

One of his crewmen shouted to him then. He bade me safe travels in turn, then stepped down from the quayside as the wide-bellied vessel cast off from her mooring. I called my thanks, and saw him wave in reply, then I watched from the wharves as *Hrithdyr* slipped out downriver, towards the sun-glistening sea, until she was out of sight.

*

It took several days for word to reach Magnus's followers, scattered as they were across the lands that lay upriver of Dyflin, and another few for word from them to return. In the meantime Magnus showed us to his ship, which was grounded a half-mile downriver from the city, close to where the shipwrights had their slipways and their boathouses, drawn up on to the shore above a beach of mud and shingle and covered with an oilskin sheet. He called her *Nihtegesa*, which was English for 'night terror', the name that his people gave to the fear-dreams that cause a man to wake suddenly, drenched in sweat and with heart pounding. Not that she looked capable of striking dread in anyone's heart.

'This is your ship?' I asked when the tarpaulin was drawn back by Magnus and two of his retainers. I did not know much of ships, but I knew enough to be able to tell when one was seaworthy, and *Nihtegesa* was clearly not. The topmost strakes on both sides were dry and crumbling, while a few others were cracked and darkened with rot; they would need replacing, as would the rigging. 'How long since she was last out on the water?'

'A full year, nearly,' Magnus said.

'We'd almost do better to buy ourselves a new ship,' Serlo muttered, a little unkindly perhaps, though I would be lying if I said that the same thought hadn't briefly crossed my mind.

'And you have enough coin for that, do you?' Magnus ran a hand over her timbers, stroking her gently as if she were a horse, at least where barnacles hadn't encrusted her timbers. This was the first time I had seen him without a wine-jug either in his hand or close by, and he seemed a little brighter of spirit for it. 'All she needs is a little care, and she'll float again. Besides, she used to belong to my father. She's all I have left of his, and I'll not sail to war in any other vessel.'

At eighteen benches in length, she was fairly small for a warship, but she was sleek and, to judge by the waterline on her hull, would sit high on the waves. I had not measured her, but she looked to be around seven times from prow to stern what she was in beam, which were generally agreed to be the ideal proportions when building a boat with speed in mind. Assuming that Magnus was right and she could be repaired in good time, she ought to be quick enough to outpace any danger we might happen to run into. I had never fought from the deck of a ship, and had no desire to, if I could help it.

'He reckons it'll be a week's work to patch her up well enough to ride the waves,' Magnus told me later that day, after he'd had one of the shipwrights who plied their trade nearby examine her. 'Possibly as much as ten days', though he couldn't be sure.'

We would have to be content with that, I supposed, and hope that the winds didn't change in that time, because if they did then we might be waiting a while longer still. At least Magnus seemed more favourable towards this expedition than he had the other evening. The very fact that he was seeing to the repair of his ship was a sign of that, although I was wrong to assume his opinion of me had changed for the better.

'I know what you are,' he told me that night as we shared a pitcher of ale in one of Dyflin's many taverns. It was late; the others were already abed in the rooms on the up-floor, and so we sat alone at a table in an otherwise all but empty common room.

'You do?' I asked, surprised, and not just because of what he'd said, but because he had said it in the French tongue.

'I know you're no Fleming, and that your name isn't Goscelin.'

'Snorri told you, did he?' I ought to have known better than to trust the Dane, for all he had helped me.

There was fire in the young man's eyes. 'You're one of them. One of the Devil-fiends who stole our kingdom from us, who ravaged our land with fire and sword.'

I would be lying if I said that his words didn't sting. But after all these years I was well used to hearing such things from his kind. I wasn't going to waste my breath trying to explain to him that England was King Guillaume's by right, as the Pope had confirmed by giving his blessing to our invasion. Of course that did not by any means excuse the violence he had visited last winter upon the Northumbrians when he had scoured their lands. But whether I agreed with his actions or not, the fact remained that he was the lawfully crowned king.

'If you're so sure,' I asked instead, 'then why are we still talking? Why don't you kill me now and be done with it?'

'The thought had crossed my mind.'

I rose from my stool and nodded in the direction of the door. 'I'll fight you right now, if that's what you want, but not here.'

Out of the corner of my eye I'd spotted the tavern-keeper, a slight, grubby man with hair that was a tangle of red curls, glance in our direction. He sensed trouble and wanted no part of it. Better, if we were to do this, for it to be out in the street.

'Sit back down,' Magnus growled. 'If I had even the slightest chance of besting you, I might be tempted to try my luck. But I'm not as foolish as all that. I've grown up in the company of warriors. I know a swordsman when I see one.'

I remained standing. 'What, then?' I demanded. I probably shouldn't have been provoking him, in case he changed his mind and decided he did want a fight after all. Because of one killing I had already been forced to leave England; I didn't want to have to flee this place because of another. 'If you're not looking for a brawl, what do you want with me?'

Magnus rose so that we faced each other, eye to eye. 'Do you know what you and your bastard duke took from us?'

'Tell me,' I said, even though I suspected he was about to do so anyway.

'Because of you,' he said, almost spitting, 'I find myself an outlaw, a wanderer, treading the paths of exile, in flight from my own country, my halls and my home. And now you dare to ask for my help?'

'I have no quarrel with you,' I said. 'We have an enemy in common, and, so far as I am concerned, that makes us friends.'

He didn't seem to be listening. 'For years we fought against your kind, and what good has it done us?'

I wasn't sure if he expected me to answer that or not, and so kept quiet.

'All that struggle,' he went on, 'all that hardship, and all for nothing. Even if I did manage to kill you, what would it change? It wouldn't help us regain what is rightfully ours. The taking of one Norman life would not undo the slaughter your countrymen have wrought.'

I disliked his tone, but his reasoning at least showed he had a wise head upon those shoulders. Wiser, indeed, than those of many older and, one would have hoped, clearer-thinking Englishmen I had encountered in these last few years.

'Did you fight for Eadgar Ætheling?' I asked.

Magnus's cheeks flushed red, not with ale but with anger. 'That pretender? What makes you think I would ever march under his banner?'

'Then who? Wild Eadric, was it?'

'Eadric?' he echoed, frowning. 'Are you trying to insult me?'

'You tell me, then. King Sweyn? Morcar?'

'Enough,' he said, cutting me off. 'I didn't fight for any of them. I fought for myself, for my brothers, and for my family.' He stopped then, frustration writ upon his brow and in the set of his teeth. 'You still don't have the slightest notion who I am, do you?'

My patience, too, was running thin. 'Should I?'

He sat back down upon his stool and buried his head in his hands. An anguished groan escaped his lips that spoke at one and the same time of grief and fury, loss and pain. His shoulders trembled as he spoke.

'I am Magnus,' he said, so quietly that I could barely hear him, 'son of Harold.'

It took me a moment to comprehend what he was saying, a moment that stretched into an eternity as, dumbfounded, I stared at him.

'Harold?' I asked. Only one man by that name came immediately to mind, but surely it couldn't be true. 'You mean the—?'

The oath-breaker and usurper, was what I'd been about to say, but stopped myself in time. Even I was not so stupid as to deliver such an insult to the man's own son, even if both charges were true.

'Harold Godwineson, by God's grace king of the English people,' Magnus said, his voice rising. 'I am his eldest surviving son, and the heir to his realm. The realm that your bastard duke, Guillaume, stole from us!'

He was almost in tears as he said this last. That was when I remembered where I had seen the design on his signet ring, so long ago that it could have been another life entirely, and yet it was not that long ago at all. That same dragon mark, or rather its reverse, I had seen imprinted in red sealing wax on a letter written by Magnus's mother, Eadgyth, who had taken holy orders after the death of her husband, and retreated to an abbey in Wessex.

'By rights you should call me king,' Magnus said. 'By rights Eadgar and all those who flock to his banner should be swearing themselves to my service and bending their knees before me. By rights England belongs to me, and yet here I am, king of nothing. Nothing!'

How many men had falsely laid claim to England's crown in recent times? First there had been the oath-breaker Harold and his namesake, the King of Norway, and then, after each had perished to the sword, there had been young Eadgar. There was talk, as well, that Sweyn, the Danish king who last year led his raiding-fleet to Northumbria in support of the ætheling, had secretly been plotting to turn on his English ally and seize the kingdom for himself.

And now Magnus added himself to their number. Five false claimants in as many years, and those were just the ones of whom I'd heard. But where was his retinue? What host did he command?

The tavern-keeper was glancing nervously towards the door, I noticed, probably contemplating whether or not to go and fetch help. His look of confusion suggested he wasn't familiar with the French tongue, and no doubt that ignorance was only adding to his alarm. It was as well that there was no one else in the alehouse at this hour to hear Magnus's ravings, or surely our arguing would have spilt over into a brawl by now, and then the tavern-keeper would indeed have reason to be worried.

But the storm had passed. Magnus was weeping now, his hands covering his eyes and hiding his tears. '"Hu seo thrag gewat,"' he said between sobs, '"genap under nihthelm, swa heo no wære."'

How that time has faded away, dark under night's curtain, as if it had never been. I recognised the phrase from an old poem, one of many that Ædda, who was almost as fond of words and verses as he was of the horses in his care, had once recited to me. But I didn't know what to say to it, and so for a long time we sat in silence.

Magnus Haroldson. Hard to believe that the usurper's own flesh and blood was sitting here before me. I recalled having heard in passing about the raids that he and his two elder brothers had launched upon the coast of Wessex, whilst we were occupied fighting the king's wars in Northumbria last summer. Nothing much had come of those raids, and they had been repelled with little difficulty and with great injury inflicted upon the invaders' small band. Indeed, on one of those occasions the brothers' own countrymen, the folk who lived in those parts, had stood against them and helped drive them out. If the object of those expeditions had been to reclaim the crown that their father had for a brief few months worn, then they served as an example of the low regard in which the English folk held the house of Godwine. Little wonder, then, that such bitterness lingered.

Eventually, I signalled to the tavern-keeper to bring us another jug of ale, which after a moment's hesitation he did. It was thin and a little too bitter for my taste, but it was better than nothing.

'Not so long ago I happened to cross paths with your mother, Eadgyth,' I said, remembering that visit we had paid to the nunnery in Wessex a couple of years before.

To have any chance of confronting Haakon and claiming Oswynn back, I needed Magnus as an ally, and for us to set our differences aside, yet at this moment I was close to losing him. Somehow, I had to try to win back his confidence.

'My mother?' he asked, eyeing me suspiciously. 'What do you mean?'

'I mean that I met her, and spoke with her, too.'

'Spoke with her where? Does she still live at the abbey at Wiltune?'

So he knew of her whereabouts. 'This was a couple of years ago, but yes. She is safe there, and seemed in good health, too, though she grieves for your father, and greatly misses her sons.'

'She told you that?'

I nodded. That last part I had made up, although Magnus would never guess that. Fresh tears ran down his cheek.

'I have not seen her in more than five years,' he said. 'Not since she and my father left Lundene to face your duke in battle. He forbade me and my brothers from going with him, said we were too young, though I was already fifteen winters old then and they were older still. I would rather have suffered death in the shield-wall than endured the pain of exile.'

There was silence for a while. A cold draught gusted in as the door opened and two red-haired men with thick arms and broad shoulders entered. I guessed they were brothers for they shared the same wide brows and prominent ears. They caught me staring at them and I turned away. I had no wish to cause trouble here tonight.

I looked Magnus in the eye. 'You will not win back your father's kingdom,' I said, as gently as I could, in a low voice so that the Irishmen wouldn't hear.

He shook his head, but it could not be denied. These were words he needed to hear.

'You can't,' I went on. 'Not now. That battle is over. England belongs to King Guillaume. But you can win back your honour and your pride. And I will help you do it.'

'Why?' he asked. 'Why would you help me?'

'Because Guillaume is my king no longer,' I said. 'Like you, I'm an outlaw, an exile, lordless and landless. All I have left are oaths, and the loyalty of those with me. I've spent long enough fighting wars on the behalf of others, risking my life for precious little reward. But no more.'

'How do I know I can trust you?'

'Isn't it enough that we share an enemy?'

'If we're to fight alongside one another, I want to know who's guarding my flank.'

That was only fair, I thought. He had been honest with me regarding who he was, and now I would be honest with him in return.

'Snorri was right,' I admitted. 'My name isn't Goscelin. I'm no Fleming, nor am I a simple traveller.'

'Then who—?'

'Listen and I'll tell you. My name is Tancred.' I paused for a moment to see if that meant anything to him, but it looked as though I was to be disappointed. 'I'm the man who won the gates at Eoferwic, who fought Eadgar on the bridge and almost killed him. I'm the one who gave him his scar. I was the one who led the attack upon Beferlic, who fired the ships and helped destroy his storehouses. If it weren't for me, the ætheling you hate so much would be master of England by now.'

He had fallen quiet by then, his lips pursed, and I took that as a sign that my words had had their desired effect. I'd been relying on the supposition that even if news of the rebellion on the Isle hadn't yet reached his ears, he'd at least have heard the tales of how Eadgar and his allies were routed in those great battles. And it seemed I was right.

'If there's anyone who can help you do this, it's me,' I said. 'That's why you should trust me.'

Twenty-one

Fortunately Magnus seemed to be convinced by my reasoning, which was just as well, since I doubted my coin would extend to hiring for myself an army sufficient for this task, as well as a guide who knew the islands and the sea-routes of the Suthreyjar, and not to mention a ship as well. God's favour was clearly shining upon me, and I accepted with no little thanks these gifts He'd sent my way, welcome as they were after everything I'd endured in recent weeks.

Thus while *Nihtegesa* was being repaired and caulked ready for our voyage in the days that followed, Magnus rode out in person to solicit the support of those of his followers who dwelt outside the city.

'Most of them left when it was clear I no longer had the means to pay them,' he told me. 'It would have been fruitless to try to prevent them going, so I released them from their oaths. Some have taken service with other lords; a few have found themselves Irish wives and a corner of land on which to settle. Still, if I seek them out and tell them what I have in mind, I hope that a few at least will be willing to rejoin me.'

'I hope you're right,' I said.

He shrugged. 'I can but try.'

His faith was well placed. Almost a week after we had first made port in Dyflin, the first of Magnus's old retainers came to the city and presented himself at his hall. A thickset Englishman in his middle years, he was dressed in mail and armed with spear and sword, as well as a long-handled axe that he carried slung across his back. His top lip was adorned with a thick moustache, and his tangled beard was flecked with breadcrumbs. His name was Ælfhelm and he was, I soon learnt, one of the longest-serving and most trusted retainers of the usurper's family. He had been left to defend Lundene when Harold had marched to meet King Guillaume, and so had been spared a bloody end at Hæstinges.

On first seeing myself and my knights, and recognising us for the Normans we were, he reached straightaway for his sword-hilt. I believe he would have tried to face all three of us at once had Magnus not blocked his path, explained who we were and why we were here.

Ælfhelm spat on the floor. 'Why should I ally myself with these whoresons?'

'Because I wish it,' Magnus answered.

'It was men like these who slew your father and his brothers. Have you forgotten that?'

'They're friends,' Magnus insisted, and though that seemed to me a little overstating matters, given that we had met only a few days previously, I didn't argue. In any case, it seemed to put an end to the debate. The bearded one's mouth twisted into a scowl and he kept glancing suspiciously at us as Magnus led him into the hall and the two of them exchanged what tidings they had. We would have to keep a close watch over him, I reckoned.

Nor was he the only one we would have to be wary of. In all, twenty-six of Magnus's huscarls responded to his summons, each one accompanied by a manservant or stable-boy, and a couple with their lovers and mistresses. They were men of all sizes and appearances, some of an age roughly with myself, while others were older even than Ælfhelm, although he seemed to be chief among them. All, however, regardless of how many they were in years, possessed the same stiff bearing and sour temper that spoke to me of battles fought and lost, of feuds unsettled, of thoughts of vengeance rarely uttered but ever-present, of untold bitterness against the circumstances that had brought each one of them to these shores. These were the men alongside whom I would have to fight if I wanted to reclaim Oswynn.

In my time I had been forced to make cause with some unlikely allies in pursuit of common ends, but these were without a doubt the unlikeliest of all. In another place and another time, they would have had no more hesitation in cutting us down than we would them. As it was, only Magnus stood between us and a grim fate. I supposed since he was their lord and, in their eyes, their king, they were oath-bound to accept his wishes, but that did not make me feel any safer. I was not alone, either.

'I don't like this,' Serlo confessed to me when the five of us were alone later that day, having ventured down to the market to provision ourselves for the voyage north.

'Neither do I, lord,' said Pons. 'How soon will it be before they turn on us?'

'They won't,' I said firmly, more to convince myself than because I truly believed it. 'I have Magnus's word. He's someone who understands honour, and the value of keeping one's oaths.'

'Like his father kept to his oaths, you mean?' Pons asked, and there was an obvious barb to his tone. He was referring, of course, to the pledge of fealty Harold had made to Duke Guillaume, and his promise to support the latter's claim to the English crown: a promise Harold later broke when he seized the crown for himself.

I didn't offer an answer to that, for I knew there was none that would satisfy him.

Pons sighed in exasperation, and shook his head in disbelief. 'You can't rely on the word of an Englishman.'

'That's not true,' Godric protested.

'Except for the whelp here, of course,' he added. 'But he's not like them.'

'Why not?' I asked. 'And what about men like Ædda, and all the folk at Earnford?'

'You know what Pons means, lord,' said Serlo. 'The moment we're out on the sea, they'll cast us over the side, if they don't come for us sooner. In the night, perhaps, while we're sleeping. They'll kill us and then they'll have their way with the girl.'

'Then make sure your sword is always at hand,' I said. 'And stay together. They're less likely to try anything if we keep close.'

We continued in silence. I found a merchant selling the tufted cloaks that Snorri had praised so highly, and handed over a clutch of silver in exchange for five of his finest. Winter was fast approaching; almost everywhere the branches were bare, having finally cast off the robes they had clung to since summer, the robes that once had been full of brightness but which the turning of the seasons had made drab. Each dawn when we awoke was colder than the last. Across the city the thatch upon the houses and the workshops was covered with frost, and that morning we had stepped outside to find all the puddles in the street hard with ice. It was a good thing that *Nihtegesa* was, by then, seaworthy again, the rot having been discovered to be less severe than at first we'd feared.

'I'm told she's still letting in some water, but all ships leak to a greater or lesser extent,' Magnus had told me. 'So long as we make sure to bail her now and then, she'll do fine. Were we travelling to Ysland or anywhere across the open sea, I'd want her in better condition, but she'll suffice for where we want to go.'

Even so, he had insisted upon waiting another day or two in case any more of his retainers showed themselves. Had the decision been mine, I would have set out straightaway rather than delay for the sake of a couple more swords and risk the wind changing in the meantime. Since they were his men and it was his ship, however, I'd had little choice but to defer to him.

'This whole expedition is folly, lord,' Pons muttered after we had been walking a while longer. 'Coming here to Dyflin is one thing, but now you want us to venture in winter across the northern seas, and all in pursuit of a woman.' He nodded towards a slim, freckled Irish girl of perhaps sixteen summers who was helping her mother, herself far from unattractive, carry rolls of cloth. 'There are women here, lord!'

'Oswynn isn't just any woman,' I said. 'She's my woman.'

'Truthfully, lord, what chance do you think you have of claiming her back, assuming that she still lives, or that this Haakon hasn't sold her to one of his pirate friends?'

'She was alive and in his company when Eithne met them a few months ago.'

'And happy, lord?'

I stared at him. 'What?'

Serlo frowned and placed a hand on his sword-brother's shoulder. 'Pons,' he said warningly.

But Pons wasn't about to listen. 'Did Eithne ever tell you whether she seemed happy in his company?'

I glanced at the girl, who hadn't understood what we were saying, although she couldn't have failed to hear her name, spoken in harsh tones. Her cheeks had turned pale. She sensed something was amiss, even if she couldn't be sure what.

'Ask her,' said Pons. 'Ask her now.'

'No,' I said, doing my best to restrain my anger. 'I'm not going to ask her. I don't need to.'

Why? Because I was afraid of what the answer might be? Afraid to learn that all this effort to which I'd gone was, in fact, for naught? Afraid to find myself bereft of any cause to fight for?

'What is it, lord?' Eithne asked me in English.

'Nothing,' I muttered. 'It's nothing.'

'You've said yourself that it's been nearly three years since you were last with her, lord,' Pons said. 'Even if we do find her, and even if you manage to bury your sword-point in Haakon's throat, that doesn't mean she'll necessarily thank you for it.'

I stopped in the middle of the street. 'She will. I know it. And besides, what else is there for me? For us. Tell me that.'

Pons didn't answer straightaway. Men and women shouted at us in tongues I didn't understand, berating us for getting in their way as they tried to roll barrels and drive oxen up the way, but I paid them no heed. If Pons did not support me in this, then I needed to know. My mind was already made up, for I was going with Magnus to whatever fate awaited me in the north. But I had no place on this expedition for men who would not give their all in this cause.

'Well?' I demanded.

'I don't know, lord,' Pons said eventually.

'Serlo?'

He took a deep breath, and his hesitation betrayed his uncertainty. He glanced sidelong at Pons before turning back to me. 'I'm with you, lord, as always. But that doesn't mean I'm altogether happy about it.'

Pons nodded in agreement. I supposed that was the best I could hope for. That they had followed me this far, without so much as a murmur of dissent until this moment, was testament to their loyalty, and a reminder of how much I owed them.

'What about you, Godric?' I asked. 'You, at least, could return to England, if you'd rather not come with me.'

'Where would I go? Back to my uncle?' He shook his head. 'There's nothing for me there, lord. Not any more.'

It hadn't been two months since we'd first met, but already he seemed a different person. He was his own man now, subject to no one. That he nevertheless chose to stand by me, though he was bound by no oath to do so, earned my respect.

I turned to Eithne, and briefly wondered what she might say if I asked her the question Pons had wanted me to. I tried to drive such thoughts from my mind.

'Do I have a choice?' she retorted, when I asked her whether she was still willing to come with me.

'I can give you money enough for passage back home, if that's what you want. There'll be ships that can take you, I'm sure.'

'You place too much faith in other men,' she said in that mocking manner I had grown used to. 'How far do you think I would get, travelling alone, without anyone for protection? At least with you I am safe.'

That made sense, I supposed. If these last few weeks had taught her anything, it was that she could trust us. Why put herself at risk by striking out on her own? No doubt that was why she had stayed with us this long; she'd had plenty of opportunity along the way to flee if she'd wanted to.

We were all agreed, then. Breton, Normans, English and Irish would travel together into the north, albeit some more reluctantly than others.

Unspeaking, we ventured on past the rows of stalls where cloth merchants, fishmongers, wine-traders, candlemakers, wood-sellers and spicers plied their trade, until we came upon an open square close by the thing-mount, where rows upon rows of men, women and children of both sexes and all colours of hair and skin sat upon the muddy ground, bound together with ropes and chains, their heads bowed and faces leaden, huddled inside clothes that seemed either too large or too small and were dirty and frayed at the hems; all being watched over by men armed with clubs and staves.

The great slave-market for which Dyflin was renowned. Beside me, Eithne shrank back. At first I wondered if she'd spotted her former master, Ravn, somewhere among that throng, but there had to be hundreds of slaves, owners, traders and guards, variously crying and shouting and negotiating and cursing, and so I reckoned she was merely nervous.

'You're with me, so you're safe,' I told her. 'Isn't that what you said?'

'Let's leave,' she said. 'Please.'

I was about to, for her sake, when my gaze fell upon three dark-skinned young women, one short and the other two tall, all of them wide-eyed and trembling, being led away by a fierce-looking man whose arms were covered in silver rings and who was shouting at them in Danish. I'd glimpsed Moorish women before, but not often and not for long. They were a strange sight to me, and I confess that I could not take my eyes off those girls, spellbound as I was with a mixture of curiosity and admiration, for although they looked thin and ill fed, they were nevertheless creatures of wonder.

'Lord,' said Serlo in a warning tone, jolting me from my thoughts. He was gesturing down the street whence we had come, where I saw now a group of four men clad in hauberks and chausses, with swords on their belts. To begin with I didn't know why he was drawing my attention to these in particular, when so many walked the streets of this city armed and mailed, but as they stopped by the stall of one of the cloth-sellers and turned to speak with him, I saw the distinctive close-cropped hair at the backs and sides of their heads.

We were too far away to make out their features, but I knew at a glance they were Normans, and knights, too. But why were they here, in Dyflin of all places?

Only one reason came to mind. They had to be Robert's men. Who else?

I'd thought that leaving England behind and going into exile would be enough to satisfy them. Obviously I was wrong. So determined were they that I should face trial for my crime that they had taken ship across the sea in order to haul me back to England. Now they were here, barely fifty paces away, if that.

'This way,' I said to the others, my heart pounding all of a sudden. 'Quickly, but not too quickly.'

I'd realised that if we could see them, then they would just as easily be able to see us. I didn't want to linger, but at the same time knew that we would only draw attention upon ourselves if we ran. Without looking back, I slipped through the market crowds, towards an alley where the smoke of a blacksmith's forge billowed white and thick.

'Do you think they saw us?' Godric asked when we had all gathered, coughing and with eyes stinging, on the other side of that cloud, safely out of sight of the marketplace.

'I hope not,' I replied.

We pressed on in the direction of Magnus's house, which was only a short distance away, close to the city's southern gates. From time to time I risked a glance behind us, but didn't want to attract suspicion. Fortunately there were many different ways one could take through the streets, and, having spent now a little more than a week in this city, I was beginning to learn them. From time to time I risked a glance over my shoulder to see if they were behind us, until eventually I had to concede that they weren't following.

'They're determined, aren't they?' Pons remarked.

It didn't make sense. Why pursue us here, all this way? For that matter, how did they even know where we were headed? I'd held that piece of information back from Ædda and Galfrid and Father Erchembald for this very reason. Neither had I told Eudo and Wace, at least not so far as I could recall. Where were they now? Had they gone with Robert on the king's planned expedition to Flanders?

And then I remembered. I'd let it slip to Robert, on the very day that we had buried his father, in his solar at Heia.

I'd been a fool. An accursed fool. At every turn I'd given my enemies the means to ensnare me and bring about my downfall. First Atselin, and now Robert himself, difficult though it was to think of him as such. But I could hardly count him as a friend any longer.

'They're looking for me,' I said, after we'd arrived at Magnus's hall and I'd explained to him what had happened and what we'd seen. 'They've already driven me from England, and now they'll scour this town until they find me.'

'What did you do?' Ælfhelm growled. He and a number of his brothers in arms whose names I hadn't yet learnt sat along the benches, passing between them a leather flask from which they filled clay drinking pots.

'That doesn't matter. What does matter is that we get away from here, and as soon as possible.'

Many pairs of eyes had noticed us walking Dyflin's streets in recent days, coming and going from Magnus's hall, and there would be plenty of rumours passing from tongue to tongue, some of them accurate and others less so, about who we were and what our business was here in the city. Armed with a little silver, it wouldn't take all that long for Robert's men to learn where we were. When that happened, I could give up all hope of finding Oswynn soon.

'You want us to sail now, simply to protect your wretched hides?' Ælfhelm asked. 'Why should your fate concern us?'

'Ælfhelm,' said Magnus warningly.

But the huscarl was not to be deterred. 'I smell a trick, lord. First these Frenchmen come here claiming to seek your help, and now suddenly a horde of their countrymen arrive in their wake. This seems to me no accident.'

'What are you implying?' I asked.

Another of the Englishmen, a thin-faced, long-haired man by the name of Uhtferth, who was *Nihtegesa*'s steersman, had been nodding in agreement for some time, and he spoke up now.

'You, lord,' he said, addressing Magnus, 'are the one who the Frenchmen are after. They want to finish what they have been unable to do for five years, which is to make sure that no heir of

Harold lives to challenge them. Having first rooted you out, this man' – he pointed at me – 'has clearly sent word to his friends, and now they've come to kill you.'

I could only laugh at how ridiculous that sounded. 'If that were true, why would I come to warn you in advance that my countrymen are here?'

Uhtferth and Ælfhelm glanced at each other, but neither appeared to have any answer. I turned to Magnus, for the decision in the end belonged to him. My safety rested in the hands of an Englishman, and not merely any Englishman at that, but no less than a son of the usurper, who owed me nothing and had every reason to hate me. If he decided he was better off fighting Haakon without us, or even if he chose to give us up to Robert's men, I wouldn't have blamed him, or even been surprised.

It was a long while before Magnus spoke, or perhaps it only seemed that way because I knew how much rested on the next words that came out from his mouth.

'We sail tonight,' he said at last, much to my relief.

'Tonight?' Ælfhelm echoed, amidst a roar of disapproval from his comrades.

'That's right. I will not force you to come if you do not wish. So either make your peace with this alliance I've made, or else stay here in Dyflin. I leave that choice to you.'

The huscarl grimaced, but it was clear that the desire for adventure and for glory still burnt bright in his heart, despite his years. He would not abandon his lord, would not refuse this challenge.

'What about the others?' Uhtferth said. 'I thought we were going to wait another few days in case Halfdan and Beorhtred and Ecgric showed themselves.'

'If they were eager enough, they would have made the effort to come sooner, as you have all done,' Magnus said. 'We can't wait for ever. No, providing that the skies are clear, we leave tonight. At least then we'll have a full moon to light our way.' He turned to address the rest of his men. 'Are you with me?'

A murmur of less than hearty agreement went around the hall.

'Very well,' he said. 'Find those who aren't here and pass word on to them. We'll meet at the eastern gate an hour after full dark. Be ready. If you're not there, we won't wait.'

Reluctantly and with not a little grumbling, they raised themselves from the benches, leaving their drinking pots still half full as they buckled on sword-belts, donned cloaks and ventured out into the stiff breeze. Ælfhelm lingered a moment, regarding me with suspicion in his eyes, but then his comrades shouted his name and he followed. The sun was already low; they didn't have long to gather their friends and everything they needed.

'For this,' Magnus said to me after they'd left, 'you owe me.'

And I knew he was right.

We did not venture outside Magnus's hall until night had settled completely. Fortunately the skies were clear, as hoped for, with only the faintest wisp of cloud veiling the stars to the west. God was clearly with us, and the light of His favour shone milky-pale upon us.

It couldn't have been three hours since we'd spied Robert's men, but it had felt like an age. The streets were quiet now. Gone were the merchants shouting out the prices of their wares, the calls of the goats and pigs and cattle and geese. The stalls had been dismantled, the goods taken away, and the sellers had returned to their cottages to sup by their hearth-fires and count out whatever meagre coins they'd been able to reap that day. Few men and even fewer women were about at this hour, but nevertheless we pulled our hoods up over our heads lest anyone should recognise us.

Thankfully no one challenged us, and we reached the east gate without trouble. The rest of Magnus's company were already there by the time we arrived, and assured us that everyone was present, but nevertheless he counted them out: twenty huscarls, most accompanied by retainers of their own; and ourselves. The wives and mistresses that some of the Englishmen had brought with them were to stay in Dyflin or return home, Magnus having forbidden any women on this expedition, for their presence on board a warship was said to invite ill fortune. At my insistence he had made an exception for Eithne, but I could tell from the glances he gave her that the thought of bringing her with us unnerved him.

The sentries looked strangely at us when we presented ourselves at the gate, and at first they refused to let us pass, but then Magnus drew back his hood to reveal his face, and I suppose he must have been known to them, since they quickly changed their minds and allowed us through.

Nihtegesa was drawn up on to the muddy beach above the creek that ran into the river mouth, one of many vessels that lay at rest there. The tide was already high, almost on the turn. The waves lapped at her stern, and the mud sucked beneath her. Magnus had left Uhtferth the steersman and another half a dozen of his hearth-troops to guard her, as was usual. Ships, and especially warships, were greatly prized, not just for the goods that were often to be found in their holds but also for the power they represented, and for that reason they were the favoured targets of many a thief.

We passed our packs up over the gunwale to the boat guards, taking care not to make too much noise as we did so. It was not unknown for ships to leave port in the middle of the night, but it wasn't commonplace either, and we didn't want to attract more attention than was necessary. Already some of those keeping watch by the other ships were calling to us, asking what we were doing about at this hour, and their shouts were waking other crews, who yelled back in their various tongues for them to be quiet. We ignored them all as we went to work pushing *Nihtegesa* down the mud and the shingle, her keel scraping against stone, towards the blackness of the creek, until she was fully afloat. We waded out to her and those already on board held out their hands to help haul us up and on to the deck, where we shook free strands of wrack that had become stuck to our sopping trews and boots, and then set about raising the mast and the rigging, pulling on ropes according to Magnus's and Uhtferth's instructions, and tying them off where needed.

The rowers took their places on the sea chests that served as their benches, lowering their oars into the water with a soft murmur of splashes. As the incoming tide continued to surge up the inlet, they steadied *Nihtegesa*, taking care that the swell didn't take her and run her aground. It wasn't long before the waters began to ebb, Magnus gave the signal and we slipped down the creek, past the landing stages and hythes, the slipways and coves where river-barges, wide-beamed traders, rowing boats and fishing craft lay at rest, and a handful of longships, too, most around the same size as *Nihtegesa*, but one larger.

Much larger, in fact, I saw as we grew nearer. Outlined by the moon's light, she was a fearsome and magnificent sight. Probably thirty benches in length, she dwarfed every other vessel beached or at anchor in that creek; indeed she would have dwarfed most vessels in all of Britain.

To eyes untrained as mine were, there was little to tell one ship from another, especially in the dark and from such a distance. Nevertheless I realised in that moment that I recognised her, for I'd sailed on her once before. This was *Wyvern*, the ship that once had been the pride of Guillaume Malet and that now belonged to his son. Which only confirmed that the Normans we'd seen in the city earlier had indeed been Robert's men. And if his ship was here, did that mean that he himself was too?

I glimpsed a flurry of movement on her deck as men were roused and lanterns lit. Voices carried across the water, hailing us, and a shiver ran through me, for those shouts came in French. The men pulled on shoes and, leaping down on to the shingle, came running down to the shore, waving their arms at the same time. No doubt they'd worked out by then what was happening, and that we were getting away, but they were too late. We were already past them, and gathering speed, *Nihtegesa*'s prow carving through the star-glistening waters towards where the narrow creek emptied into the river mouth, and I was laughing, whooping with the thrill of the chase, of having eluded them.

'You'll have to try harder if you want to catch us!' I yelled at them, into the breeze gusting from astern, and Serlo and Pons were quick to join in, hurling insults at the Frenchmen, who could only watch, powerless to do anything, as we pulled away. They shouted something in reply, but whatever it was they said, I couldn't make out. I saw some of their comrades labouring to float *Wyvern*, but she was easily half as large again as *Nihtegesa*, and they were clearly struggling.

That was the last I saw of them. A moment later the creek opened out into the bay, we rounded a headland and they were lost from sight. Breakers foamed as they met the shore, whilst *Nihtegesa* rode the swell, the salt spray crashing into her bows and her gunwales, luminous in the moonlight. With one hand Magnus beat a small drum that hung by a leather strap around his neck, keeping the oarsmen in time, while Uhtferth kept a steady head on the steering-oar, his thin face drawn in concentration.

Ahead the open sea beckoned, stretching as far as the eye could make out. Somewhere out there, among the islands known as the Suthreyjar, was Haakon, the man whom I had been seeking for a year and more.

I hoped for his sake that he slumbered soundly while he still had the chance. For all too soon we would be descending upon his halls, wreaking our own night terror, inflicting upon him the same despair as he had inflicted upon me. He had taken something that did not belong to him, something precious to me. Now I would take it back, and make sure that he paid for the suffering he'd inflicted.

He had no way of knowing it, but we were coming for him.

Twenty-two

Whether I truly believed that was the last we would see of our pursuers, and that we had shaken them off our trail for good, I can no longer remember. If I did, however, then I was not only foolish but also gravely mistaken.

In those hours after our flight from Dyflin, though, I found no place in my thoughts for worry or doubt. The seas were calm that night, which meant that for once my gut was not churning, and so instead of sickness swelling in my stomach, there was hunger. My heart was filled with delight, my head giddy not just with the salt air but with the prospect of adventure and the feeling of freedom: a feeling I hadn't experienced in a long time. Tancred a Dinant, the Breton, the lord of Earnford, was once more going to war, but this time it was different, for this was a war of my own choosing.

Under the cover of night, we ran north for a couple of hours or more, taking advantage of the stiff breeze that blew athwart our course, until the clouds began to veil the stars, when Magnus at last took us in towards shore, where a wide beach stretched between two high cliffs. We pushed *Nihtegesa* high up the sand, then took down her mast and made a tent over her deck with an oilskin sheet to keep out the thin rain which by then was beginning to fall, and bedded down under it for shelter, with our cloaks rolled up as pillows. By morning the skies had cleared, and with the sun glistening off the wave-tips and a favourable wind filling our sail, we set off again, following the whale-road north.

The sun was past its highest when first we glimpsed the ship on the horizon. It lay some way off our stern, and a little out to sea, on our steerboard side. The keenest eyes among us could not make out whether she was trader or longship, however, and we soon lost sight of her. Still, it served to put me on edge all that afternoon and the evening too, which was probably why I was in such a foul mood as we sat around the campfire, where Ælfhelm and his comrades were cooking some kind of stew made from fish and beans that was apparently a favourite dish in Defnascir, the place many of them hailed from.

'What was it that Haakon stole from you?' Magnus asked me later that evening, when the last light of day was all but gone. I was sitting upon a boulder high up on the beach, above the tideline, running a whetstone up the edge of my sword, the one I'd brought from Earnford. It was not as well balanced as I would have liked, and I was still getting used to its weight, but the least I could do was keep it sharp and free of rust.

'Why?' I asked. 'What business is it of yours?'

'It's my business because it's my ship.'

I didn't answer straightaway, but simply took an oilcloth from my pack and worked at polishing the flat of the blade until the coiling, smoke-like pattern ingrained in the steel glimmered in the moon's wan light.

'Well?' Magnus asked.

'He took my woman.'

At first he must have thought I was joking, for he gave me a strange look. 'Your woman?' he asked with a snort. 'Is that all?'

'If you had ever seen her,' I said, 'you wouldn't be laughing.'

'It's not my place to judge, I suppose,' said Magnus. 'All I can say is that she must be a precious jewel indeed if you're travelling to the ends of Britain just to find her.'

'She is,' I answered, closing my eyes, recalling her face, just as I had many times during the dark, lonely nights since she'd been taken from me. I remembered the wild gleam in her eyes that spoke of her mischievous, restless spirit, the feel of her skin upon my fingertips, her round, firm breasts that I had caressed so many times in those short months that we had been together.

How I missed her.

It was often said that only for the sake of reputation will a man risk everything, but now I realised that wasn't true. For here I was. What fame I'd earned myself was all but squandered, and my name tarnished, perhaps for ever. But if it wasn't riches or land or duty or honour that had set me on this path, then what? Love? That was one name for it, I supposed, although this didn't feel to me like the love that the poets often sang of: overpowering, obsessive and jealous. No, this was different. Even though we had not been together long, somehow with Oswynn I had sensed a kinship of souls, a closeness that I had never been able to forge with any other. Not even with Leofrun, for all that she had been dear to me. That closeness was what I yearned for above everything. All my striving for fame and glory had not made me happy. Now I went in search of the one thing that would.

The boulder on which I perched was wide enough for two, and Magnus sat down beside me. 'I got into a fight over a girl once myself,' he said as he gazed out across the cove at the breakers lapping gently upon the sand. 'I didn't know she was married until her husband stumbled upon us while we were tumbling together. I was fortunate to get away without a scratch upon me. He wasn't.' He shook his head sadly. 'It always seems to end badly when there are women involved. And yet we never learn, for we're always fighting over them, aren't we?'

I thought back to that summer's day, long years ago. The day when I had claimed my first kill. That fight had been over a woman, too.

I was nearly twice the age now that I'd been then, but clearly the last twelve years had taught me nothing, nothing at all. For I was back where my journey along the sword-path had begun, as reckless and as dim-witted now as ever, and with barely anything to show for all my struggles.

'How did Haakon take her from you?' Magnus asked.

I sighed, and told him about the ambush that night at Dunholm, and how my friends and I had barely managed to escape with our lives, and how that had been the last I'd seen of her for a year and a half, until she had appeared at Beferlic. 'How she came to end up in his company, I don't know. Possibly one of Eadgar's men captured her during the ambush, and later sold her on as a slave.'

'I can think of a simpler explanation than that,' Magnus said. 'Haakon was at Dunholm.'

I shot him a glare. 'What?'

'He was there. He was pledged to Eadgar at that time, as were many other sword-Danes from Orkaneya and the Suthreyjar. He was one of those leading the attack. Or at least so he's now claiming.'

'Whoever told you that obviously wasn't there. It was Eadgar and the Northumbrians who led the attack that night. I saw his purple-and-yellow banner.'

'I'm not denying that Eadgar was there, but he wasn't the one who broke down the gates of the stronghold and torched the mead-hall. That was Haakon's doing.'

I stared at him, confused. 'No,' I said, surprised that Magnus could have heard it so wrong. 'It was Eadgar who stormed the gates. He burnt the mead-hall.'

With Robert de Commines, my lord, inside. Had I not, weeks later, stood face to face with the ætheling whilst he bragged of how he had murdered him? Had all that been but a dream?

'So Eadgar would have everyone believe. He wanted to be the one to kill Earl Robert, but Haakon desired the glory for himself. What I've been told is that while the aetheling was occupied elsewhere in the town, he took it upon himself to assault the stronghold.'

I couldn't believe what I was hearing. 'If that's true, then why haven't I learnt of this before now?'

'Because Eadgar paid Haakon and all his followers to keep their mouths shut, and paid them very generously at that.'

My mind was reeling. None of this was making sense. 'Why would he do that?'

'At the time he was seeking the support of a number of the great Northumbrian lords, many of whom still doubted Eadgar's stomach for a fight, and didn't believe in his conviction or his ability to mount a full campaign. The ætheling needed them to believe he was the one, and he alone, who burnt Dunholm, who killed Earl Robert and destroyed his army, if he was to bring their spears under his banner.'

'But why should the truth only come out now?'

The Englishman shrugged. 'Now that Eadgar's rebellion has been crushed and he's fled to the protection of the King of Alba, most of those supporters have deserted him. I suppose Haakon thought there was no need to hide it any longer. Probably he was tired of keeping it a secret and wanted, finally, to boast of his triumph. I only heard this from someone who learnt it from a passing trader, so how much of it's true, I can't say. Still, it would explain how your woman came to be with him.'

It was as if a veil had been lifted from my eyes. At a single stroke most of what I thought I knew about what had happened that night was swept away, revealed for the lie it was.

How many times had I played over those events in my mind, trying to think of some way that it could have been different, something I could have done to turn the battle and save my lord? How many times had I dreamt of exacting my revenge upon Eadgar for what he'd done, for all of my sword-brothers he had slain, for all the Norman blood he had spilt?

All this while I had been swearing vengeance upon the wrong man. It wasn't Eadgar I needed to kill, after all. It was Haakon Thorolfsson.

Until now, though I would never have admitted it to Magnus, I'd been wondering whether it would even be necessary to mount an attack on the Dane's fortress if I could negotiate with him a price for Oswynn's release. Now, however, I realised that nothing less than his blood would satisfy me.

And I, not Harold's son, would take his life. My hand would deal the telling blow. I would do it slowly, and make him suffer as he had made my lord suffer. I'd do to him all the things that, long ago, I'd sworn to do to Eadgar. I would put out his eyes and sever his balls, cut out his tongue so that he could not scream, and only then would I kill him, slicing open his belly and burying my sword-point deep in his chest, in his heart, and when I was done I would leave his broken corpse for the carrion birds to feast upon.

Even then it wouldn't be justice. Not after what he had done. Nothing could be.

But it would be enough.

The following day we saw the ship again, only this time she was a little closer than before. Close enough, at least, that we could make out the black and yellow stripes of her sail.

Wyvern.

She must have seen us, for she stayed on our tail for more than an hour that afternoon, gradually overhauling us, until a sudden squall blew in, lashing us with rain and hail and churning the waves into a foaming tumult that harried *Nihtegesa*'s hull and splintered into trails of froth that cascaded up and over the gunwale and soaked us to our skin. The timbers creaked and shudders ran along the whole length of the ship. We shipped the oars so that they did not shear, and had to bail water out of the bilges just to stay afloat, but one good thing came of it, for amidst the low clouds and the heaving waves we managed to lose *Wyvern*. When finally the rain ceased and the clouds passed over and we saw the evening sun disappearing over the thickly wooded lands that lay to larboard, there was no sign of her.

'Your friends are certainly determined,' Magnus said that night when we lay at anchor. He'd brought us into a narrow cove, which was difficult for anyone who wasn't familiar with the land and its rivers to spot from out at sea, but which offered good shelter from the wind. 'It's lucky for you I know these coasts, or else there's a good chance they'd have caught us already.'

I couldn't argue with him on that, although admittedly there'd been a moment earlier that day, before the squall, when I had doubted him. In an effort to maintain some distance between us and our pursuers, he had ordered Uhtferth to steer us hard by a headland, too close for my liking to the looming crags and sharp rock stacks that jutted proud of the waves. The wind had gusted in *Nihtegesa*'s sail and more than once I'd murmured a prayer to God, thinking it was about to take her and dash us against those cliffs in a tangle of broken timbers, but fortunately Uhtferth and his crew had a good feeling for the currents and the swell, and we'd raced swiftly past without coming to harm.

'I've been thinking,' he said.

'About what?'

'About how much easier it would be next time not to try to evade these friends of yours, but to hand you over to them instead. How much do you think they'll offer in return?'

'They won't give you anything,' I said. 'You'll be fortunate if you manage to escape with your life, once they learn who you are. And you can be sure that I'll tell them, if you dare betray me.'

He contemplated that for a moment, unspeaking, as *Nihtegesa* bobbed on the tide.

'That's why you wanted to flee Dyflin that night, isn't it?' I asked. 'Not for my sake, but because, even now, you fear what they would do to you if they ever caught up with you.'

Again he didn't answer me, and I took that as a sign I was right. Water slapped against the hull and the anchor chain grazed the timbers. Some of the crew were still awake, but most had fallen asleep, huddled beneath blankets next to their sea chests, while Godric, Eithne, Serlo and Pons had bedded down on the bow platform. Even after spending two days at sea in close quarters, my band and Magnus's tended to keep themselves apart as much as possible, with at least one man from each party staying awake at all times to keep lookout during the night. Tonight, partly to ease the lingering hostility between English and Normans, among whom Magnus's men counted Godric for having thrown in his lot with me, we had each nominated ourselves to take the first watch.

'I should have left you there,' Magnus said ruefully after a while.

'Why didn't you?'

'Because . . .' he began, and then hesitated. 'Because I have few enough allies left these days. I knew that if I was to do this, I'd need all the men I could muster, and another four swords could prove useful. You seemed every bit as desperate as myself, and for that reason I felt I could trust you.'

How flimsy were the bonds that held us together. Perhaps that had always been so. Alliances were rarely forged through mere friendship, after all, but out of convenience, in the hope of mutual gain, and because both parties shared a common interest. He owed me nothing; he didn't even like me, not really, despite the many ways in which we were similar. For the time being we were useful to each other, and that was all that mattered.

For two more days we ran north with a swift following breeze, and saw no more sign of *Wyvern*, but on the third day the wind dropped and there was barely enough to make the sailcloth flap, which meant we were forced to go under oar alone. Each of us, even Magnus, took our turn to sit upon the sea chests and bend our backs to the waves. It was hard work, even for one like myself who was well used to long days of exertion, spending almost every day practising at arms or in the saddle. When my stint had finished and it was time for someone else to take my place, my hands were raw, my forearms glistening with sweat, my bones aching and my throat parched. I was searching for some water with which to moisten my lips and tongue, for they had grown dry with the salt air, when Ælfhelm, who was keeping watch on the steering platform, gave a sharp shout.

'It's them,' he said. 'The Frenchmen!'

I glanced up and saw him pointing towards the southern horizon, where once more the black speck of a ship was visible. Her sail was furled, and so it was hard to be sure, but there was little doubt in either my mind – or Magnus's – that *Wyvern* had returned. At once he began barking orders to his crew and beating a quicker time upon the drum. He realised, and so did I, that we couldn't rely on another squall blowing in to help us escape, not this time, and so if we were to have any chance of outrunning them, it would have to be through our own toil.

'Row,' Magnus roared. 'Harder, you bastards, you sons of whores, you lice-ridden dogs!'

Quickly, though, it became clear that it wouldn't be enough. Before, with the wind behind us, we just about been able to keep pace with *Wyvern*, for we were lighter and narrower and shallower of draught, and therefore easily able to skip across the waves. But when it came to a battle of oars alone we could not compete, for she had almost as many rowers on one bank as we had on both larboard and steerboard together.

'Faster!' Ælfhelm bellowed, adding his exhortations to those of his lord. 'Faster, you wretches!'

But it was no use, and they both realised it, too, as *Wyvern* continued to bear down on us. We were steering as close to the rocky shore as Uhtferth dared, yet still she was closing. The other ship's thirty pairs of oars rose and fell in steady rhythm, like the beating of wings, as she soared across the blue-grey waters, gliding through the spume and the spray, while desperately we floundered. She was little more than an arrow's flight away now, close enough that I could hear their shouts, though not close enough to hear what it was they were saying. They had chased us across the kingdom of England, from the fenlands to the Marches, across the sea to foreign shores, and now finally their doggedness was to be rewarded, for they had caught us.

'To arms,' I shouted, not just to my knights but to those of Magnus's huscarls who weren't at oar. I'd already donned my helmet and buckled my sword-belt upon my waist, and now snatched up one of the round shields that I'd purchased in Dyflin, gripping the leather brases firmly in my hand.

I'd never had to fight aboard ship before, although I had come close to doing so on occasion, and didn't much relish the prospect, especially when it meant coming to blows with fellow Frenchmen and even, possibly, the man who had been my lord. But if a battle was what he wanted, a battle was what he would get. He wouldn't take me without a struggle.

'*Scyld*,' Magnus shouted to one of his men, cursing violently. '*Bring me scyld!*'

My eyes met his. I saw the grim look upon his face, and wondered if he remembered our conversation the other night, and whether he still had half a mind to turn me over. His huscarls closed ranks around him, beating their sword-hilts, the flats of their blades and their spear-hafts against their shields, raising the battle-thunder.

'*Acwellath hi!*' Magnus roared in his own tongue, and the cry was taken up by the rest of his men. *Kill them*. He wasn't about to forsake me, then. Not yet, anyway.

By then the remaining rowers had realised they faced a struggle they could not win, and had hauled in their oars, abandoning them in favour of knives and axes and whatever other weapons were to hand. They rushed to form a line along *Nihtegesa*'s broadside, making ready to face the onslaught as the ship heaved and rolled in the swell. The deck was slippery and I almost fell, but managed to recover my balance in time.

'To arms,' I yelled at Serlo and Pons and Godric, thinking that perhaps they hadn't heard me, then in English to Eithne: 'Get below deck.'

'I can fight,' she protested. 'Give me a knife and I'll fight.'

Having heard the tale of how she had resisted her captors in the battle for the Isle, I didn't doubt her, but whatever others might believe, I held to the opinion that a battle was no place for a woman.

'Do as I say,' I roared. 'Now!'

Beneath the platforms at either end of the ship there were compartments where supplies were usually stored so as to keep them dry, each of them large enough for a person, or several people, to hide in. She scowled, but thankfully didn't need telling again, which was as well, since I had no more time for her then.

'What are you standing there for?' I asked the others, who still hadn't moved.

'You want us to fight them, lord?' Serlo asked. 'Our own countrymen?'

'Do you have something else in mind?'

'We can't win,' Pons shouted as spray crashed over the prow. 'There are too many of them.'

'We've faced worse odds than these, haven't we?' I shot back. 'We can hold them off, I know it.'

'They've caught us, lord,' Serlo said. 'It's over. There's no shame in yielding.'

'We don't have any choice, lord,' Pons added.

My blood boiled. I couldn't believe what I was hearing. My own knights, oath-sworn to my service, were turning against me.

'Lord—' Godric started, but I was in no mood to listen to their protests any longer, least of all from him, the runt on whose behalf I had fought and killed Guibert. He, ultimately, was the reason why we were here, and yet, in spite of everything I'd done for him and the protection I'd given him, he still had the nerve to question me.

'No,' I said, interrupting him. 'I haven't come this far to give up now. So tell me, are you with me, or against me?'

It must have seemed to them as if a kind of madness had taken hold of me, that I'd taken leave of my senses, although it did not feel that way at the time. Rather, it seemed to me that everything had suddenly become clear. I could not let Robert and his men take me. I had come too far now to be steered from this course, to let this undertaking come to naught.

'Lord!'

'What?' I demanded, as I turned to Godric, who was pointing eagerly out across the wide blue-grey expanse, his eyes bright, his voice filled not with alarm but with joy. For while we had been arguing, I realised, he had been watching *Wyvern*, and now I saw what he had spotted.

For she wasn't closing as if to attack us, as I'd expected. Her oarsmen had slackened their rhythm, and rather than drawing directly alongside us, as they would have done if they'd wanted to grapple and board us, they seemed to be keeping their distance. Instead of presenting a wall of painted leather and a forest of steel, the men aboard her were waving towards us, hailing us, although their cries were all but drowned out by Magnus and his men. They were still beating out the battle-thunder upon their shields, roaring insults and taunts at our pursuers, swearing death upon them. I could barely hear my own thoughts, let alone make out what those on the other ship were trying to say.

But then, through the din of steel and limewood and jeers and curses, I heard what sounded like my name. The sun was behind the other ship, casting her crew in shadow, and the sea all around was flashing bright, so that for an instant I was blinded. With my free hand I shielded my eyes from the glare, and that was when I saw two figures standing at *Wyvern's* prow. They were both waving, trying to catch our attention, one a little taller than the other, both with scabbards hanging from their waists.

The taller of the two cupped his hands around his lips. 'Tancred!' he yelled, and this time he was close enough that I recognised his voice.

'Eudo!' I said, and no sooner had I done so than I realised who the second figure must be. 'Wace!'

The other ship drew closer still. The sun disappeared for a moment behind a wisp of cloud, and suddenly I was able to see them clearly.

At first I thought my eyes had to be deceiving me. How long was it since I'd last seen them? Not since that night at Heia, more than a month ago, I reckoned, although I'd lost count of the days. All at once the battle-anger that until then had been coursing through my veins vanished. But surprised as I was to see them both here, to say I was overjoyed would be false. They were still sworn to Robert, after all. Wasn't that why they had followed me?

'Do you know these people?' Magnus asked me as he made a sign to his huscarls, who ceased clattering their weapons against their shield-rims, although they continued to regard *Wyvern* and those aboard her warily.

'I know them,' I answered, but he didn't look much reassured, and understandably so, as the other ship, easily within range of a javelin's throw now, moved alongside us and it became clear just how much larger she was than *Nihtegesa*, and how many more men she carried. But still none of them were rushing to arms, as I might have expected.

'God's teeth, but you're persistent, aren't you?' Eudo shouted across the water, laughing. 'We were beginning to think we'd never catch up with you.'

'I was hoping you wouldn't,' I replied.

'Are you going to let us come aboard, then?' Wace asked. 'Or are you and your new friends going to keep waving your weapons at us until we all perish of old age?'

'That depends,' I said, although what I meant by that exactly, I wasn't sure.

'On what?'

They were my two oldest and most loyal friends in all the world, and I wasn't about to take up arms against them. Unable to flee and unwilling to fight. What choices did that leave us with?

'Is Robert with you?' I asked, glancing along the length of their ship, looking for him. If he was there, however, he wasn't showing his face, which was probably as well. As hard as I'd tried to bury my anger in the past few weeks, I still hadn't forgiven him for driving me from Earnford, from the lands that I had striven hard first to earn and then to defend.

'No,' Eudo said. 'We came alone.'

'He sent you, did he?'

'All this way? What makes you think he would do that?'

Little more than a couple of oar's lengths separated *Nihtegesa* and *Wyvern* now. 'To take me back to Heia, so that he can further humiliate me,' I said bitterly. 'Has he not inflicted enough punishment on me already?'

'Robert hasn't forgiven you for what you did,' said Wace. 'He's angrier now than he was then, too, since with you being gone, he's the one who's had to pay the blood-price to Guibert's kin. But no, he didn't send us.'

'If he didn't,' I asked, 'then what are you doing here, and in his ship?'

'If you'll tell your friends to sheathe their blades and let us come across, then we'll tell you. We don't want a fight any more than you do.'

'If you want to come aboard, you talk to me, not him,' Magnus called out in French. 'I understand well enough what you're saying, so don't think that I don't. This is my ship. I alone decide who's allowed to tread her decks. No one else.'

'And who are you?' Eudo asked.

'Magnus,' he replied, not daring to give his full name to them as he had to me, and then, for want of anything else to say, added, 'This is *Nihtegesa*.'

'Order your men to lay down their weapons, Magnus, and I promise you there won't be any blood spilt this day.'

He seemed to consider this for a few moments. He signalled to me and I jostled my way past his sweat-reeking huscarls towards him.

'When you said you know these people,' he said, keeping his voice low so that only he and I could hear, 'does that mean you trust them?'

'With my life,' I replied. 'And I know that they don't make promises lightly. If they say there'll be no bloodshed, they mean it.'

His eyes were hard, his expression stony. 'Before I met you I'd almost begun to believe that I'd never have to lay eyes upon a Frenchman again. Now it seems that wherever I go I find myself plagued by your kind.'

'Do we have an answer, then?' Wace called.

Magnus let out an exasperated sigh and returned to the gunwale. 'Do I have much choice?' he shouted back with the weariness of one who was well used to defeat.

'You get to choose whether you want to live or die,' Eudo said. 'Is that choice enough for you?'

When the question was put to him that way, there was really only one answer the Englishman could give. Reluctantly he bade his retainers sheathe their swords and put down their spears and axes, while *Nihtegesa* and *Wyvern* steered closer to one another. The crews on both sides threw across coils of rope, which they used to lash them together. Timber thudded and scraped against timber as the two hulls met, and first Wace and then Eudo came aboard, both of them accompanied by their household knights.

'So,' I said, not even caring to greet them properly. 'Now that you've travelled the length of Britain to hunt me down, perhaps you'll tell me what it is you want.'

Twenty-three

And so they did, and it was exactly as I'd thought. They wanted me to return to England with them.

'I thought you said Robert was still angry,' I said. 'That he hadn't yet forgiven me.'

'He is, and he hasn't,' said Wace. 'You don't know the storm you've stirred up. It's not just that Robert's been forced to pay the blood-price to Guibert's widow; many of his vassals are saying he should have been quicker to act, and more severe in his punishment. They say he should never have allowed you to flee Heia, let alone England.'

'You think that's going to encourage me to come back with you?' I scoffed.

'All these quarrels can be settled in a single stroke, if you only show a little contrition,' Eudo said. 'If you return willingly, do the penance that the Church requires and recompense him for the money he paid out on your behalf, then all those barons can be satisfied that justice has been done in the proper manner. There's no reason then why Robert shouldn't accept your submission and restore you to your lands.'

'Is that what he told you, or just what you believe?' I asked, and I took the silence that greeted my question to mean that he had made no such assurances. 'Anyway, if it were as simple as that, don't you think I would have done it already?'

'You killed a man,' Wace said. 'There is no disputing it. Many witnessed it happen. This matter will not be forgotten easily. Not unless you at least demonstrate some humility, so that people see you feel remorse for what you did.'

I rounded on him. 'Don't think for a moment that I don't regret what happened that night.' Guibert had been a boor, but he hadn't deserved to die, not by anyone's estimation. The knowledge of what I'd done had hung like a shadow over me ever since.

But remorse would not bring him back. Nor did I think that mere gestures would heal these wounds, though they might well restore Earnford to me. For I was tired. Tired of the obligations with which I'd long been burdened. Tired of risking my life time after time under the banner of a lord who could not provide, in the name of a king who was as cold-hearted as he was capricious, for a country that, a few good men and women aside, hated us and whose people would slaughter us in their beds if they had half a chance.

'Even if I had the silver to pay him,' I said, 'I'm not about to prostrate myself before him and beg for the restitution of what by right is already mine.'

'You have no right to that land,' Eudo pointed out. 'Not any more. Robert expelled you from his service, or have you forgotten that?'

'You should count yourself lucky,' Wace said. 'If Guibert had been better liked while he lived, there might have been even more of an outcry. There'd be no hope of you returning in that case, and we wouldn't have wasted the last two weeks pursuing you all this way across the sea.'

'Why did you, anyway?' I asked. 'I thought Robert was leaving for Flanders, and both of you with him.'

'He was,' Eudo said. 'But when the Flemish count heard rumour that King Guillaume was planning a foray against him, he quickly offered a truce. In return for peace, he agreed not to go raiding.'

'You mean the expedition never went ahead?'

Fate can at times be cruel, and never had it felt crueller than at that moment, as I thought back to my quarrel with Robert, in his solar at Heia all those weeks ago. A quarrel over nothing, as it now turned out.

If only I could have known. For if we had not argued so bitterly that day, then perhaps I wouldn't have been in such a foul mood that evening. Perhaps I wouldn't have let my temper get the better of me, and Guibert's blood wouldn't be on my hands, and none of this would have happened.

But then I wouldn't have learnt about Haakon, or discovered the truth about what had happened at Dunholm. Was that knowledge worth the price I'd paid? Had it been worth Guibert's life?

'What brought you here to Yrland, then?' I asked, trying to shake such thoughts from my mind.

'Robert sent us across the Narrow Sea,' Eudo said. 'He wanted us to bear news of Malet's death to his vassals in Normandy. But we decided to do otherwise.'

'You seized his ship?'

'Not exactly. When we told Aubert what we had in mind, he was only too willing to help. As soon as we were out of sight of land, we changed course.'

'Aubert?' I asked. 'He's here?'

'Aye,' I heard the shipmaster call, no doubt having heard his name. I looked up to see him waving from *Wyvern*'s deck, a broad grin upon his face. 'You've been making trouble, or so your friends have been telling me.'

I'd last seen him over two years ago, but he hadn't changed much in that time, save for being a little greyer around the temples than I remembered, not to mention a little fuller in the stomach, too. He also hailed from Brittany, although, like me, it was some time since he'd been back to the place of his birth.

'Robert told us you had it in your head to go to Dyflin, though he didn't know why,' Wace said. 'We reckoned that was where we would most likely find you.'

'And we nearly did,' Eudo added. 'But then you left that night.'

'How did you know we'd be travelling north?'

'The winds told us,' Aubert said by way of explanation. 'We followed where they took us.'

'That's our tale, anyway,' Wace said. 'Now maybe you'll tell us yours.'

I was in no mood to recount everything, not again, but I could hardly not tell them, and so I repeated exactly what Eithne had told me about Oswynn and Haakon, and how she'd helped set me on their trail.

'We both wondered where she'd appeared from,' Wace said, meaning the girl. 'You never said anything, though, so I reckoned it was better not to ask.'

Eudo shrugged. 'I assumed she was helping to warm your bed, although I admit she seemed to me a bit fierce-looking for your tastes.'

I glanced at Eithne, who had emerged from the compartment beneath the bow platform. Her mouth was once more twisted into her usual scowl. She must have guessed from the looks they were giving her that we were talking about her, even if she couldn't know exactly what we were saying.

Eudo laughed. 'Even Oswynn never glowered like that one does, and she wasn't exactly an easy one to tame, from what I remember. And now you're saying you know where to find her?'

'I don't, but he does,' I said, gesturing at Magnus, and introduced him to them, saying merely that he was a ship's captain from Dyflin, whom Haakon had wronged in the past, which the Englishman seemed to be content with. I also gave them the names of Ælfhelm and the rest of his huscarls, all of whom continued to regard the newcomers with suspicion. Not that I blamed them.

'You understand, then, why I can't go back,' I said. 'Not now. Not having come this far already.'

'How do you expect to be able to mount an assault on this Haakon's stronghold with a single ship's crew?' Wace asked.

'Do you remember when we stole our way into the enemy camp at Beferlic last autumn? There were only nine of us then, and only six when we took the gates at Eoferwic the year before that.'

'And both times we nearly got ourselves killed,' Eudo reminded me.

'No man ever won himself fame without taking any risks,' I said, repeating the old proverb that was often spoken amongst warriors. 'What do I stand to lose?'

'Everything,' Wace said, no longer caring to disguise his frustration. 'And this has nothing to do with winning fame.'

He had every right to be angry, I supposed. They both did. They had ventured all this way, hundreds of leagues from the manors they called home, in hope of talking some sense into me, and all for naught.

'I've made my decision,' I said, tight-lipped. 'If Robert expects I'll happily don a penitent's robe and bend my knee before him, he's wrong. Besides, you should be coming with me, not the other way around.'

Eudo frowned. 'What are you talking about?'

And that was when I told them what Magnus had related to me only a few evenings ago. That it was Haakon who burnt the mead-hall that night at Dunholm. That he was to blame, not Eadgar Ætheling, for the death of our former lord, Robert de Commines, the man who had in so many ways been like a father to me, to us, who had provided for us and inspired us and trained us in the ways of war.

I didn't expect them to believe me to begin with, just I had refused to believe the Englishman when he first told me, and so it proved. But I called Magnus over and had him confirm everything I'd said.

'So Earl Robert was your lord?' he asked when he'd finished, glancing at us all.

'He was,' I answered. 'A good lord, and a good man, too. He didn't deserve to die.' I turned to Wace and Eudo. 'Unless you're going to throw me in chains and forcibly drag me back to England, that's where I'm going. Are you with me?'

The two of them exchanged uncertain glances. They knew as well as I did that this was far from the first time I'd tried to persuade them to follow me on one of my reckless adventures, and knew, too, how that same recklessness had almost been their deaths. And the truth was that, in all the years we had known each other and trained and sparred and ridden and feasted and laughed together, this was one of the most desperate endeavours I'd ever asked them to join me in.

Even if we were to succeed, I couldn't promise that the poets would write songs of these deeds of ours, songs that would be sung across Christendom for years to come, for this was no glorious battle on the outcome of which rested the fate of kingdoms. Nor could I swear that victory would bring us much by way of riches. But we didn't even have to succeed. The mere willingness to fight was enough to win ourselves something immeasurably more precious than reputation or glory, silver or jewels, horses or ships, halls or castles, and that thing was honour. Even if this road only led to failure or, worse, death, at least we would have tried. More noble, in my eyes, to meet our ends fighting for a cause we believed in than to refuse the challenge because it was too arduous. Nothing worth having ever came easily.

'Well?' I asked, growing impatient, for the longer I waited, the less sure I was what their answer would be. Neither of them would so much as meet my gaze.

I don't doubt that it was a more difficult decision for them than it was for me. Although I was no longer oath-bound to Robert, they still were. Already in coming here they had defied his wishes. What would he say if he discovered not only that they had taken his ship away into the north for their own ends, but then that they had joined forces with me, the murderer he had so recently cast out from his service, to pursue our own feud, our own private war?

Whether by choice or by necessity, we had taken different paths. Our loyalties, our obligations, which for so long had been the same, were now opposed. I might have nothing more to lose, but they did.

Wace gave a shrug of resignation as he glanced at Eudo, who sighed through clenched teeth. Suddenly I felt a stirring of hope.

'We'll do this. For Robert,' Eudo said, by which he meant, of course, not Malet's son but our former lord: he who had led us on so many campaigns across the length and breadth of Christendom. And now, one final time, we would fight in his name.

'For Robert,' Wace agreed, albeit not without some reluctance. Stern-faced, he came to clasp my hand at last. 'You owe us. You realise that, don't you?'

That was a phrase I'd grown all too used to hearing. 'I know.'

I did not for a heartbeat think our task would be easy, but with the two of them by my side, we stood a far better chance than if

Magnus and I were to do this by ourselves. Not for the first time it struck me how fortunate I was to have friends as faithful as they.

'What about you?' I called to Aubert, who had been watching on. 'Will you join us?'

The shipmaster looked apprehensive, and I didn't blame him. This wasn't his battle. He had done Eudo and Wace a favour out of friendship, but the prospect of risking his lord's prized longship on a voyage far beyond familiar shores was another thing entirely.

'I'll have to ask my men,' he said. 'They're honour-bound to follow my orders, but I also have a responsibility towards them. Bear in mind as well that many of them didn't even want to come this far.'

'I understand,' I said, and waited while he went and spoke with the members of his crew, some of whom I recognised from the last time I'd set foot on *Wyvern*'s deck, and several more that I didn't. I saw lots of shaking heads and heard snorts that I took for disapproval, until one, older and more weather-worn than the others, whose name, if I remembered correctly, was Oylard, stepped forward. He began remonstrating with them, calling them cowards, saying they were unfit to call themselves Normans, and that their fathers and their grandfathers would be ashamed to see them shrink from such a challenge.

He pushed his way through the throng towards us. 'Is it true?' he called across from *Wyvern*. 'Is it true that this Haakon was responsible for what happened at Dunholm?'

'That's what I've been told,' I replied, raising my voice for the benefit of the others, who were watching, listening. 'He was in the vanguard. He was the one who stormed the fastness and set fire to the mead-hall.'

Close to two thousand Normans had met their deaths that night when Eadgar and his allies had attacked. Men, women and children alike been cut down without mercy; the streets had run with their blood. No army of ours had ever suffered such a reverse on English soil. It was a humiliation that most of us would rather have forgotten, and yet how could we forget it? Even now, three entire campaigning seasons later, Northumbria remained unconquered;

the king's efforts to scour that land last winter had not made him its master nor brought the instigators of the rebellion to justice. And so the stain of that defeat lingered, while those who had inflicted it continued to live.

'My cousin was at Dunholm,' Oylard said as he turned to address his fellow boatmen. 'A farrier's apprentice, he was, no more than a boy. I later found out that he never came back. Dead at only thirteen summers old.'

They couldn't fail to have heard about what happened that night three years ago. Many had probably heard it firsthand, from those like Eudo and Wace and myself who had been there and who had survived, although such had been the slaughter the enemy had wrought that we were few in number. No doubt Oylard was not the only one to have lost a friend or relative to the enemy's sword at Dunholm, or at the very least knew someone who had.

One of the others, bald and thick-necked, spoke up. 'I don't know about you, Oylard, or any of the rest of you, but I for one won't be risking my neck unless there's the chance of reward at the end of it.'

'There'll be spoils enough to go around,' I said. 'From what I hear—'

'From what you hear? What kind of an assurance is that?'

'You have my word,' Magnus interjected before I could answer. 'He stole from me, as he has stolen from many others over the years. His treasure-chests brim with silver and gold, so rich has he grown profiting from the triumphs of others. I can promise that there'll be no shortage of plunder should we succeed.'

'And you're willing to share in that wealth, are you?' asked Bald-head.

The Englishman hesitated, and I understood why. Naturally he didn't want to have to share, not if he could help it. If *Wyvern* were to join us then whatever booty did come our way would have to be divided more than a hundred ways. And yet another ship's crew worth of allies would undoubtedly prove useful. There was much more to this expedition than pursuit of riches, and so if that was the price we had to pay for their help, then so be it.

That was how it seemed to me, anyway. But the decision was not mine alone to make. Magnus was chewing his lip, his face drawn as if contemplating.

'Well?' asked Bald-head.

'If you'll join us,' Magnus said after a moment's pause, 'then, yes, we'll share that wealth with you.'

He glanced at me to make sure that I was in agreement, and I nodded. The bald one went to confer with Aubert, Oylard and his fellow boatmen. Again there was grumbling, and again voices were raised, but at the end of it the shipmaster came forward.

'Have you decided?' I asked.

Aubert smiled. 'We've come this far, haven't we? It seems to me we might as well venture a little further. If Robert has anything to say about it later, well –' he shrugged and gestured towards Wace and Eudo '– I can always claim that they forced me to come north against my will, can't I?'

'If you do, those will be the last words ever to come out of your mouth,' Eudo warned.

His expression suggested he was only half joking, but Aubert laughed all the same.

'So,' the shipmaster said. 'Where do we find this Haakon?'

After that day's calm, the wind picked up again on the next. A fierce storm blew in that made it impossible to sail, but we came upon a village close by the shore whose folk proved friendly enough, once they realised that we weren't interested in robbing them. There we put what coin and goods we had to good use, exchanging them for a barrel of salted pork to replace one we'd lost overboard whilst riding out the squall several days before, as well as two more of ale in place of some that the seawater had spoiled. Our purchases made, we waited for the gale to subside, for the rain to cease lashing down, and for the skies to lighten once more.

I thought of old Snorri, and hoped *Hrithdyr* was safe in port rather than having to weather out this storm on the open seas that lay between here and Ysland. Assuming that they had made it without harm through the Suthreyjar, that was, although if there was anyone who would know which passages were safe to take and which islands to avoid, it was probably him.

'He wouldn't have lived as long as he has, doing what he does, if he didn't know how to take care of himself,' Magnus assured me. 'He'll be all right. If he's sensible he'll have sought out a travelling companion or two for the voyage. At this time of year the sea wolves are beginning to slumber, but nonetheless you'll often find traders will band together for protection.'

'As we have,' I said.

'True, but no one's likely to attack us, are they?'

'Why not?'

'You'll find easy spoils aboard a trader, but on a longship all you'll find are warriors. You never see wolves preying upon their own kind, do you? Why should they waste their time fighting each other when there are more than enough pickings to allow them all to grow fat?'

That made sense, although even so I found myself more than a little nervous when the next morning, after the sea-mist had lifted, our two ships left the shores of Yrland behind us, for I knew we were venturing further north than I or any Norman had ever been before, into waters unknown even to Aubert.

I only prayed this latest undertaking did not prove to be a mistake on my part. The Danes were renowned across Christendom for being hard men to kill, and if the stories about him held any grain of truth, we were pitting ourselves against one of the fiercest and most ruthless of them all.

Winter was almost upon us. Even hours after the sun had lifted above the hills off our steerboard side, my breath misted before my face, while the wind bit through my cloak, working its chill through my flesh and deep into my very bones. This was the time of year when most sensible folk were slaughtering what animals they couldn't afford to keep fed through the winter, mending holes in their warm clothes and caps, and huddling down close by their hearths.

But we were not most folk.

The further north we sailed, the steeper and darker grew the islands that rose like jagged mountains out of the sea, the more thickly wooded they became, and the fewer signs we saw of anyone living there. No wisps of smoke rose towards the slate-grey skies; no sheep grazed upon the hillsides; no fishermen's hovels stood above the shoreline. These were sparse, barren lands, where the inhabitants of the one village we did come across were subject to no king that they knew of, whether English or Scots or Irish or Danish. Indeed, if any lord at all held sway in these parts, they had not heard of him. They tended their chickens and their few goats, and sometimes sold their goods to passing merchants and other travellers, though not often, and for the most part those were the only souls they saw outside of their own valley. But when Eithne and Magnus, who both happened to speak their language or something very like it, mentioned to them the name of Haakon Thorolfsson, and asked if he had been heard of recently, they all made the sign of the cross and began babbling at once.

'He came to these parts only a week ago, they say,' Eithne told me. 'They all started running as soon as they saw the crimson sails of his ship appearing from the mist, but it turned out he hadn't come with any intention of raiding.'

These people had precious little that was worth stealing, so that was no great surprise. 'What did he want?'

'He was looking for men who could hold a spear. He offered to give two sheep and five geese to every man who would go with him for the winter, although naturally they were all suspicious of him, and so none accepted.'

'Why would he be looking to hire spearmen?' Magnus wondered aloud. 'He can't be planning on going foraging at this time of year, surely?'

'Maybe he's looking to bolster his defences,' I said.

'But why?' The Englishman hesitated. 'Unless—'

'Unless he knows we're coming,' I finished for him.

And I could explain, too, how he knew. Only one person who wasn't a part of our expedition was aware that we were seeking out Jarl Haakon, and why. I wondered how much he'd been paid for his information, and felt embarrassed at having only the other evening been concerned for him out there on the wild and open ocean. Now I hoped that he choked on his next meal.

Old Snorri, who had deceived us with his friendly manner, had betrayed us to our enemy.

Haakon knew, then, that Magnus was coming for him, and that was why he was looking to purchase the services of fighting men, to help guard the walls of his stronghold. But I hadn't revealed my real name to the trader, so Haakon couldn't yet know that accompanying Harold's son was the knight Tancred, nor that he brought with him a second shipload of warriors, allies from England. He remained ignorant of exactly how many we numbered, and that was one advantage we still held over him.

Events in England had been moving apace in the short time that I'd been away. During those days as we crept up the coast of northern Britain, Wace and Eudo related how King Guillaume had accepted the submission of the principal leaders of the Elyg rebels, granting forgiveness and receiving them at court. No sooner had they dismissed their armies and sent all their followers home in time for the ploughing season, however, than he cast them all in chains and confined them to the castle dungeon at Cantebrigia until he decided what to do with them.

'He did that?' I asked, having joined my countrymen on *Wyvern*. I found it difficult to believe that the king, who was not usually one to break a pledge, and indeed prided himself on that reputation, would go back on his word, and in so blatant a fashion.

'That's what we've been hearing,' Eudo said. He turned to Godric. 'It means there'll be no earldom for your uncle. All Morcar's estates and those of his vassals have been confiscated.'

Godric grunted. His lips were set firm, his expression unfeeling. 'It's no more than he deserves.'

Wace grinned and clapped a hand on his shoulder. 'It's lucky that you're with Tancred now, isn't it, whelp?'

'Otherwise you'd be rotting away along with Morcar in whatever dank prison the king finds for him,' Eudo added.

Godric said nothing, and I wondered if he wasn't perhaps feeling a little guilty at having evaded such a fate, at having turned his back upon his uncle, who had, after all, sheltered him for so many years. Yet he had nothing to feel ashamed of. Morcar had broken promise after promise, first to the king and then to the rebels, committing one betrayal after another, playing both sides to his advantage. In hindsight he'd been foolish to think that the king would act any more honourably towards him. He had brought about his own ruin.

'They're still looking for Hereward, you know,' Wace said.

'Still?' I asked. 'They haven't given up?'

'The king is convinced he's out there somewhere, hiding, plotting. Several bodies were pulled from the marsh in the week or so after the battle, we're told, one of which was supposedly about the same size and build as Hereward, but his flesh was too bloated and his skin was peeling away, so no one could tell for sure. Most people seem to think he's fled England altogether. In the meantime the king's keeping up the search, and will probably do so all winter.'

King Guillaume was well known for his bullheadedness, as we had seen for ourselves during the campaign in the fenlands. If he had decided that Hereward remained alive and a threat, then he would do everything he could to hunt him down, even if that meant scorching the Fens to draw him out, in the same way that he'd ravaged the north during his campaign last winter.

News wasn't the only thing they'd brought from England, either. 'We have something else for you,' Eudo said.

Beckoning me to follow him, he made his way to the hatch that led to the hold space beneath the steering platform, from which, with my help, he hauled out a small chest about half as long as a man was high, with iron handles mounted on either end.

'What's this?' I asked. 'A gift?'

He didn't answer, but untied the leather thong that was attached to his belt and held out the key that had been hanging from it. Not quite sure what to expect, I took it from him, eyeing him suspiciously, then knelt down, placed it in the lock, twisted until I felt it click, then lifted open the lid—

To find my packs, just as I had left them at Heia, as well as a sword in its scabbard, wrapped in a bundle of white cloth. And not just any sword. Its hilt was decorated with a single turquoise stone, set into the centre of the disc pommel.

A turquoise stone that I recognised at once.

'We both reckoned that if you were to go back to face Robert, it would be better if you didn't arrive looking like a flea-ridden beggar, but had your blade and all your other belongings,' Eudo said with a grin.

I was too surprised and overjoyed even to think, let alone find the words to thank him. Laughing in delight, I lifted the scabbard, still shrouded in its cloth, out from the chest, laying it on the deck beside me, and drew the blade from the sheath. The steel had been recently polished so that, even in the small light of that dull day, it gleamed like silver.

'Open out the cloth,' Wace said, having come to join us.

'What?' I asked. 'Why?'

'Unfurl it, and you'll see.'

Carefully I unwound the thick bolt of linen from around the scabbard, wondering if perhaps there was something else wrapped inside, although I couldn't think what. It only took me a moment to realise what I was holding, as I glimpsed first a wing and then the head with its short, curved beak, the bird emblazoned in black upon a white field, in flight with talons extended as if stooping for the kill. The hawk of Earnford – and of Commines, too, for it had also been the symbol of our former lord. When the time had come for me to choose a banner of my own, I'd adopted the device as a mark of respect, thinking that I would thereby serve his memory in the same way that I had served the man himself.

'I almost forgot,' I heard Eudo call, as he disappeared back into the hold space. 'There's one more thing.'

He emerged a moment later holding a shield, which like my banner bore the symbol of the hawk, although rather more crudely depicted, since whereas I'd entrusted the task of making the banner to the women of Earnford, I'd insisted on painting all my shields myself, and had spent long hours working under the sun and by the light of the hearth-fire daubing white and black on to the hide that faced the limewood boards until they appeared how I wanted them, or close enough to the image I held in my head as to satisfy me. Some laughed when they saw my efforts, reckoning that my hawks looked more like magpies or moorhens, but I didn't care.

For a shield is not only a knight's protection, it is also his pride, and any warrior who values his life knows to pay as much attention to his shield as to his mail and his blades. That said, even the sturdiest of them rarely lasts long in the hands of one who lives his life by the sword, and this one had seen happier days. The boss was scuffed and dented, and there were grimy marks upon the paintwork, which might have been mud or blood or a combination of both. How much longer this one would last until the iron rim cracked and the limewood began to splinter, I couldn't say with any certainty, but none of that mattered right now. Eudo held it out to me and I took it gratefully, passing the long guige strap over my head and then working my forearm through the brases, adjusting the buckles with my other hand until it felt secure.

And all the while I could not stop smiling. I might have been landless and lordless, lacking so much as a horse to ride and a hall to call my home, with hardly a penny left in my coin-purse and so few friends that I could have probably counted them on my two hands alone, yet in that moment I felt rich beyond imagination. For those friends that I did have were worth more to me than all those other things put together. On my behalf they had taken risks that other men would baulk at. After everything that I'd done, they were still prepared to fight by my side.

And that thought alone was enough to give me confidence that we could do this. That somehow, I did not know how, but somehow, we would prevail.

Twenty-four

The last thing we wanted to do was to rush in, in the hope of gaining the advantage of surprise, only to find ourselves caught in a snare. Thus we proceeded cautiously, with lookouts posted at all times at bow and at stern.

More than a week after leaving Dyflin, we found ourselves entering a narrow strait between two islands: one of gently sloping hills that Magnus called Ile; and another that he called Dure, which was steeper, with slate-grey peaks that rose like the burial mounds of giants, dwarfing us and our tiny craft. There was, Magnus had told us, a shorter route we could have chosen, to the east of the steeper island, which he had used once before and where there was less chance of being spotted, but those were treacherous waters. A vicious whirlpool churned off the northernmost point of Dure, around which waves had been known to rise to the height of ten men, enough to overwhelm even the sturdiest vessel and cause it to founder and sink.

'Some believe that on the sea floor dwells a sea serpent whose jaws are large enough to swallow even a forty-bencher whole,' he said solemnly, and I wasn't sure whether he meant that was what he believed. 'Others say it's the washtub of an ancient hag-spirit, who comes down at night to clean her filthy, lice-ridden robes in its waters, although no one has ever seen her.'

Whether either of those stories was true or not, since Magnus was our guide and he knew these waters better than anyone else among us, I thought it wise to take his advice. Even for those who knew the currents well, he said, that was a dangerous channel, for the winds and the tides could conspire to dash unlucky travellers upon the rock-bound shore, on the sharp skerries that rose out of the water, and the dark shoals that lay just beneath the surface.

Instead, then, we took the safer, longer route, although as we neared the strait that joined the two passages, we glimpsed one of those whirlpools from afar, and saw those immense waves of which Magnus had spoken, rearing up like wild sea stallions that charged at one another before erupting in clashes of white-glistening spume, as if the sea were at war with itself. Even from several leagues away the roar of that maelstrom was loud enough to make many men cross themselves against the evil of that place.

No evil befell us, however, nor did we spy any other ships approaching, and so that same afternoon under grim skies Aubert steered *Wyvern* to the north-east, following *Nihtegesa*. With a gusting breeze at our backs, we sailed into a wide sea-lake, bounded on both shores by dark-towering mountains the likes of which I had never before seen, whose peaks were lost amidst the clouds. And in the middle of that sound, stretching along the length of the fjord, rose a long, low finger of land, its crags and grassy slopes dotted with wind-stunted, bare-branched trees. From the other ship, one of the Englishmen waved to attract our attention, pointing towards that island as his crew reefed her sail and the oarsmen slackened their pace.

'That's it,' Magnus called to us, once Aubert had brought us level with *Nihtegesa*, and even above the gusting wind I could hear his excitement. 'That's Haakon's isle.'

'What now?' I shouted back.

'We find shelter!' He spread his arms wide and gestured upwards to the darkening heavens. The upper slopes of the mountains had suddenly become lost amidst the swelling cloud, and with every moment the wind was increasing in strength, turning white the tips of the waves that ran up the fjord, a sure sign of worse weather on the way. Perhaps that was the reason why we hadn't spied any other vessel out, not even a coracle or fishing boat, although it still concerned me that the waters were so quiet. I wasn't alone in that opinion, either, as Magnus told me after we had steered our ships into a bay on the fjord's northern shore that offered a good natural harbour. There, with the light fading, we dropped anchor to ride out the coming squall, and conferred on our best course of action.

'He knows we're coming,' Magnus said. 'He must do. So why hasn't he shown himself yet?'

'Perhaps he's weaker than we've been led to believe,' I suggested.

'Or else that's what he wants us to think,' Wace put in, 'so that he can draw us in closer.'

'Into his snare,' Eudo added, his expression sour.

'What would be the purpose of that?' I asked. 'He has no need to risk an open battle with us. More likely he's simply decided to stay behind his walls at Jarnborg, and wait to see what we do.'

They all were silent for a few moments while they contemplated that. We sat in a circle on oak sea chests aboard *Wyvern* as she rocked gently from one side to another on the incoming tide. The wind was up, howling through the bare branches of the trees on the shore.

'How do we find this fortress of his, then?' Wace asked.

'Finding it is easy,' Magnus said. 'If you sail a few miles further up the fjord you can see it clearly from the water. It stands atop a rocky promontory that juts out to the north, at the far end of the island from here, overlooking a wide bay where he keeps his ships.'

Eudo raised an eyebrow. 'You know it well, do you?'

'I came here once before, two years ago,' Magnus said flatly. 'Just as Haakon murdered your lord, so he was responsible for the deaths of my two brothers. I wanted revenge, and tried to storm Jarnborg, but only succeeded in leading several of my retainers to their deaths. Now their blood is on my hands.'

Suddenly I understood what he'd meant before, when he'd told me that hosts numbering in the hundreds had not managed to take Haakon's fortress. The thought that he himself had been there, had thrown himself and his army against its walls, hadn't so much as entered my head. But if he had already tried and failed, what made him think things would be any different this time? Even with Eudo and Wace and the crew of *Wyvern* to swell our numbers, we only had around one hundred and thirty men at our disposal, and he could not have expected their support when he had first agreed to this venture, back in Dyflin. Was it desperation that had driven Magnus on this course, as it had driven me?

'In that case you'll be able to tell us the best way of approaching Jarnborg,' Eudo said.

'There's a sandy cove about halfway along the island, on the north-western side, if I remember rightly,' Magnus replied. 'It can't be much more than an hour's march from the fortress. We can land there, providing that he doesn't send forces to drive us off.'

'He won't,' I said. 'Not if his nearest refuge is an hour's march away. He'll wait for us to come to him.'

'Assuming that we land without meeting any trouble,' Eudo said, 'what then?'

'Somehow we have to draw Haakon out.'

'Either that, or find a way into his stronghold that doesn't involve a direct assault on its walls,' Wace suggested.

I turned to Magnus. 'Is there such a way?'

'Not that I can recall. The promontory's summit is ringed all around with a high palisade, beyond which steep bluffs lead down nearly all the way to the water's edge. There's only one gate leading in, and only one way, too, of reaching that gate, across a narrow neck of land to the south of the crag. It's exposed, and the enemy would see you coming from half a mile away or more.'

'What about an approach by water?' Wace asked. 'Is that possible?'

'There are landing places at the foot of the bluffs, yes, but you can only reach them in a rowing boat or coracle or some other small craft. You couldn't get a whole army up that way.'

'Perhaps not, but Haakon is less likely to be expecting an attack from that direction,' I said. 'Could a handful of men make the climb, using the cover of darkness?'

'By night?' Magnus asked scornfully. 'You'd be as like to slip and break your neck. Besides, even if you did manage to make the ascent, how then would you get inside the fort? The gate is the only way in or out, so far as I know.'

That was a problem, certainly, and one to which it was hard to see a solution. It looked as if our only hope, then, was to try and draw Haakon out. But how?

One thing was for certain. We needed to see this place for ourselves, and try to ascertain just how many men he had, so that we knew exactly how strong a foe we faced. Only then could we start thinking properly about a strategy that would either get us inside Jarnborg, or else entice them out, so that we could give battle on our own terms.

'If there's a way, we'll find it,' I said, and wished that I felt more sure of that. We were close, so close, yet victory still seemed a distant dream. To think that Oswynn, my Oswynn, was only a few leagues from where we now lay at anchor. How many times this past year had I dreamt of holding her, embracing her? Now she was almost within reach, and yet at that moment she seemed further away than ever.

Tiredness clawed at my eyes that night but I could not sleep. Instead I lay awake, shivering beneath a swathe of winter blankets, my breath misting in the light of the waning moon as I thought of her and tried to imagine her lying beside me, the two of us sharing in the warmth of each other's bodies. For some reason, though, her face would not come to my mind, and that troubled me.

Somewhere towards the prow a man began to snore. I tried to bury my head in the blankets to shut out the noise, but even then I couldn't settle. It wasn't just that the deck was hard and the cloth coarse and uncomfortable. My mind was filled with a thousand knotted thoughts that I could not tease apart. What if we failed? What if, in spite of all our efforts, this expedition came to naught? What if Jarnborg remained unbroken, Haakon still lived, and we were forced to leave this place, bruised and bloodied, humbled and empty-handed? What was to prevent Pons and Serlo forswearing their oaths and leaving my service? I could hardly expect them to remain bound to me for ever if I had nothing to offer them, any more than Robert could expect me to obediently follow him everywhere he led. But if my sworn swords deserted me, and my friends sailed back to England, what would become of me? Where would I go? If revenge and victory were denied me, and if I could not have Oswynn, what was there left for me?

Only then, as I lay there, eyes closed in the darkness, waiting for sleep that would not come, did I truly understand what it was I'd committed myself to. This was more than a simple feud over women and honour between rival warlords on the fringes of Christendom. What tattered scraps remained of my pride, my dignity, my reputation depended for their survival or the success of this endeavour. It was I who had started us all on this road. My shoulders would bear the responsibility if we failed, and mine alone.

But how would I be able to go on, knowing that I'd given my all and still it had been for nothing? Although I wouldn't admit it to any of the others, in that moment I saw that, for me, there were only two ways this could possibly end. Nothing less than success would be enough for me.

It was victory, or it was death.

Eventually sleep did take me, although it was a fitful sleep in which fragments of half-formed dreams bled one into another. I saw the faces of old sword-brothers long dead, whose names no longer came to mind. I walked through places long forgotten, places I hadn't visited since my youth: the woodlands near to the castle at Commines where the other boys and I had played and practised ambushes and, later, taken girls for secret trysts; the abbey in Brittany where I had grown up under the care of the monks. And I saw Robert, the first by that name to whom I had been sworn, but he was an old man, wrinkled and hoary-haired, which even in the midst of the dream I thought strange, since he had only been around forty years or so when he met his end. He would hardly meet my gaze, would utter not a word, and I didn't understand why.

I woke still bone-tired and with a chill in every corner of my body, to a morning veiled by a white sea-mist that made it hard to see more than fifty paces.

'It's like this every morning in these parts,' Magnus told me as we huddled in our cloaks, waiting for it to clear.

'Every morning?' I asked.

'All through the winter, from when the leaves begin to fall to when the first green shoots burst through the soil. And the winters last a long time this far north.'

It must have been another hour before the fog had cleared enough for us to raise the stone rings that served as anchors and, on the ebbing tide, leave the shelter of that harbour.

And so we set out for the isle without a name, Haakon's isle, keeping close formation as we watched that land carefully for any signs of the enemy. I glimpsed farmsteads, barns, woods, sheep-pens and pastures, cairns and burial mounds, but no scouts or sentries, until we passed a headland where stood the crumbled ruins of an old stone roundhouse. There, on the cliff-top, waited a rider mounted on a white horse. He watched us as we drew closer, no doubt counting the number of oars on both ships and trying to guess from that how many we numbered, until suddenly he kicked on and galloped away, no doubt to Jarnborg, to tell his lord the news.

If Haakon didn't already know we were coming for him, he would shortly.

Not long after that we came upon the cove Magnus had mentioned. As expected, there was no one to prevent us landing there, and so we ran both ships aground on the sand next to one another, close to where a narrow rivulet emptied into the sea. The day was silent, save for the plaintive cries of a pair of buzzards as they circled over a small clump of trees that stood a little way to the south, and the cawing of rooks gathered in its branches.

'I don't like this, lord,' Serlo, ever the morose one, muttered. We jumped down from the ship, our boots sinking into the wet sand, and trudged up towards dry land. 'He's plotting something. He has to be.'

'Maybe,' I said. 'Or else our arrival has frightened him.'

I didn't believe that, not for a moment, but didn't want to admit that the silence unnerved me too. Did Haakon have a war-party hiding in that copse, waiting for the right moment to attack us? It seemed unlikely, unless they were keeping very still indeed so as not to disturb those rooks. It didn't look big enough to hide more than fifty men, and we had more than twice that number. Not all of those were warriors, of course, but every oarsman and deck-hand knew how to handle a spear or a sword. It was no great army, not by any means, but it wasn't a force to be dismissed readily either. I only hoped it was enough.

After holding another council, we agreed that a small group should go on ahead to scout out the island and see if we could get close enough to Jarnborg to be able to ascertain its strength. Leaving Serlo, Pons and Godric with Aubert and most of the rest of our party to help defend the ships in the event that the enemy did come, Wace, Eudo and I donned hauberks and helmets, knives and swords and shields. Together with Magnus and ten of his huscarls, Ælfhelm among them, we set out across the grassy tussocks and the outcrops of grey, lichen-covered stone that jutted from the earth, making our way towards higher ground where we might gain a better view of our surroundings.

In all that time we saw no more sign of our enemy, and none of the local folk dared approach when they saw us, instead running in from the fields to the safety of their homes. Probably they thought we were raiders, come to steal their flocks and their women. We left them alone, following Magnus as he led us half marching, half scrambling over that stony, broken land, until we descended towards a broad, flat plain that was crossed by countless tiny streams and hemmed in on both sides by high crags, and which ran for about a mile towards the sea. A few scattered barns and round wattle-and-thatch hovels lay close to the shore, where spindly-legged wading birds dug their bills into the mud in search of worms, and where a number of small fishing boats together with four longships were beached.

'Those are Haakon's ships, for certain,' Magnus said, his expression darker than ever I had seen it. 'I'd recognise them anywhere.'

By my reckoning, four longships meant at least two hundred men, and possibly as many as two hundred and fifty. I guessed the true number was smaller rather than larger, since each one would be an additional burden on his storehouses, representing a mouth that had to be fed and kept well watered, but I couldn't be sure.

'We've been seen,' Wace said, and pointed up towards the crags on the northern side of that valley, perhaps a quarter of a mile away, where the same rider on the same white horse had stopped and seemed to be gazing down towards us. At least, I assumed it was the same man.

He must have known we were looking at him, but strangely he did not bolt at once as I might have expected. Instead he stayed where he was for a while longer, before once more galloping away, soon disappearing over the crest of the hill.

'We ought to turn back, lord,' Ælfhelm said to Magnus. 'We're too exposed here. If Haakon has a trap laid for us—'

'He hasn't,' I interrupted him.

'How can you be so sure?'

'What would be the point of sending us such a warning if he meant to ambush us?' I countered.

'A warning?'

I sighed. 'That horseman wasn't trying to stay hidden. If he were, he'd have kept to the trees, and wouldn't be riding anything as visible as a white steed. No, he wanted us to see him.'

'Where's the sense in that?' Ælfhelm asked.

For all his years, the huscarl still had much to learn, but I was too tired to explain it myself. 'Wace?' I asked. 'Eudo?'

It was Wace who spoke up first. 'Haakon wants only to remind us that he's still watching us and that he knows what we're up to, and so make us a little more cautious.'

And his warning was working, too, on Ælfhelm at least, for although he said nothing more on the matter, I could see from the look in his eyes that he remained less than convinced.

So much in war comes down not to individual prowess of arms, or weight of numbers, or deftness of strategy, but to confidence. Confidence in one's scouts and their information. Confidence in one's ability to survive and succeed against the odds. Confidence in one's friends and allies to stand firm in the shield-wall and protect one's flanks in the charge. Even small raiding-bands can accomplish momentous deeds if they have sufficient nerve, while I'd heard tales of great hosts that in times past have been cowed into fleeing without so much as giving battle, merely because their commander lacked the stomach for the impending clash of arms, or because the enemy by their clever ruses had convinced him that victory was impossible.

In the end, it is very often not the side that is largest or most experienced that gains possession of the field of slaughter, but the one that is most confident. For that reason we did not turn back, but chose to carry on, keeping to the open where the enemy could clearly see us and where, if they did show themselves, we would be easily able to spot them coming. In doing so, we were letting Haakon know in turn that we had no fear of him.

We trudged on down that valley, across lush grassland made soft and heavy by the previous day's rain. We watched the crags on both sides lest any more riders should appear, but they didn't, and before long we glimpsed the forbidding slopes of the promontory rising to the north, just as Magnus had described it, ringed by steep scarps and crowned with a high stockade. A gatehouse looked out over the neck of land that lay to its south, and the golden, freshly laid thatch of the halls inside was just visible above the sharpened points of the walls' timber posts.

Jarnborg.

This, then, was the iron fortress about which we had heard so much. I'd harboured half a hope that Magnus had been exaggerating, and that it would turn out to be little more than a simple ringwork of banks and ditches surmounted with stakes, like the refuges in which the folk who lived on the Marches sometimes sought shelter from the marauders who came across the dyke. But that half-hope was stifled the instant I set eyes on Jarnborg, and my heart sank, for it was every bit as impressive as its name suggested, as formidable a fastness as I had ever seen and easily a rival to any castle that we Normans, who were known and admired across the length and breadth of Christendom as master builders, had ever erected. Indeed it might as well have been wrought from iron, for it seemed like a place that could withstand the passing of ages and perhaps even the world's end itself.

'There it is,' Magnus said. 'Haakon's winter stronghold.'

Desperately I scanned its walls, searching for some weakness we might exploit, but could find none, not from this approach at least. A cart-track wound its way up the incline towards the gates, between the boulders that everywhere jutted up from the ground, but it was narrow, the land on either side falling away sharply towards the shore, where the waves pounded and the seabirds flocked to feast upon whatever the tide had washed up.

And it was while we were all gazing, unspeaking, upon that fortress, that the gates opened, and from them issued forth seven horsemen. Too few to pose much threat to us, and so we waited to see what they would do, watching them carefully as they descended the track that led down towards the valley, until there could be no doubt that they were making towards us. They made no particular haste; even once they were on the level ground they rode merely at a gentle trot, as if enjoying a morning's ride around their estates.

They hadn't come to fight, I realised, but to talk.

'Keep your eyes open and your wits about you,' I told the others nonetheless.

'You think this might be a ruse?' Eudo asked.

'I don't know,' I said as the wind flapped at our cloaks and buffeted our cheeks. 'But keep your hand close by your sword-hilt just in case.'

Six of the riders halted around two hundred paces away, close to where a wooden bridge crossed one of the many streams, leaving the seventh to ride on alone, giving flight to the banner in his hand. The black dragon, exactly as I remembered it, with eyes of fire and an axe gripped in its claws. The man who carried it was powerfully built and broad of shoulder; his greying hair was tied in a braid in the Danish style at the back of his head. A thick beard adorned his chin, his arms were decorated with rings made from rods of gold twisted around one another, and he wore a sealskin cloak over a mail shirt that looked in places to be missing a few links, but which nevertheless had been polished to a shine. His face was lined with the creases of age, but there was a wolfish keenness to the way his eyes darted about that somehow made him seem younger than his years.

And I recognised that face, for it was the same one that had haunted my dreams for a year and more, ever since that night at Beferlic.

Haakon Thorolfsson.

How many nights had I lain awake, thinking of the ways in which I would wreak vengeance upon the one who had murdered our lord? And now at last here he was, brazenly riding towards us. He grinned broadly, although there was no humour in his eyes. He checked his mount about fifteen paces away: close enough to be able to converse without needing to shout, but far enough that if any of us charged him he would easily be able to turn and gallop safely away. He wasn't stupid.

'I was wondering when you'd come,' he said. There was a rasp to his voice that perhaps was a mark of the cold, wind-blasted lands from which he came. 'Although I confess I'm disappointed. I thought that, between you, you might have been able to muster more of an army.'

I think we all knew there was no point in answering that, for none among us spoke. Haakon was well aware how large was the force we had brought with us, and we weren't in the mood for playing such games.

'Magnus Haroldson, my friend,' he said, spreading his open palms as if in greeting. 'It's good to see you again after so long. Come to break your army against Jarnborg's walls once more, have you?'

'What do you want, Haakon?' Magnus asked. 'Or have you left the comfort of your hearth merely to insult us?'

'Insult you?' the Dane asked, and managed somehow to laugh and look affronted at the same time. 'Why should I want to insult you? We are old allies, are we not?'

Magnus spat in his direction. 'You stole everything from me. My brothers are dead because of you.'

'If you thrust your hand into a wasps' nest, then it is your own fault if you are stung. You and your brothers were foolish enough to leave your spoils unguarded, and so I took them. There is no more to it than that. I had nothing to do with their deaths. If anyone should bear the blame for that, it is these Frenchmen you call your friends. They were the ones who deprived your family of everything it had, and who drove you from England. Is that not true?'

I glanced at Magnus, but couldn't read his expression. I understood, of course, what the Dane was trying to do, and only hoped that the Englishman understood it too, and that his hatred for Haakon outweighed his hatred for our kind.

'Very well,' the elder man said when it was clear that Magnus had nothing more to say. 'You ask me what I want, and this is my answer.' He turned his gaze towards myself, Wace and Eudo. 'I want to know which one of you is the Breton, Tancred of Earnford.'

That surprised me, for I hadn't expected him to have come by that information.

'I am,' I said curtly as I felt my sword-arm itch and imagined how, if I could only get close enough to him, I would slice my blade-edge across his steed's neck, unhorsing him. Then, while he lay on the ground, I would drive the point down into his mailed chest, using all my strength to bury it deep. One strike was all it would take to puncture his heart. One strike, and we could end this now. But he was too watchful to allow that to happen. I only had to take a couple of paces towards him and he would retreat at once.

He smiled with the warmth of an old friend who had not seen me in years. 'So,' he said, 'you are the one I have heard so much about. The one who gave Eadgar Ætheling his scar. A worthy warrior.'

I wasn't about to confirm or to deny it for him, and so instead I said, 'How do you know my name?'

At that Haakon gave a laugh. 'You cannot send your spies, your knowledge-gatherers, all across Britain, and yet expect me not to hear that you've been seeking me out. I've suspected for months that you'd be coming. It was only a question of when. To tell the truth, I didn't think it would take you this long.'

'They told you I was paying them?' Not only had those whoresons failed to bring me the information I wanted, but they had in turn sold what they knew about me to my enemies.

The Dane breathed a sigh. 'It tires me to relate how it all happened, so let us not waste our breath discussing it. Suffice it to say that you are not the only one who has his spies. I've heard the tales of your deeds. I know who you are, Tancred, and what brings you here.'

I wondered how much he did know. Certainly I wasn't about to let slip anything which might turn out being to his advantage. Did he think I had come because of the life he had taken, or because he had stolen my woman from me?

'You killed our lord,' I said, deciding that, of the two reasons, that was the one he was more likely to know about. 'You killed Robert de Commines.'

He stared at me for long moments, that wolfish look having returned. 'Yes,' he said at last.

'You admit it, then?' Eudo asked.

'Why shouldn't I?' Haakon countered. 'Yes, I killed him. I watched the mead-hall burn and I heard the screams of those inside. I remember how he stumbled out with the smoke billowing around him. I remember how easy it was for me to ram my sword home. I remember how he died with barely a whimper.'

'You don't deserve to live,' Eudo said. The wind had dropped and in the stillness I heard the hiss of steel against his scabbard's wool lining as he drew his sword.

'Eudo,' I said warningly. The Dane had clearly come to parley with us for a purpose, and I wanted to know what that was, not to scare him off.

Wace laid a hand upon our friend's shoulder. 'Put your sword away.'

Eudo hesitated, but eventually he must have realised that it was a useless gesture, for he slid the blade back whence it had come.

'Even if you did kill me, it wouldn't bring your lord back to you,' Haakon said. He turned to Magnus. 'Nor your brothers.'

'That doesn't mean we wouldn't enjoy watching you squirm while your lifeblood dripped away,' Harold's son retorted.

The Dane smiled. 'The young pup has a loud bark, I see. It's a shame that he lacks the bite to match it.'

'Enough of this,' I said, growing impatient. 'Have you come with anything worthwhile to say?'

'There is one thing.'

'Then spit it out.'

A smirk was upon his face. 'Vengeance isn't the only reason that brought you here, is it?'

So he knew. Knew why I had come here, what it was that had brought me on this journey in the first place.

'Where is she?' I demanded.

Haakon didn't answer, not in any words. Instead he merely raised a hand in what I took for a signal to his six companions waiting by the bridge. Still mounted, they advanced now. Suspecting a trick, I laid my hand upon my sword-hilt, and out of the corners of my eyes I saw the others doing the same. If the Dane was at all concerned, however, he didn't let it show.

I fixed my gaze on the six figures as they approached, realising as they did so that only five of them were men. For in the middle of them rode a woman, and not just any woman either. Long before she was close enough for me to make out her features, I knew who she was.

As if it could have been anyone else.

Oswynn.

Twenty-five

'Oswynn,' I said, under my breath at first, and then more loudly, so that she could hear: 'Oswynn!'

Her hands were tied in front of her and her mount was being led by one of the riders flanking her. She wore a cloak that might have been otter fur over a fine-spun woollen dress, but all that expensive garb did not disguise the bruises on her face, which was thinner and paler than I recalled. Her head was bowed as if in submission, and when she did look up her eyes were hollow. All the fire she'd once possessed seemed to have been extinguished. The summer when we met had been her sixteenth, and three more summers had come and gone since then, but she looked much older than her years might have suggested. And yet she was still as beautiful as ever. Her hair, black as the night when the moon is new and cloud veils the stars, which I had liked her to wear unbound, was braided like that of a married woman.

'I presume she's the one you came for,' I heard Haakon say, but I was not paying him attention, not really, for I couldn't tear my eyes from her.

I willed her to say something, even just my name, but she did not utter any sound at all, nor so much as smile, which I ascribed to fear of what they might do to her if she did, rather than because she didn't recognise me. She did, I was sure of it, just as I was sure that even in those hollow eyes I spied a glimmer of something like relief or hope. I tried not to imagine what the Dane had done with her in the years we had been apart, but it was impossible. The way she held herself told me all that I needed, or wanted, to know.

'Striking, isn't she?' Haakon went. 'Prettier than any Danish girl, for sure, and I've known my share of them. I can well understand why you would want to come all this way to steal her from me.'

'You're the one who stole her,' I said. 'She's my woman, not yours.'

'Is that so? Where were you that night to lay claim to her?' He gave a flick of a hand, beckoning her forward. Reluctantly, she came sidling up alongside him. 'She belongs to me,' he said, reaching over and untying the bonds around her wrists. A gasp of surprise or protest escaped her lips as he seized her forearm and held up her left hand. 'Here is the proof.'

A marriage-band glinted in the cold light of that winter's day. Oswynn, in tears now, tried to snatch her hand away, but Haakon's grip was firm and all her struggling was in vain.

My blood boiled and I set my teeth in anger, but somehow I held myself back. I didn't believe for a heartbeat that she had become his wife out of choice, nor do I think he expected me to. All he wanted was to taunt me, but I refused to rise to the bait. Losing my temper would achieve nothing, and indeed could end up costing me everything. Haakon's men were close; if I came within five paces of their lord, they would strike me down without hesitation.

'I don't want to see blood spilt upon my lands any more than you wish to lose good hearth-troops,' the Dane said as he released Oswynn's wrist at last. 'Better men than you have tried to take Jarnborg from me, and all have died by my sword-edge. For that reason, and because I am a generous man, I will give you one piece of advice. Do yourselves and your followers a favour, and leave these shores.'

'What happens if we don't?' asked Magnus.

'You aren't the only one who has friends,' Haakon replied mildly. 'I sent word to mine three days ago. They will be here within the week, if not sooner, at which point we will not hesitate in crushing you and making drinking cups of your skulls. So you have a simple choice. If you value your lives then you'll leave. Otherwise I can promise you only death.'

'You lie,' Wace said. 'You have no friends coming to lend their swords in your support.'

'Believe what you will,' Haakon said, 'so long as you're prepared to wager your life on it. I have given you my advice, for whatever it might be worth. I leave it to you to decide whether or not you heed it.'

With that once more he smiled that humourless smile, then turned and spurred his steed into a canter, followed by his retainers, and by Oswynn, who cast a desperate glance over her shoulder, holding my gaze for as long as she was able as they led her away, back across the bridge, across the valley, up towards the gates of the iron fortress.

'I'll come for you,' I called after her, using the English tongue. 'I swear it, Oswynn, I'll come for you!'

I didn't know whether, above the wind and the thudding of hooves upon turf, she managed to hear me, but I hoped she did.

'He's bluffing,' Wace said later, when we had returned to the beach where the crews of both ships had set up camp, and spoken to the others. 'He must be.'

'How can you be so sure?' Eudo asked as he tore off another hunk of bread and crammed it into his mouth. The sun was high and we hadn't eaten since daybreak, but I couldn't so much as think about food. Seeing Oswynn, only to have her taken away yet again, had left me feeling empty and despondent.

'If Haakon knew he had help on the way, why would he care to warn us?' Wace asked. 'Why not let those allies of his come, and try to catch us by surprise?'

'Because he has nothing to gain by attacking us,' I said. 'If he can make us leave without having to risk battle, so much the better as far as he's concerned. He's made it clear that whatever our quarrels with him, he has no interest in us. Unless we come assaulting Jarnborg's walls, there's no pressing reason why he or his friends need cross swords with us at all.'

Like his countryman Snorri, Haakon was proving to be a cautious one, far from the reckless adventurer that I had expected. Undoubtedly I could have learnt much from his example, were I not so intent on killing him. As it was, I was wondering only how

355

we might take advantage of that caution to bring about his downfall.

'I think he'd prefer to destroy us if he can, rather than risk the possibility that we might return in the spring with an even larger fleet,' said Magnus. 'For that reason I'm inclined to agree with Wace.'

That was the first he had said in a long while. No doubt he was still thinking about those crags and that palisade, and whether there was any way of scaling them, without any siege towers or ladders, that wouldn't cost the lives of half our retinue. As too was I.

'What I don't understand', Eudo said, 'is why he should feel the need to bluff at all, assuming he has the strength in numbers that we think he has.'

I mulled over that for a few moments, and then it came to me, and I gave a laugh. 'Of course,' I said. 'That's it exactly.'

For Eudo had as good as answered his own question. Haakon must be worried to some extent about his ability to defend his stronghold, or else surely he would not resort to such ruses. Did that mean his defences were perhaps not quite as sound as we had supposed?

To begin with Eudo gave me a strange look, but then he too must have realised, since he began to smile, and Wace and Magnus and Ælfhelm as well.

Four longships we had seen drawn up on the sand in the bay beneath Jarnborg at the north of this island. We'd assumed that meant he had four full ships' crews at his disposal, but what if that weren't the case? What if he didn't have the ten score spears I'd hazarded, but only half that number?

Naturally all this was guesswork, and didn't mean that Jarnborg was ours for the taking, not at all. A mere thirty spears could probably hold its gates, so strong was its position upon the promontory. But it all helped add to my conviction that, providing we could only find a way inside, we could do this. We might have struggled to hold our own against two hundred, but against a hundred, anything was possible.

Confidence. As so often, it came down to that. Haakon was trying to play on our doubts, to make us lose heart, but it hadn't worked, and in so doing he had betrayed his own unease.

'What do we do next, then?' Magnus asked.

I considered. 'If he's bluffing, then nothing has changed as far as we're concerned, so there's no reason why we should go anywhere.'

'And if he's telling the truth?'

'Then we know we have only a few days in which to make our assault, if we're to do it at all, before his allies arrive.'

'A few days?' Ælfhelm asked. 'How can we possibly defeat him in that time?'

He was right to have his misgivings, and yet a new sense of purpose had stirred within me, and I was not to be discouraged. 'We'll find a way,' I answered.

We had made it this far, after all: further than I would have dared imagine was possible even a couple of short months ago, during the struggle for the Isle. Back then I'd all but given up hope of finding Oswynn again in this life, and this morning I had seen her with my own eyes.

'One thing's for certain,' said Aubert, who must have overheard our conversation. 'We won't be going anywhere this afternoon.'

'Why not?' Eudo asked.

'The winds have been gusting hard all morning and I've watched the waves growing choppier by the hour. There's a gale on its way. Trust someone who's spent more years out on the sea than you've even lived.'

'In that case,' I said, 'we'd better make use of the time we have, and see if we can find Jarnborg's weakness.'

Provided, that was, that it had one.

As unlikely as an attack by Haakon seemed, we nevertheless took care to post sentries along the ridge that overlooked our landing place, as well as further inland, so that those back at the ships would have plenty of warning if indeed he came. Then, while Magnus took a handful of men with him to try to get closer to Jarnborg, I set off with Serlo and Pons and Godric to learn what we could from the folk who lived close at hand: those who did not flee at the first sight of us, and whose speech Eithne could understand. I'd brought her with us, thinking she might be familiar with whatever tongue was spoken in these parts, which she was, but only barely.

'I can only understand half of what they're saying,' she explained to me after we'd managed to accost a grey-bearded cowherd, whose name we learnt was Tadc, and his trembling, bone-thin wife, Aife. 'Some of the words they use are unknown to me, and they have a strange accent.'

'What do they know about the fort?' I asked.

Eithne put the question to them, and I sensed her frustration both in her voice and in the set of her lips. Although I couldn't understand her tongue, I nevertheless recognised the name of Haakon's stronghold, at the mention of which Tadc and Aife suddenly froze, their eyes wide, before both began to babble at the same time, talking over one another, gesturing wildly with spindly fingers towards the north and all the while shaking their heads.

'They dare not so much as set foot upon its slopes, or come within an arrow's flight of the bay where he keeps his ships,' Eithne said. 'They are frightened of Haakon and his fellow warriors, with their pagan amulets and their foreign speech. He asks them for payment and they give him what he demands, but otherwise he ignores them, and they are happy enough at that. They have no reason to venture anywhere near his stronghold.'

'So they rarely meet Haakon or his men?'

I waited, trying my hardest to remain patient while Eithne attempted first to make herself understood and then in turn to understand the answers they gave.

'The only time they ever speak to them is when they come to collect each month's tribute,' she said. 'A party regularly comes down from the fort to collect water from the spring, although no one dares disturb them.'

'What spring?' I asked.

Eithne translated for me, and after a few moments both husband and wife pointed towards a copse that stood on a rise some distance to the north, which I reckoned could be little more than half a mile from Jarnborg's gates, if that.

'Amidst those trees,' Eithne said. 'They come twice every day, perhaps an hour or so after first light, while the fog still lingers, and again at dusk, and lately a third time as well, around midday.'

'Always at the same times?'

Eithne nodded. 'It seems so.'

'How many?'

Again she conferred with the couple, and again I waited for the answer to come back.

'Three slave-girls, usually, sometimes four, with pails that they carry on poles across their shoulders, together with the same number of guards to stop them from running away.'

'Danish girls?' I asked.

Eithne shook her head. 'Irish, Aife thinks. He brings them back when he returns from his travels, from places across the water. She believes they are badly beaten, since she's sometimes heard them crying.'

From Dyflin, I'd wager, like Eithne herself. Was it possible that the girls were kinswomen of hers?

And suddenly the beginnings of an idea began to form in my mind. Clearly there was no ready supply of water on the promontory, save for what they could harvest from the rain. But whatever army Haakon was hiding behind those palisades would need plenty, not just to drink and to brew into ale, but to wash and to cook with as well.

'How old are these girls?' I asked.

'What?' Eithne asked, confused.

I was in no mood to explain at that moment. 'Just ask them.'

After some discussion between the cowherd and his wife, the answer came back that, although they couldn't say whether it was always the same ones who came, they tended to be young, somewhere between twelve and eighteen summers, by their reckoning. Around Eithne's age, in other words.

'What are you thinking, lord?' she asked.

I only smiled in what I trusted was an enigmatic fashion, waved my thanks to Tadc and Aife and beckoned for the others to follow as I set off back in the direction of camp. I didn't want to say, not just yet. Not until I'd had the chance to consider exactly how this might work.

Even so, a shiver of exhilaration ran through me. Exhilaration at the thought of the battle to come. Exhilaration because I sensed that vengeance, justice and honour were at hand.

Because I knew how we would get inside Jarnborg.

'There has to be another way,' said Wace, shaking his head, once I'd begun to tell them all of my plan. 'A simpler way.'

The day was growing old, and dark clouds once more hung over us, threatening rain at any moment. We were gathered by the campfire, sharing bread and passing around flagons of ale: Magnus and Ælfhelm, Eudo and Wace, Aubert and myself.

'Is there no other way in or out of Jarnborg?' Eudo asked Magnus, who had been scouting the surrounding land that afternoon.

'None,' Ælfhelm growled.

'We ventured as close as we dared to its walls,' Magnus offered more helpfully. 'We spied what looked like a doorway on the north-western side, with a path leading down to a sandy cove where they could unload supplies, but it's been blocked up, while the cliff-face below it has crumbled away, and most of the path with it. The approach might still be climbable, for someone with sufficient knowledge and experience, but not in mail and with a shield strapped to one's back. The only other way in or out that we could see remains through the gatehouse.'

'You're certain of that, are you?' Wace asked, regarding him dubiously.

'As certain as I can be,' Magnus replied. 'Would you rather go scouting those slopes yourself?'

To that Wace made no reply.

'If we're to have any chance of victory, we need to bring him out from behind the protection of his palisades,' I said. 'As I see it, there's only one certain way of doing that.'

'Attacking his ships,' Eudo murmured.

I nodded. 'What are Danes known for, if not their love of their boats? Without them Haakon can't very well go raiding in the spring, can he? So if we make an attack on them, I'll wager that he'll come running to defend them.'

'They're well guarded,' Magnus said. 'He already has forty-one sword- and spear-Danes posted there. We counted them.'

'That won't be enough to fend off two boatloads of battle-hungry warriors,' I replied. 'For that he'll need to send the larger part of his host down from Jarnborg.'

'Which he'll do as soon as he guesses what we're up to,' Aubert said. 'And from atop that promontory, he'll be able to see us coming from miles away. Even before we've entered the bay, he'll have gathered enough spearmen to make a landing all but impossible.'

'So long as we can scare him into coming out from his fortress, nothing else matters,' I said. 'The point is not to bring him to battle, at least not at first.'

Aubert frowned. 'If the point isn't to bring him to battle, then what is?'

'To distract him.'

'Distract him from what?' Wace asked.

I grinned. 'From the second prong of our attack.' And I told them of my plan to slip unnoticed, together with a handful of men, inside Jarnborg.

'You'll never manage this,' Wace said when I'd finished. 'This is reckless beyond belief.'

Reckless it was, certainly. I'd be the first to admit that much. Nor could I remember having ever devised a more elaborate plan than this. Not one that had worked, anyway. But if there was ever any strategy that guaranteed success without involving some measure of danger, I was yet to hear of it.

Eudo stared at me in disbelief. 'And what would be the purpose of this? To capture it?'

I shook my head, aware that I was grinning like a fool.

'What, then?'

'To burn it.'

I would do to his hall what he had done to the fastness at Dunholm three winters ago. Or try, at least, knowing that if it worked, it would surely shatter the spirit of Haakon and his host. For if what

Magnus had told me was right, everything he held dear was contained within those walls. It was his home, where his treasure hoard was kept, and it was his pride, too.

And I would be the one to destroy it.

Eudo gave a chuckle as a grin spread across his face. Like me, he had always possessed something of a rash streak, and revelled in causing chaos where he could. Of the rest, only Wace did not look entirely convinced, and I supposed that was only to be expected. He had ever been the most level-headed of all my friends.

'This can't work,' he told me. 'You're a fool if you think it can. How long do you think you can survive inside the enemy camp? How will you even get past the sentries on the gate? You don't look like a Dane, nor do you speak even a word of their tongue.'

'I'll take with me someone who does,' I replied, 'and make sure to keep my own mouth shut. I'm not asking any of you to come with me, not if you don't want. I'll do my part, providing that you do yours. Speak now if you have anything better in mind. Otherwise this, as I see it, is our best chance of victory.'

Wace breathed a tired sigh. 'I won't even try to sway you, Tancred, not this time. But you must understand that if anything goes wrong and Haakon's men discover you, you're all dead men. You and whatever band of fools you can convince to accompany you.'

'I know that,' I replied tersely. 'Don't think I don't.'

I glanced at Eudo and Magnus, willing them to challenge me, but neither uttered a word. How long we remained there in silence, I couldn't say, but it felt like an eternity. For the first time doubt began to creep into my mind. Perhaps Wace was right. What if Haakon refused to be drawn out? What if he had enough spears at his disposal to defend his ships and his stronghold both?

'How many men would you need for this?' Magnus asked after a while.

'Six or seven at most,' I answered. 'The smaller the party, the better.'

He seemed to consider this for a moment. 'Very well,' he said at last. 'I'll join you.'

'Lord—' Ælfhelm protested.

But Magnus's eyes were gleaming with the prospect of adventure, and he ignored his countryman. 'You said yourself that you'll need someone who speaks Danish. If this is our one chance to destroy Haakon, then we might as well give it our all. If nothing else, at least we'll die knowing that we did everything we could. There is honour in that.'

There was indeed. I grinned back at him and held out my hand. He clasped it firmly, and so it was settled. Our destinies were bound, and we would go to Jarnborg, Haakon's stronghold, the iron fortress, together.

Fate can lead a man upon many strange and unexpected paths, and I confess that this was one of the strangest I'd ever embarked upon. Before me was someone who not so long ago I'd have counted among my enemies, whom I wouldn't have hesitated in killing, and no doubt the feeling was mutual. However, just as a storm will scatter ships to the wind and carry them far from their intended courses, so fate had carried us both far from the places we called home and into this alliance, with circumstance and common cause the only things binding us. Now as sword-brothers we were going to war.

I only hoped I was not making a grievous mistake.

And so it was agreed. Magnus and I would stay behind to lead the raid on Jarnborg itself, while the others, led by Wace and Eudo and Ælfhelm, would mount the feint on Haakon's ships. The next morning, then, we parted ways. We would make it look as though we had heeded the Dane's warning after all, decided against trying to fight him, and thus quit the island.

'As soon as the fog starts to lift tomorrow morning and it becomes safe to sail, that's when you'll need to begin your approach,' I told Eudo and Wace. We stood on the beach above the tideline while *Wyvern*'s crew pushed her out on to the water. 'By that time we'll either be inside Jarnborg, or we'll all be dead. Haakon's men always come to the spring in the morning, an hour or so after first light, or so we've been told, anyway.'

'I hope your information is sound,' Wace said. 'For your sake, not ours.'

I hoped so too. Only now, as we were about to embark upon this strategy, did I realise what a fragile thing it was, and how much we were relying on matters beyond our control: on the trustworthiness of the information given us; on the water-carriers coming to the spring at the right time; on Haakon doing exactly what we expected of him.

'Remember,' I said, 'don't commit yourselves to battle unless it's clear that the numbers are in your favour. I don't want any more Norman blood spilt than is necessary. Enough good men have wasted their lives because of me in the past couple of years.'

'So tell us again,' said a confused-looking Eudo. 'If we're not going to fight Haakon's forces, then what? Are we simply to lie in wait off the shore?'

'That's right,' I said. 'Wait until you see the flames licking above Jarnborg's palisade. In the confusion that follows, with any luck our enemy will be distracted. That's the moment when you strike.'

'Luck is the right word,' Wace said bitterly. 'We'll need some, if this plan of yours is to bear any fruit.'

Was that not true, though, of every struggle that had ever been fought? No strategy could account for every possible course of events, nor make order out of the turmoil of the mêlée, nor allow for the courage of the few or the timid hearts of the many. So much in battle was a question of luck, and every warrior needed good fortune, no matter whether he was a fresh-faced youth standing in the shield-wall for the first time, or a knight who had spent more than half his life travelling the sword-path. The poets who write the songs that pass into legend would have it differently, of course, but every man who lives his life by the sword knows it well.

Yet I still believed that the best warriors were those who made the most of their luck, who grasped in both hands the opportunities given them, who saw their enemies' weaknesses and how they might be turned to their advantage. That was why I refused to believe that our cause was as desperate as it might seem.

'What about the Englishman?' Eudo asked, nodding his head towards Magnus, who was embracing his huscarls down by the water's edge. *Wyvern* and *Nihtegesa* were already afloat, bobbing in the swell as they lay at anchor. The sea-mist had cleared to reveal skies heavy with the promise of rain to come, and I only hoped that another storm was not on its way. 'Do you really trust him?'

'Only about as far as I could throw him,' I answered. 'But he wants the same thing as we do. Until we achieve it, there's no reason why we can't depend on him.'

Wace didn't look convinced. 'What did Haakon mean yesterday when he called Magnus the son of Harold?'

'Did he say that?' I said, doing my best to feign surprise, although the looks they gave me suggested I hadn't succeeded.

'Don't play games with us,' Wace said in a warning tone. 'You know something. He didn't mean *the* Harold, surely?'

I met his stare, but realised it was pointless to try to keep the truth from them any longer.

'Is he, or is he not, the son of the usurper?' Wace asked.

'So he claims.'

'You knew?' asked Eudo, while Wace simply turned away, cursing under his breath. 'Why didn't you tell us?'

'Why do you think? If you'd found out he was Harold's son, would you have come this far, or would you have taken *Wyvern* back to England?'

He didn't answer, but they knew as well as I did what they would have done.

'I don't believe this,' Wace said. 'It's one thing to be fighting shoulder to shoulder with Englishmen, but I never thought I'd find myself sharing bread and ale with the usurper's own blood.'

'Quiet,' I hissed, aware that Magnus and his huscarls were not far off. 'Don't forget that we outnumber them by three swords to every two of theirs. If anyone has any reason to be worried about being murdered in his sleep, it's him, but he obviously trusts us, or else he wouldn't be here, would he?'

'He has the oath-breaker's blood running in his veins,' Eudo said. 'What's to say he won't turn on us, just as his father turned on King Guillaume?'

'He hasn't yet.' It was a poor answer, and one that even I was not convinced by, but it was the only one that came to mind. 'If he'd wanted to kill us, he'd have found a way to do so before now.'

'And on that reasoning you're prepared to stake your life?'

Truth be told, I wasn't sure, not entirely. What I was sure of was that if I gave up now, when we were so close, the knowledge that I had fled from this fight would forever haunt me. Never would there be a better opportunity for us to slake our thirst for vengeance, or for me to take back the woman who was taken from me, the woman whom I had yearned for above all others. That was why I had to do this, and that was why it had to be now.

'So long as you know what it is you're taking on,' Wace said. 'From the moment we're out on the water, you'll be on your own. We won't be able to help you.'

'I know,' I replied. 'But hopefully you won't have to, and the next time we meet we'll be celebrating a great victory.'

'I only hope so,' Wace said.

We embraced then, but they didn't bid me farewell, nor I them, since that would have seemed too final. For all the doubts that plagued me, I still believed we would be victorious and that we would all be standing come nightfall tomorrow. Nor did I stay to watch them cast off from the shore, although that was for a different reason, since there was a chance that Haakon's scouts might be watching, and that would only have aroused their suspicions. Instead Magnus and I and the small band we'd gathered slipped away one by one into the copse overlooking that inlet, where we intended to lie in wait the rest of that day and the night as well. But between the trunks I was just able to make out the blue-grey waters, and *Wyvern*'s black-and-yellow-striped sail billowing, and the flecks of white as the oars of both ships broke the surface. I watched until they were out of sight.

There was no turning back now. The next morning we would strike at the very heart of Haakon's power, and take the fight to him. Three long years had passed, but tomorrow, I promised myself, I would have Oswynn back, and Robert de Commines would at last be avenged.

Twenty-six

We waited until well after night had fallen before making our way across that still and silent land to lay our snare. The skies were clear and the stars cast a chill light upon us. Everywhere the branches, the fields and the meadows glowed white with frost. There was no wind to cut through our cloaks, for which I was glad, but nevertheless I could feel winter's icy tendrils wrapping themselves around me, drawing the heat from my limbs.

Eventually we found the spring Tadc and Aife had told us about, although not without some difficulty, even following the directions they'd given, since it lay close to the summit of a low rise, at the heart of a dense thicket which the small light there was barely penetrated. In darkness as deep as pitch we scrambled through leaves and mulch, while branches and thorns scratched our arms and our faces. We climbed up the sharp crags, sometimes feeling our way on hands and knees, our leather soles slipping on the lichen-covered boulders, all the while listening for the trickle of water. After what seemed like hours of searching, we eventually found it burbling forth from a crevice in the rock. Surrounding it, forming a crown upon the brow of that gentle hill, stood a wide ring several dozen paces across of rough-hewn stones, most of them half as high as a man and a few even taller, which I supposed had been left by the ancient folk who were the first people ever to live in Britain, before even the Romans had come and wrought their great works.

There, taking shelter amidst the hazel and the holly, the oak and the ash, huddled in our cloaks and with our breath misting before our faces, we lay in wait for our prey, taking it in turns to keep watch. There were nine of us in all: Magnus and myself; Serlo and Pons; Godric and Eithne; Ælfhelm, and two of the huscarls under his command, neither of whom seemed to have proper names. The first was known as Sceota, which was the English word for a trout, on account of the fact that he had a reputation as a strong swimmer, while the other was called Dweorg, which meant a dwarf, even though he was a giant of a man and easily the tallest of all of us, taller even than Serlo.

I lay awake for a long while that night, and not just because of the cold and the damp that was soaking through my cloak into my tunic, but also because my mind was racing with thoughts of Oswynn, of the fastness upon the crag and how we would take the torch to its halls so that the flames would leap high enough to be seen the length of the fjord. I smiled as I closed my eyes and thought, too, of Haakon himself, and how I would take pleasure in gutting him like a fish and watching his lifeblood slip away. Blood that should have been spilt a long time ago. That was the last thing to cross my mind before finally sleep claimed me.

A sound sleep it was, too, strange though that might seem, since the ground was wet and I never usually rested well when wearing mail. It was filled with dreams of Earnford as I remembered it from the early summer, shortly before we had ridden to join the king's army in East Anglia, when the wheat was still green and the days were growing long, and for some reason Oswynn was there too, her hair flying long and loose behind her as we rode from the woods down to the river. Her laughter filled my ears as with a spray of sun-glistening water we crashed through the ford, except that when I arrived upon the other side and looked back, there was no sign of her. All was still, the sun had disappeared behind dark, fast-moving cloud that obscured the sky, the crops were withering in the fields, and I was calling her name over and over and over as I whirled about, searching for her. I was still calling when I felt a hand upon my shoulders, shaking them roughly, jolting me from sleep.

Instinctively my hand leapt to my knife-hilt at my waist and drew it free, thrusting the point in the direction of the blurry shape that was my assailant.

'It's me, lord,' said the one standing over me, drawing away from my blade, and as my eyes adjusted to the dimness of the morning I realised it was Serlo. 'It's me,' he repeated.

A grey half-light filtered through the mist that hung all about, obscuring the trunks of the trees and making it difficult to see much more than a hundred paces.

My head was spinning, my throat parched, my sight still a little blurry, and under my tunic my skin was soaked with sweat. 'What—?' I began as I withdrew my blade and, blinking to clear my eyes, slid it back into its sheath.

He put a finger to his lips. 'They're coming.'

'Already?'

That was when I heard, somewhere down the slope a short way to the north, the familiar jangle of horse harnesses, a peal of laughter and the sound of voices in a tongue I couldn't understand but which had to be Danish.

At a guess I reckoned it was barely after dawn, which meant that they were early, although the enveloping mist obscured everything beyond about forty or fifty paces, even the sun, so probably it was not quite as early as it seemed.

Without wasting another moment I hauled myself to my feet, at the same time shrugging off my cloak, which was sopping and covered all over with leaves, and letting it lie where it fell. Pons, who had joined Serlo for the final watch of the night, was busy waking Godric and the other Englishmen. I checked to make sure that my sword slid cleanly from its scabbard. How long had it been since last I'd drawn it in anger, since last her edge had tasted enemy blood?

Eithne, lying wrapped in blankets by the trunk of a wide-bellied oak, was beginning to stir, and I laid a hand on her shoulder.

'They're coming,' I said. 'Hide.'

She woke with a start, wide-eyed in panic, at first not seeming to understand what I was saying, but then quickly she rolled up the blankets and scrambled for cover. The voices were growing closer with every passing moment, and I knew we didn't have much time before they were upon us. I crouched down behind one of the frost-covered standing stones. Magnus had taken cover behind a holly bush to my right, and I held up a hand to catch his attention.

'On my signal,' I whispered, as loudly as I dared, which was not very loud at all. 'Make sure the others know.'

Magnus nodded. This was his fight as much as it was mine, but there was no disputing whose sword-arm was the more experienced, and in any case he understood that this was no time to argue. Each of us knew what he had to do. The others took position behind the stones, amidst the undergrowth, in the crevices between the outcrops of rocks and wherever else they could hide themselves. I glanced to my left and my right to see who was beside me, and found Dweorg and Godric.

'Stay close to me,' I told the latter. 'Remember everything I told you and you'll do well.'

He looked every bit as nervous as when I'd first met him. This would be his first taste of battle since that day in the marshes when he'd slain Hereward. His first fight as a true warrior, as a full-fledged killer. Only too well did I understand the burden of expectation that placed upon a man, and yet I had every faith that his nerve would hold and that he would not fail me. He knew what was at stake, and knew what he owed me, too.

The voices came again, closer than before, and I risked a glance around the edge of that standing stone in the direction from which they were coming.

In the dim light I saw their shadows emerging from out of the fog. They came in a line, each following carefully in the footsteps of the one before them, trudging up the stony ground to the summit of that little hill. Four slave-girls, each with two wooden pails that they carried on poles across their shoulders, were in the middle of that column, with two of Haakon's men leading and two more behind, preventing them from running away. One of the girls yelped as she stumbled and fell, her pails clattering upon the ground, and then a second time as one of the Danes hissed some manner of curse and hauled her up. She rubbed her elbow where she had fallen on it, and gingerly, stifling a sob, proceeded to pick up the fallen containers from where they lay. She was small and slight of stature, about Eithne's age, I reckoned, although it was difficult to say for certain.

Keeping still, hardly daring to breathe, I watched as the two leading Danes, swathed in thick cloaks of grey fur clasped at the shoulder with silver disc-brooches, with helmets upon their heads and wearing necklaces made from beads of amber, jet and ivory, approached the spring, murmuring to one another in low voices. One of them gave a curt snort of laughter, although at what I could only imagine. In the belief, perhaps, that our ships and their crews had been fooled into leaving their shores. Their manner and the fact that they wore no mail told me they had come without any expectation of trouble.

My hand, dry and cracked from the cold, tensed, my numb fingers curling around the corded grip of my sword-hilt. Slowly, so that it made not even a whisper, I slid the steel from the scabbard's lining of oiled fleece, all the while keeping my gaze on the party of men and girls. They were inside the stone circle now, not thirty paces from where we were hiding. So close, and yet not close enough.

Beside me, I sensed Dweorg growing impatient as he shifted uncomfortably behind another of the standing stones. The tall huscarl's sword was in his hand, and he kept glancing at me, ready for the signal, eager to spill some Danish blood. I glared sharply at him, knowing that the slightest sound now could give us away. I wanted Haakon's men to know nothing of us until we were already upon them, so that they had no time to so much as draw their weapons before we cut them down. We were barely half a mile from Jarnborg's walls. In the stillness of the morning their cries and those of the girls could easily carry, and it would be unwise to rely solely on the fog to mask the sound. No, we had to pick the right moment to attack, when the guards were least expecting it, when we could be certain of making this quick.

I kept a careful eye on them as, taking it in turns, the girls knelt down next to the spring. While one of the Danes kept watch, the other three paced about, drawing their cloaks more tightly around them and blowing warm air into their cupped hands, mumbling to one another. They were still more than twenty paces from us, and I knew it would be hard to come upon them by surprise across such broken ground, but it didn't seem that we had much choice. Already two of the girls had filled their pails. We were running out of time. I had to make a decision quickly, or else squander this chance we'd been given and let our one slender hope of victory slip away.

It was now, or not at all.

I glanced to my left, at Dweorg, and to my right, at Godric, nodding to each of them, then gave a wordless roar as I sprang to my feet, scrambling through the mass of branches before me, rushing out from my hiding place with steel in hand and the blood-lust coursing through my veins, pounding behind my eyes.

'Kill them!' I heard someone call in the English tongue, and it sounded like Magnus, but I didn't see him or indeed any of the others, only the four Danish men as I, their death-bringer, charged upon them.

They stood before us, startled and slack-jawed, but not for long. As soon as they realised how many of us there were, good sense prevailed and they turned in flight. One alone remained, his feet seemingly having taken root. He stared at us, unspeaking, as his hand moved to his hilt, but not nearly quickly enough, and he was still staring when I ran him through, plunging my sword deep into his gut. Blood gurgled forth across my hand, dribbling on to the frost-hardened earth. A gasp escaped his lips, his knees gave way, and I kicked him hard in the chest as with a sharp wrench I freed the steel from his belly.

'Go,' I shouted to the others, who were with me now, and indeed overtaking me in their pursuit of the fleeing guards, and of the slave-girls as well, who were shrieking as they dropped their pails and fled down the rise, deeper into the woods, albeit in a different direction entirely to the men. 'Don't let the girls get away. We need them!'

While Serlo, Pons, Sceota and Ælfhelm went after them, the rest of us charged on after Haakon's men. Two were making for the edge of the copse where they'd tethered their horses, at the foot of the hill, while the other was striking out through the undergrowth.

'Go after that one!' Magnus yelled to Dweorg and Godric. 'Leave the other two for us,' he added, by which I guessed he meant himself and me.

Leaving the corpse of that first Dane behind me, we crashed on down the slope after our quarries, between the birches and the elms, hacking a path through the brown bracken, strumbling across the uneven ground. We were gaining on them, and they knew it, too. Each risked a glance over his shoulder, and I glimpsed the whites of their eyes. It was a risk too many for the shorter, dark-haired one. He gave a cry as his knee twisted and he tumbled forward into the undergrowth. He struggled to get up, shouting for help, but either his friend didn't hear him or else didn't care enough, and he was still prone on the ground when Magnus's seax found the back of his skull, silencing him.

The taller one ran on towards the nearest of the four horses. I wasn't far behind him. No sooner had he vaulted up on to its back and, red-faced and sweating, pulled his knife from its sheath, ready to cut through the rope tethering the animal, than I was upon him, seizing his leg and with my other hand grabbing his sword-belt, dragging him from the saddle. He landed awkwardly, falling on his shoulder as he struck the ground, and I would have finished him then had not his mount, panicked by the commotion and the sight of naked steel, suddenly reared up, pummelling the air with its forelegs. I threw myself backwards, just in time, as an iron-shod hoof passed inches in front of my face, before landing on my arse on the hard earth.

Straightaway I scrambled to my feet, expecting to find the Dane striking out across the open ground that lay beyond the woods in the direction of the fortress. But the fall from the saddle must have injured him worse than I'd realised, for he was still on the ground, lying on his back, his chest rapidly rising and falling as softly he whispered words I could not understand. I stood over him, staring into his fearful eyes. Fearful, because he knew that his end was at hand. Blood, thick and dark, burbled from his nose and mouth, streaming down his cheek and his chin. He clasped his hands together, imploring me to grant him mercy, to grant him his life.

In vain. He must have seen the look in my eyes and realised this, for suddenly he tried to scramble backwards in crab-like fashion. He didn't get more than a couple of paces before I laid my foot upon his chest, pinning him to the ground, and he had enough time to let out a yell before the point of my sword came down on his neck, piercing flesh and bone. At once his flailing limbs were stilled, his chest ceased moving, his eyes glazed over and his lifeless head lolled to one side.

Silence. Breathing hard, my lungs burning with the cold air, my sword's fuller dripping with crimson, I gazed out into the mist in case these Danes had any friends nearby, but no one came to challenge us. Hurriedly I sheathed my blade, although not before wiping it upon the grass to clean the worst of the blood from it, then set about dragging the man's corpse back into the woods where it would be less easily spotted.

'Help me,' I said to Magnus, who was with me now. The Dane was heavier than I'd imagined. The Englishman took hold of the feet while I lifted the shoulders. Together we carried him back up the slope a short way into the copse, where no one was likely to happen upon him. We threw him down amidst the bracken so that he was hidden from sight, and there we left him, although not before stripping him of his cloak, his silver brooch, his boots and his necklace of ivory beads. We did the same to the one Magnus had felled as well as the other two, not as spoils but as preparations for the next part of our plan. Having found Godric and Dweorg again, we ventured back towards the hill's summit, where Pons, Serlo, Ælfhelm and Sceota were already waiting for us with the four trembling slave-girls, who sat around the trunk of the broad-bellied oak, keeping close together, regarding us with wide eyes.

'Did you catch them all?' Serlo asked when we reached them. 'Are they—?'

'All dead,' I replied as I let the collected garb of the Dane I'd slain fall in a heap on the ground. I cast my gaze over the girls, who looked down, doing their best to avoid my attention. They looked pale, and freezing in their thin, mud-stained dresses. Terrified, too, and I supposed they had every right to be.

'Have you told them who we are and why we're here?' I asked Serlo.

'Not yet. We were waiting for you and Magnus.'

I glanced around. 'Where's Eithne?'

She rose from the rock on which she was sitting. For the first time since that day we had met at Alrehetha, the Irish girl was about to prove her worth. This was the reason I'd brought her with me, rather than let her go with Eudo and Wace.

'I need you to speak to them,' I told her. 'They'll understand you.'

It was a reasonable assumption that they understood Danish, too, if they served in Haakon's household, so I could have asked Magnus instead, but I thought the girls would be more reassured if Eithne were the one addressing them, not just because she was a country-woman of theirs but because she was of a similar age.

'What exactly do you want me to say?' she asked.

'First give them our names and tell them why we're here,' I said. 'Tell them there's going to be a battle, that we mean to destroy Jarnborg and Haakon too, but that for all of those things to happen we need their help. The rest I leave to you to explain however you can.'

More than anything we needed a way to gain entry through the gates, but beyond that we also needed a guide, or guides, who knew the fortress and could show us where to go once we were inside. Although they didn't yet know it, the four of them provided our answers to both problems.

I waited, watching them closely, while Eithne related everything to them. At the mention of Jarnborg they all jumped up in alarm. Tears spilt down the cheeks of the youngest. She was probably no more than eleven or twelve summers old, with a thin, pointed face, hair as bright as gold and eyes the colour of sapphires. One of the others got down on her knees before Eithne, clutching at the sleeves of her cloak, while the two elder ones, who with their round, freckled faces and dark, tangled hair were so alike that they were probably at least cousins if not sisters, beseeched her with words I couldn't understand.

'Quiet,' I said, marching forward, hoping that even though they might not understand what I was saying, the force of my voice would be sufficient to still them. I wasn't disappointed. At my approach they quickly fell silent.

'What's the matter?' I asked Eithne, although I could readily guess.

'They don't want to return to Jarnborg, lord.'

I didn't blame them, but we didn't exactly have a lot of choice. Since they were our prisoners, neither did they.

'If they want their freedom, they'll help us,' I said, and hoped that would prove incentive enough for them. 'And not just their own freedom, either, but that of every slave in Haakon's household. Tell them that.'

It was a lofty promise to make, and even as the words left my lips I wasn't sure it was one I could keep. Still, I needed to win them over somehow, and things would go much more easily if we had their willing support and didn't need to coerce them.

Again I waited while Eithne, her hands raised in a calming gesture, passed on my promise, and for the answer to come back. For a few moments the slave-girls exchanged nervous glances, whispering to one another and shaking their heads. They had no reason to trust us, no reason at all. Why should they believe anything we told them?

Eventually one of the two elder ones with the freckled faces came forward, her chin held high as she addressed us, though of course we had no idea what she was saying.

I glanced at Eithne, seeking her translation. 'They'll do this,' she told me after a moment. 'Any foe of Haakon's is a friend of theirs, Derbforgaill says, and if they can be a part of his destruction, they will.'

'Derbforgaill?' I asked, to which Eithne nodded. I still struggled to get my tongue around these Irish names. 'Give her our thanks, and tell her that we're indebted to her. To all of them.'

Eithne did so, and thus it was settled. After that we wasted no time. The mist was already thinner than it had been, or so it seemed anyway. Perhaps it was only my imagination, but I didn't want to take any chances. *Nihtegesa* and *Wyvern* would be sailing soon, and we needed to be inside the stronghold's gates before Haakon's sentries sighted them entering the bay. Before the alarm was raised and Jarnborg rose in arms.

The others had drawn lots beforehand, since that seemed like the fairest way of deciding who would accompany Magnus and myself, and who would stay behind. Four Danes there had been guarding the slave-girls on their way to the spring, which meant that only four of us could go to Jarnborg; the rest would stay behind and join up with the others when they arrived in the ships. Godric and Ælfhelm had drawn the shortest twigs from the bunch that I'd held in my fist, and so they would join us. I'd rather have had Pons and Serlo alongside me in a fight, but I was hoping it wouldn't come to that. For there would be only four of us against a horde of the best warriors that Haakon, one of the most feared pirates of the northern seas, could muster.

I must be stupid to have considered this, I thought. But it was too late to turn back. And we had already travelled so far. Not so long ago I had been with the king's army in the marsh-country, embroiled in a struggle for power and in the name of the kingdom. Hardly two months later here I was, hundreds of leagues from any place I could call home, in this frozen, wind-battered island on the northernmost fringes of Britain, beyond the dominion of any king or prince: the sole Frenchman in a company of Englishmen, waging a desperate fight against a Danish warlord who until a few short weeks ago had been little more than a face to me.

What strange tapestries our lives weave. I only prayed that Jarnborg did not turn out to be the place where my own tapestry reached its end.

Trying not to dwell on such things, I shrugged on the grey cloak of the man I'd killed and fastened the brooch at my left shoulder in the Danish manner. A few drops of blood had stained the fur on the collar, spilt when I had plunged my blade into his throat, but they were small and hardly noticeable except from close at hand.

Nothing could be done about it now. It was a little too large for my frame, but hopefully no one would notice. I belted it tightly so as to conceal my hauberk. None of those we'd killed had been wearing mail, but I wasn't about to venture into the enemy camp without it. Lastly I removed the garnet-studded golden cross that Father Erchembald had given me and handed it to Serlo for safe-keeping. In its place I fastened the leather string with the ivory beads around my neck, noticing as I did so that some of them were inscribed with strange, spindly runes. Perhaps they spelt out a good-luck charm. If so, it hadn't worked for its owner.

I turned to Magnus, who had similarly attired himself in the garb of the man he'd slain, the one difference being that the necklace he wore was threaded with small pieces of amber and jet rather than ivory.

'How do I look?' I asked.

He grinned. 'Like a Dane.'

I hoped he was right. As disguises went, these were hardly the most elaborate we might have devised, but with any luck we wouldn't need to fool Haakon and his men for long. I was relying on them believing that we had quit the island, and for that reason being less watchful than perhaps they ought to have been. The last thing they would expect, surely, would be for their enemies to saunter in by the main gates.

And that would be their mistake.

Twenty-seven

And so we set out: Magnus, Godric, Ælfhelm, Eithne and myself. We needed someone who could speak both English and Irish to act as interpreter, and so she took the place of the one called Derbforgaill, since they were not dissimilar in height and in build. She had undone her braid, rubbed dirt into her hair and smudged some across her cheeks too so as to make herself look more like the slave-girl, and then they had exchanged clothes: Eithne's fine-spun woollen garments for the other girl's coarse linen shift and tattered, mud-stained cloak.

If putting on a slave's garb brought back unwelcome memories of her own thralldom, I saw no sign of it. Certainly she seemed nervous, but then so were we all.

'God be with you, lord,' Pons said when the time came for us to part ways. Often the light-hearted one, his mood was solemn now.

'And all the saints too,' Serlo added. 'May they keep you safe from harm.'

We could well do with their favour this day. Indeed I reckoned we would need every ounce of aid that the heavenly kingdom could offer us, and more besides.

The same thought was running through my mind when, not long after that, we began the climb up the crumbling track that led towards the iron fortress. The eastern skies were markedly brighter than they had been earlier, and across the fjord the mist was just starting to clear, although it still hung thickly around the crag on the promontory, veiling the tops of its palisades and the gatehouse, which had the strange effect of making them seem taller. A grim sense of foreboding gripped me then, as I gazed up at those dark walls and realised that, one way or another, this was where my fate would be decided.

We'd retrieved the horses that Haakon's men had arrived upon, but while the path was wide and even enough for us to ride up it, I was all too aware of the sharp precipice to our right, where the ground fell sharply away towards the rocks and the pounding waves below, and so we dismounted and went on foot. Magnus and Ælfhelm led the way, with the girls behind them, bearing their now-filled pails of water on the short poles across their shoulders. Godric and I brought up the rear.

With every step we took towards Jarnborg's gates, my heart thudded harder in my chest, and my throat grew drier as my doubts began to multiply. All it needed was for one person to challenge us, and they would surely see through these feeble disguises of ours at once. And mine was feeblest of all. While the Englishmen's longer hair would allow them to pass, at a glance, for Danes, my own, cut short as it was in the French style, clearly marked me out as a Norman. Fortunately one of the corpses had been wearing a helmet with a chain curtain to protect the neck. It was a little too large for my head, but it was better than nothing.

The palisade loomed ever larger before us. Yesterday, from half a mile away, it had seemed formidable enough. Now that we were almost upon Haakon's winter fastness, however, it became clear just how powerful a position it commanded, perched as it was atop the rocky promontory. Gradually I began to make out the rough shadows of two sentries standing atop the gatehouse, behind the parapet, with spears in hand, the points presented to the sky. They saw us as surely as we saw them. Recognising us for the party that had been sent to the spring, straightaway they called down to whoever was manning the gates. With a long creak of timbers, those great doors swung open. This was the moment of reckoning. All our careful planning would be for naught if we failed here.

Loose pebbles crunched beneath my feet as I led my horse up the track towards the open gates, and I breathed deeply to try to still the pounding in my chest, convinced that someone would hear it.

The sentries on the gatehouse called out something that might have been either a greeting or a challenge; I guessed it was the former, because Magnus, at the head of the column, raised a hand in acknowledgement. He and Ælfhelm passed beneath the gatehouse's arch, followed by Eithne and the girls, and then Godric and myself. Two fair-haired boys, both no older than thirteen or fourteen, their cloaks huddled about them to guard against the cold, stood just inside the gates. From the red rims around their eyes, the sorry-looking expressions on their faces and their unsteadiness on their feet, I reckoned they were suffering from having over-indulged the previous night. Perhaps that was why they had been placed on gate duty this cold morning, as a punishment for their drinking, and perhaps if they had been more awake then they might have spotted that we were not the same men who had ridden out from the fortress earlier. But, as I'd often found, folk will often see only what they expect to see. The thought that we might attempt such a ruse wouldn't even have entered their heads, and so they had no reason to pay us close attention.

Nevertheless I dared not meet their eyes, but instead fixed my gaze on the way ahead, concentrating merely on putting one foot in front of the other, and on coaxing my stubborn horse on. Behind us, I heard the great oak gates creak as they were closed once more.

We were inside Jarnborg. Against the odds, against even my expectations, we had done it. I could scarcely believe it. Under the very noses of Haakon's men, we had slipped inside his precious stronghold, his so-called iron fortress, against the walls of which Magnus's assault had been broken and scores of his loyal followers had been killed. The place that not so long ago we had considered all but unassailable.

All was deathly still, and strangely so, considering that it had to be more than an hour since first light. Usually by this time I would have expected to hear shouting and laughing as men trained at arms in the yard, and the steady ring of hammer upon anvil as a farrier worked at his forge. But there was none of that. Save for those at the gate, no one seemed yet to have risen. Instead there was only an eerie hush, broken occasionally by a dog's bark or a cock's crow, as if the whole of Jarnborg were still asleep, its defenders all snoring soundly in their beds.

'Where is everyone?' I murmured to Eithne once we were far enough away from the gate and the sentries posted there that we could talk without fear of being overheard.

Even as I spoke, through the lingering mist, I spied an array of tents, more than I could easily count but numbering in the scores, arranged in rings around burnt-out campfires. A few men had emerged from them, but not many, and they looked barely able to stand. They sat upon the muddy ground outside their tents, groaning and holding their heads in their hands. One lay curled on the ground, his dog licking his face, eagerly trying to wake him from his stupor, while a pair of hogs that must have escaped their pen wandered the wreckage in search of morsels. Everywhere the ground was littered with wineskins and ale-flasks, with chicken bones from which strings of flesh still hung, with half-eaten hunks of bread, wooden bowls in which the remains of some kind of bean stew had frozen, browned apple cores, broken clay cups, knives and skewers, iron ladles, spoons carved from antler and bone, and empty casks half the height of a man, some of which had been overturned.

'There was a feast last night,' Eithne said at last, after passing on my question to the other girls. 'A celebration.'

'A celebration?' Godric put in, frowning. 'Of what?'

A smile crossed my face then, and I had to stifle a laugh as, even before Eithne had the chance to explain, I realised what had happened. Our ploy had worked better than I could ever have dared imagine.

Hardly had our two ships been sighted leaving his shores, she said, than Haakon had ordered two dozen barrels of ale brought up from his cellars, and another dozen of wine, and haunches of meat and rounds of cheese and all manner of other foodstuffs from his storehouses. There had been dancing and there had been singing, as the Dane and his followers savoured their victory and fell about with laughter at how he had driven us off with mere words, at how he had frightened us into fleeing. And so it had gone on most of the way through the night, until, insensible with drink, they had eventually given themselves up to sleep.

The deceiver had himself been deceived. He had been too ready to believe in appearances, and so he had let down his guard. He had underestimated us, underestimated our cunning. Now we would make him pay for that blunder.

A thrill awakened within me: a thrill of a kind I hadn't known in what felt like an age. All the doubts, all the fears, all the misgivings that I'd harboured suddenly fell away. With every heartbeat, as I stared out across the yard and the debris left over from the feasting, my confidence grew.

For that was when I truly began to believe that we could do this. Victory was ours for the taking. All we had to do was to seize the opportunity we'd been given.

'What now?' Ælfhelm growled under his breath. He kept glancing about, as if expecting hordes of foemen to descend upon us at any moment.

'Now we find my woman,' I said, knowing that we had no time to lose. The past few days at sea had taught me that once this early fog did start to lift, it lifted quickly. Already it was decidedly thinner than it had been when we'd ambushed Haakon's men. Whereas before we could barely see further than a stone's throw, now I was able to make out on the far side of the enclosure the faint outlines of barns and storehouses, halls and workshops, stables and chicken-pens. Above the palisade to the east, meanwhile, the sun's disc was struggling to make itself shown, its feeble light just about visible through the gloom.

Earlier, with Eithne's help, I'd described Oswynn to the slaves, and asked if they knew her. It was as I'd feared when Haakon showed me the marriage-band on her finger. He wasn't keeping her as a mere house-servant, or a dairymaid or corn-grinder or washer-woman. As if I'd believed for a heartbeat that he would. Rather, she was one of the chosen few he often liked to take to his bed. They were quartered separately from the other thralls, in a building close by his own hall, from which they could be readily summoned at a moment's notice whenever Haakon's lusts consumed him. My blood boiled at the thought.

'They're well treated,' Eithne had added. 'They're fed well, better than his other slaves, at least, and he makes sure they always have the finest clothes—'

I'd stopped her before she'd been able to go on. Eithne hadn't been with us when we'd met Haakon the previous day. She hadn't seen the bruises decorating Oswynn's cheek, or how thin she looked.

Those thoughts were foremost in my mind now, as I bade Eithne ask the slave-girls where I could find this building where Oswynn was being held. No sooner had she finished speaking than they began pointing in the direction of a long stone-and-thatch hall in the far corner of the enclosure, and the squat, low-gabled house that stood beside it.

So near. Little more than a hundred paces stood between myself and Oswynn. My throat was dry and I swallowed to moisten it. Soon I would be able to hold her, as I hadn't held her in three long years.

'Go with the girls,' I told Eithne. 'Get word to the other slaves. Tell them there's going to be a battle, but that they have nothing to fear from us. They'll be safe provided that they stay out of sight of Haakon's men. So long as they're ready to leave this place when his hall goes up in flames, I can guarantee them freedom. Can you remember all that?'

'I think so,' she replied, somewhat stiffly. 'I'm not stupid, you know.'

'Then don't waste time quarrelling with me. Go now.'

Her eyes betrayed her anxiety, but she did as she was told without further argument. I watched the four of them go, still carrying those pails lest anyone looking on suspected there was something awry.

'Come on,' I said to the others. 'We can't tarry here.'

A cock crowed, heralding the morning, but that was the only sound to break the stillness. Leaving the horses tethered to a post, we trudged across the muddy yard towards that low building. Icy water seeped into my boots, making my toes numb, as we skirted our way around the tents and the men camped there, walking with purpose but at the same time trying not to make it seem as though we were in a hurry.

Two of Haakon's huscarls were posted outside the entrance to the stone hall, decked out in mail hauberks that fell past their knees. Their long-handled axes and bright-painted round shields rested up against the wall and they were pacing about, rubbing gloved hands together and blowing into them to try to warm them, muttering to one another and occasionally snorting in laughter. They must be the only people in the whole of Jarnborg, I reckoned, who were not still nursing the effects of the previous night's feasting. They both cast a glance in our direction as we approached. I tensed, but then after a few heart-seizing moments they turned away to resume their conversation, and paid us no more attention. And why should they? We were, by all appearances, merely four of their countrymen, stretching their limbs on a cold winter's morning. If they'd seen us at close hand they might have thought differently, but most likely they saw our helmets and guessed we had simply decided to rise early for some sword practice in the yard. Perhaps if they had dwelt on that assumption a little longer, they might have questioned why it was that we four were so keen when everyone else in camp still lay huddled in their blankets. Perhaps then their suspicions might have been aroused. Obviously they were too concerned with other things, however, since no challenge came.

We rounded the main hall, past the stables and the mounds of dung that had been shovelled into heaps outside, towards that low-gabled house. There was no sentry guarding the entrance here, but the door was stout, built of oak or some other heavy timber, and fitted with a sturdy iron lock and ring-handle. I glanced back over my shoulder to see if those two huscarls had followed us, but could not see them, although I heard their laughter from around the corner. Satisfied that no one was watching, I descended the steps towards the door, which was slightly below the level of the ground. I gripped the cold handle, gently twisting it until I heard the latch lift, then pushed, slowly but firmly, more in hope than in expectation, for I didn't expect to find it unlocked.

But unlocked it was. Silently, without so much as a creak of hinges, the door swung open, much to my surprise. Truly God's favour was shining upon us that morning.

Without further hesitation we ventured inside. A small, sparsely furnished chamber greeted us. A pair of stools stood in the middle of the floor, on one of which was a lantern, the candle within burnt down to its last inch, while on the other rested a knife with a short, curved blade and a thick handle, and a crude wood-whittling of what I supposed was meant to be a horse, since it had a head and mane and bridle, and the beginnings of a saddle, but for some strange reason the animal had not just four legs, but eight. There was no sign of anyone. Perhaps the sentry had gone to find another candle to work by, in which case we probably didn't have much time before he returned.

Another door led off this small guardroom, but Magnus tried it and found it locked. 'No luck,' he said.

'We'll break it down,' Ælfhelm said as he shrugged off his cloak. 'Let me—'

'No,' I said sharply. 'If you do that, someone's bound to hear. You'll end up bringing every single sword-Dane in this place upon us.'

'What do you suggest, then?'

I glanced about the chamber, in case perhaps the key had been left lying somewhere, though I knew it was a futile hope.

'If we had a fishhook we could pick it,' Magnus said, glancing around as if half expecting one of us to have one hidden somewhere on our person. 'Or a nail, maybe. Anything like that.'

I looked doubtfully at him. Somehow it seemed unlikely that one of noble birth such as he, the usurper's son, would have had reason to learn the art of lock-picking. 'And you know how to do that, do you?'

'No, but we could try.'

'I've seen it done, when I lost the key to my chest last winter,' Ælfhelm put in. 'Dubgall the smith's son showed me how.'

'You've done it before?'

'No, but if a boy of eleven can manage it, then it can't be that difficult, can it?'

'We don't have time for this,' I said with mounting frustration. I didn't know who Dubgall the smith's son was, and even if he happened to be the wiliest thief in Christendom, I didn't much care, for he wasn't here, and this was no time for us to begin teaching ourselves his craft. At any moment the Dane whose wood-carving that was could return.

'Do you have any better suggestions?' Magnus asked.

I gave a sigh. 'Go outside and keep watch,' I told Godric. 'If you see anyone approaching, come and let us know straightaway.'

'Yes, lord,' the boy said, and scurried back out into the open. Daylight flooded in briefly before we were plunged back into lantern-light as he closed the heavy door behind him.

I snatched up the whittling-knife that rested on the stool and passed it to Ælfhelm. 'Will this work?'

He took it, turning the stubby blade over so that it caught the light. 'We can try it,' he said, kneeling down in front of the lock, and with his free hand gave a click of his fingers. 'I need light. Bring me that lantern.'

I did so, holding it up so that its faint light shone inside the keyhole, while he peered at whatever levers and springs were housed within. I wondered that he could see anything at all, but after a short while he lifted the curved blade, which was just narrow enough, and slid it into the lock. His brow furrowed. Listening carefully for the sound of the mechanism, he turned it first in one direction, then in the other, muttering curses to himself.

'Faster,' I hissed in between glances towards the door. 'If this is going to take all morning—'

'Don't hurry me,' the huscarl said. 'Give me time.'

'We don't have time,' I muttered, but he didn't seem to hear me. His eyes narrowed in concentration as, using both hands to steady the handle, he turned the blade upwards, then widened again as a hint of a smile appeared at the corners of his mouth. He twisted again—

There was a click, so faint as to be almost imperceptible. Ælfhelm's smile broadened. Beaming from ear to ear, he looked up, first at his lord and then at me.

'And to think you doubted me.' He withdrew the blade and gave the door a gentle push. It swung open into darkness.

I went first, holding the lantern high so as to light up the chamber beyond. 'Oswynn?'

I tried not to speak too loudly for fear of being overheard. Sweat was running from my brow and the breath caught in my chest. A dank smell hung in the air, as if a fire hadn't been lit in some while. The hearth had been recently swept and fresh rushes had been laid. A tall ewer stood in the middle of the floor, next to an iron pisspot that needed to be emptied, for as I took another step inside I caught a whiff of its contents. Benches ran down each wall, and on each one were heaped crumpled blankets. I cast the lantern's light down their length, until at the far end I found, huddled together, their eyes wide and white-glistening in the candlelight, three women who, had they not been trembling in fear, I would probably have called pretty.

Oswynn was not among them.

Before we could speak with them and try to find out where she was, however, I heard the sound of feet descending the timber steps that led down to the outer door. Godric had come to tell us that the guard was on his way back, I thought. I turned back into the guardroom as the door opened and frigid air flooded in.

The figure who ducked beneath the lintel wasn't Godric. Round of stomach, he had long, fair hair that trailed from beneath a woollen cap, with a moustache and beard to match. In one hand he held a whetstone and, in the other, a lump of cheese from which he was just about to take a bite when he saw us. And froze.

His jaw hung agape in surprise and confusion, and I saw the half-chewed remains of his last mouthful. He stood there, blinking, for what felt like an hour but could only have been a heartbeart, his expression slowly hardening.

'Hverir eruth er?' he barked. 'Hvat gerith er?'

I glanced at Magnus, who was the only one among us who spoke their tongue, but it seemed he had no reply to whatever it was the Dane had said. That was when the round-bellied one noticed the door to the other chamber lying open. Whether he quite realised we were foemen or not, he saw that we meant trouble. Suddenly alert, he reached for the sword belted to his waist. He took a deep breath as if about to call out, and I knew that if he did our plans would be dashed like a ship against a cliff-face, and we would all be dead men. I started forward, reaching for my hilt, hoping to run him through—

I never had the chance. Before I had even got within five paces of him, he stopped mid-movement. His eyes glazed over abruptly and rolled back in his head. The faintest of gasps escaped his lips as his sword-hilt slipped from his limp fingers and tumbled with a dull clang to the hard floor, and then he too collapsed forwards, landing in a crumpled, bloodied heap, revealing the knife in the back of his neck.

In the doorway stood the one who had killed him. Godric. As if it could possibly have been anyone else.

'You seem to be making a habit of this,' I said drily.

'Of what, lord?' Godric asked.

I bent down to drag the Dane's corpse away from the doorway, lest anyone walking by should see it, although of course we could do nothing about the blood pooling amidst the woodchips.

'Help me move him,' I said to Ælfhelm, who was closest to me. 'If you take his legs, I'll take his shoulders,' I added, before answering the boy's question: 'Of striking down your opponents from behind. You know that sooner or later you're going to have to learn how to kill them from the front as well, don't you?'

'At least I did kill him, lord,' he replied. 'Now you owe me again.'

I glanced up. 'For what?'

'For saving our lives.'

I supposed that was only fair. 'I'm sure I'll have the chance to repay the favour before long. Now, close that door,' I said, and tossed him the ring of keys that I'd removed from the foeman's belt. 'Lock it, too. I don't want his friends stumbling upon us.'

Godric didn't need telling twice, but did as instructed, while the huscarl and I hauled the Dane's corpulent frame through to the second chamber. No sooner had the women set eyes upon the dead guard, than they began shrieking, loud enough to wake the dead. It was a good thing that the door was indeed closed. As it was, I could only hope that no one heard.

'Keep them quiet,' I told Godric and Magnus as we laid the pot-bellied one down on one of the benches and then covered him over with some of the coarse blankets.

The women quickly shut up as the others approached, but I didn't want them to fear us. We needed their help, just as we had needed the help of the water-carriers. Ælfhelm fetched the lantern, and brought it in so that we might have some light.

'Tell them we don't mean them any harm,' I said to Magnus. 'Tell them we're looking for someone.'

'Who are you?' the middle one of the three women asked after I'd finished speaking. Dark-haired and generously endowed both in chest and in the hips, which I supposed must be how Haakon liked them, she regarded us uneasily. 'What do you want with us?'

I stared dumbly at her. For some reason I'd assumed that, Oswynn excepted, we would find only Danish and Irish girls, since they were the most often captured and traded in these parts. She had spoken, though, as I had, in English.

'We're here to kill Haakon,' Magnus said. 'We want nothing from you, we swear upon our lives.'

Her eyes held an expression I couldn't read, although it was somewhere between shock and joy, and closer to shock. 'You're going to kill him?' she asked. She had a voice like a summer's breeze, I thought: warm and soft and light.

'If we can,' I answered.

'The four of you, alone?'

'We have friends on their way,' I said. 'There's no time to explain everything. What do they call you?'

'Eanflæd,' she replied.

A pretty name, I thought, for a girl who, even though I was in the middle of searching for another, I admitted was attractive.

'Tell me, Eanflæd, do you know of an English girl by the name of Oswynn? Do you know where I can find her?'

'Oswynn?' she repeated, and my heart stood still. 'Y-yes, I know her.'

'Where is she?'

'Haakon took her, last night.'

'Took her where?'

She looked at me as if I were stupid, and I suppose I was, but only because love had made me that way. 'Where do you think?' she asked. 'To his chamber. After the feast was over, he called for her—'

I held up a hand to stop her from going on. How we were going to get inside Haakon's hall, when there were two of his household warriors posted at the entrance and undoubtedly countless more inside, I didn't know. Soon, of course, they would spot *Wyvern* and *Nihtegesa* approaching, and I was counting on exploiting the resulting confusion to allow us to do what we had come here for. But what if something went wrong, or the waters were too rough or the wind gusting too strongly? What if Haakon didn't react in the way that we hoped to the threat to his ships? How then would we be able to find Oswynn, let alone get out of Jarnborg?

All these thoughts were running through my mind when the knocking began. At once I stopped still. There were men outside, shouting in words I didn't understand, pounding on the oak door. A shiver ran through me. Some of the dead man's friends must have heard the women's screams, and had come to find out what was happening.

'Quiet,' I hissed, pointing at Eanflæd. 'Not a sound.'

She nodded and then whispered in the ears of the other two, in whatever language it was they spoke. There was no other way out of this place. I swore violently, under my breath.

'I could talk to them,' Magnus offered.

'And say what?' I countered. Would the Danes be so dim-witted as to mistake his voice for that of their pot-bellied friend? Even if they did, how was he to explain why the door was locked, or the reason for the screaming?

Outside, the pounding grew more insistent, the shouts louder and angrier. They couldn't yet know there were four of us, or guess who we were, or why we were here. All of those things they would soon work out, however, as soon as they came through that door, realised that they didn't recognise our faces and that we didn't speak their tongue. When that happened, we could abandon all hope of leaving this place alive.

Every man's luck ran out eventually. There were few truths greater than that. We had done well to make it this far, but I ought to have known this could only end badly. Now we would pay the price for our recklessness.

Yet I would not give up easily. Not without a fight.

'Barricade the door,' I said. 'Bring that cooking-pot across, and anything else we can use.'

The inner of the two doorways could only be locked from the outside, which meant we had no choice but to make our stand in the small guard-chamber. While Magnus and Ælfhelm together manoeuvred the iron cauldron across the floor, Godric and I set the heavy bar in place across the door, so that even if they did manage to unlock it, they would still have to break it down.

'What can we do?' Eanflæd called from the other room.

'Nothing,' I said, 'except pray for our sakes that they don't get in.'

I helped Magnus and Ælfhelm overturn the cauldron on to its rim so that it would be more difficult for our foes to tip over, and then we set about piling whatever other obstacles we could find against the door. Some of the benches were fixed to the walls, but some were not, and we dragged those that we could in front of the doorway so that anyone coming through would with any luck trip and make it easier for us to kill them.

There was a jangle of metal as the enemy tried the lock. I heard it click, and heard, too, their cries of success, short-lived as they were as the foemen found the door barred against them. The oak rattled against the stout plank, and through the gap between the door and its frame I heard them shouting. How many were out there, it was impossible to say, but from the noise I reckoned there had to be at least half a dozen already, and such a commotion would only attract more. What they thought was happening in here, I could only guess. Maybe they thought that their friend the wood-whittler had allowed his lusts to get the better of him and had decided to have his way with his lord's most prized bed-slaves.

In the other room, one of the women began shrieking again, and I cursed.

'Keep her quiet,' I called through to Eanflæd, although by then it was already too late.

Sooner or later the enemy would break through and slaughter us. They had to, for they were many and we were few. Nonetheless, if this was my day to die, then I was determined to take as many as I could with me to my grave.

Swords drawn, we stood facing the door, watching it shudder. I imagined a horde of flaxen-haired Danes lining up outside, each waiting for his turn to test his shoulder against the timbers. Then, without warning, the pounding ceased. I glanced at the others, raising a hand so that they knew not to speak. But the respite was only brief. The silence was broken by the unmistakable sound of an axe-blade biting into wood. Again the door shook. It wouldn't be long.

'I didn't think I'd ever go to my death fighting shoulder to shoulder with a Norman,' Magnus said to me in what was barely more than a whisper. 'But you have been a steadfast ally, and for that I thank you.'

'And you,' I replied solemnly, without looking at him, without glancing either to left or to right. My gaze was fixed firmly on the door as I waited for the timbers to give way and for the first of our foemen to burst through. 'May God grant our sword-arms strength.'

Neither Ælfhelm nor Godric spoke. Possibly they were both lost in prayer or thought, rehearsing in their minds what they would do when the enemy came upon us, imagining how they would strike and how they would spill Danish blood. Or possibly they simply realised, as I did, that there was nothing more to say.

All I could think about were the things I regretted. Not being able to see Oswynn one last time. Not taking my vengeance upon Haakon for what he had done. Bringing Godric with me on this expedition. For all that recent weeks had changed him, he was still not much more than a boy, eager and full of promise. Now that promise was to be snuffed out because of me.

Beneath my helmet my brow was running with sweat. It trickled off my brow, stinging my eyes. The dim lantern-light played across the surface of my blade and lit up the turquoise stone decorating the pommel, and I felt the cord wrapped around the hilt digging into my palm as I gripped it tight. Like Rollant defending to the last the pass against the pagan hordes of King Marsilius, so I too would go bravely to my death. This was my stand, my Rencesvals, I thought bitterly.

The door timbers flexed as the axe struck again. The door couldn't hold much longer, surely. In another few blows splinters would fly, the enemy would be through. And then the killing would begin.

'Stay close,' I murmured. 'Don't let them draw you out. If they break through the barricade, fall back to the second room. Remember that each one we cut down is another corpse that his friends will have to climb over before they reach us. We will hold fast. We will fill the morning with their blood.'

I almost followed that by raising a cry for Normandy and for King Guillaume, so familiar had those words grown in recent years, so instinctive had they become, just as the movements of the thrust and parry, the cut and the slice were ingrained through long hours of practice into my limbs, into my soul. But I choked them back, realising even as the phrases formed upon my tongue what an affront to Magnus it would be to utter them, and indeed how little they now meant to me. The friends and allies, present and absent, who had supported me in this endeavour were the only men, the only causes, in whose names I now fought.

For Magnus and Ælfhelm. For Godric, Serlo and Pons. For Aubert, for Eudo and for Wace.

The door flexed once more. The hinges made a terrible shearing sound, and the bar that we'd set in place trembled. Another blow followed, and suddenly the planks were cracking along the grain, buckling under the force of the impact. I closed my eyes and inhaled deeply, letting the sweetness of the air roll across my tongue, quelling the fears that dwelt at the back of my mind and burying them deep, doing my best to still my fast-beating heart and allow the battle-calm to overtake me, steeling myself for what was to come. Readying myself to meet my God.

Then the sound of steel upon oak ceased, and I opened my eyes, expecting to see the first of the foemen staggering beneath the lintel. The first who would die.

But though the shouting continued, the door still stood. At first I couldn't understand what was happening, why the enemy seemed to have given up. I glanced at the others and saw the same bewilderment in their expressions. Only then did I hear the horns sounding out across the camp: a series of rapid, insistent blasts followed by a single sustained note. Again the pattern was repeated, and again, and a fourth and a fifth time as well. And though their words were a mystery to me, I realised from their tones that the Danes standing beyond the door were suddenly crying out for a different reason: no longer out of haste to break down the door and discover what was going on in this hall, but in confusion and alarm.

Feet thudded upon turf, steadily growing further away from us. From the din that was erupting outside I reckoned the whole camp had to be rising. It didn't take me long to guess the reason why.

They had come. *Nihtegesa* and *Wyvern* had come, and not a moment too soon.

Twenty-eight

As impatient as we were, nevertheless we dared not emerge until we could be sure it was safe. Across the yard the war-horns continued to blast out their warning notes, hooves pounded, men shouted to one another, dogs barked in excitement. But no more axe blows came, and no longer could I hear footsteps outside the hall.

Trying to make as little noise as possible, I climbed across the crude barricade we had thrown up. With Godric's help I lifted the bar from across the door and tentatively opened it, by only the smallest fraction at first, but enough to be able to see out. I half expected to find at least one of the Danes left guarding the entrance to the hall, but there was no one.

Elsewhere across Jarnborg, all was disorder. Men, some only half-dressed, were scrambling from their tents into the morning light, struggling to their feet, running back and forth, swigging from leather flasks to lend them courage, hurriedly tugging on leather jerkins and mail shirts, belting scabbards upon their waists and snatching up spears and shields and whatever other weapons they could find to hand. Meanwhile their lords were yelling for order, trying to gather their hearth-troops around their banners even as they poured out through the gatehouse: an unruly horde sallying forth with blades drawn and raised to the sky.

And then, striding out from the great stone hall, came Jarl Haakon himself, he of the black-dragon banner. He wore a helmet with a nasal-guard, so his face was partly hidden. Nevertheless I recognised him not just by the greying braid at his nape and the keenness of the eyes that stared out from beneath his helmet's gilded rim, but also by the rings of twisted gold he wore upon his arms, by his silver-gleaming hauberk, and by the dozen or so huscarls guarding him. His cheeks were red as he barked instructions to those around him, doing his best to ignore the hounds who were racing around him and his men, their tails up, occasionally leaping up to paw at their chests and lick at their faces. They sensed that something was afoot, and they wanted to be a part of it.

'What's going on?' asked Magnus, who was behind me, but I waved him silent.

Haakon's stable-boys brought him and his retainers their horses. Without hesitation they mounted up and rode out, bellowing at all the others making for the gates to get out of their way. The black dragon was flying to battle, flying to vanquish his foes and drive them from his shores once and for all.

Or so he thought. Hooves thundered as he galloped through the midst of his followers, closely followed by his huscarls, and still I kept my gaze upon them until they had disappeared through the gatehouse arch, with the rest of his army charging on foot in their wake.

'Come on,' I said to the others as the last of the enemy filed out from the fortress. Even in the short while that we had been holed up inside this hall, the mist had lifted considerably. The skies had grown lighter, and there was even a small patch of blue through which the sun was breaking. If we were looking for a portent, there could be few better than that.

Throwing the door open, I ran up the wooden steps into the yard, which was strangely quiet now. Only a few stragglers remained: those for whom the previous night's celebrations had proven too much. Bleary-eyed and pale of face, they staggered about in search of weapons. Some were doubled over, spewing forth long trails of vomit on to the muddy ground. They didn't notice us; or else, if they did, they didn't think anything of us. They had more pressing concerns.

'Where are you going?' Eanflæd called as she came rushing after us, clutching her skirts to avoid tripping on the steps. 'What about us? Are you just going to leave us here?'

'You'll do best to stay here, where you're safe,' I replied. 'We're going to find Oswynn.'

'And then to burn this place to the ground,' Magnus added grimly.

I tossed the keys to her and she caught them neatly in two hands. 'Lock yourselves in if you have to, if you feel safer that way, although that door won't hold much longer,' I told her. 'We'll come back for you, I promise.'

'Wait,' she said, just as we were about to set off. 'Who are you?'

'My name is Tancred,' I replied. 'And this is Magnus. Haakon wronged us both, and we're here to take our revenge upon him. But we have to go now, or else everything we've done so far will have been in vain.'

She seemed content with that explanation, and she would have to be, for that was all the information I was prepared to give her then. I signalled to the others and we set off across the yard, past the stables, towards Haakon's hall. Taking care not to make a sound, keeping low so as to be less easily spotted, we moved along the side of that long stone building towards the gable end where the two huscarls had been posted earlier. I led the way, creeping towards the corner of the hall, where some dozen or so empty barrels were stacked. I crouched behind them, peering through the slightest gap, and saw that of the two guards, only one remained, looking more than a little agitated as he glanced around, his long-handled axe in hand. He was probably a few years younger than me, around the same age as Magnus, round-faced and looking uncomfortable in his hauberk.

'How do we get past him?' Ælfhelm murmured, startling me, for I hadn't noticed him beside me.

It was a good question. The entrance to Haakon's hall lay in full view of most of the rest of the fortress, and I couldn't see how we could kill him without attracting unwanted attention.

'I have an idea,' Magnus said. 'Wait here.'

Before I could say anything to dissuade him, he was rising to his feet and darting back the way we had come.

'Magnus,' I hissed in warning, but he was already too far away to hear me. Rather than heading back towards the building where the bed-slaves were quartered, though, he disappeared instead around the far end of the hall. Silently I cursed him for not telling us what he had in mind, for leaving us here.

That was when I heard what sounded like his voice, calling out in what must have been the Danish tongue from the opposite side of the hall. Ducking as low as possible so as not to be seen, I watched the entrance to see what the young door-guard would do. Whatever it was Magnus had said, suddenly the Dane was turning towards the source of the noise. Again the Englishman called out, and this time it was enough to draw the guard from his position. He ventured round the corner and out of sight.

This was our chance.

'Now,' I said as we scrambled from our hiding place, making for the doors to the hall. I thrust them open, and burst inside, with the two Englishmen behind me, into a long, dark feasting-hall. The wreckage of the previous night's celebrations lay everywhere: broken pitchers, abandoned ale-cups and drinking horns, rushes stained with the contents of several men's stomachs, and, suspended on an iron spit over the still-smoking hearth, the almost bare carcass of what had once been a pig, but was now hardly more than bone, with scraps of charred meat hanging from it. A putrid stench of piss and vomit filled the room, causing the bile to rise in my throat, but somehow I managed to hold it down.

Nothing moved, save for the mice scrabbling among the rushes in search of crumbs of food, and a scrawny cat that was licking its lips as it padded the length of the long trestle table that stood on the dais. A pair of torches in sconces mounted on the walls offered the only light. Apart from us the hall was empty. Behind us I heard the door open and I tensed, my hand leaping to my sword-hilt, but it was only Magnus.

'Is he—?' I began.

'Dead,' he confirmed.

I nodded. 'Build up that hearth-fire, and do it quickly,' I called to the three of them as I took one of the torches from the wall and marched towards the dais end of the hall, where I saw a flight of stairs leading up. 'Anything that you think might burn, throw it on. We don't have long.'

Haakon's bedchamber would most likely be on the up-floor. Hurriedly I picked my way through the remains of the feast, over ale-soaked bedrolls and puddles that might have been water but which could well have been piss, then ran up the stairs, shouting: 'Oswynn!'

No answer came. I reached the top; the faint light of my torch flickered across the roof-beams and the sloping thatch above. Richly embroidered tapestries in bright hues hung upon the walls to keep out the draughts. A squared tæfl board lay on the floor, the ivory and jet playing-pieces scattered everywhere.

And then, at the far end of the chamber, I saw the bed, and curled up beneath the blankets and the furs, sobbing, a figure I knew only too well, for I would have recognised that black hair anywhere.

'Oswynn,' I said. 'Oswynn!'

There was a stand for the torch at one side of the hall, and I set it down there before rushing over to her.

'No,' she said as I approached, shaking her head wildly and retreating further beneath the coverlets, and I wondered if she'd mistaken me for Haakon. 'No, please.'

'It's all right,' I said as I knelt down at the bedside. 'It's me.'

She raised her head from the pillow then and looked at me through red-rimmed eyes, a fearful look upon her face. For long moments all she did was stare at me in shock, as if I were an apparition, but then her expression began to soften as recognition took hold.

'Tancred,' she said, sitting up suddenly and blinking as if she couldn't believe what she saw. 'You came.'

'I came,' I replied, smiling gently.

In truth I could hardly believe it myself as she threw her arms around me and I held her close for the first time in nearly three years, wondering how it could have been so long, feeling her form beneath her rough linen shift, thinner than I remembered, and breathing in the sweet scent of her skin. She began to cry, and that was enough to set me weeping as well. Tears cascaded down my cheeks, and they were tears of relief, tears of love, tears of joy. After all this while, all this searching, hoping, dreaming, we were once more together. I thought of all those bleak hours in recent months when I'd despaired of ever being able to find her again, when the grief and the pain had been almost too much to bear, and I remembered the darkness that had often descended upon me. A darkness that now was banished. For here she was.

'I didn't think you would . . .' she began, but couldn't go on as a fit of sobbing overtook her. 'He told me you'd left,' she said once it had subsided. 'He said—'

'He was wrong,' I said. 'Whatever he told you, it was a lie.'

I gazed into her soft, glistening eyes, wondering what she must have seen in the past three years, what she must have endured, though at the same time I did not even want to imagine.

'Come on,' I told her. 'We have to go.'

She wiped a hand across her moist cheeks as she raised herself, somewhat stiffly, I noticed, from the mattress. Haakon had hurt her and for that, I promised myself, I would make him suffer, just as soon as I caught up with him.

'Go where?' she asked.

'Anywhere but here. My friends have ships. They'll take us to safety, if we can only get out of this place.'

To tell the truth I wasn't quite sure how we were going to reach them, given that the whole of Haakon's army lay between us and the bay. As always, getting inside was the easy part. But I knew that somehow we would do it. We had to, for the only alternative was death.

Taking Oswynn's hand in mine, I led her towards the stairs, lifting a sealskin cloak from where it lay atop a chest and wrapping it around her shoulders, then taking the torch from its stand. Down in the feasting-hall the hearth-fire was crackling and smoking. Godric, Magnus and Ælfhelm had tossed armfuls of the drier rushes on to the smouldering embers, and now bright flames were sparking into life, already causing some of the larger kindling and timbers they had thrown on it to blacken and catch light.

'Grab that torch,' I said to Godric, pointing towards the second of the two wall-sconces, and to Magnus and Ælfhelm: 'Take some of those timbers from the fire.'

They didn't need telling a second time. This was the moment we had been waiting for. The moment when we would send our message to Haakon, when we would destroy his famed stronghold, and all he held dear.

We carried those firebrands out into the open and then tossed them high up the thatch on both sides of the hall so that it would catch all the quicker. Then, while Godric went to fetch Eanflæd and the other women from the building where we'd left them, Ælfhelm, Magnus, Oswynn and I set about spreading flame to some of the other storehouses, sheds and outbuildings that abutted the palisade.

I knew it wouldn't be so long before we were spotted. And so it proved. Of the two hundred or so warriors who must have comprised Haakon's army, only perhaps a score still remained in Jarnborg, and they were clearly the worst afflicted, since many were barely able to stand and even now were continuing to empty the contents of their stomachs all over the yard. No sooner had they seen us, however, and realised what we were doing to their lord's halls than they raised a cry and began coming at us: a swarm of wild spear-Danes and sword-Danes and axe-Danes in various states of undress, some in only their trews, most without even a shield to protect themselves.

We, however, were armed and ready for a fight, eager to free our sword-arms, our blood already up.

'Stay back!' I yelled to Oswynn as the enemy charged. 'Stay behind us!'

Some tripped over their own feet as they ran, while others could only manage an ungainly stagger, which meant that instead of all attacking together, they came in ragged fashion, in ones and twos. The first of them rushed towards me, yelling wordlessly, aiming a swing at my shoulder. Steel shrieked as I met his weapon with my own, and then I was turning the flat of my blade against the edge of his, forcing it down and out of position, before jerking my elbow up and into his chin. Stunned, he staggered backwards, and instantly he was forgotten as I spun out of the path of the next man's axe and whirled about his flank. This one was not quick either in wits or on his feet, and before he'd even realised where I had gone, I'd sliced across the back of his thigh, sending him sprawling.

'No mercy,' I shouted. 'No mercy!'

The battle-calm was descending, the sword-joy filling me, and I gave myself over to instinct as I stepped deftly from one opponent to the next, cutting, parrying, thrusting, scything through their midst, as easily as if it were a dance. All about me the blade-song rang out. I was dimly aware, at the far end of the enclosure, of Eithne and a band of the slave-girls, a dozen of them and more. With knives in hand they rushed from one of the buildings. Even as we tore into the enemy from the front, they assailed them from behind, hurling themselves into the fray, setting upon those Danes who had tripped and fallen, plunging steel into their throats, and I was laughing as I saw we were winning, cutting them down on all sides, wreaking a ruin amongst Haakon's troops, filling the morning with our fury.

The fire was taking hold now, sweeping across the thatch of the feasting-hall and the other buildings. Bright tongues of flame licked at the sky, while thick clouds of black smoke billowed up, wafting across the enclosure, stinging my eyes and making me cough, but I did not care as I released the anger that for so long had been building and let my sword do its work, until suddenly the enemy, the ten or so that remained, were falling to their knees, or else fleeing across the yard.

Behind me I heard Oswynn scream, and my heart all but stopped as I turned, thinking that she had found herself some trouble. They were not screams of alarm or pain, though, but of hatred. In her wide eyes was a fury I'd never before witnessed. Rushing forward, she snatched up the sword of one of the fallen Danes, and then, as he tried to rise, stamped her foot down on to his chest, pinning him to the ground. He gave a yell, but it was short-lived, as Oswynn gripped the hilt in both hands and drove the point down, hard, into his face, all the while shrieking in triumph as tears streamed down her cheeks. Her teeth gritted, she tugged it free, then plunged it into his chest where his heart would be, and again and again and again, until finally I managed to drag her away.

'He's dead,' I said, though still she struggled. 'Oswynn, he's dead!'

Eventually I was able to prise the weapon from her grasp. I tossed it aside and she fell into my arms, pressing her face against my shoulder, weeping uncontrollably. By then the fight was all but over, and those few who hadn't surrendered were being chased down by the slave-girls. In all the years I'd trodden the sword-path I'd never seen anything like it.

'He was one of Haakon's friends,' Oswynn said. 'Sprott, his name was. Many times he—'

But whatever it was she had been about to say, she couldn't go on, for fresh tears spilt forth.

'It's all right,' I said, caressing her head. 'You don't have to tell me.'

Given what she had seen and what she had been made to do, it was a wonder that anything of her old spirit remained. At least she had not forgotten how to wield a blade. A long time ago I'd gifted her with a knife and spent long afternoons teaching her how to use it, so that she would be able to protect herself if ever she needed. A keen learner, she had picked up the rudiments far quicker than many boys, and I was pleased to see that those skills were as sharp now as they had been then.

'Lord,' I heard Godric call, and looked up to see him returning with Eanflæd and the other two women close behind him.

Haakon's hall was by then nothing but a writhing, twisting tower of flame, a beacon blazing out across the fjord. Around it the many stable buildings and workshops that we had also fired were aflame, and even some that we hadn't, as the breeze spread glowing ash from one to the next. Smoke swirled all about, growing thicker with every heartbeat. Jarnborg, Haakon's home, his pride, his so-called iron fortress, was burning.

This was no time to revel in our achievement, however. We had to leave while we still could, before any of his men rushed back to rescue their prized possessions from the blaze.

'This way,' I called, waving to Oswynn but also to Godric, Ælfhelm and a grimacing Magnus, who was hobbling, the leather of his shoe covered with blood where he had been wounded. He was clearly struggling, and I knew he would never make it out of Jarnborg alive on his own. But I wasn't about to leave him. Together we had planned and plotted this victory, and together we had risked all. Together we had fought, and together we would see it through.

'Go with them,' I said to Oswynn, meaning Godric and Ælfhelm. I picked up a spear that a dead Dane had no more use for and thrust it into her hands. She could hardly go without a weapon, and that would be better suited to her than a heavy sword. 'You'll be safe so long as you stay close to them and don't leave their sight.'

'No,' she said, her eyes beseeching. 'I want to stay with you.'

'Don't argue with me,' I said. 'Not now.'

I wiped away the tear rolling down her cheek and kissed her then, kissed her hard, savouring the feel of her lips pressed against mine, and with that I tore myself away from her embrace.

'Go,' I said. As she turned, a shiver ran through me, for I remembered only too well what had happened the last time I'd left her to the protection of others. But it would be different this time.

I rushed to Magnus, placing one arm under his shoulder and lending him my own for support, allowing him to take the weight off his injured foot. Out of the corner of my eye I saw Ælfhelm hurrying towards us, and I knew that it was the oath binding him to his lord that had made him turn back. At the same time Godric too was hesitating, as if uncertain what to do.

I waved them on. 'Lead the women away from here,' I shouted. 'Get them to safety. Go!'

Fortunately the huscarl soon saw sense. After a moment's hesitation, he turned, raising his sword and pointing it towards the gatehouse. I was relying on him, as doubtless the most experienced warrior among us, if not necessarily the best swordsman, to keep his head.

The guards at the entrance, seeing how we had possession of

the place of slaughter, had already fled, leaving the gates open. All we had to do was reach them. One step at a time, I helped Magnus across the yard, through the mud and the puddles, around the bodies of the slain. The usurper's son wasn't heavy, but he wasn't light either, and I soon felt the strain on my back and shoulders.

'Thank you, Tancred,' he said through clenched teeth when we were rounding the pig-pens and halfway to the gatehouse.

'Don't thank me until this is over,' I replied curtly. 'We haven't survived this yet.'

Close by the gate, Eithne was marshalling the slaves, yelling at them to follow Godric and Ælfhelm and Oswynn. As well as women and girls, there were a few men and boys, I saw now, all recognisable by their short-shaven hair and all armed, some with spears and axes taken from Danes they had killed, but most with fish knives and meat cleavers, hayforks and iron pokers, implements that in the right hands were as good as any weapon.

'Lord!' Eithne shouted when she saw me. Quick-thinking as ever, she ran to the horses that we'd tethered not far from the gate. The sight of the flames, the smell of the smoke and the clash of steel had spooked them, but she clearly had a way with the animals, for by the time we'd reached her she'd managed to soothe one so that it would let Magnus mount it. Together we helped him into the saddle. He winced as he placed his injured foot in the stirrup.

Teeth gritted against the pain, he clasped my hand in thanks. 'I'll live,' he said. 'So long as I can hold a sword, I'll fight.'

Eithne and I turned our attention to the other horses, doing what we could to calm them before mounting up and slicing through the ropes tying them to the post. Then the three of us kicked on, cantering through the smoke, beneath the gate-arch and on down the track, riding hard to catch up with the rest of our party.

The wind buffeted my cheeks and stunted trees flashed past on either side. The mist was clearing; through the bare branches I could see all the way down the slope towards the bay. *Nihtegesa* and *Wyvern* were drawn up on the shore, with hundreds of footprints leading away from them across the sand, towards drier land.

Where battle had been joined. Already on both sides the ordered lines of the shield-wall had broken and men were running among one another, hacking and thrusting and laying their enemies low, filling the morning with howls of agony and cries of rage, with the clatter of steel upon limewood and the screams of horses. Across the bloodstained field lay crumpled bodies in their dozens, with their weapons and their pennons lying beside them. And then, in the middle of the fray, I caught sight of Haakon's banner, the black dragon with the burning eyes and the axe in its claws. It was all but surrounded, with both Eudo's tusked boar and Wace's rising sun harrying it, although from such a distance I couldn't pick out either the Dane or my friends amidst so many mail-clad warriors.

'For Robert!' I yelled. Those on foot ahead of me heard our hoof-beats and my cries and made way. I kept looking for Oswynn and Ælfhelm and Godric, but I didn't see them, and I could only suppose they were somewhere further ahead. 'For Robert de Commines!'

'On!' Magnus cried, exhorting our band. Cheers erupted from the slaves as he and I rode past them to lead the charge. 'On, on, on! For Eadmund and for Godwine!' yelled Magnus, and I guessed those must be the names of the two brothers he had lost.

We had reached the flatter, open ground at the foot of the promontory on which Jarnborg stood. Ahead, three foemen were stumbling away from the fray: one clutching his arm; another whose face was entirely covered with blood and was missing several of his teeth; a third who had lost an eye. Too late they saw us coming. Too late they raised their weapons. My steed did not falter as I brought my weapon to bear, slicing across the shoulder of the first at the same time as Magnus battered his blade across the second's helmet. The last, the one with the missing eye, threw himself to one side, just in time, and we left him for those behind to finish as we rode on across the open meadow, towards the heart of the struggle, towards the dragon banner, which was beginning to waver as our forces pressed at it on all flanks, from the front and from behind.

Worse was to come for Haakon, too. Some of his followers had decided their lives were worth more than their oaths to their lord, for suddenly they were breaking and running. They hadn't been expecting a battle this morning; they had no stomach for the struggle, nor in truth were they in any fit state to wield a blade, and their nerve was failing them. Their side still held the advantage in numbers but, as I'd found, numbers alone will not win a battle. Confidence is everything, and theirs had been shattered. Where bloodlust and battle-fury had reigned, now there was only fear. And just as one man's resolve can provide inspiration for his sword-brothers, and make their hearts swell with belief both in themselves and their cause, fear can do the opposite. So it was then. Man by man, the enemy host crumbled. As each spear-Dane saw his companion deserting his side, abandoning the struggle, so he too realised his efforts were in vain. He saw the hordes of Englishmen and Normans bearing down on him with sharpened steel in their hands and death in their eyes, and he fled, spreading his panic in turn to the next man and the next and the next, until, like sparrows fleeing the hawk's shadow, suddenly the enemy were scattering, running anywhere they could, so long as it was away from their foes.

Into that tumult, roaring, swearing death upon them, invoking God and all the saints to aid us in the slaughter of our enemies, Magnus and I charged, with the rest of our small army behind us. On horse and on foot, men and women alike, we hurled ourselves against the enemy tide, adding our numbers to those of our allies, striking out to left and right, losing ourselves to anger, to the wills of our blades, revelling in the joy of the kill. Over the heads of the enemy I glimpsed the dragon banner on the move, heading further inland, across the boggy valley to the higher ground and the safety of the woods that lay at the heart of the island. Somehow Haakon had managed to break out from the midst of the Englishmen and Frenchmen surrounding him. I made out his gleaming mail, bright beneath the morning sun, as he struck out with only his standard-bearer and a bare handful of his loyal huscarls for protection. They were on foot, having clearly lost their horses during the fighting, and were now running like the rest of their countrymen. Like cravens.

We had done it. Hard though it was to believe, we had done it. In every direction I turned, the rout was under way. Haakon had been not just crushed but humiliated.

'Lord!'

I glanced about, saw Pons waving to me, his sword in one hand, his helmet in the other. Blood was smeared across the front of his hauberk, his hair was flattened against his head, and there was a broad grin on his grimy face. Some fifty paces further away, Wace and Eudo and their knights had managed to surround a group of Haakon's huscarls, and I took them for such because of the long-handled axes that they each bore. These they now threw down on the ground as a sign of their surrender.

'Where's Serlo?' I asked Pons. 'Dweorg? Sceota?'

'I don't know, lord. I lost sight of them during the fighting.'

I glanced about, but could not spot them anywhere. I could only hope Serlo was all right.

'We need to get after Haakon,' I said. 'We need to finish this.'

'He won't get far,' Pons replied. 'Where can he possibly go?'

He had a point. Even if the Dane did escape into the woods, sooner or later he would have to show himself if he didn't want to starve. When he did, we would be ready, waiting to cut him and his retainers down. He had fought and he had lost, and he would die by one means or another, sooner or later.

At the same time, though, I knew I wouldn't be able to rest until that murderer, that defiler, that vile heathen lay lifeless with my sword buried in his gut. For three years already I'd thirsted for justice. No longer was I to be denied.

I glanced at Magnus, and he at me, and saw that he was of the same mind.

'Vengeance,' he said.

I nodded in agreement. Wheeling about, I coaxed my horse into first a canter and then a gallop, drawing all the speed I could from his legs as we took off across that field of death in pursuit of Haakon and his band. All around rose the familiar battle-stench of blood and shit and mud and piss and horse dung and vomit, all intermingled.

'Haakon,' Magnus yelled, trying to catch his attention as we left the scattered, crimson-soaked corpses behind us and charged across thick tufts of grass. The Dane's standard-bearer had at last thrown down the cumbersome banner and we rode over it, trampling the once-proud dragon and axe into the mud.

'Come and face us, you whoreson,' I called out. 'You can't run from us!'

The ground was soft and once or twice my mount almost stumbled, but nevertheless we were quickly gaining on them. They were five in number: his erstwhile standard-bearer, a fair-haired boy who could not have seen any more than twelve summers; his three hearth-troops; and, lagging a little behind them, the Dane himself, half running and half limping in a way that suggested he must have been wounded in the battle. They still had a few hundred paces to go until they reached the safety of the trees, and they must have been beginning to doubt whether they could manage it before we fell upon them.

To my flank there came a piercing shriek and a yell. Magnus's horse must have tripped, for I glanced over my shoulder and saw it had gone down, and he with it. Hooves flailed and turf flew, and in the midst of it all the Englishman was struggling to extricate himself from the saddle.

'Magnus!' I said, but he didn't seem to hear me. He had other things to worry about.

As did I. Brief thoughts of going back to help the Englishman were swiftly forgotten. Something much more important was at stake. It fell to me now to kill the Dane, to claim revenge on behalf of us both. That was the promise I'd made myself. Here was my chance to make good on it.

'Haakon!' I roared.

With every heartbeat I was growing closer, while the clash of arms and the shouts of men were growing more distant. He couldn't ignore me any longer. At the sound of his name this time he stopped and turned to face me. Even though the nasal-guard of my helmet obscured my face, he must have recognised me.

He must have seen, too, that there was no longer any use in running. Fixing his gaze upon me, he drew his bloodied sword and stood his ground as I charged towards him. He knew that his time had come, but he was proud. I'd heard long ago that amongst the heathens to die without a weapon in one's hand was the worst dishonour, for it meant they would not be permitted to dine with their gods in whatever afterlife it was they believed in. Whether that was true or not, and whether that thought was in his mind, I don't know. More probably, like any man whose life had been spent travelling the sword-path, he considered it nobler to go to his grave fighting, a warrior to the end, rather than suffer the coward's death and be cut down from behind.

A howl left his lips as he ran, staggering, at me, his sword raised high, his golden arm-rings shining. His braid had come loose and his greying hair flew behind him. He realised, I think, that I was responsible for burning his hall, for destroying everything he had spent so many years fighting to gain. He knew now what I had felt that night at Dunholm, when so much had been taken from me, when my own world had crumbled about me.

Our blades clashed with a shriek of steel, and then I was past him, turning sharply before coming at him again. I parried the blow he aimed at my horse's neck, and the one after that, and the one after that, trusting in the steel not to shear, all the while waiting for my opportunity to come, as I knew it must. Waiting for him to give me the opening I needed. Blood trickled from a gash at his hip, and each movement he made seemed unsteadier than the last. He was slow to turn, and slower still between each sword-stroke.

'Die,' he yelled in that coarse voice of his, and he was weeping now. Weeping because he knew that his end was near. Weeping because he knew that I was toying with him. 'Die, you bastard, you Norman filth! Die!'

He swung at my thigh, but it was the swing of a desperate man. Again I met his blade with mine, and this time I was able to force his down, out of position, before backhanding my sword-point across the side of his head. He was only just within my reach and so I managed only a glancing blow, but it was enough to rob him of his balance and send him to the ground with limbs flailing and teeth flying. His sword slipped from his fingers, falling away uselessly into the grass. I slid from the saddle and stood over him. He gazed back up at me, rasping heavily, his eyes moist. A bright gash decorated his cheek, and a crimson stream ran from the corner of his mouth.

Some way off, Danish voices shouted out in despair. So desperate had they been to reach the sanctuary of the woods that his remaining huscarls hadn't noticed that their lord was no longer with them. Not until it was too late. They turned, and began rushing back to try to save him, but they were too far away to do anything.

I pointed the tip of my blade at the pale skin at Haakon's neck. 'Aren't you going to plead for mercy?'

He stared up at me, not in fear but in something more like resignation. 'Would you grant it if I asked for it?'

'No,' I replied. 'But I want to hear you beg.'

He smiled that humourless smile I'd seen before. Of course he would not beg. Nor, had I been in his place, would I.

'She moaned like a whore,' he said instead.

'What?' I'd thought he might ask me to make his end quick, or say any number of other things, but I hadn't been expecting that.

'Night after night, she moaned when she was in my bed, when I was inside her. She was my favourite. Did you know that?'

'Enough,' I said. Tears welled in my eyes, and my throat stuck. 'No more.'

'I loved her,' he murmured, a hint of sadness in his tone. He closed his eyes as if recalling some long-cherished memory. 'Yes,' he said with a heavy sigh, 'I loved her.'

I couldn't bear to listen any longer. Summoning all my strength, all my hatred, I plunged my sword into his throat, thrusting it hard so that it tore through flesh, sliced through bone, and I was roaring as I did so, roaring for all the world to hear, allowing the anguish that for so long had been buried within my heart to finally let itself be heard, until there was no more breath in my chest, and I had nothing left to give.

Gritting my teeth, I ripped the blade free. My heart was pounding, my whole body trembling and dripping with sweat. Falling to my knees, I wiped the moisture from my eyes and gazed down at Haakon's bestilled, bloodied corpse. In that instant, all the grief and pain and doubt and despair that for three years had plagued and tortured me were at once dispelled.

It was done.

Twenty-nine

With Haakon dead, the rest of his retainers fled. Jarnborg was ablaze, sending up great plumes of smoke into the sky. A bitter wind gusted from the west, carrying those plumes across the water along with the cries of the injured and the dying. Sword-blades and spear-hafts clattered against iron shield-rims as our men raised the battle-thunder in triumph.

'Sige!' I heard some of Magnus's men roar. 'God us sige forgeaf!'

God has given us victory. Indeed it seemed little short of a miracle. After so long dreaming and hoping and praying, Haakon had fallen. The field of battle belonged to us.

I was still kneeling beside the Dane's limp body, hardly daring to believe that it was true, that he was dead and that our struggle was at an end, when Magnus called my name. He hobbled towards me, wincing with every step, his horse having bolted. Luckily he'd managed to free himself from the stirrups before it did, and apart from the injury to his foot I was glad to see he was unharmed.

'I only wish I could have killed him myself,' he said as he stood beside me. Together we stared down at the Dane: at his face, strangely serene in death; at his unmoving chest.

I nodded but said nothing. Had it been the other way around and his been the hand that slew Haakon, no doubt I would have felt equally cheated. But I also knew that only one of us could have delivered the killing blow, and I was glad it had been me.

He must have guessed my thoughts. 'You did the right thing, Tancred,' he said, and clapped a hand on my shoulder as if to assure me that he did not bear any resentment. 'If it had been your horse that had fallen, I wouldn't have turned back to help you. So I don't blame you. You did what had to be done, for both of us.'

His tone was not grudging, but sincere. He smiled, and it was a smile of relief as much as anything else. Relief at having survived this day. Relief that justice, at long last, had been done.

We ventured back towards the rest of our host. Some of the enemy still lived, but not many. Magnus's huscarls remembered only too well how Haakon had betrayed their lord, and held anyone who had thrown in their lot with him in the lowest contempt, while the men that Wace and Eudo and Aubert had brought with them knew of the Dane's part in the massacre of near two thousand Normans at Dunholm, and were not inclined to show forgiveness. And so the slaughter still went on as our men set about pursuing the enemy, cutting them down from behind and decorating the backs of their skulls with bright gashes. A handful had fled on to the sands, perhaps hoping to reach their ships drawn up further along the shore and make an escape by water. When they realised how few they were in number, though, they abandoned their weapons and whatever armour they possessed, deciding instead to try to swim across the bay to safety. They waded out from the shore, crashing through the waves, but they didn't get far before our men were upon them, staining the foaming sea-froth pink with Danish blood.

'No mercy!' I heard a familiar voice shout from across the field, and saw Eudo on a horse that he must have seized from one of Haakon's hearth-troops. In one hand he held a bloodied spear, while his banner was in the other. Gradually those around him took up the cry, until a dozen Normans were chanting as if with a single voice: 'No mercy!'

Wace was with him, albeit on foot, and Tor and the Gascon and Serlo too, all charging behind the tusked boar, filling the air with their battle-joy, delighting in the glory of the kill.

With those roars and chants ringing out, Magnus and I trudged across a meadow trampled flat by the passage of hundreds of feet. Men cheered as they recognised us, and yet I hardly heard them, for my mind was elsewhere. I glanced about, searching for Godric, Ælfhelm and Oswynn. Until I knew she was safe, I would not celebrate. But amidst everyone running back and forth, amidst all the panicked horses, I couldn't spot them, and the longer I kept searching, the more my concern grew. I could feel it stirring in my breast, clutching at my heart, and I tried to bury it, not wanting to let even the possibility enter my thoughts. She was safe, I told myself. She had to be.

To left and right, English and French were throwing their arms around one another, slapping each other on the back, punching their comrades on the shoulders, lifting fists to the sky, sharing in the delight of a hard-earned victory, celebrating together as allies and brothers in arms. I had seen some strange sights in my years, but never any as strange as this.

'Lord!'

Over the laughter and the singing and the whoops of joy, I made out Eithne's voice. She stood amidst a crowd of men, perhaps a hundred paces away, close to a jagged outcrop of dark rock, waving both her arms, trying to attract my attention, and at once I felt my worries easing, my heart lifting.

But only for an instant.

'Lord!' she cried again, as she beckoned me over, and this time there was no mistaking her tone, which was insistent rather than jubilant. With her, crowded close, were Godric and Ælfhelm, who was nursing a wound to his shoulder, his fellow huscarls Dweorg and Sceota, and Pons too. Of Oswynn, however, there was no sign.

And I knew.

My skin turned to ice. My heart all but stopped, and the breath caught in my chest. No longer were all those men shouting and rejoicing; or perhaps they were, but I did not hear them. Around me the whole world seemed to slow.

'Lord!' Eithne was shouting still, her voice desperate, as I pelted towards her as fast as my legs could carry me, nearly tripping over the corpses in my way but somehow managing to stay upright.

'Where is she?' I roared as I grew nearer. 'What happened?'

She stared, terrified, at me, but though her mouth opened, no words came out. Instead, after a moment's hesitation, she and the others simply stepped to one side, making way and allowing me to see for myself.

Oswynn, my Oswynn, lay on the ground, her head of pitch-black hair resting upon a bundle of folded cloaks, her eyes closed, her chest rising and falling. Her breath misted in front of her face, but there was so little of it, and it came only in stutters.

'No,' I said, barely able to manage even a whisper, so numb, so devoid of strength, so helpless did I feel. 'No.'

Eanflæd, the English girl, knelt beside her, pressing a bloodied cloth against Oswynn's lower torso, whilst at the same time stroking her brow. Her eyes were red and her cheeks wet with tears. No sooner had she noticed me approaching than she rose to her feet and made way.

'She wanted to kill them all,' I was dimly aware of Ælfhelm saying. 'We tried to stop her, Tancred, but there was a fury in her, a fury such as I've never seen in a woman. We tried, but before we could even—'

He kept speaking, but whatever he said, I didn't hear. My mind was running with a thousand thoughts and I was deaf to his explanations, blind to everything except for my woman as I fell to my knees by her side and took her cold hand in mine, squeezing it as I tried to coax her back to me. Her eyelids fluttered, and a drawn-out moan escaped her lips. Beneath the rag Eanflæd had been using to staunch the flow, Oswynn's shift was torn where a spear or a seax had dealt its blow, and the linen around it was crimson-dark and sodden. I pressed the cloth firmly against the gash, refusing to admit to myself what my eyes and my heart were telling me, which was that it was no use, that the blood was burbling forth too freely to be stemmed. She was gut-stricken, wounded deep, beyond the ability of the best physician or leech-doctor in Christendom to help, and experience had taught me that no one who suffered such an injury ever lived long. With every trace of mist that escaped her lips, it seemed that a little more life went out of her. Breath by breath, she was slipping away. From the world. From me.

This couldn't be happening. Not after everything we had done; after the many leagues we had travelled across field and marsh, river and storm-tossed sea; after the countless foes I'd laid low in order to find her and bring her back. Did all of that count for nothing?

'Oswynn,' I said desperately. This had to be some dream, some *nihtegesa*, I thought, except that I couldn't find a way to wake from it.

At the sound of her name she stirred. Her eyes opened, just by a little, but enough to see me kneeling over her.

'Tancred,' she said, and she was weeping, her voice weak, little more than a whisper. 'I'm sorry. I'm so sorry—'

'No,' I said, and suddenly I was weeping as well. To hear her say such a thing was more than I could bear. She had no reason to apologise. If anyone was to blame, it was I, not her. 'I should never have left you. I shouldn't. It's my fault.'

I wasn't only thinking of that moment earlier this morning when I'd entrusted her protection to Godric and Ælfhelm. I was also thinking back to that night at Dunholm. If only I'd been there to defend her, none of this would have happened.

'You came, though,' she whispered, managing something like a smile, although there was such pain in it.

'Of course,' I said, but I wasn't sure if she heard me. Her face was pale, her skin cold to the touch, her chest barely moving, her breathing light, and growing lighter. She closed her eyes and I gripped her hand more tightly, trying to hold on to her. To prevent from happening what I could not prevent; to stave off fate. To keep her with me a little longer.

'Oswynn,' I pleaded, as if that would help, as if it would change anything. 'Don't go.'

The smile had faded from her expression; her fingers grew limp in my grasp. Her eyelids trembled, and her mouth opened by the tiniest sliver. She was trying to say something, but whatever it was I couldn't tell, for at the same time from somewhere close at hand a sudden cheer rose up, drowning out the sound of her voice. Doing my best to stifle my sobs, I leant closer, until my ear brushed against her lips.

'—for me,' she managed to say, and I thought I must have missed something, or else misheard, so quiet was she. But then she spoke again, and this time I did hear her. 'You came for me.'

'Yes,' I said, unable to hold the tears back any longer. She gave a long, slow sigh, and through watery eyes I gazed down at her, waiting for her to say more, to say anything at all.

Her mouth was still. Her eyes were closed.

'Oswynn!' I said, but no matter how loudly and how many times I repeated her name, she could not hear me. Grief overtook me then, and I let it pour out, spilling down my cheeks as I hugged her close and sobbed into her hair and into her cheeks and her neck. Over and over I begged her to wake, to come back to me. But she would not wake, nor would she come back. Her soul had fled her body, fled this world for whatever place it is that souls are supposed to go.

The sun shone in a bright, clear sky, but a chill had descended upon me, a chill that seized my whole body and wrenched at my heart, and I could not stop trembling. I clung to Oswynn, the one woman in all the world that I had ever truly loved, and I did not want to let her go, or move, or even walk this earth any longer. All I wanted was to die, so that I could be with her.

For she was gone, and my world had grown dark.

We buried her.

A few miles from Jarnborg there was a tiny timber building, not much bigger than a cattle-shed, that passed for a chapel amongst the island folk. We laid her in the earth in its grounds, beneath the winter-green boughs of a hollow yew. The priest, a wrinkled greybeard with a lame leg who walked with the aid of a crutch, recited the necessary liturgy. He had no Latin learning and so spoke in his own tongue, but even if he had, the words would have meant nothing to me, so lost was I in thought, in regret, in sorrow.

Afterwards, when the earth had been placed over her body and everyone else had left, I alone lingered, kneeling by her graveside for how long I cannot say, only that it seemed like an eternity. Clouds scurried from the sea up the length of the fjord, thick and brooding. They billowed and tumbled and blotted out the sun, which grew ever lower in the west. A drizzle came and went; the wind rose and settled and rose once more, tugging at my cloak and buffeting my cheeks, brushing clear the tears that I did not care to wipe away. I thought of her, and remembered the times we had shared, short though they were, and the many happinesses of those times. I prayed for her soul, and prayed also that when the day of reckoning arrived we would be united again in the heavenly kingdom, small comfort though that was to me in those lonely hours, as I thought of all the years stretching ahead that I would have to spend without her. Everything that had seemed so certain in the wake of Haakon's death, in the wake of our victory, was thrown into confusion. The future that I had hoped for, that I had dreamt of, was not to be.

'She was a good friend,' came a voice, startling me. I turned in the direction it had come from, and had to raise a hand to shield my eyes from the setting sun, which was just above the figure's shoulder.

My eyes adjusted, and I saw it was Eanflæd. She brushed her dark hair from where it had fallen in front of her face. I wondered if she had anything more to add, but when she said nothing, I looked away, embarrassed that anyone should see me so affected, and angry too that she had intruded upon me.

Eanflæd did not come closer, though, nor did she kneel down next to me by Oswynn's grave, as I'd half expected she might, and I took that as a gesture of respect.

'She had a child. A girl. Did you know that?'

'No,' I said, surprised. Oswynn had not spoken to me of any child, although in our haste to escape Jarnborg we hadn't had the opportunity to exchange stories. 'The child was Haakon's?'

'He certainly thought so,' Eanflæd said. 'He named her Alfhild, and doted on her whenever he returned to Jarnborg. She was born in the autumn after Oswynn came here, on the feast day of All Saints.'

It took me a moment to understand the import of what she was saying. The feast of All Saints took place on the first day of

November, while the ambush at Dunholm had happened nine months earlier, in late January.

'What did Oswynn think?'

Eanflæd shrugged. 'She never liked to say what she believed, or if she did, not to me. As for the rest of us, we always did say amongst ourselves that the girl had more of her mother than of Haakon in her looks, but who knows? Oswynn certainly didn't, no matter what she might have hoped.'

'What about the girl?' I asked, sensing the slightest glimmer of hope. If there was something that remained of Oswynn, even if she were not a child of my blood—

'She died,' the Englishwoman said. 'She was a sickly thing from the day she entered the world, although God granted her the strength to see through her first year and more. But then the winter came, and the snows, and she caught a fever, and there was nothing that could be done for her.'

No sooner had that candle been lit, than it was pinched out. 'And after that?' I asked.

'What do you mean?'

'Did she ever bear Haakon a child after Alfhild?'

Eanflæd shook her head. 'Nor did any of us, lord.'

'None of you?'

'Not one,' she confirmed. 'God alone knows why. Although that never stopped him from trying.'

I nodded, not knowing what to say. To tell the truth I wasn't sure quite what to make of this new knowledge, or even whether there was anything to make.

'She never stopped believing that you would come for her,' Eanflæd said, and now at last she did come to kneel beside me, gazing down at the broken earth beneath which Oswynn lay. 'Especially after she saw you at Beferlic. She often confided in me, and I in her. She told me you would come sooner or later, and I never had the heart to say otherwise. Every time we were allowed to venture beyond the fortress's walls she was always looking to seaward. I knew she was hoping to spy a ship headed for the island, a ship of warriors who would kill Haakon and free her. She held on to that hope; it was what kept her alive through the dark nights, and there were many of those. It made her strong, and we in turn took our strength from her.'

Eanflæd stopped, for she was sobbing. Her hands covered her face and her whole body shook. I placed an arm around her shoulder in reassurance.

'She was right,' she said, between sniffs, as she wiped her sleeve across her nose. 'In the end, she was right, and it shames me that I never believed in the same way she did.'

'She always was strong,' I replied, not knowing what else to say.

Someday, I resolved, I would come back here; I would make the pilgrimage north and find this island again. It didn't matter that there was no shrine, no altar, no great minster church to mark the site where she lay in the ground. To me, if to no one else, this humble place would always be sacred: here, beneath the eternal yew, the tree of ages, where the leaves never fell or lost their shade, where life was ever-present. Wherever my travels took me in future, to whatever far-flung parts of Christendom, always I would hold this place in my mind, in the same way that my memories of Oswynn would never fade, but instead would remain as vivid in the years to come as they did now. That was the solemn oath I swore to myself, and it was a pledge that I knew I would have no trouble keeping.

As long as I lived, I would not forget her.

'Where will you go?' asked Eudo the next day. We stood on the sands beneath the still-smoking ruins of Jarnborg, listening to the waves lapping on the shore and gazing out over the bay, across the choppy waters sparkling beneath the light of the sun, towards the distant peaks thickly robed with cloud. We had done what we came here to do; now the time had come for us to part ways, and to venture where we must.

'Not back to England,' I said. 'That much I know. There's nothing left for me there.'

'You can still try to make amends,' Wace pointed out. 'Robert might yet decide to accept you back into his service, if you come with us and seek his forgiveness.'

On that, at least, I had made up my mind, and I think they both realised it, even if they didn't want to admit it.

'No,' I answered firmly. 'He doesn't need me, or my sword. Not any more. He's made that clear enough. He will do his own thing, and I'll do mine. Maybe in time these wounds will heal and we'll be able to see eye to eye once more, but until that happens, no.'

I would not humble myself before him. I would not beg forgiveness. What respect I'd had for him, recent events had steadily ground down. Until he earned it again, I would not bend my knee nor offer my oath to him anew. I couldn't. Not without losing all respect for myself.

I would not go back. I only hoped that Eudo and Wace understood, and did not think any less of me for that decision.

'If not England, then where?' asked Eudo after a while. 'Back to Normandy, or to Brittany?'

I shook my head. 'First of all I'm going to take Eithne home, to reunite her with her kin, providing they still live. I promised her that much, and it's time for me to make good on that promise.'

Since Haakon and his men had no further use for them, I had claimed the largest of his four longships. It turned out that one of the slaves we had freed from Jarnborg, a lank-haired, bone-thin countryman of Eithne's by the name of Domnall, had been steersman to a wealthy merchant from Haltland before he was captured by pirates and thrown in chains. He, together with a good number of the other former thralls, had agreed to join us, partly because they had nowhere else to go, and partly because I think they sensed with Magnus and Aubert and myself opportunities to seek out their fortunes anew.

'And after you've taken her home?' Wace asked. 'What then?'

I could only shrug in answer. In truth I was in no mood to think about such things, although of course I would have to decide before long. A man cannot spend his life forever dwelling on the past, wondering about what might have come to pass that didn't, and wishing things were different. Sooner or later he must turn his mind to what lies ahead.

Wyvern's crew, directed by Aubert, were loading supplies for the voyage back to England. The island folk had bestowed food and fleeces and other gifts upon us, which at the time I'd taken for tokens of their gratitude for ridding them of the Danes. Later, though, I'd wondered whether in fact they meant it as tribute, fearing that if they did not placate us, we would soon turn our attentions to their steadings and their homes, and raid them just as we had raided Haakon's hall. However those offerings were meant, we'd accepted them with gratitude, adding them to what we had managed to recover of the jarl's treasure hoard. For rather than immediately killing those who had surrendered to us, we had given them the chance first to show us where their lord had buried the chests containing all the silver and the gold that he had reaped on his expeditions. Only after they'd done so did we condemn them to the ends they deserved. Afterwards we shared the booty out as fairly as we could, so that both crews were rewarded and every man in our party, whether English or French, received a portion. Once divided out between so many coin-purses, it looked like a paltry amount for a warlord of Haakon's repute to have amassed, and I suspected he had other hoards that his men hadn't known about or else, if they had, simply hadn't told us of, both here on this island and elsewhere. Nonetheless, it was hard-earned recompense for the men who had toiled so tirelessly in our cause with oar and sail, spear and sword, risking everything. But naturally there were many whom we could not reward: those who had lost their lives to Danish steel, far from any port they could call home. All we could do was honour them, as we had honoured Oswynn, and give Aubert money that he could pass on to their families.

'Robert won't be best pleased when he learns you took his ship without his permission,' I said to Wace and Eudo. Nor that *Wyvern* would be returning with fifteen fewer men than it had set out with, and a number of the rest still recovering from various small wounds taken in the battle.

'It'll be some weeks before we arrive back at Heia,' Eudo said. 'We still have to visit Robert's barons in Normandy and bring them the tidings of his father's death, assuming that they haven't yet heard. The Christmas feast might have already passed by the time we see home again. Between now and then, we'll have plenty of time to think how we're going to explain it all.'

'He can have our share of the plunder, if that'll help soothe his temper,' Wace added. 'There's always more silver to be made. Besides, we didn't come here for riches, but for something greater than that, and we found it. That's all that matters.'

As usual he spoke good sense. Still, I didn't envy them facing Robert, for he would surely hear the tale of their exploits before long. Even if they were able to swear *Wyvern*'s crew to silence, someone was bound to let slip at some point. What Robert would do then, I could only guess. The two of them had taken a great risk on my behalf, and I lacked the words to thank them as they deserved. Better, more loyal friends than they I'd never known.

'Wherever you end up going, take care,' Eudo said as we embraced, to which Wace, when it was his turn, added:

'God be with you, Tancred.'

'And with you,' I said solemnly. 'Both of you.'

As sword-brothers, we three had grown up together in our lord's houschold, had fought alongside one another on occasions without number, and it was a strange feeling to part company without knowing exactly when I would next see them. That fate would bring us together again, and that our paths would cross sometime, I had no doubt. When that happened, I would make sure to repay the debt I owed them. But even so it seemed a turning point not just in my life, but in all of our lives.

Thus it was with heavy heart that, later that day, I took one of Haakon's horses and rode to the cliff-top at the island's southernmost point. There, with the wind gusting in my face, I watched *Wyvern* as she put out to sea. Her long, narrow hull rode the swell as her oarsmen bent their backs to the waves, her proud dragon-prow cutting through the blue-grey waters. Not once did I take my eyes off her, but kept waving in the hope that Eudo and Wace would see me, and it seemed that they did, for after a while I spotted two figures waving back. Smaller and smaller and smaller the ship grew, until she was no more than a faint speck on the horizon and then not even that. The wide sea beyond the fjord glittered beneath the afternoon sunshine, and amidst all those shards of light I soon lost sight of her.

I was alone.

Even long after she had vanished from sight, I remained there. While my mare wandered, I stood by the cliff-edge and stared down the length of the fjord towards the sea, searching for I knew not what, listening to the waves crash and froth against the rocks below, feeling hollow inside.

How long I spent standing there, lost in my thoughts, with the cold winter wind tugging at my cloak, I don't know. By the time I heard the hoofbeats approaching from behind, cloud had come across the sky, veiling the sun, and a soft drizzle was beginning to fall.

'Lord!'

I glanced over my shoulder. It was Godric.

'We were starting to get worried,' he said as he checked his horse, dismounted and came to me by the cliff's edge. 'No one knew where to find you.'

'Well, you've found me now.'

The words came out more sourly than I meant them, although if Godric noticed, he didn't seem to take any offence. Sighing, I gazed out across the waters once more, doing my best to ignore the Englishman, hoping that if I paid him no attention he would simply leave me be.

'Are you all right, lord?' he asked, clearly sensing the disquiet raging within me.

'I'm thinking,' I replied.

'About what?'

I hesitated, unsure whether to trust with my innermost thoughts someone who only a few weeks ago had been a stranger to me. 'About whether I'll see Earnford, or so much as set foot on English shores, ever again.'

Godric did not answer straightaway, and I wondered if his mind was on the estate at Corbei that his uncle had granted him, which the king had seized along with the lands and properties of all Morcar's followers.

'You will, lord,' he said after a short while. 'I know it. We all will, someday.'

He smiled gently, but the firmness of his tone told me that he was not simply trying to lift my spirits, but that he truly believed it. I wished I had his confidence. Still, perhaps he was right. Perhaps in time I would find myself feasting in my own hall once more, with my friends around me, music filling the air and ale and wine flowing, and all would be well with the world.

I smiled in return as I tousled Godric's hair. He tried to squirm away, protesting, and I chuckled. He had done more in my service than I could ever have expected of him. Of course he had much to learn still, but he was eager and showed promise both as a swordsman and as a rider. In years to come he would make a good warrior, I thought. And I would be proud not just to teach him but also to count him as a friend.

For the truth was that I was not alone, nor would I ever be. Not as long as I had men like Godric, like Serlo and like Pons. They had followed me to the ends of Britain, and I had no doubt that they would follow me still, to the farthest parts of Christendom and even beyond.

The sun broke through a crack between the clouds, and I felt its slight warmth penetrate the chill that, until then, had held me in its grip: a chill that had first descended as I'd held Oswynn, dying, in my arms, and which had not left me since. And as that warmth touched my skin, so something stirred within me. To call it a thrill did not seem right, for my heart was still too full of grief to allow that. Still, as I looked out over the wide, shining waters, it struck me that beyond them existed a whole world I hadn't yet seen. A world beyond England, beyond Normandy and France. Lands I'd seen in my dreams, of which I had heard tales, but which I had never glimpsed with my own eyes. And, for the first time in my life, I had both the means and the opportunity to see that world.

'Come on,' I said to Godric as I turned away from the cliff's edge and marched towards my horse, which was grazing contentedly close by. 'It's time we left this place.'

'Where are we going?' he called after me.

'Wherever the winds take us!" I shouted above the gusts as I mounted up and coaxed the mare into a canter back in the direction of our camp.

For I had a ship. I had silver. I had men who were loyal to me. What else did I need?

If experience had taught me one thing, it was that the sword-path is never a straight road, but rather ever-changing, encompassing many twists and turns. All a man can do is follow it and see where it leads. I had followed mine, and this was where it had taken me. But my journey was not over yet. Whatever fate awaited me, I was still to find it.

The sword-path beckoned, and so, for good or for ill, I would keep on following it. Wherever the promise of glory and riches took me, that was where I would go. To live. To fight. To strive. To forge a reputation that would live on long after I had departed this earth.

That was who I was, and who I would continue to be.

I, Tancred.

Historical Note

F ew people today have heard of Eadgar Ætheling, Wild Eadric and the other leaders who instigated the series of rebellions during the years immediately following the Normans' arrival in England. One name that continues to resonate, however, is that of the outlaw Hereward, later known by the epithet 'the Wake', whose stand in the Fens against the invaders has become the stuff of legend.

Much mystery surrounds Hereward, who first appears in the historical record in late 1070, when his sack of the monastery at Peterborough is mentioned in the entry in the Anglo-Saxon Chronicle for that year. Of his life and deeds, there is little that is reliably known. The Chronicle's only other reference to him is in the following year, when it records his courageous escape from Ely, together with 'all who could flee away with him', even as the rebellion around him was crumbling. As David Roffe suggests in his entry on Hereward in the *Oxford Dictionary of National Biography* (OUP, 2004), the brevity of this mention might imply that, at the time this passage was composed, the tale of Hereward and his exploits was so well known that no further explanation was needed.

Due to the lack of information given in contemporary accounts about Hereward and the Ely rising, we are largely reliant on later, twelfth-century sources, including the *Liber Eliensis* (*Book of Ely*), the *Gesta Herewardi* (*Deeds of Hereward*), and Geoffrey Gaimar's *L'estoire des Engleis* (*The History of the English People*). All three appear to have been influenced to a greater or lesser extent by a now-lost chanson cycle about the life of Hereward. Their versions of events incorporate a significant dose of romance, and draw heavily on contemporary heroic tropes and literary devices, and, furthermore, contradict each other on several crucial aspects, all of which means it is difficult to reconstruct a coherent narrative of Hereward's life and the siege of Ely. In writing *Knights of the Hawk*, I have been selective in my use of these sources, borrowing certain elements while at the same time choosing to reject others.

What seems likely is that Hereward was not in overall command of the rebellion, or at least if he was, only for a short while. While his role in Ely's defence was obviously significant enough that his name was remembered in legend, he was certainly not the highest-ranking individual present, and it seems more likely that if the rebels looked to anyone for leadership, it would have been Earl Morcar. However, given that we do not know whether the rebels all shared the same cause, or were ever anything more than a loose coalition, it might be that no single person was in charge.

Regarding the events of the siege and the reasons for the rebellion's eventual downfall, the sources disagree. It is possibly significant that the historian Orderic Vitalis, also writing in the early twelfth century but whose account of these early years of the Norman Conquest is generally considered reliable, does not mention Hereward at all in his short summation of the siege of Ely. Instead he records only that 'crafty messengers' proposed 'treacherous terms' to Morcar, in order to deceive him with false promises into surrendering to the king. Around the mention of these anonymous messengers, I have woven the fictional tale of Tancred's capture of Godric, and his use as a go-between and hostage in the exchanges of information between King William (Guillaume) and Earl Morcar.

The exact details of how, in the end, the Normans managed to capture the Isle, however, are unclear. The *Gesta Herewardi* implies, somewhat implausibly, that the Normans' capture of the Isle occurred without much bloodshed at all, after Abbot Thurstan of Ely submitted to the king and invited him to come in secret to the Isle. But it says nothing of the means by which King William was able to cross the marshes that for so long had stood in his way. Earlier, it mentions a causeway that he'd ordered built, across which the Normans had attacked unsuccessfully, the structure having collapsed under the weight of men and horses, resulting in a great loss of life. This story is corroborated by the *Liber Eliensis*. However, in contrast to the *Gesta*'s assertion that William arrived in secret, the *Liber* has a much more dramatic tale, telling of a final assault across a pontoon bridge, although whether this followed the same route as the first causeway is not clear. Having traversed the marshes, the *Liber* further relates that the king and his army faced a battle against a large rebel army comprising 3,000 men, who had fortified the Isle's shore. Since it seems unlikely that the Normans faced no resistance at all in their crossing of the marsh, I have preferred this version of events to that provided by the *Gesta*. However, the details of this struggle are extremely sketchy, and so I have elaborated in order to harmonise it with Orderic's story of Morcar's submission to King William.

What became of Hereward after his famous flight from Ely, we can only surmise. The Anglo-Saxon Chronicle has nothing more to say about him after this incident, and our other principal sources are once again in conflict. The *Gesta Herewardi* suggests that, following several more adventures, he was imprisoned by the king, then set free by a band of his followers, before at last reaching a rapprochement with the king and being restored to his familial lands, where he lived out the rest of his life in happiness. In Gaimar's version, too, Hereward is reconciled to the king, but there is an additional coda, in which the former rebel is set upon and killed – albeit after a valiant last stand – by a band of Norman knights. It's possible that Hereward's fate was a mystery even to most contemporaries, which is why we have such varying accounts. Alternatively, after his escape from the Isle, he may have sought refuge overseas, like many dispossessed Englishmen in the years after 1066. Into this gap in our knowledge I have inserted my own tale of Tancred's pursuit of Hereward through the marshes, the skirmish, and Hereward's death by Godric's hand.

Regarding the fates of some of the other rebels, we can be more certain. We know, for example, that whatever accommodation the king reached with Morcar, it was swiftly revoked. Hardly had the earl submitted than he was cast in prison, where he would remain for the rest of his life. Another prominent figure among the rebels, Bishop Æthelwine of Durham, whose role in events is unclear and whom I have mentioned only in passing in the novel, was sent to Abingdon Abbey, where he was held in captivity until he died the following winter. Of the rest, some were imprisoned, while others were allowed to go free, although not before having their hands severed and their eyes gouged out.

One individual who is believed to have met his end during the siege of the Isle is Guillaume Malet. We know from a few short references in Domesday Book (1086) that 'he went into the marsh' and that he died during his service to the king, and it seems probable that both statements refer to the Ely campaign. It has been suggested by Cyril Hart in his article 'William Malet and his Family' (*Anglo-Norman Studies*, vol. 19, 1996) that his role would have been administrative rather than military, given his previous failures as a commander in the defence of York, but the truth is that we simply don't know. The circumstances of his death are likewise a mystery; my contention that he was already dying as a result of illness contracted during his imprisonment by the Danes is pure invention. At any rate, we hear no more of his whereabouts after 1071. The location of his grave is unknown, but given the relative proximity of Ely to Eye in Suffolk, which was the family's chief estate in East Anglia, it is entirely plausible that his body would have been laid to rest there.

As well as Hereward, Morcar, Malet and the various kings mentioned in the novel who ruled during this period, many of the other characters are based on real historical persons. These include both Roberts – de Commines and Malet – Beatrice and her husband Guillaume d'Archis (William d'Arques), Elise, Thurcytel and Magnus. Tancred's young charge Godric is also based on a real figure, albeit one who appears in the sources as little more than a name. The *Gesta Herewardi* lists him among Hereward's companions, and describes him as a *nepos* of Morcar – a term that many medieval writers used to describe various familial relations, but which is often translated as 'nephew'. Aside from this brief mention, however, we know nothing of the historical Godric, and so the character I've constructed is essentially fictional.

Magnus was probably the third son of Harold Godwineson by his first wife, Eadgyth 'Swan-neck'. Following their father's death at Hastings, he and his two elder brothers, Godwine and Eadmund, appear to have fled to Dublin, from where they staged two raids on the south-west of England. The first of these took place in 1068, but achieved little. Entering the River Avon, the three brothers proceeded to Bristol, possibly expecting a warm welcome as the heirs of the former king and Earl of Wessex. If so, they were disappointed. They were resisted by the townspeople and met in battle by a prominent local landowner named Eadnoth the Staller, whom they killed before venturing back to Ireland with their plunder. In the summer of 1069, the brothers returned with either sixty-four or sixty-six ships, hinting at a significant force numbering perhaps as many as 3,000 men. Again, however, their efforts came to nothing. They were repelled, this time by a certain Count Brien, who was able to surprise them, inflict heavy casualties in the ensuing skirmish, and drive them off. After their defeat, they withdrew once more to Ireland, and, with that, Harold's sons disappear into obscurity. About their further activities or their ultimate fates, the sources offer no information, and we can only speculate.

Orderic tells us that Harold's sons were given support by King Diarmait and other Irish princes, which has been interpreted as meaning ships and men, although how many is unknown. It seems likely that their raiding-force would also have included other exiles from England, as well as Hiberno-Norse freebooters looking for the opportunity to win plunder. There was no individual by the name of Haakon Thorolfsson in real life, although there would probably have been many warlords like him who plied their trade by selling their swords to the highest bidder. At this precise point in history, it isn't clear what ruler, if any, held sway over the Hebrides, and it may be that there existed a vacuum of power along this vital sea route from the Continent to Iceland and Orkney: a vacuum that would have allowed pirates and petty kings alike to flourish. Readers familiar with the geography of the region might have been able to spot from the descriptions offered that Jarnborg, Haakon's fictional 'iron fortress', is sited on the island of Lismore in Loch Linnhe, across the water from modern Oban.

The verse recited by Eudo on the eve of the battle for the Isle is excerpted, of course, from *The Song of Roland*, the heroic poem concerning the last stand of its eponymous hero in a remote mountain pass in the Pyrenees. The oldest surviving manuscript of this text dates from sometime between 1130 and 1170, but there is good reason to suppose that the *Song* itself was composed earlier than this, perhaps as early as 1060, although the generally accepted date is around the time of the First Crusade (1095–99). Two twelfth-century authorities, William of Malmesbury and the Norman poet Wace – no relation to my character of the same name – state that a certain Taillefer sang of the deeds of Roland as an exhortation to the Normans immediately before the Battle of Hastings. It might well be the case that certain elements of the Roland legend had already been committed to verse by the time of the Conquest, even if the full *Song* as we know it today didn't yet exist in its final form. The text I have quoted is derived from John O'Hagan's verse translation of 1880, published by C. Kegan Paul & Co., although I have adapted it slightly.

The poetry spoken by Magnus in Chapter Twenty, meanwhile, is excerpted from an Old English elegy known to modern scholars as 'The Wanderer'. The poem is narrated from the perspective of an exiled warrior whose lord and companions have been killed. Plagued by sorrow and by memories of former glories, he finds himself wandering the cold seas, bemoaning the situation to which *wyrd* ('fate' or 'destiny') has condemned him. I have referred to this text once before, in *Sworn Sword*, but it seemed especially appropriate that Magnus should quote from it here as well.

With hindsight, it might be argued that the suppression of the Ely rebellion marked the culmination of King William's bitter wars of conquest, which had lasted five years and resulted in the deaths of thousands of Normans, Bretons, Flemings, English, Welsh and Danes. But we should not suppose that, even by the end of 1071, he felt entirely secure. No one could know, after all, what plots were afoot beyond the boundaries of his realm: in Wales and Scotland, France and Denmark. Peace rarely lasted long, and as will become apparent, there was no shortage of troubles in the years to come.

Whether Tancred decides in the end to return to England, or whether he ventures forth to seek his fortune elsewhere, time will tell. One thing is for certain, however, which is that he will ride again soon.

Acknowledgements

As always, I'd like to take the opportunity to thank several individuals without whom this novel would not have been possible.

Knights of the Hawk sees Tancred venturing further from home than ever before: into distant lands filled with people whose languages are unfamiliar to his ear. Once again I'm indebted to Richard Dance of St Catharine's College, Cambridge, for being my guide through the linguistic patchwork that was eleventh-century Britain, and for taking the time to translate several passages of modern English dialogue into Old Norse and Old English.

Many thanks also to my editor, Georgina Hawtrey-Woore, to Katherine Murphy, Amelia Harvell and everyone else at Random House for all their hard work in bringing these books from manuscript to bookshelf, as well as to my copy-editor, Richenda Todd, whose close attention to detail has helped to make this the best work it can possibly be.

For their generous feedback, I am once again grateful to Jonathan Carr, Liz Pile, Beverly Stark, Tricia Wastvedt, Joanne Sefton, Jules Stanbridge and Gordon Egginton, who all took the time to read extracts from the novel at various stages during its development, and whose insights and advice have proven enormously helpful.

Final thanks, as ever, go to my family and to Laura for all their unfailing support and encouragement through the course of writing the novel.